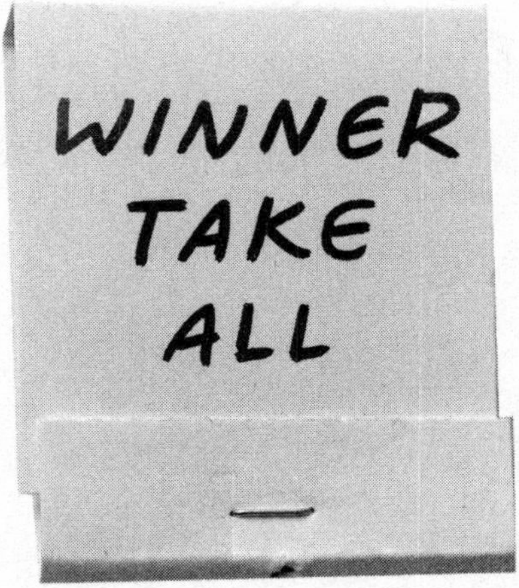
WINNER
TAKE
ALL

WINNER TAKE ALL

LAURIE DEVORE

[Imprint]
MAKE YOUR MARK

NEW YORK

[Imprint]
MAKE YOUR MARK

A part of Macmillan Publishing Group, LLC
175 Fifth Avenue, New York, NY 10010

Library of Congress Control Number: 2017945056

ISBN 978-1-250-08288-6 (hardcover) / ISBN 978-1-250-08289-3 (ebook)

Our books may be purchased in bulk for promotional, educational, or business use. Please
contact your local bookseller or the Macmillan Corporate and Premium Sales Department
at (800) 221-7945 ext. 5442 or by e-mail at MacmillanSpecialMarkets@macmillan.com.

Book design by Ellen Duda

Imprint logo designed by Amanda Spielman

First Edition, 2018

1 3 5 7 9 10 8 6 4 2

fiercereads.com

If you take this book, keep in mind—you're starting a game you will never win. And you're
not the only one willing to play dirty.

To any girl who's ever been too much.

1

I can't stop staring at the back of Jackson Hart's head.

Trust me, it's something that most of the girls (and I'm sure some of the boys) at Cedar Woods Preparatory Academy would admit to—in fact, a few have probably made it a pastime. But I have very little interest in the back of Jackson Hart's head or much else about him. I'm not staring because he is six foot two with hair so dark it might as well be black, or because of his pretty blue eyes and tanned skin, altogether making him look like a beautiful boy raised on the river. I couldn't care less that he's amazing at baseball or can talk any girl out of her dress faster than you can say *skinny-dipping*. And you'd never catch me saying Jackson Hart is charming, though I might admit he's too smart for his own good.

I'm staring because what's coming out of his mouth right now is so ridiculous, I can't believe it's real.

"I mean, at its heart, isn't *The Scarlet Letter* really about our worst impulses as a society?" Jackson is saying. "Puritanical viewpoints controlling female sexuality? We always seek out what's forbidden. Alcohol. Sex. Sin. And then we condemn those who want it. Commit violence in the name of hypocrisy. One could argue it's a historical dystopia."

"That's an interesting point, Jackson," Mrs. Wesley says.

I raise my hand.

The thing is, I can't let something so utterly, immensely wrong go unchallenged. And no one knows that better than Jackson Hart.

"Yes, Miss Becker," Mrs. Wesley says.

"On a fundamental level," I say, and the class's eyes turn to me, "calling *The Scarlet Letter* a historical dystopia doesn't make any sense, since that's how things *were* in the past. Most times in history would be considered dystopias by today's standards."

"Well, of course the struggle of these characters doesn't feel as reality-based for Nell, but consider reading this in conjunction with something like *The Handmaid's Tale* and examining it from that angle. As for Nell, she's so perfect that she doesn't experience temptation," Jackson says, and the class laughs. I bite the inside of my cheek. "Which is, of course, an admirable quality, but maybe limits her ability to relate to the point I'm making—"

"I understand the point just fine." I cut him off. "And yes, I agree that Hester Prynne is asked to bear the sins of a puritanical society, with its secrets and hypocrisy—but your reducing the entire thing to 'keeping female sexuality down' and equating that with all of society's worst impulses is so completely intellectually lazy, especially in relation to *The Handmaid's Tale*. What about Hester's own agency? She chose to have sex, and she lives with that decision. Look at the way she isn't afraid of these men who are so terrified of *her*. She's not *ashamed*. She bears the brunt of what she and Dimmesdale did and what all the men around her have done. And that's why you're fundamentally wrong."

Jackson looks back and grins with all of his white, white teeth, his thick dark hair effortlessly messy on his head. He's always purposely baiting me in this class. His whole face comes to life when he sees a chance to refute me—just last month, we had it out over the role of imperialism in the absolutely wretched *Heart of Darkness*. He enjoys it: the way our classmates always turn on me, the fact that he can pull any ridiculous interpretation out of his ass and everyone—even the teachers—will be mesmerized by his words. The way I can't ignore him.

I won't stop until I win. It's my fatal flaw, and Jackson Hart reads me like a book.

He's a monster.

"I just think if Nell were to take a step back and see things from, I don't know, *my* perspective," he continues now, "she could see why this still feels so relevant and hits home in an environment like Prep."

"Yes, let's hear how the twenty-first-century rich boy relates to the nineteenth-century man writing about feminism through the lens of male pain. Spare me."

"The isolation Hester suffers for her actions—"

"Is just a punishment for having sex and being a woman, you said that already," I tell him. "I know. *We all know.* Seriously, Jackson, no one believes you read the book."

I appeal to Mrs. Wesley as Jackson turns away from me in his seat, looking, if anything, more pleased than when we began the conversation. "Surely you can't buy this."

I can feel the rest of the class laughing at me. Know-it-all Nell Becker. Boring, perfect Nell Becker who wears her school uniform exactly as per regulations. Whose mom is head of school and whose family is hilariously middle class.

Boring, perfect Nell Becker doesn't even belong here.

Mrs. Wesley is looking at me as if *I'm* the one making a mockery of the English canon. "Mr. Hart is making a solid analysis, Nell. To presume he didn't read the book because he disagreed with you is not scholarly and not acceptable in this classroom."

One of Jackson's best friends, Doug Rivera, is laughing behind his hand because he knows the same thing we all do. Jackson couldn't give a shit about *The Scarlet Letter* and he certainly wouldn't waste his valuable time reading it. Not when he could be playing the part of a Quintessential Rich Kid, drinking and getting laid and being his typical giving-zero-fucks self.

Jackson somehow manages to stay right behind me in the class rankings, sleepwalking through every subject with perfect grades. Sometimes I swear he does it just to annoy me, too.

"I think you need to apologize," Mrs. Wesley says.

I sit back in my seat, waiting.

"Nell?"

I almost laugh. She can't be serious. "You think *I* need to apologize?"

"Yes, to Jackson."

I do laugh.

"It's fine, Mrs. Wesley," he has the nerve to say. "Don't worry about it."

"*Nell?*" she repeats.

The only thing I can't stand more than the idea of Jackson getting away with the world's most absurd faux-feminist nonreading of *The Scarlet Letter* is the idea that I might be the one to get in trouble because of it. I bite back the thrum of anger coursing through my veins as I say, "My apologies, Jackson. Your reading of the book is certainly just as . . . valid as mine, if somewhat shallow." A piece of auburn hair has escaped my long, messy ponytail and I moodily attempt to shove it back into place.

"Thank you," Mrs. Wesley says. I feel the happiness radiating off the class. Perfect, know-it-all Nell Becker got what was coming to her.

"Clearly this book has inspired passion in some of you, which is all I could ever really ask for as an English teacher." As Mrs. Wesley turns to walk to the front of the room, spouting nonsense, Jackson looks over his shoulder one last time and winks at me.

The bell rings ten minutes later and I shove my used copy of *The Scarlet Letter* into my worn-out book bag, stalking out the door before anyone else can say something preposterous to me. I stop at my locker halfway down the hall and switch the book out for my precalc and biology textbooks.

A smooth voice comes from my right. "You know, it's really simple, actually." Jackson is leaning into the locker next to mine, watching me.

"In the environment of *The Scarlet Letter*, a man could show half the mental fortitude and bravery of a woman—if any at all—and would be praised for it. A society that praises male voices over female ones. I was only testing the text in a modern setting."

I slam my locker door. "Are you seriously trying to make me believe you were being a jackass as some kind of clever meta statement on society?"

"I thought it was a compliment," Jackson tells me with a shrug. "The patriarchy is keeping you down, Nell. I didn't even read the CliffsNotes."

"Really? Were those above your reading level, too?"

"Oh, come on, Becker," Jackson says. "I'm one measly hundredth of a GPA point behind you."

I decide to exit the conversation, marching away from him down the hall, my fingertips skimming the edge of my navy plaid uniform skirt. He tails me like some sort of megalomaniacal puppy. He's got two inches on me tops, so I take the steps two at a time to make sure he has to work a little to keep up. "Do you want something?"

"You shouldn't let me get to you."

I stop so fast he almost walks right past me. I face him. "You honestly think *you* get to me?" I can feel the heat building, my fair skin turning red.

He grins. "I know it."

"You're delusional. We both know I'm the best, and deep down, you can't stand it."

"You can't stop arguing with me, can you?" he asks as if he's genuinely excited by the prospect. "You want to feel like you're somehow superior to me even though we both know that I'm enjoying life in a way you can't even imagine. Someday I'll look back and have interesting stories to tell, and all you'll be able to talk about is when you were stressing over my fake interpretation of *The Scarlet Letter*. That's kindergarten-level jealousy, Becker."

It is physically painful to stop myself from arguing again, but I have to let it go. It's a psychological game: If I don't let him have the last word, I'll be proving him right.

Instead, I roll my eyes, walking around him to my class. My skin is practically vibrating with irritation against the textbook I'm holding, as if the book itself is holding me together. And I realize that, by not getting the last word, he still got me—I can't win.

Dammit.

I glance behind me to see he's already engaged in something else, his arm thrown around one of his friends as they walk away, talking animatedly, as if whatever he's saying is the best thing anyone's ever said.

I hate everything about him.

2

I hit the ground hard, diving for a ball on my left side, and then roll back over my right shoulder, getting both my feet back under me as I spring up again, teetering slightly.

"Too slow, Becker," Coach Madison yells at me, slamming the volleyball with her open-handed palm, the *crack* telling me to clear out of the way. I shake my head, running to the end of the line behind Lia Reagan, towering over her by about eight inches.

"You're fine," Lia says preemptively. I sigh, tugging on my ponytail. "You're *fine*," she repeats because she knows I need to hear it. I wish I didn't. "You rolled over the wrong shoulder. It would've been faster over your left but you're afraid to go to your weak side."

"I'm not *focused*," I say, my voice rising with frustration.

"Anything to do with your little tête-à-tête with Jackson Hart in Mrs. Wesley's class today?" Lia asks, careful not to smile.

"You heard about that?" I ask, staring straight ahead as I edge back to the front of the line. Lia dives for the ball ahead of me, her curly blond hair bouncing on top of her head.

As I take my turn, I swear Coach Madison puts my ball five feet farther out than anyone else's has been, but I do my very best to catch up to it, flipping over again. Not bad.

Lia turns around to me once I follow her to the end of the line. There's a bruise blooming against the pale skin on her knee. "Everyone was talking about it."

"About how I'm a freak?"

Lia doesn't look me in the eye. "People just think you're intense."

"Right." I nod. "Intense."

Coach Madison blows her whistle, signaling the end of practice. She gathers the team in a circle and proceeds to tell us we're "shit," yelling so much, I'm worried she may go into labor. Spring conditioning is supposed to go through the end of the school year, but there's no way she won't have her baby before then. We have club ball practice—our competitive summer league—starting up soon, but not soon enough, considering our first major tournament of the summer is in less than two months. All the biggest college scouts from around the country will be there. I've been training overtime for it: runs in the morning and conditioning plus spring drills with the volleyball team in the afternoon.

It never feels like enough.

Coach Madison releases us, and Lia and I walk side by side back to the locker room like we always do. "Why did you get into it with him again? After the great *Heart of Darkness* meltdown of April, I thought you weren't going to do that anymore. Because it's not worth it, remember? Any of this ringing a bell?"

"Should I let him spit out lies, then?" I ask. "Like complete nonsensical bullshit? Is that *fine*?"

"It's fine with everyone else," Lia says, reaching into her locker. I can tell she's trying not to laugh.

"Y'all talking about Jackson?" our other middle hitter, Michonne Tyler, asks from the locker next to mine, shaking her braids out of her ponytail. I yank my gym bag free.

"No," I mutter.

"I heard you won the argument, even though no one knew what you were talking about," Michonne says. I grin to myself.

"See?" Michonne tells Lia. "I know how to make Nell happy." Michonne is the only other Prep player on our club team. Her dad is an investment banker, a prominent member of the southeast chapter of the National Association of Black Finance, and her mom a well-known artist, a Taiwanese immigrant. Like most people at Prep, Michonne has been tapped to grow up to "be somebody."

"*See*, Lia?" I ask.

Michonne grabs her gym bag, pushing it up onto her shoulder. Her naturally light brown skin has darkened from days on the river, a telltale sign of the upcoming summer break. "I'll see y'all later," she says, throwing one last look at us.

"It's pointless, Nell," Lia singsongs to me as her locker door closes. I sigh, giving in at last. "I know."

"Do you?" she asks, almost under her breath, still shaking her head.

"*What?*" I ask.

"Nell. You're obsessed with him."

"Oh, get off it," I respond, closing my locker with more force than necessary. I shove my fingers through my hair, pushing it back. "Exams are in a few weeks and he's breathing down my neck. He's just trying to get under my skin. And his whole 'I don't care' thing is such bullshit. He has to study sometime. He can't be *that* much smarter than me."

Lia looks at me with a slightly kinder expression, something like pity. "He's not. You'll beat him. Don't stress so much." She touches the side of my face. "It'll get stuck like that."

I swat her hand away playfully, and hip-bump her. I know she means well.

"Are we riding with Taylor?" I ask, putting my armor back up. The exposed cracks feel too much like weakness.

I'd ridden to school with my mom this morning—Mom made a comment about how it was probably a good idea I get in early to study and *have you thought about putting on some lipstick?*—but Lia usually gives me a ride home from practice. This week, though, her car is in the shop, so her brother is our ride.

She nods and starts walking to the exit of the locker room. I follow her.

Outside, we hear spring sports under way. Tennis racquets hitting balls hard, a pitching machine whirring on the softball field in the distance, and the sound of a baseball colliding with a catcher's mitt. All of the equipment state of the art, all the athletes top caliber, built on years of private lessons paid for by their parents. Cedar Woods Prep—the most hated school in lower-state South Carolina.

They pay the best athletes to come to their school—we can't compete with their facilities, the public school parents say. *They have donors; they'll always win.*

I know what the public school kids hear. I used to be one of them.

Before Mom got the head job here, that was me, always a couple of steps behind the Prep volleyball players on the court. I may have been the cream of the crop at Cedar Woods Middle School, but that wasn't enough. I had transferred to Prep with Mom and done what I did best, risen to the top. To my prep classmates, I was the middle-class head of school's jumped-up daughter, rated only slightly higher than the scholarship kids in their minds, but even in a world where legacy kids were always expected to win, I never went down without a fight. I still remember meeting with the freshman guidance counselor on my first day, staring down at my transcript.

"Smart girl," he said. "You'll fit in just fine here—keep your head down, and Cedar Woods' prestige will put you on your way to a good college."

I remember, too, scanning the sophomores', juniors', and seniors' class rankings posted right outside the admin hall. At the top, all the boys' names. Right next to pamphlets for the best schools in the country. Not just *good* colleges.

He'd had no idea: I don't fit in, and I don't keep my head down.

Luckily, despite being in a place where I didn't make friends easily, I had Lia, who oftentimes still thinks she's protecting me from myself.

We'd been best friends since I moved to Prep freshmen year and have played volleyball on the same club team for longer than that.

In the bullpen off the baseball field, Lia's twin brother, Taylor, is throwing pitches. He's much taller than Lia, almost exactly the same height as me and built skinny as a rail, like his mom. The twins' freckles, blue eyes, and curly blond hair match up perfectly, though, and their pale skin picks up color with even the most limited exposure to the summer sun. Each of Taylor's pitches hits the catcher's mitt with a loud *thwop*. Lia and I make our way over and I prop my chin up on the yellow plastic covering the top of the fence, watching him go. I've heard he throws high nineties on a good day.

He doesn't look at me, but I think he sees me when he sends one way over his catcher's head.

"What was that, Reagan?" I call with a grin, goading him.

"He doesn't perform well under pressure," Jackson, who is of course the star catcher, calls out, fetching the ball. He sheds his mask before throwing the ball back to Taylor.

Lia catches my eye, smiling. "You gonna be done anytime soon?" she asks Taylor. He catches the ball from Jackson, looking annoyed.

"Give me fifteen," he says.

"Okay," she says just to me. "In that case, I'm going to go see if I can catch Andrea before she leaves. She said she'd lend me her history notes."

I nod. She runs off, and I sit back on a hill leading down to the baseball field, admiring the grass, which is perfectly maintained by the Prep grounds crew. I watch Taylor throw a couple more pitches before I pull out my bio textbook and start reading that night's assignment.

"We're done," someone says around the time I hit the third page. I look up to see Jackson, walking up the hill with a bat bag over his shoulder. "You look pretty transfixed," he goes on. "Most exciting thing that's happened to you all week?"

"Yeah. Totally." I slam the book shut.

"Do you ever stop studying?" he asks, nudging my book with his foot. I yank it away and slide it back into my bag. "That's cute. Almost as cute as it's going to be when I take valedictorian."

I push myself up from the ground, putting my bag over my shoulder. "Sorry," I tell him. "My time spent engaging with you for the day has officially run out."

He grins. "I had a chance to speak to the illustrious Mrs. Becker today."

"Right."

He goes to leave, but then turns all the way around, talking to me while walking backward with an amused look on his face. "She says I'm a compelling young man."

"I'm sure she didn't mean it as a compliment."

"Probably not," he concedes. Then, with a smile like poison: "Bye, Nell."

I go the other way down the hill, annoyed again. I hate that he knows how to get under my skin.

Taylor is coming through the gate as I reach it. "You look pissed," he says.

"Jackson," I reply. That's enough. As Lia's twin, Taylor's known me long enough to know the way I feel about Jackson. Our lives have always intersected at sleepovers at the Reagan house, long trips to volleyball tournaments, and questionable bouts of teenage rebellion. To Taylor, I'm another one of Lia's extremities. He gives me a half smile as we walk toward his car.

"Did you hear he broke up with Shauna?" Taylor asks.

Shauna Meyers is a cute junior with a huge house on the river. Her family has something like two boats and three Jet Skis, and she'd been latched on to Jackson like a parasite for the past three months. "Can't believe that didn't work out," I say, like I absolutely can believe that.

Taylor chuckles. "I can't help but wonder how he does it. How he gets away with it."

"With what?"

"Shauna's, what? His third girlfriend of the school year?"

Fourth. But I'm not going to admit I know that.

Taylor continues on. "He treats girls like they're disposable and yet there's always one waiting to be next in line. You know he's not good to them. He's way too self-involved."

"That's psychology I can't even imagine digging into," I return. I hear the arrogance in my own voice, judging those girls. "But I kind of do know how he does it. He sees through people to what they want and gives it to them. They *need* to believe him. You should have heard the interpretation of *The Scarlet Letter* he gave in class today. It was complete nonsense but he had Mrs. Wesley eating out of his hand." I actually *have* spent a lot of time thinking about it. Too much, clearly.

Taylor laughs, running his hand through his hair. "Oh my God, are you still on about that?"

"Don't be an asshole."

"I heard a phenomenal retelling of the whole incident from Doug Rivera earlier."

"This school is too small," I say as we get to Taylor's SUV. He hits the Unlock button.

"You're right, though," Taylor says. "Everyone at this school fawns all over Jackson like he's the Second Coming—and, like, just because he's good at stuff, we're all supposed to worship him?"

I step up onto the passenger's-side floorboard, watching Taylor over the car. "I thought you liked him."

"I guess he's fine," Taylor says, hedging. It's so aggressively Taylor— he's the definition of nice, which will get you run over in this world. He's all floppy hair and easygoing smiles and he wants to like everyone.

What a waste of time.

Finally, Taylor sums it up. "But he gets whatever he wants. He does whatever he wants."

To be honest, that's pretty rich coming from Taylor. The Reagans may not have as much money as the Harts, but they're on the "rolling in it" side of well-off. Their house had its own spread in *Charleston Home+Design* last year. Before his dad started making headlines for other reasons.

"I think it's pretty simple. He believes he deserves whatever he gets, so everyone else believes it, too," I explain to him. "I keep trying to use that strategy myself, only everyone thinks I'm an overeager bitch."

"You're not, though," Taylor says sincerely, as if I wasn't just deflecting my jealousy. "You're smart. You can see through him and most people can't. Even people I really like."

I can't help but think it then. That I want to pry underneath the surface of Jackson and tear him apart, examine the pieces. Find what makes him weak and use it. I want to beat him.

I'm *going* to beat him.

"Can you imagine that kind of power?" I ask him, hearing the longing in my own voice.

"You'll have all the power you want one day," he answers me confidently.

"Taylor!" Lia yells in the distance, and we both look up as she comes running from the fields. "Are you leaving me?"

I give him a smile as if Jackson doesn't matter at all and slide into the front seat.

3

Mom's still at work when I get home, and Dad's grilling burgers on the back porch. Already changed into gym shorts and a T-shirt, with a beer in one hand, he looks more like himself than he ever does in the suits he wears to work. I dump my backpack and gym bag on the kitchen floor and go out to join him.

"There she is," Dad says as I lean over his shoulder to check out the burgers. "Don't sweat on the goods."

I laugh, falling into a chair at the table on the screened-in porch. "How was your day?"

"Finally got an offer on this house I've had on the market for the last month," Dad tells me as he flips a burger. Well. That explains the good mood.

"Congrats," I say as he chugs his beer. He's built tall and stocky, like me but with lighter hair, a rounder face. I look sharp; he looks kind.

"I think it's the worst stretch I've had since I started," he goes on, explaining himself to me like I've questioned his commitment. "Even during the recession, I was making my numbers, but with the way everyone's using the Internet now, it's different." He sighs. "But enough about me. How was school, kid?"

I start to answer him, but the sound of the door opening as Mom joins us on the porch distracts me. She's still in her Head of School Mary Becker pantsuit with a crisp white sleeveless blouse and stockinged feet, only missing her jacket and shoes. Mom's back is always straight. She doesn't need to ask for respect—everything about her demands it.

"Nell, can you please not throw your bags in the middle of the floor when you come in? I almost tripped over them." She goes to Dad and grabs the beer from his hand, taking a swig, and gives it back to him. She turns to me. "Oh, honey, you look exhausted."

I wilt under her gaze. That doesn't sound like a compliment.

She falls in the chair opposite me but I can feel her scrutiny all over me. "Your mascara's running," she says after a minute.

I wipe it away with the pad of my thumb, black streaks rubbing off onto my skin. "So it is. Thank you for pointing that out." My words are flat.

Mom's eyes flick back and forth over the rest of me, looking for imperfections, no doubt. She leans against the rocking chair, sliding her feet onto the seat so that it sways with her shift. "I got a text ten minutes ago. Coach Madison went into premature labor. She told me earlier that she thought it would be a good idea to give you girls the rest of the spring off, and with so little of the semester left, I tend to agree."

I blow out a long, loud breath, tugging at the roots of my hair. "I'm going to have to figure out another way to keep in shape until club season starts."

She levels a look at me, and I can tell I said the right thing. "I can ask Coach Montoya if you could work out with the baseball team during seventh period. I heard his conditioning is tough. And you can keep up drilling with Lia. It's not like you've got anything useful to do after school now that the yearbook's done, right?"

It's not like whatever it was would meet her definition of *useful* if I did. Besides, working out with the boys will be a good challenge for me. "Do you think he'll mind?" I ask, noncommittal. I don't completely love the idea that I could potentially make a fool of myself in front of them, either.

"I don't care if he minds," she says. "It's my school and despite what anyone in this community thinks, girls get the same opportunities as boys." She shrugs. "Being in charge has its advantages."

Dad snickers, but I watch her. It's strange, but I teeter right on the edge so much of the time. Of whether I want to please her or be her.

Dad comes to stand over Mom's chair. "I don't know. It might not be a bad idea if Nell took a break from constant training for a couple of weeks with exams coming up. She could use the study time. And the break, to be honest."

"Hmm." Mom frowns. "Is that what you'd prefer?"

My eyes move back and forth between the two of them, feeling like I'm caught in some game. I grapple with the suddenly too intense feeling that I don't know what I'm supposed to want at all, and that feeling weighs on me, my mind racing away. *Breathe. Nell. Think. Nell.* "I shouldn't take a break this close to club season," I say at last, and I see the way Mom's eyes shift ever so slightly. I breathe. But Dad watches me steadily, and I almost hear what he doesn't say.

"There's something else I heard," Mom continues, grabbing Dad's beer again. "I think they're adding another charge to Arnold Reagan's trial."

I try not to react. "Where did you hear that from?"

"One of the teachers. And if it's reached them, God knows how long it's been buzzing around."

"How are Lia and Taylor doing?" Dad asks. I can tell he feels as uncomfortable as I do.

"I guess the good news is that rich people never have to go to prison for very long," I say.

"Don't be callous," Mom says, and then I can't stand feeling like I'm not doing right by either of them. Sometimes I don't know how else to be but callous, to force my emotions off.

"I need to go study," I tell them, pushing through the door back into the house.

4

When one of the richest families in town is prosecuting one of the most established families in town, school functions get complicated fast. Lia and I are at Taylor's baseball game the next night, seated on the opposing team's side to avoid the Proctors. Columbus Proctor is Cedar Woods' starting shortstop, six and a half feet tall with a smile that could break your heart. The Proctors are one of the few black families at Prep, but we aren't supposed to talk about it. Besides Michonne, who is mixed race, there's only one other black student in the entire junior class, and I'd heard white classmates make jokes in front of all three of them that they wouldn't dare make in polite company. The lack of diversity was old, ingrained into the walls, and chipped away only little by little. Columbus's dad, Everett, is a retired NFL lineman and current motivational speaker, twice as big as most of the parents in Cedar Woods, with a laugh to match. I'd seen so many of the other parents suck up to him to his face, reliving his best college and professional plays, and then mock his rags-to-riches story and family barbecues behind his back, as if he wasn't as smart as them, despite the fact he'd graduated cum laude from Georgia. Columbus's mom, Carla Proctor, is the lead solicitor for our district—the lead solicitor who brought corruption charges against the mayor two months ago.

That would be Mayor Arnold Reagan. Lia and Taylor's dad.

The truth is, these little soapy family dramas aren't exactly uncommon in Cedar Woods. Mom jokes that she has to track shifting allegiances and newly formed enemies among the parents like a list of dramatis personae in the front of a fantasy novel. But this one had shaken the community—the Reagan family had always had a pristine reputation; Lia and Taylor's dad had followed in the footsteps of Reagan mayors before him, an upstanding rich man who still cared about the little people.

And there, on the other side of the field, fiercely independent Carla Proctor, dressed in her Cedar Woods Knights best. I can still remember her election commercials—her smiling, someone who actually felt like a real person, like you or me, who'd married into money and was going to use that influence to take down the self-satisfied Cedar Woods government. The Cedar Woods electorate—who, up to that point, had always been smart enough to do what they'd been told—had rebelled and elected her, and she'd done exactly what she promised.

I'd never tell Lia, but I so admired her.

Mom would say it was a low goal to aspire to: to *marry* into your wealth and then choose to be a public servant. I guess that's true. But, I think, as I so often do, that the chance to bring down these people who've had the world handed to them on a platter would be worth it. Especially boys like Jackson. There had been a scandal in Cedar Woods when I was in middle school—a hazing by the now-defunct Cedar Woods Prep lacrosse team that had left a scholarship student named Bryce McCabe dead, with no one sure exactly what had happened. His teammates said Bryce had been walking along the railing of the bridge across the river and fallen in, hitting his head on the way down. His family said he'd never have been on the railing if he wasn't forced.

Tensions had been high at the time, but the boys were never charged with anything, despite the family's pleas. I saw one of them had been hired at a prominent tech company recently.

Prep hired Mom the next year, mostly to get the town off its back, to look like they were cleaning up the toxic-masculinity culture that had permeated the school for years. She was the first ever female head of school. Since Prep had gone coed only twenty years earlier, it was an even bigger deal.

I still think about Bryce sometimes when I'm driving over the river, crossing that divide. I wonder if Carla Proctor does, too.

I wonder if she was thinking of Bryce when she filed the charges against Mr. Reagan.

I pull myself back into the present as Taylor throws the final pitch of the game—I could tell it would be from the way it left his hand. The batter swings desperately but the ball is already hitting Jackson's glove. Jackson throws off his helmet, running forward and giving Taylor a high five before literally jumping into Columbus's arms. Of course, Jackson has to display his best friendship like he's performing in an exceptionally entertaining movie about himself. Taylor and Columbus avoid each other as the rest of the boys congratulate one another on their natural winner genes and superiority. I glance at Lia and catch her watching everyone cheering on the Cedar Woods side of the field with longing. Without thinking about it, I reach my hand across to hers and grab it. She looks down gratefully.

"It's fine," she tells me. It's her common refrain.

Normally, Taylor's girlfriend, Amanda Yee, would at least come over during the game and sit with us for a couple of innings, but she's already left for the weekend to visit her little brother, who has been in the hospital in Charleston for the past two weeks, receiving treatment for leukemia. Somehow, without her bubbliness around, the whole thing feels even more miserable.

As the team exits the dugout, Lia and I hang back waiting for Taylor. I haven't seen either of their parents at a game this season. Mr. Reagan is still for all intents and purposes the mayor, but completely out of the public eye. Annie Reagan, on the other hand, has fallen back into her worst habit. Namely, the project of replacing her entire bloodstream with white wine.

But still, there are plenty of Cedar Woods residents on the Reagans' side because well-off and white doesn't fold easily—they weren't likely to say it out loud, but Mom told me many of the Prep parents implied to her that they thought Carla Proctor had taken it "too far". I tried not to take sides, here more for Lia's emotional support.

The boys file out slowly. It's the usual crowd of parents; I've been to enough games to have a pretty good idea about exactly who is too checked into their kids' lives, who isn't at all, and the small few with good sense. But tonight there are two I don't recognize: a tiny little waif of a woman with salon bottle–blond hair, her skin still a little pallid under makeup, and her tall, dark, and handsome husband. He'd been on his phone for the entire game.

Jackson and Columbus come out of the dugout together. I find myself studying the easy way Jackson carries happiness on his shoulders, always seeming so carefree. Columbus's parents go over to them, Mrs. Proctor giving Jackson a hug. Then I see Jackson notice the other couple, and shake the Proctors off in the nicest, easiest way before approaching the other two. Of course, now that they are next to one another, the relationship comes into stark focus. He's an older version of Jackson, the way his mouth moves, his gestures. His hair is graying slightly, and he's wearing a jacket with no tie. Jackson stands straighter in front of his dad than I've ever seen him.

"You were great, honey," his mom says, her voice slight. He gives her a smile that would probably melt a lesser person's heart. He glances over at his dad and then averts his eyes.

"I'm glad y'all came," he says to them. Even though I can acknowledge something deeply depraved in it, I can't stop watching him. Like I'm looking through a funhouse mirror at a different version of Jackson Hart, one who's missing color around the edges, who lacks clarity. "Hungry?" he asks then, putting his arm around his mom like a person who's overcompensating. "I'll take you to dinner. My treat. Maybe Dad will even look up from his phone when the food comes out."

His mom is totally enthralled by him, I can tell, but his dad's face doesn't twitch in the slightest. "Do you have to be cute about every goddamn thing?" he asks, as if he's been holding it in the whole time.

"There it is," Jackson says. He glances over at me, and I look away. "That was fun. What did that take, Dad, only two minutes?"

His dad sighs, takes his phone back out, and starts walking toward the parking lot. His mom hardly falters at all. "Don't be like that. He always looked up when you were coming to bat." She touches his cheek. "You're so talented, my dear."

His eyes are soft. "Thanks, Mom." He kisses her on the cheek. "I'll meet you in the car," he says in a way that is clear he is dismissing her, and she seems more than happy to be dismissed. She walks the way his dad went, and Jackson stands there, alone. He smiles at Columbus's parents as they file by and grabs on to Columbus's hand as he passes. I see Columbus's eyes go to Lia and me, and as if he can't help it, he says, "Hey, Nell. Hey, Lia. Hope y'all have a nice night," and then his mom puts her arm around him and they head in the direction of the cars.

Lia sighs, rubbing her hands over her arms. "Where is Taylor?" she asks.

I glance at Jackson again, standing still, eyes on the ground. His hands are working at his side, his fingers twisting around one another. And then he sees me watching him; a light clicks into place behind his eyes.

Taylor comes out of the dugout and Jackson looks away, staring down at his hand, flexing it into a fist. "Hey," Taylor says, bending to give his sister a hug. "Thanks for waiting."

"Nice pitching, Reagan," I compliment him.

He gives me a weak smile. "Thanks." Then to Lia, "You okay?"

She shakes her head and says something quietly back to him, and I step over to give them their space.

"What'd you think?" Jackson calls to me then, his voice low.

I look off, away from him. "About what?"

He puts both hands out at his sides. "The show."

I know he's referring to his parents and I force all my features into a straight line. "You're always exactly who I think you are, Jackson."

He tips his cap at me and then follows everyone else, whistling all the while.

It's unfair of him, really, even at his worst, to barely flinch at all.

• • •

My family has always jokingly referred to the Reagans' house as the White House for obvious reasons. Namely that it's white—shining white—and because their status as the First Family of Cedar Woods has been around longer than I have.

It's less funny now, with the Reagan name so tarnished.

Lia, Taylor, and I are spread out on Mrs. Reagan's exorbitantly expensive white couch eating pizza and watching a movie. Taylor has mixed himself a vodka and something, and he's finding the lines in the movie funnier as time goes on.

After a particularly loud guffaw, Lia cuts her eyes at him. "You need to put that back in the liquor cabinet," she tells him. "And lock it."

"So she can drive to the store? Brilliant idea," Taylor says, his voice meaner than usual.

I've seen the current look on Lia's face often—it's when she's ready to destroy someone. "I think this type of behavior is called *mimicry*."

Taylor stares at her, his eyes narrowed, and sips his drink.

"You're going through a stressful situation, so you're drinking to deal with it. Like Mom," Lia goes on, as if explaining it to him will help.

"Lia," I start.

"What?" She throws her hands up. "I'm the bad guy for pointing out the self-destructive tendencies in this fucking family?"

"No, Lia, as ever, you're the one true hero for us all," Taylor replies.

"Oh, you're one to talk," she snaps. "It's not like people didn't notice you not speaking to Columbus the entire game."

Taylor laughs, flattening his back on the couch. "Or you sitting on the opposing team's bleachers. I mean, poor Columbus. How does he make it through his day knowing the family his mom's ruining won't talk to him?"

"We need to maintain appearances."

"And that's what I do," Taylor says, "for the other twenty-two hours of the day. I won the game for us, didn't I? Look at me. I'm fucking perfect. Now let me have a couple of minutes to not be."

My eyes go back and forth between the two of them. My family is all passive-aggressive insults and usually the Reagans work the same way, so this outright hostility between Lia and Taylor isn't something I'm used to.

There's been a lot of it lately.

Lia turns off the movie, flouncing through the family room and out the back door. I give Taylor a look and move to follow her.

"It's *one* drink, Nell!" he calls behind me. I hear him reaching for the remote as I follow Lia outside.

The Reagans' backyard is pristine, the local landscapers visiting once a week to keep everything clean. Mom keeps a garden in our backyard; it's a mess of mismatched plants and trees growing in unexpected directions, twisting around one another, the pruning somewhat sporadic. But in Mrs. Reagan's garden, everything has a place: rows are planted carefully, and shrubbery is maintained as if it's open for public viewing. There's a table and chairs on the patio, with a brick path cutting through the garden and leading toward a koi pond.

Lia is in front of the pond, staring down into it. I go stand beside her and look down, but the fish are doing the same old thing they always are. I wait a moment.

"I've always hated these fish," she says to me, not looking up. "Whenever Mom is sober, she becomes obsessed with them. She's always all, 'But what about the fish?' and 'Who will take care of the fish?' and out here feeding them and shit, and I'm like, you know, where is that ounce of care for me? Would she like me better if I was a fucking fish? Because then I wouldn't be quite so complicated, right? I would just swim around and eat. That'd be ideal for her, don't you think?" She glances up at me. "If Taylor and I didn't feel anything, and were just here to calm her and be perfect. And we both try. So. Damn. Hard."

"Do you want to kill one?" I ask her. "We could get like a fishing rod or something."

Her whole face shifts into disgust. "*What?*"

I shrug. "I don't know. You hate the fish, and I'm a problem solver."

She laughs. A little bit at first, and then it keeps building until she's laughing so hard she doubles over, taking in small hiccups of breath. The more she laughs, the funnier it gets, and then I can't stop laughing, either. We collapse next to each other on the ground beside the pond, Lia's curly hair tickling my skin. Our laughter fades out slowly, along with the sunlight. Finally, Lia manages to say, "You are so twisted." She pushes a tear from under her eye. "And that was a really poetic speech, too."

"I know," I tell her. "It was good. I was honestly moved."

"To commit fish murder," she says with another laugh. "Which you'd rather do than talk about my feelings, apparently."

"I'm sorry." I squeeze her shoulder. "I didn't know what to say."

"Clearly." Her smile fades slightly. "Do you think Taylor's okay?"

"He's fine," I tell her, confident. "Taylor's so even-keeled all the time, of course he needs to act out every now and then. If he didn't, he would explode."

"This is going to be the death of us all." She sighs, staring up at the pink-streaked sky. "Sometimes, I wish I could be more like you. Know what I want, not be so caught up in appearances."

I glance at the back of the house, at Mr. Reagan's dimly lit office window and then at Mrs. Reagan's dark bedroom window. I don't see much of either of them anymore, even less than before—which still hadn't been that frequently.

"It's not as great as it looks," I admit to her at last. But Lia knows. That's why she's always trying to pull me back from the edge.

"You get to be your own person in the world. Not so tangled up in who your parents are. Do you know what my mom would say to me if she found out I was telling off Jackson Hart in English class? 'No one wants to marry a girl like that.'"

I laugh, loud. "To be fair, she's probably right."

"'Be smart but not too smart. Be a leader but step aside. Be an athlete but never look too strong.' It isn't all about the trial. It's about playing a part, and I'm tired of it. Taylor, too. Mom and Dad can go make a scene whenever they like, but we're not worth anything unless we look good."

I shrug. "You don't have to play a part for me."

"It's nice," Lia answers. "To really feel like myself sometimes." She sits up, hugging her legs.

"Why don't we watch a really bad movie?" I suggest. "Or you could tell me more about all your feelings. I don't know. Whichever."

She laughs again, a crisp sound in the settling dark.

5

Smoke curls into the air, fire reaching out and grabbing at every last bit of wood on the bonfire at the Waccamaw River shore. I watch it go up up up in flames, everyone stepping back as much as they can from the heat because it's way too damn hot on an April Tuesday night this close to the beach.

"Burn, baby, burn," Lia says, falling into my side and pushing me away. I laugh, shoving her back.

The bonfire marks the beginning of spring sports playoffs this week, when the proud Knights of Cedar Woods Prep will destroy every poor bumpkin school in the state of South Carolina who deemed themselves worthy to put another team on the field. It is a metaphorical funeral, really, for the hopes and dreams of those sickeningly average kids who would never be asked to stand in the heat with Prep's best and brightest.

"You look like you're having a dark thought," Lia says to me then.

The flames dance in my eyes. "No more than usual."

"Are you girls having fun?"

We both turn around to find Lia's mom over our shoulders, dressed in all white. The bonfire is a storied occasion, too important to miss. I'd also heard her say something about not being scared off by a bunch of sanctimonious low-country Democrats. Mrs. Reagan's red Solo cup of Chardonnay sloshes to and fro as she puts an arm around Lia's shoulder.

"So much fun," Lia says in a clipped voice as she pushes Mrs. Reagan's cup of wine aside to give us a wider berth from any spillover. "The time of our lives."

"Nell, you look very nice," she says, removing her arm from Lia's shoulder and resting a hot hand against the side of my face. "You put yourself together very carefully, don't you?"

I look at her, not sure if it's some sort of passive-aggressive insult or not. Her eyes are kind of sharp, the way she's always looked at me, even during her sober stretches. I have on a tasteful sundress and a headband holding my auburn hair in place, understated, unlike what some of the other girls showed up in.

"Jesus Christ, Mom," Lia says, pulling her mother away from me. "I'm taking her back to Dad," she adds, to me.

"Well, Nell knows it, sweetie," I hear Mrs. Reagan still saying as Lia ushers her off. "She's perfect. She's got everything all planned out."

I roll my shoulders, staring into the flames. Mrs. Reagan has always been like that, since I met Lia in seventh grade. I was never sure if she liked that Lia and I were best friends when there were so many better-bred options around the halls of Prep. But Lia and Taylor had adopted me, given me a place in this world, and never looked back.

Sometimes, I think that I should appreciate what they've given me more.

"Perfectly Planned Nell."

Goose bumps rise all over my body. I glance over my shoulder, then back out at the fire and the water. "God, are you following me?"

Jackson steps beside me. I can smell the alcohol in the cup he's holding. "You wish I was following you."

I press my lips together. Sigh. "Do you want something?"

"She's right, you know. Annie Reagan might be turned up to ten, but she's right about you."

"Oh, yes, please psychoanalyze me some more," I say. Then I look him over. "Are my feelings toward you not clear enough?"

"You're so dull," he says, sipping on his drink, continuing to stand next to me.

I laugh. "And you're so obvious."

"What does that mean?"

I shake my head.

"What, Becker?"

I face him. He has on a nice light blue button-down, a pair of khaki shorts, and ridiculous boat shoes. His dark hair is perfectly tousled, sticking up at angles as if the wind helped him plan it. "You're doing this on purpose. You're antagonizing me because you're bored."

His eyebrows go up.

"Your fan club isn't entertaining enough for you so you have to come over and pick a fight with me. You guys are all the same—your games can only entertain you for so long. But please, go on about how *I'm* the dull one."

Jackson opens his mouth for what I'm sure he thinks will be a devastating rebuttal, but I never hear what he would've said because at that moment, Taylor calls my name.

"Nell!" He's jogging over to the two of us. "Lia just texted me. Everything all right?"

I shrug, stepping back from Jackson.

Taylor nods at Jackson the way boys do. "Hart."

Jackson sips his drink in a maddeningly superior way. "Reagan."

"Sorry about Mom," Taylor says, looking only at me.

"I'm used to her," I say. "It's not a big deal."

Taylor gives me this look and I realize *I'm used to her* probably wasn't a thing I should have said.

"Are you coming to the game on Friday?" he asks me. He sips from a cup of water.

"Yeah, for sure." I look around at everything but Jackson. "I'm wondering how long before it will be socially acceptable to leave this thing. I've got a bunch of work to do before tomorrow."

Jackson laughs. "Of course you do."

I narrow my eyes at him. "I have a lot going on," I say.

He offers me his drink and I bat it away.

The wind carries a voice up from down near the water where most of the parents are standing. It takes a minute before I'm able to track it to a woman yelling. All I can see from here is that she's petite and blond, which puts her in the majority of women at this event, and that quite a few people are looking at her in alarm. The tall dark-haired man with her looks to be on the receiving end of her anger.

"Oh shit," Jackson says next to me. He drops his cup right in the sand and takes off running toward the fray. Taylor exchanges a look with me and we follow him, watching with interest. Us and everyone else in the general vicinity.

I catch some snippets of what the woman is saying as we approach. Something about how *no, I won't calm down* and *no, I don't need a drink* and to *get out of my face before I throw it on you.* Jackson grabs her before she can say something else and he's mumbling to her and then she bursts into tears, and he momentarily pulls her into his chest. He pushes her through the crowd of staring people, right in our direction, and the man trails behind them. I recognize Jackson's parents from last week's baseball game. As the trio approaches us, I hear Mr. Hart say, "You two always have to go and make a damn scene." Jackson laughs at that, and I watch the lines of his face, the way he doesn't think it's funny at all. He's rubbing his mom's back.

"It's just the antidepressants," she's saying to him. "Throwing me all off."

Jackson's eyes catch mine as he brushes past Taylor and me. I open my mouth like I'm going to say something helpful but then close it and let them walk away. For a moment, everything around the bonfire stays quiet, but slowly the conversation builds back up, leaving the incident forgotten and Jackson long gone.

Just another night in Cedar Woods.

"What was that?" I ask Taylor.

"The Harts," he says darkly. "I've never seen them do *that*. They're usually the most normal parents at any given party."

I swallow the sympathy bubbling up in my chest. For Jackson. *Screw that.* "Do you think they'll be all right?"

"Yeah." Taylor nods. "I saw Doug running after them. I'll shoot him a text, though."

That's Taylor—determined to help everyone. I watch him type up the text, refusing to show any curiosity.

"I know what that's like, you know? When your parents become the scene," Taylor says at last. It isn't polite for me to agree with him, so I don't. Progress.

I stare off at where Jackson's mom was standing, remembering the wind whipping her blond hair around her face. I wonder if she's okay.

But I don't ask Taylor. I get the feeling from his expression that the answer is probably no anyway.

• • •

Our street looks cheerful as we pull back into the driveway. Cozy, even. It would seem like a nice place if you hadn't just been on the other side of town with all its landscaped lawns and beautiful architecture and perfection.

After that, our street looks inferior.

I get out of the backseat and follow my parents into the house.

"Are Lia and Taylor okay?" Mom's asking me as we walk up the steps. I eye her cautiously as Dad fits his key into the lock. Everyone saw Mrs. Reagan at the bonfire, sloshing her wine.

"They're . . . fine." It's the polite way to say it, I guess. Nothing out of the ordinary here. "Lia got her mom out of there before she could really make a scene." Then I absentmindedly tug on my dress, thinking about what Mrs. Reagan said to me.

"Thank God those two were born with some sense," Mom says as

31

she kicks her heels off at the staircase. "Because neither of their parents have a lick of it. One can only assume it's recessive and nature prevailed over nurture at some point."

"We should have them over for dinner sometime," Dad says. He presses his fingers into my back in a way that feels protective.

I don't answer.

"I'm opening a bottle of wine. I hate those godforsaken events," Mom says. "Nell, honey, can you unzip my dress?"

I do as she asks and the zipper exposes her freckled back. She rolls her shoulders up and down in a familiar motion and then saunters off into the kitchen, coming back with a bottle of white and two wineglasses, her entire back and her bra just exposed like that's good enough.

"You're in a good mood," Dad says as if it's an unusual thing, taking the wineglass Mom passes to him. He flips the television on.

"Must you watch TV?" she asks, and he resumes ignoring her. Mom narrows her eyes, twisting the top off the wine bottle rather aggressively. "Only three more ridiculously overproduced ceremonies to go before this school year's over. Nell, why are you standing there? Why don't you come sit down?"

I look over at her, already drinking her wine, and Dad, already watching something like there's nothing in the conversation for him, sipping absentmindedly on the glass she poured him.

"Did you see the Harts tonight?" I ask her.

She drinks her wine slowly, not answering.

"I have seen more ridiculous fights between adults in front of their children in Mary's three years at Prep than I have in my entire life," Dad says, not looking away from the TV. "The maturity level. What my dad would think of that, if he were still alive." He whistles and shakes his head.

Mom continues sipping her wine. Her not having an opinion is unusual. She loves judging people.

"Taylor said he's never seen the Harts act like that," I continue, stuck on the point.

"Are you concerned?" Mom asks as if she's uninterested. "You see the Reagans like that all the time, don't you?"

"That doesn't make it okay," Dad replies to Mom, a challenge in his voice. "I can't stand that Nell has to be around that. It was never like that where I'm from."

"Oh, yes, life was so much better in Buckley, South Carolina," Mom says sarcastically. Mom grew up half an hour outside of Cedar Woods—her family was old money, but her dad had lost most of it in business ventures—while Dad is from a small town a few hours away. They met in college.

Them ever having been in love isn't something I can imagine.

"People respected family," Dad bites back at her. "They respected privacy."

"*Look*," I cut in between the two of them, hoping to defuse. I know Dad doesn't see why I need to go to private school, why we're suddenly too good for the public school our taxes pay for. He didn't grow up middle class, and even though he never actually says it out loud, it's clear he thinks this whole town and this elite Cedar Woods world is a betrayal of his values. "I wasn't trying to start something. I was just wondering if something happened with the Harts. I don't know—it seemed hostile."

"Nell," Mom says, cutting a sharp look at Dad before she continues, "you're going to see people like the Harts for the rest of your life. You'd do best to forget it. It's none of our business what goes on behind closed doors." Dad looks like he wants to say something but doesn't.

I think about that, nodding my head slightly. "So I should pretend it never happened? That doesn't seem right."

"It doesn't," Dad mumbles. "Maybe you should check on the kid tomorrow."

Mom sighs. "I don't think Jackson Hart needs our help. You know he's the one right behind Nell in the class rankings," she informs Dad.

"I don't see what that has to do with anything."

Mom sips her wine. "Only that our daughter has a chance to be the third female valedictorian in Prep history, so I don't think she needs to be wasting her time cheering up Jackson Hart. Or had you forgotten that?"

I don't see how he could. I've heard it so many times, it's basically carved on my brain.

I watch Dad's unimpressed face, and then start, "Maybe I should—"

"Nell," Mom cuts me off with a tone of finality. "Mind your own business."

6

I'm walking toward the weight room before seventh period the next day when I see Jackson walking in the opposite direction. I slow down. He doesn't look any different from every other day. Arrogant and annoyingly superior in his regulation khakis and white Oxford, his sleeves rolled up to expose his tanned forearms. But I hear my dad's voice the way I do sometimes—his voice imploring me to take his side every now and then—and stop.

"Hart," I call.

He diverts from the straight line he's walking through the hallway and comes over to me, his blue eyes already looking bored with the conversation we're not having. "Can I help you?"

I blink slowly, looking up at him. I wish this were anyone but him, because the last thing I want is for Jackson to think I care about his well-being. I just want to be the kind of person my dad would be proud of, to show I haven't lost myself in Cedar Woods. "Look, I know it's none of my business, but is everything okay? Taylor said your parents . . ." I trail off. I don't even want him to know I asked about him to begin with.

He rubs his eyes. "Jesus Christ, you're really this clueless, aren't you?"

"Excuse me?"

"How could you possibly have been going to school here for this long and still have absolutely no idea how to deal with people?" Everything in his tone is condescending. My blood runs through my veins hot and angry.

"I seem to do all right," I shoot back.

"Ignore it, Becker. Just like every other person besides you in this school knows how to do. Even your precious Taylor. Look at what the Reagans are doing every day. Why must you make it so obvious you don't belong here?"

I curl my fingernails into my palms. "My valedictorian spot and All-State volleyball nomination seem to disagree."

"And what are those things going to do for you in the real world?" He shakes his head. "You are *so* ignorant."

"You just keep hoping that if you give me enough shit, eventually I'll roll over and let you win, don't you? Like, I'm so sorry my parents know better than to embarrass me in front of the entire school."

He gives a dark chuckle in response to that. "Let me give you a helpful tip: Try and understand how this place works before your accomplishments no longer mean anything."

"You think I don't know how it works? How you cover up your sad little hurt feelings by insulting me? Like I'm the damaged one for asking."

He stares at me and I stare back, waiting for something I don't think will ever come. Finally, he blows out a sigh. "One day you'll figure out how to leave well enough alone."

"Get out of my face," I say at last.

"With pleasure," he answers, stepping around me as he goes. I watch him continue down the hall, moving slowly at first, different from before. But gradually, it comes back. The shoulders, the bored posture. The arrogance. So simple.

I turn around, frustrated. Don't care. Don't show emotion. Stay on top.

Easy enough.

7

On Friday the baseball team wins their game, the poor little public school they play handily dismissed. After the game Taylor and Lia talk me into going, just this once, to a party at Alston Marcus's house. We have a late club volleyball practice tomorrow and *don't I want to celebrate the awesome victory?* And I agree, mostly because I think they just don't want to go home.

Alston Marcus graduated from Prep last year and instead of doing the college thing, decided to strike out on his own, move from his parents' house, and live like the common people. Or his dad threw Alston out after he caught him dealing prescription pills out of their house—whichever version you prefer. He lives in a falling-apart two-story on my side of town and hosts parties on an almost-weekly basis. I do not attend these parties.

Taylor finds a parking spot down the street and the three of us make our way to the house.

"This seems like a bad idea," I say, watching a group of older kids walk up onto the porch and inside. College semesters are ending and Prep alumni are flocking home for the summer to enjoy their parents' speedboats and a summer of endless booze and weed.

Life is so perfect for them.

We follow the kids' path up the stairs of the caving-in front porch, practically hidden thanks to huge, untrimmed bushes in front of the house. We're right across the street from Cedar Woods High, the public school in town—Alston's parties are usually the perfect place for rich Prep kids to pick out public-school prey. Raise them up to high-class status and then dump them without a second thought.

I think of Jackson's words to me earlier this week: *You don't belong here.* I shake my head to push the thought away.

The house smells like stale beer and weed. It's so grunge chic. As if Alston Marcus's parents aren't paying for anything except the state-of-the-art blender caked with fruit chunks and the one-hundred-dollar liquor coating the flaking linoleum counter. Kicked out didn't mean cut off in Cedar Woods. The heat inside is oppressive and the fans running in three corners of the room aren't doing much more than pushing the hot air around.

I grimace.

"Oh, come on, Nell," Lia says with a laugh. "Don't look so horrified."

"It's even dirtier than it looks when people post pictures." I'd never been to Alston's house but I'd obviously seen it via everyone post-ing ridiculous videos and pictures on social media, desperately seeking attention.

"It's all part of the charm," Taylor tells me. Then he stops, his eyes falling on Columbus mixing drinks at the bar.

"Hey, Reagan, my man, you pitched a great game tonight," Columbus says, reaching out to shake Taylor's hand, as if everything is normal. Taylor offers his hand back begrudgingly. "Good to see you. Lia. Nell." He gives us both a wave, flashing his hundred-megawatt smile—he's one of those people who always finds a smile easily. He is skinnier than his dad but almost as tall. His black hair is cropped close to his head, his white Cedar Woods T-shirt in sharp contrast to his rich brown skin. "Y'all want anything? I don't see you around these parts much."

With good reason. Nothing good happens at a place like this. I rock back on my heels.

"Where's the keg?" Taylor asks.

"Down in the basement, I think," Columbus answers. Lia is looking at the drinks cautiously, and Columbus is looking at her. "Can we talk really quick?" he asks, and I see the desperation in his eyes. Columbus isn't used to being disliked by anyone.

"Sure," Lia says, confidence covering up any nerves. To Taylor and me, she says, "I'll meet you in a bit."

I run myself a cup of water from the faucet of the questionable-looking sink, and Taylor and I head down the dirty staircase in the corner. "What do you think Proctor wants?" Taylor asks me.

"To talk?" I guess.

"I wish he wasn't so nice," Taylor complains. "I can't hate anybody, much less nice people." He rubs his hands through his hair.

"Relax."

"I'm always relaxed, Nell," he tells me. "Can't you tell?"

"Likewise," I answer. Then after a second, I laugh and he does too. We hit the floor of the packed basement that is, if anything, hotter than upstairs. The lights are dim everywhere except the entrance, and the music blasts as people dance practically on top of one another. The concrete room is nothing but an empty bar, a keg, and one huge speaker.

"So, this is what you do on the weekends, huh?" I ask as we go. Taylor smiles guiltily.

"Usually when Amanda goes to visit her brother for the weekend. But I actually think she's coming tonight. It's a nice break for her sometimes," he admits. Amanda's six-year-old brother is currently being treated for leukemia at the Medical University of South Carolina in Charleston. "She's going through so much. It's tough." I nod, as if he's said something not completely generic about Amanda's situation.

"It's good you guys have each other," I answer, wincing at my clichéd response.

"Amanda didn't cause her own problems," Taylor replies darkly. "My dad did."

We walk together over to the keg and he pumps it expertly before pouring himself a beer. He tries to hand me one, and I shake my head.

"You're so good, Nell," he tells me.

"Don't remind me." Damn, do I get sick of hearing it.

"Do you want to dance?" he asks, gesturing at the floor with his beer. I cut my eyes at him and he laughs. "No, I guess not," he answers his own question.

"I'm sorry I'm no fun," I tell him.

"No-Nonsense Nell."

I grin and bear it.

Taylor looks at his phone, searching for an escape I assume. It's not that he doesn't like me—Taylor and I are friends—but Taylor is the person people want to hang out with at a party. I'm the one who calls the cops.

I should go home so my friends can have fun.

"Amanda's here. I'm going to go find her. Are you good?"

I'm about to tell him I'm leaving when someone grabs me from behind, hugging me. I turn to see Michonne holding on to me. She has her braids pulled up into a bun, and is wearing a bright yellow crop top, revealing her flat stomach. She smells of some kind of liquor.

"Nellllll!" she yells. "What are you doing here?"

"I think I'm good," I tell Taylor with a smile. And stuck.

"You need a shot," Michonne tells me as Taylor walks up the stairs.

I shake my head. "I am *not* drinking."

"Fine," she says. "Wait, do you see that tiny, dark-haired girl over there? She found out that I broke up with Brad and has been flirting with me allll night. Stay right here really quick." She runs over to the girl, roping her into a shot instead. I decide to make my escape anyway, but as I'm headed back to the stairs, Jackson comes down them. How can he be everywhere?

He stops in front of me. "What are you doing here, Becker?" he asks me, a smile playing at his lips. "Columbus said he saw you, and I told him he'd had too much to drink already. And it's early yet."

"That's funny," I say, laughing like I actually think it is. "You think we're speaking."

"Are you mad?" he asks, rubbing his hand over his chin as if interested. I stare at him because he's finally completely lost it. What little of it he had to begin with.

"You think you can talk to people like you talked to me the other day and then be like, 'Are you mad?'"

"I don't know." He shrugs. "I never really talk to other people like I talk to you. May I?" he asks, and he nods toward my drink. It happens so fast that I let it. He takes a sip out of my cup and hands it back. "Water. That's what I thought. It's like I told you," he goes on without a beat passing, "just pretend it never happened. It works for everyone else except you."

"That's what you do, isn't it? Pretend none of it ever happens." I stare at my cup, thinking it's tainted now. He doesn't move out of the way.

"Do you want something?" I ask him at last. It works about as well as it usually does, because he keeps standing there looking at me.

Finally, he winces as if in pain. "I'm sorry."

"You're *sorry*?"

He looks around, like he's waiting for an escape route to open up to him. "For the other day. For laying into you. I've got some stuff going on."

I snort. "You're not sorry," I tell him.

He raises an eyebrow, takes a sip from the drink in his hand.

"Why did you say it, then?"

"All right, fine." He tilts his cup up, draining the whole thing in one go. Then he flings the red Solo cup to the ground, looking straight at me as if readying himself. "Maybe it's because I didn't want to talk about my parents having a fight in front of everyone I know with the person who admits she hates me the most of anyone at Prep. Maybe some extremely small part of me felt just a little horrified by the whole thing and needed some space. Maybe I took some of my anger out on you. Maybe part of the problem with us rich people is that we don't talk about our problems, so we don't have a sweet fucking clue how to handle them. And maybe, Becker, the one thing I can't stand worse than anything is that *you*, of all people, might pity *me*."

I bite into my lip, mostly to have something to do. He's looking at me and I want to look away, but I don't. "I didn't feel sorry for you," I say.

"God," he says, rolling his eyes. "There it is."

"Okay," I admit. "It didn't feel right to me to just ignore what happened. Which makes me weak, apparently."

He shakes his head. "Just naïve."

"Yeah, this is why I came to this party. So you could corner and insult me. This is good fun, I can see why you do it."

"Actually, I'm bored." His eyes flash as he looks at me.

I hear the way he says it, the way he repeats the word I'd said to him at the bonfire. Almost like an admission. Or a challenge.

"I'm listening." I glance at my phone screen. "But only for a limited amount of time."

"Tristan!" Jackson calls over my head. Behind me, Tristan Kaye is walking around looking so jaded, it's as if she practices in the mirror daily. Her objectively amazing eyebrows knit and she heads over to where Jackson is standing.

"Tristan, you know Nell?"

She looks at me with interest. "What's that short for, anyway?" she asks without pretense. "Nell." She glances at Jackson. "That's weird, right?"

"I like it," Jackson says. "Sounds classic."

They're trying to intimidate me, which I at least find amusing. "Eleanor."

Tristan nods. "It is classic," she says, shooting Jackson another look.

I know Tristan Kaye, but not well. She's the kind of girl who comes with a reputation and a hell of a lot of baggage. The rumors about her—or more specifically, her long list of trysts—run wild in the halls of Cedar Woods Prep, but she has the effortless cool to pull off a pair of cutoff jean shorts and gladiator sandals up to her knees. She's a member of Jackson's band of misfits, but she isn't in the AP classes with Jackson and me. Everything I know about Tristan Kaye comes from the fact that her legend precedes her.

Mostly I know that Tristan Kaye is not the kind of girl I'd ever want to be.

"What do you want?" she asks Jackson. I'll give them this—they fake not giving a shit perfectly. Like they know something about life that no one else does.

Or maybe they really don't give a shit. I don't know what that would be like.

"Can I have your drink?" He points to his discarded cup. "I'm all out and I'm working on limited time here."

"How much have you had already?" Tristan eyes him warily. Her hair is all long, black, wavy, and perfect in contrast to her bronzed skin. They look amazing together.

"Enough."

"I'm not giving you my drink," Tristan tells him.

He points. "It's for her. She needs it."

"Fine," Tristan says. She shoves the drink in my hand before I can protest and walks away. I stare down at it, unsure of how to handle the whole situation.

"We can share, right?" Jackson asks me.

"It's so easy for you, isn't it?"

"What?"

"Everything." He blinks. "Here." I hand him the cup. "I should go."

"You ever been in love, Becker?"

I stop, because what even. "Excuse me?"

"I don't know," Jackson says. "I was thinking about that book we read—*The Scarlet Letter*—and what you said about bearing the weight of other people's sins, and I was just thinking. About love."

"You didn't read that book," I correct him.

He laughs. "Okay, but I figure"—and he sips—"you know, I've let that marinate a bit, and I don't think love is that complicated or complex or whatever. Like, give me a couple more cups of this and an hour tops, and I could be in love with any girl here."

"That's not what it's about. Hester's sacrifice—"

"Right, right, right," he cuts me off.

"And that's not love. Nothing you feel is love. That's lust. And that's all the girls feel back. They don't *love* you—they *want* you." My eyes scan him. "For whatever reason."

"Fine, I could be in lust with any girl here, and she'd, as you so eloquently put it, want me back." He snorts into the drink. "Please. Have some of this. You need it."

I take it and sip without thought, pulling back from the cup as soon as the bitterness hits my lips. I've tasted alcohol before. The fruity, bubbly stuff that Mrs. Reagan keeps at their house. But this is all hard edges and burn all the way down. "Oh, right—the irresistible Jackson Hart. I've changed my mind. I think I do know what they want. Money. Attention. That nice name recognition. And you've got it all. Who wouldn't want that?"

His face darkens ever so slightly. "So you think I'm only good for my name?"

"I mean," I say, looking away, "I guess you're conventionally attractive, but there are plenty of girls who need a little more than that."

I swear he doesn't blink for a full minute, but then he says, "Well, let's find out."

"I don't—" I start to say, but he's already walking away from me, and then, desperate to know what he's trying to do, I follow him. I follow him right into a group of girls I don't recognize, probably CW'ers. They don't look quite as comfortable in this setting as the other party-goers—that is, except the small, tanned blond girl in the middle—she oozes confidence. On one side of her is a girl with dark brown hair in a side braid and slightly oversized front teeth and on the other, a thin girl in a pair of large-frame glasses.

Jackson says to the friend in glasses, "Would you be able to settle a debate my friend and I are having?" The girl eyes me and laughs sort of softly. Glances at her friends. The ones who usually get hit on. "Sure," she says, taking a sip of her drink. "What's up?"

Jackson says, "Tell them, Nell."

My eyes cut to him, but he's just smiling affably at me, waiting for my explanation. I clear my throat once, then twice. "Are you guys familiar with *The Scarlet Letter*?" I ask them, and Jackson can't help it. He starts laughing.

The girls laugh, too, as if we are all in on one big joke. I don't. "God, I hate that book," the tiny blond girl in the middle says to Jackson. She leans in, blinking slowly.

"What about you?" Jackson asks Glasses, nodding his head at her. I watch as a pink tint crawls up her neck.

"If we're talking Hawthorne, I prefer his short stories," she says, going with the intellectual angle. I want to tell her it will never work.

"'The Minister's Black Veil,'" Jackson concedes, tilting his head to the side as if in interest. I refrain from rolling my eyes.

"I like the Brontë sisters," Blonde says.

"Austen," Glasses says. "Every day." *How trite*, I can't help but think.

"How about something from this century? Morrison? Rushdie?" I say.

"Don't be so superior, Nell," Jackson says to me like we're in on the same joke.

"No, I agree," the quiet girl with the braid answers, looking at me. I like the way she turns away from Jackson. "I'm so damn sick of reading books by dead white guys. Austen and Brontë are great to get into the mix but where's the perspective of diverse writers, especially women, women from this century? Instead, we keep talking about the same dated stuff year after year."

"Don't do that, Avery," says her friend in the middle, but I see the way a smile creeps onto Jackson's face. "I'm Serena," the blond girl says, sidestepping the literary conversation. "May," she introduces the girl in the glasses.

"Nell." Jackson points at me. "And I'm visiting for the weekend. Our parents are old friends."

I hear the ridiculous lie, but I can't help it. I want to play along.

"I go to Prep," I tell the girls. "I like to scope out Alston's on the weekends sometimes." Then I shrug. "I mean, it's kind of boring and stereotypical, but I need someone to judge." I briefly try to channel Tristan and Jackson, loving the feeling of wearing someone else for a change. And besides—I do judge everyone here. "I've never seen you guys before. Are you from out of town?" I ask like I don't care.

"No," May says. "Not really. We came with some of our friends, like, a girls' night or something and it's just"—she gives the place a once-over—"gross, to be honest."

"It is," I agree wholeheartedly.

"You look kind of familiar," Serena says to Jackson. "Have I seen you around here?"

Jackson exchanges a look with me. "I've been told I have one of those faces. Nell tells me I look just like her boyfriend," he says, grinning at me. Despite myself, I feel my face go hot.

"We go to CW," May says to me.

"Don't worry," I confide in her, ignoring Jackson. "I might look stereotypical Prep, but I hate those Prep kids as much as all of you do." I like the way it feels, like I could be a poster Prep child, even for a moment.

Like I could have everything.

"We're always willing to make exceptions," Serena says, glancing over at her friend Avery with the braid. I doubt she means exceptions for me. "Right, Avery?"

Avery shakes her head at Serena. "Don't even get me started on that right now. I'm not in the mood."

"Nell," Jackson says, staring down into my drink, "you're on empty. Let's go see about filling this up." And then he's off and I'm impulsively following him again.

"What the hell was that?" I mutter to him as he leads me over to the keg.

"Remember what I said?" he asks. He takes the cup out of my hand and pumps the keg, pouring me a beer I don't want. "About lust?"

"Great, you've proven your point—girls want you." I shake my head. "For your next trick, are you going to continue to lie about who you are and take Serena home?"

"You're sick," he tells me. "I'm just showing you. I'm more than a name and money. I actually listen to people. And Serena's not the one who's going to want me; it's Avery."

I snort. "Oh my God, you're delusional. She would never go for you."

"I feel sorry for you. You have so little imagination," he returns.

"She's too smart to fall for that," I tell him. "I know girls like that. They don't let themselves get distracted."

He watches me. "You don't know anything about that girl, you know? Everyone has their weaknesses."

I grab my drink from him. "Why do you do this?" I can't help but ask.

"Because it makes me feel good, okay, Becker? I like when people like me." I can practically feel his annoyance. It makes me oddly pleased.

I bite into my nail, watching him, hating myself for watching him. He moves ever so slightly from the table.

"Can I touch you?" he asks.

"*What?*"

"It's part of the game," he tells me.

I glance over at the three girls, catch them watching us, and then I look back at Jackson. "Fine," I say through gritted teeth.

His whole body changes, softens. He reaches out and pushes an escaped piece of my hair out of my face, smoothing it in place behind my ear, feeling too close. His fingers trail back and then are on my cheek like a whisper. He doesn't break eye contact—his eyes are on mine like he wants something that he can't get from me—and he's still touching me. Then he drops his hand, looking away quickly.

I take a deep breath.

"Not bad," he says after a minute, going back to his casual stance. "I almost believed you for a second."

"But none of this is real," I say, trying to recover. "Whatever happens. Whoever you kiss. It's all fake."

He bites into his bottom lip, giving me a smile. "There you go again, Nell. Believing the lie. It's always fake. Whether you realize it or not."

"So the chase is all you need?"

He frowns at me, turning his drink up and giving me no answer.

8

It's an hour later, and I'm standing with Michonne, talking volleyball, drunk on a heady feeling of triumph more than alcohol. The girl—Avery—is watching Jackson like she doesn't care while her friend continues to talk his ear off. I knew it.

"Are you listening, Nell?" Michonne asks me.

I snap my head back around fast, nodding. "Yeah. Definitely."

She checks her watch. "It's getting late. You want to get out of here? I have to call my brother to pick us up." She's squinting at her phone. I only live a few minutes from Alston's house, an easy detour for most Prep students on their way over the bridge, so I told Lia and Taylor to leave without me earlier, promising to catch a ride with Michonne. I'd muttered something about team bonding, but the truth was that gloating over Jackson's failure was too tantalizing an opportunity to miss.

I glance back over and all four of them are gone. Briefly, I let my eyes wander, searching for any of them. And then I spot Avery's friends, Serena and May, over by the keg. I crush the cup I'm holding, irritated.

She wouldn't.

"Yeah, we should go," I say to Michonne. I need to get out of here before I do something really stupid.

Michonne nods, turning back to say good-bye to her friends. "I'll meet you upstairs," I tell her. "I'm going to go to the restroom."

Things at Alston Marcus's house are going to hell pretty quickly,

I note as I pound up the stairs. Past spilled drinks and kissing couples and sloppy kids tangled up in arms and legs and alcohol. I push through, trying not to let the chaos swallow me whole.

Someone appears to have taken up residence in the bathroom off the kitchen, so I plow straight through a door with a sign that says *Don't come in* into a hallway, and there at the end, like a mirage in the barely lit heat, is Jackson. His hand is cupping a girl's face, and she's touching him back, and they're kissing. Really kissing. I can't tear my eyes away, the way his hand moves and tangles up in the back of her hair as her head is turned to the side.

Avery. I can't believe it.

They presumably feel me staring at them and pull apart. A smile spreads on his face when he sees me.

"Sorry," I say, flat.

"Oh, Nell!" he answers cheerfully. "Great timing. C'mere, I need a favor."

I step forward, keeping my face straight. He tosses me his phone, and I catch it. "I need a picture. Commemorating my time in Cedar Woods. At . . . What's this guy's name?"

I grind my teeth together. "Alston Marcus."

"Right, at Alston Marcus's house," he says.

"Oh, don't," Avery starts to say.

"I have to make my friends back home think I'm having a good time." Jackson gives her a smile, and she shrugs, laughing, and then shakes her head. "Fine."

Jackson puts his arm around her, and she leans up to give him a kiss on the cheek, and it's so fucking cute I feel sick. But I can't stop playing along now. Good winners are gracious in defeat.

I throw the phone back to him. "I need to go," I say, turning away.

"I better go with you," Avery says, sliding away from Jackson. "Serena and May will be looking for me." I let her follow me.

"Becker," Jackson calls to my back. I glance at him. "Until next time." He says it like a challenge, and I incline my head. Avery is watching me.

Once we're out of earshot and I'm almost free, I can't help but ask her, "Why would you do that? He's so obvious."

"Of course he is." She laughs, watching me, and I feel stupid for a minute. I thought I knew who she was. "I did it because," she says, "it felt good."

I leave her back at the entrance to the basement, push my hair away from my face, and walk out onto the front porch. Finally I'm free from the oppressive heat. I can breathe.

It's already in the air. We're in for a long, hot summer.

9

I haul my book bag in through the front entrance of Prep Monday morning. Signs of the baseball team's triumph are all over. The pep squad has done up each team member's locker with his name and number in these felt baseballs, and I can smell baked goods wafting through the hallway. There are too many housewives at Prep ready to bake cookies for the triumphant team. Like so much else at Prep, baseball's just another vehicle for students to bring glory to their parents.

Taylor's girlfriend, Amanda Yee, is at her locker, which happens to be the one located right next to mine. I go over, resigned to the fact that I'm going to have to talk to her.

"Morning, Nell," she says cheerfully. I pop my locker open and shove my gym bag into the top before shifting my regular backpack around to take some books out. "Busy weekend?"

"Yeah, definitely. What about you?"

"Good. We drove down to see Joseph at MUSC on Saturday morning and stayed for the weekend. Little guy's hanging in there." She says this all in a painfully upbeat tone, her blunt black bangs falling into kind eyes.

There's certainly nothing wrong with Amanda—she's one of the nicest people at Prep as far as I'm concerned. But she is so profoundly sad and so happy in spite of this sadness that it has a tendency to break my heart. She wears her emotions on her sleeve, and that is something that makes me terribly uncomfortable.

"How is he feeling?" I say, trying to follow a script I know most people would.

"He's always in the best spirits. Such a joy. Like, even though everything is so hard for him and it tears me up to see his little body hurting so badly, I always leave feeling more alive, you know?"

I nod, unsure of what to do with that.

"There's my girl!"

I recognize Taylor's voice with relief as he slides in behind Amanda, wrapping his arms around her like some sort of oversized protector. I close my locker, doing my best attempt at a smile. "Missed you," Taylor whispers in her ear loud enough for me to hear, and she turns her head to give him a quick kiss. "Nell?" he says then. "Heard you were the life of the party after we left."

"Am I not always?" I give him a careless reply, feeling free to dig around in my locker as I talk to him.

"Someone said they thought they saw you sharing a romantic moment with Hart."

I turn my head sharply. "*Who* said that?" I ask. Then, thinking better of it, I go back to my digging. My locker is a complete disaster area. "Never mind, I don't want to know. I did no such thing."

Taylor laughs. "I know."

"How's Joe?" he asks Amanda as I search for a homework assignment I did last week—it wasn't due until today, but I finished it on Thursday and threw it in here for safekeeping. I shift my biology book and a folder goes tumbling out.

Amanda repeats her go-to line, and I feel kind of bad for the both of them, honestly. How can you enjoy a relationship when there's always a dark cloud like that over you?

I bend down to pick up the folder.

"I want to go with you next weekend," Taylor is saying. I side-eye him as I stand back up. No way in hell he's going anywhere until baseball season is over.

"You're so sweet," Amanda tells him anyway.

Aha! I had put the assignment inside the folder when I finished it last week. So it'd be easy to find today. I unfold it and try to straighten it out by running it over the side of the locker door.

"What are you looking at?" Amanda asks Taylor as he peers at his phone. They are both pretty thoroughly ignoring my antics at this point.

"Someone just sent me a picture," he says.

"Oh, weird," Amanda replies. "Me, too."

I look over at both of them as together they stare at the picture on Taylor's phone with interest. "What the hell is this?" Taylor asks, squinting. "Some girl kissing a guy on the cheek?"

"Isn't that Jackson?" Amanda asks. My skin starts tingling uncomfortably.

"Yes," Taylor says, his voice dark as he comes to a realization. He sighs. "And that's Jordan Allen's girlfriend."

"Jordan Allen as in the senior Jordan Allen?" I ask. He is one of the Prep hotshots, already headed to Duke University, the Harvard of the south. Despite being a loudmouth, from what I can tell, he is widely beloved and on the road to becoming another male Prep valedictorian to add to the list.

Amanda's mouth falls open comically. "Oh my God. He signed the text, 'Anything you can do, I can do better, Allen.'"

Taylor looks up. "Did you get this, Nell?"

I slam my locker shut, finally, and wriggle my phone out of my school jacket to see that I have one unread notification. I click it open, and sure enough, there it is. Avery and Jackson. And she's Jordan Allen's girlfriend, because of course she is.

Taylor's watching me. "See? Now no one will think you were being romantic with Hart."

"I wouldn't let him touch me," I say, a bald-faced lie, apparently.

Then I hike my bag up on my shoulder and take off in the opposite direction, shaking all over.

Jordan Allen.

I walk so fast, I practically run to the cafeteria, where I know Jackson and his friends camp out before class every day. Well, they call it a cafeteria. There's one regular cafeteria option, a premium salad station, a McDonald's, and the nicest dessert bar I've ever seen. There's also a Starbucks kiosk because what rich kid can go a day without that.

Jackson is sitting with his group—Doug Rivera, Columbus Proctor, and Tristan Kaye. I go over and stand at the end of the table, wearing a murderous look.

"Oh shit, Jackson," Columbus says, correctly reading my face. "What did you do?"

"Can I help you, Becker?" He has a huge box of snickerdoodles open in front of him along with a card decorated with his number. It says *We* ♥ *Jackson!*

"I need to speak to you privately."

Tristan whistles. "Shit's serious," she says to the rest of the boys.

Jackson gets up with a smile, grabbing his Starbucks cup to take with him. I walk to the other side of the cafeteria where the salad station is. He rests his elbow on the counter, drinking his coffee as if bored.

"Mind telling me what the fuck your damage is?" I ask.

He snorts. "My damage?"

"A picture? That only you could have sent to everyone in school this morning? That was *Jordan Allen's* girlfriend. And you knew the whole time."

"Oh. That?" He thinks about it a minute, and then laughs. "Yeah, I did. Though I'm not sure I could've pulled it off without you, so thanks for that, Becker. She wanted to hurt Jordan, but she needed to want someone else, too. I only had to encourage her to let her guard down, and luckily, when she saw that someone like you might be interested, she did."

My blood boils, trying to burn out any guilt on its path through my capillaries. "I didn't want to be a part of this. You humiliated that girl."

"I humiliated Jordan," he tells me. "If anything, Avery was necessary collateral damage. She made her own choices."

"You're a goddamn sociopath," I say. "And you dragged me into it."

"That's a pretty egregious rewriting of history there."

"I can't believe—" I start to say. But I'm not sure what it is that I can't believe. That I played along? That I fell for his shit?

Or maybe that I was responsible, too.

"What?" he says, watching me closely. "That you got off on it? We both know that's really why you're pissed. You loved it." He looks me in the eye as he speaks, and it takes everything I have not to break eye contact, because I think he might be right.

"Why do you care so much about this, anyway?" he asks, genuinely puzzled. "Trust me, Jordan is an asshole. Everyone knows he cheats on her. That's probably exactly what he was doing on his trip to Duke this weekend. She's better off without him. Besides, it is *so* worth it to humiliate him. Prick."

My heart is pounding against my rib cage like I've run a sprint. "Like what you did to Avery is any better than what he did. She's a person, not a pawn in your ridiculous scheme. What gives you the right to make that decision for her?"

"She wasn't exactly an unwilling participant, if you remember," he cuts back at me.

"You *lied*. And it's just, like—she's not an object to be traded between guys so you can prove your point."

I can tell he doesn't like that by the way his dark eyebrows come together. "You never had to get involved at all."

"You're right," I say at last. "And fuck you for trying to turn me into that kind of person."

"I didn't *turn* you into anything, Nell." He takes another sip of his coffee. "Nothing you aren't already."

I shove past him toward the swinging cafeteria door. I kick it open in front of me with my foot and head toward something I understand. Something I can control.

And I get the hell away from Jackson Hart.

10

And so it goes. The days start to run together after that and pretty soon, I forget all about Jordan Allen and his (ex-)girlfriend. Jackson keeps his distance from me. School, conditioning, volleyball, homework. Rinse. Repeat. Two-a-days for volleyball every weekend heading into the season—one practice in the morning and one in the evening. Some people might suggest I am trying to do too much, and those people might not necessarily be wrong, but with exams playing such a huge role in final GPAs, class rankings on the line, and all the college scouts attending the Charleston Volleyball Invitational in a month, there is too much at stake. And with only three weeks left in the school year, I know I don't have to put up with it for much longer. The end is in sight. I just have to keep going until then.

Honestly, being a part of baseball conditioning is starting to be my favorite part of the day. The boys' meteoric rise to the state championship continues full speed ahead, and I can tell most of them love that hour of punishing workouts as much as I do—it is the only time no one asks them to worry about their throwing form or where to place a curve ball or which base they should cover. In conditioning, there's nothing but a battle between your body and your willpower. There's something extremely gratifying in that.

It's Friday afternoon, and we have the day off from club volleyball practice. The workout isn't too hard, and I know I'll be going all weekend—the school and volleyball one-two punch—so I'm losing myself in the ache of my muscles.

My group is on the treadmills and I decide to just break the damn thing. I push the speed up to max and fly, leaving everything else behind me. Jackson is in my group, and has unfortunately ended up on the treadmill next to me. I watch out of the corner of my eye as he increases his speed to match my own.

It's only a one-minute circuit and none of the other boys are touching our speed. In fact, I can see them fading, watching the clock as it ticks down as if begging it to move with their eyes. Screw that.

Nell. Go. Nell. Run. Nell. Don't stop. I keep commanding my body to *go go go* even though it is like *screw you* right back. It hurts like hell, and my legs are imploring me to stop, but it's not going to look like Jackson fucking Hart works harder than me.

"Whoa," Coach Montoya calls, like he's just been clued in to our unspoken contest. "Show them up, Becker! Let's see it, Hart!"

I glance at Jackson again and his eyes connect with mine. Then I turn back to watch myself in the mirror as I run before he can get a better look.

The buzzer goes off, and automatically, I know he won't stop. So I don't. I can barely catch my breath, but I'm still going, following a primal instinct. I can feel everyone watching us trying too hard to beat each other and I can hear him breathing and hear myself breathing and I am nothing but the treadmill, a pair of shoes. I am speed and competition and superiority. But then I. Just. Can't anymore.

I hop off the running belt onto the sides, grabbing on to the apparatus in front of me to collapse with my head against my forearms, panting. I realize then that I can't hear Jackson's feet hitting the belt anymore, either.

Dammit, only needed to go one more second. I almost beat him.

"Becker! Hart!" Coach Montoya barks out. "Good God, what's

the matter with you two? Go take a water break. Cool off. I've never . . ." He trails off.

With much effort, I push myself away from the console and shimmy off the back of the treadmill, heading out the door without holding it open for Jackson. He's not far behind.

I walk down the empty hallway to the water fountain and drink from it for as long as I can stand. Then I wipe my mouth off with the back of my hand and fall against the wall, sliding down it to sit on the ground. I stare straight ahead while Jackson drinks his water, and then he drops down beside me. We're both still sucking in air.

Finally, he says, "I think I went one or two more seconds than you."

I snort.

"You don't like to lose," he tells me.

"You can't lose something that's not a competition."

"Sure you can."

He's right, of course. I'm not telling him that.

"But it's probably best if we don't kill each other right now," he continues.

"I'm not—" I start to say.

"I just mean, if we push it too hard, one of us could get injured, right? And you've got your club volleyball season or whatever and I have baseball, so I think we just need to call a truce. It's conditioning. There's no reason to put ourselves out of commission over it."

I am loath to concede this point to him, but it is a good one. I can't get hurt before the season. I need to be perfect.

"Yeah," I say at last. "But you started it."

He shrugs that off. "It's good to push each other as long as we don't go overboard. I think it could be helpful for us both. We should have each other's backs."

"I don't have time for your games, Hart."

"It's not like *everything* I say is a lie, you know." I can feel him looking at me. "I really don't have a problem with you."

I laugh out loud at that. "Are you joking?"

"Nell, I do not have a problem with you," he says very seriously. "I kind of admire you, actually."

I do look at him, then. His face is flushed and his throat is pulsing, but his blue eyes are steady. Damn him. "I don't know what scheme you're trying to run this time, but I'm not falling for it." *Not again.*

He laughs, leaning his head back against the wall. "You wouldn't. You take everything way too seriously and that's kind of useless. But—okay—there are worse things you could do."

"I don't take everything too seriously. I just don't have what you've been given in life, so I take staying ahead of the curve seriously."

"I can understand why you might feel that way," he says, as if considering an alien idea for the first time. "But there are so many people here who are worse off than you. You still treat everything like it's life or death, whether you need to or not."

I feel a flash of anger that surprises me with its intensity. What can he know about what I need? My parents can't make a choice donation if I don't get into the right college. He's never had to *earn* the respect of the Prep teachers and coaches, who never seem to be able to quite wrap their heads around a girl who wants as much as I do. He can't possibly understand that. Not him or any of the other Prep boys who are always being told how special they are, how much they deserve.

They have private jets and thousand-dollar watches and their parents' friends are always politicians. And people like Jackson Hart see the whole world as one giant chessboard to be manipulated for their own gains. We're nothing alike.

But I can't help but think, that night at the party, we weren't so different. And I *totally* got it. I wanted it. I felt so alive.

Sometimes, hidden away in the dark of the night, I'm even able to admit it to myself. That some part of me wants everything they have.

I hate that version of myself.

"I've gotta go," I say, abruptly pushing myself up from the floor and walking off toward the gym.

"Nice talking to you, Becker," he calls after me.

I pull open the door to the weight room and leave him without a backward glance.

11

By Thursday night, my body is aching. Having both conditioning and club practice every day is starting to get to me. I'm trying to study at my desk, to process information, but I'm to the point where that's no longer possible. I need to sleep.

But that's tricky as well, I think, staring over at my bed, unmade and inviting me to climb in, because I can't. My mind is alive in a way that simply won't be put to sleep. I can feel it whirring, going through everything as I lie there. Equations and European history and volleyball coverage and that insistent ache in my shoulders.

How can I sleep when there is so much to *think* about?

It's not a new thing, but it's worse lately. My brain feels too foggy in class and my body hurts in new and interesting ways. I'm pushing myself too hard.

I know my mom has old painkillers from when she had surgery a few months ago. I snuck them when I twisted my ankle during last volleyball season, and they definitely made me drowsy. I can't imagine a better feeling than that right now.

My parents' voices are floating in from the screened-in porch in the back so I know I'm safe as I tiptoe down the stairs. I slip into their bedroom and their bathroom beyond, crouching down and pulling things out of the medicine cabinet. The pills are behind the first-aid kit so I fish one out and stare at it in my palm. I take it right then to be safe.

I dry swallow and make my way back through their bedroom. My luck; in the last two seconds, they've apparently come into the den from the porch.

"I don't know why you're nagging me about this," Dad is saying.

"I reminded you a hundred times that your mom's birthday was coming up soon," Mom replies, her voice sharp. "But you still expect me to do everything—to get a present and send a card. Why won't you take responsibility for anything?"

"Jesus, Mary, I'm sorry," Dad responds, though he sounds more pissed than sorry.

"You've promised me you were going to do so many things lately—" Mom starts.

"Oh, here we go with that shit again!" Dad answers. I have to get out of here and fast, but I really don't want to walk through the middle of whatever this is. "I *know*. I know I don't do enough."

"You just love to throw that fucking line around like this is my fault. I can't be responsible for all the household chores and keeping up with every little thing on your schedule. How about for a change *you* keep up with your families' birthdays and your appointments and the bills? You are unbelievable."

"C'mon, you know none of it matters. Nothing I do is ever going to be good enough for you. Even if I spent every day of the rest of my life miserable, selling every overpriced property across the river, and had this house in perfect shape, you wouldn't be happy. What about me? I need some relief. I need *something* to change. I'm so sick of this goddamn town."

"Give me a break. You know what? That's fine. Please go enjoy your midlife crisis!"

They're yelling at this point, so I guess I wouldn't have missed this anyway. Though usually I prefer to tune it out, throw on some headphones, and blast music into my head or whatever.

"I won't say anything at all. *You* can explain to Nell where you're going," Mom continues.

"Don't give me that garbage," Dad dishes right back, but his voice is fading. "I swear, you're forcing her to live the life you wish was yours. Jesus, it gets sicker every day watching you push her."

Mom goes quiet. After a moment she says, "If you hate it here so much, why don't you leave? Maybe you can go back to the country where things were apparently so goddamn quaint, since it's all you talk about now." She pauses, and then she's speaking again, her voice tripping over itself. "Don't you dare—" but apparently he does dare because the front door slams. I hold back, maintaining my composure, pretending none of it happened, waiting for Mom to make a move. Praying it's not to the bedroom because I don't know what to say to her. She'll turn it on me. Make me feel like I'm not good enough, either.

I don't have that fight in me right now.

Instead, I hear the cork of a wine bottle pop and her footsteps receding until the back door slams as well.

I'm up the stairs as the lights of Dad's car fade from the driveway and get in my bed fast. My mind keeps on whirring, but I hope that in a minute, the pill will kick in and it all won't hurt so bad anymore.

12

Coach Montoya works us hard the next day.

I love it, proving I can keep up with them, feeling like I'm always getting stronger. I'm exhausted but the exertion keeps me grounded in a way nothing else does.

The boys' state championship game is a week away and it's our last good workout before. I don't mention the pinch in my shoulder to anyone. It'll go away eventually—it always does. I'm stretching out after, purposely not making eye contact with the guys, when someone clears his throat behind me.

I turn around and Jackson is standing there.

"Go away," I say, reaching down to touch my toes somewhat self-consciously.

"I'm feeling not done," he tells me matter-of-factly.

I don't look up. "I don't know what that means."

"You want to go for a run?"

I do look up. "Now?"

He nods. "Yeah. Come on, it'll be fun. I'll tell you all my secrets."

His face is set like he really is serious. I have a couple of seconds to consider it before I am obligated to give a response. And I'm thinking about how it's the strangest thing ever and if I say no, I'll never know what it's about.

"Okay."

"Sweet."

"Let me just . . ." I glance back at him as if he's going to change his mind. "Grab my phone."

He waits while I do. I meet him at the door and stick an earbud in. Together, we walk down the hall, our arms practically brushing against each other.

"What are you listening to?" he asks me.

It's something poppy and frothy—the song of the summer. A song I would never admit to. "Something good," I say instead.

His lip quirks, but he doesn't answer as we open the double doors.

We hit the sidewalk winding through the school athletic complex and find the cross-country trail through the woods behind the school. Our sneakers strike the dirt path in unison. The truth is, my body is exhausted, and this is past the point it wants to go. But right now, it's a nice thing. It means my brain is at least not spinning out in circles, creating imaginary scenarios where my whole life falls apart—usually from one mistake I make. Ruining my grades or breaking my leg or watching Dad pack up all his belongings.

Besides, what does Jackson want?

The path takes a downward turn. "You're wondering," he says to me.

I look over at him, leaping past a rock in my path. "What?"

"Why I asked you."

I put my eyes back on the trail. "I'm not."

" 'Cause I knew you would. You're the only one who would still go running after that brutal workout."

I lift my ponytail away from my neck, a new layer of sweat forming on top of the current one on my forehead. Summer is settling in, making itself at home. "You shouldn't be doing this, you know? During the playoffs. You said it yourself, if we get hurt now we're out of commission. Twist your ankle and you screw everyone."

"Wouldn't screw me."

"Not *you*? You're the offensive MVP." I throw my hands up. "*Why* are you such a selfish jackass?"

"Why does it bother you so much that baseball isn't everything to me? It's like you feel like you're good so you owe them something. I don't owe anybody shit."

I open my mouth and close it. He's trying to project his own thing onto me and that isn't going to work.

"No." He keeps his head down, charging forward. "Say it."

"You're making some existential point about how I have terrible priorities because I think that goals and commitment are important."

"I'm not even going to read into how much you just read into that."

I hit my stride a little harder, subconsciously at first but then I lean into it. I'd never admit it, that I love the way volleyball makes me feel about myself. Like I was made for something, like I have a purpose. It's something I'm the best at, and when other people see me play, they can't deny it.

I spend so much time trying to prove my worth, trying to climb to the top, but that's the only time I feel truly acknowledged. *Seen.*

Middle school was the first time someone told me how good I was. Mom had smiled when I told her what my coach had said. "You're not just good," she'd told me. "You're better than anyone else." I've held on to that memory forever, nurtured it. That memory is me.

"You like it, don't you?" he asks after a moment. "That it hurts. I saw you favoring your shoulder during the workout. You should lay off it for a while."

"Dude." I pop my other headphone in so I don't have to talk to him anymore. But I feel him tug on the cord until it falls out of my ear.

"Look . . . I need to talk to someone, if that's okay. Someone who doesn't know or care about me and my family or anything else."

I'm instantly more suspicious about why Jackson is choosing me to be his confidante, but this is what I came to hear so I don't make a move to put the earbud back in. I can't help it; I want to *know*. And more than anything, I want to know if I can use it to beat him at his own game.

"I like it, too," he continues, working a little harder to talk with the new pace. "Pain helps me think. It reminds me that I'm not controlled by my body. That my mind puts me in control of any situation. So when things are really fucked up, I can find my center." He spits then. "Slow down, for God's sake."

I pull up, placing my hands on top of my head and sucking in a breath. He slows to a walk, keeping pace beside me. "So, tell me," because how can I not ask, "what unsettles the most secure person in Cedar Woods?"

He glances up at the sky, a smile on his face as if he can't believe what he's going to say. "My dad," he says, still watching the clouds.

I knew his dad from name alone—Atticus Hart. Super-rich businessman, travels all the time, has that asshole "I'm not really into whatever you're saying" look. Recent indiscreet fight with his wife. This is an easy solve.

"Cheater?" I say, and immediately internally cringe. There was probably a more delicate way to put that.

Our eyes meet, and then he turns his head. He nods in the other direction. "You ever been to the old tennis court?"

"I've heard rumors," I say, which is only kind of true. What I do know is that somewhere around here, there used to be a tennis court and that somewhere along the way, the carefully planned vegetation of Cedar Woods Prep grew up around it. It's popular with smokers, drinkers, and stoners alike.

"Becker," he says. "I *am* the rumors."

I roll my eyes at that.

"C'mon," he says, and abandons the cross-country trail, stepping over a fallen branch. I look at the bramble all over the ground and then back at him. It's a twisted ankle waiting to happen. But he holds out his hand and against my better judgment, I take it and allow him to pull me over.

We walk through, farther out. Finally, I see a fence, ivy winding through it, pulling the mesh of chain links away from the poles holding it up.

"What're you doing this summer?" Jackson asks me.

I walk up and grab on to the rusty steel of the gate. "Wouldn't you like to know?"

He kicks a piece of trash off the crumbling edge of the court. When I look closer, I see it's a ripped condom wrapper. God. "Don't take offense, but I can't imagine it would be that exciting."

"Close your eyes and imagine I have hidden depths, Hart."

And he actually does. He closes his eyes. Then he grins. "I like it."

"Stop trying so hard. I know you don't like me. In case you haven't noticed, a lot of people don't like me very much. I'm too 'intense.'" I put air quotes around the word.

"I do like you. Why do you insist I don't?"

I roll my eyes again and work hard not to smile, pulling open the gate and walking inside. A persistent flower is pushing up through the clay. I turn all the way around, taking it in. "This is it, huh? Charming."

He leans back against the fence, facing me. "'This is it?' This is where I've made all my best, most cherished high school memories."

"Gross." He wants me to ask for details, so I don't. "Is that what you're doing this summer? Making more 'cherished high school memories'?" I tilt my face back, the sun warming it. When I look down, he's looking at me.

"We'll see."

"Don't try to pull your shit on me."

"You can't blame a guy for trying," he says.

"So. Your dad?"

"Oh. That." Looping his fingers through the fence, he rocks back and forth; it shakes in a metallic wave, making a rattling sound. I watch him without speaking, a useful trick for getting people to talk that I learned in a journalism class last year. "I mean, even you know his deal. It's literally that obvious."

"But why do you care now? This isn't, like, brand-new information to you, is it?" I ask, crossing my arms. Stupidly getting invested.

"You." He points at me. "You're charming, you know that?"

I shrug.

"He really doesn't care, though," Jackson goes on. "When we were younger, my sister would always make comments, like, 'Dad's had a lot of overtime this week' or 'He always did have a soft spot for brunettes,' but at least some part of him tried to be subtle then. He doesn't hide it at all now. Coming in with this horrible perfume all over him. Leaving me to deal with Mom." He breathes out deeply. "She can't fucking stand it. She's always angry or depressed or some toxic mix of both. But she lets him. She just lets him." He embraces his anger, gripping the fence tighter even though the metal has to be hurting his hands, almost as if they are no longer in his control. "I lost my temper with her last night. Completely. And now I feel like shit, like I only ever make everything worse exactly the way Dad says I do."

"Why?"

"What do you mean, 'why?'"

"Why should you feel bad? For once in your life, you probably did the right thing. She *allows* herself to be disrespected by some . . . some"—I search around as if for a word bad enough, and then one comes to me, as if from the sky—"dickhead. And that's why she gets treated like shit. Why should you have to keep acting like it's okay?"

His head tilts to the side like a confused, miffed puppy. Then he shakes it and walks out of the tennis court.

"Jackson." I say it in the shape of an apology, following him. He holds up a hand, still moving away from me.

"I don't want anything from you, Becker."

"*You* wanted to talk to *me*," I say. "Remember?"

He stops, facing me, frustration pouring off him. "You can't blame my mom for him. Maybe she doesn't stand up to him, but it's not her fault. She can't just turn her emotions off like you can. Most people aren't like you, you know?"

A miraculous breeze gives me goose bumps from the sweat dripping off my skin. I hold my ponytail up off my neck. "I do."

"I really do hate her sometimes. Because she sits back and watches when she should be doing something, *hurting* him. But she can't help how she feels, so what kind of person am I if I blame it on her?"

I want to say, *Why are you telling me this?* But I don't want him to stop telling me this. So I bite my tongue and watch watch watch.

"You ever hated anyone, Nell?"

I'm so busy watching, I almost forget to answer. "Not a lot of room for hate when you've got so much to do," I equivocate, not wanting to admit I hate *him*. Then I think a little bit more and find my answer changing, shifting into something else. "Maybe. I guess. Not one person, but, like, everyone."

He looks briefly amused as he barks out a laugh. "Everyone?"

I shrug. "People here. With all their money and fake talk about meritocracy. I know I'm not badly off, but I hate the way you—the way *they* look at me and people like me, like we're just pieces to be moved around. I never want to be like them, but I feel like I need to impress them? Always trying to climb to the next rung of something.

"So I don't really specifically hate them, but I hate what they are, what I feel myself becoming sometimes. Sorry." I shake my head. "I know that's not what you meant."

But he looks interested. "That completely makes sense, actually." His tone is almost warm for a moment.

I skip right past it, though, because I'm obligated to ask the part that comes next—it's what he's waiting for. "You ever hate anyone, Jackson?"

His face kind of clouds over. I imagine it's what he looks like when he decides to hurt someone. Like he can't be bothered to be charming because he's got a mission. "Him. My dad. I hate him."

It was the answer I was expecting, so I'm not sure what to say.

"It's all a game to him. These other women. Win them over. Play with them for a while. Leave and move on."

I swallow. Try to swallow it back. Don't say the thought pounding into my brain, demanding to be heard. Except I don't swallow it back at all. "Like you," I say.

He goes, if anything, darker. "Really, Becker?"

His incredulity doesn't calm me down; it wakes me up to him. To the fact he's still dangerous. "You can't tell me you don't see it."

"See *what*?"

"That you act just like him," I spell out.

"I'm not cheating," he tells me, defiant.

I bark out a humorless laugh. "So that's the only part you have a problem with? Treating girls like objects doesn't bother you? You're a hypocrite, Hart," I tell him.

"That pedestal is pretty high, isn't it?"

"You're good at deflecting." I can't stop looking at him, waiting for him to see it. "But you can't be that oblivious. You've seen those girls you mess with cry. You've seen their hearts get broken. You hate your dad so much? I think you hate yourself."

I'm not sure what I expect him to do when the words leave my mouth. Wildly, I think he might hit me, but no, that's not what Jackson is like. That's not how he retaliates. But I won't absolve him.

His eyes are ice-cold when he says, "You can find your way back from here?"

I set my jaw. "You didn't want my pity. I gave you what you came for," I remind him.

He turns and walks in the opposite direction from the trail, pushing his way through the vegetation that grows wilder the deeper he goes. I head the other way.

That was not what I was expecting.

13

The next week, the baseball team wins their Monday night game and loses when they travel upstate for the Wednesday game. Everything comes down to Friday.

Coach Montoya canceled conditioning for the week so the team could stay focused, which means I haven't spoken to Jackson and he hasn't had any trouble ignoring me, either. I wish it wasn't bugging me so much. I spend my time running drills and studying with Lia.

On the Thursday before the game, Taylor catches me at the end of sixth period.

"Hey, Coach canceled practice today. He said, and I believe these were his exact words, he 'figures we suck now about as much as we're ever going to so we might as well have the afternoon.' Some of us are going to go down to the riverbank to unwind. You want to come?"

I consider the offer. "I should really be studying."

"You need a break worse than we do. Come on, I know you have volleyball at four. It's just a couple of hours."

I think about it for another minute, decide he's not wrong, and then say, "Fine."

Twenty minutes later, Taylor is pulling his SUV up to the riverbank park on my side of town. It's a long sandy beach, divided off from the wooded area around the river. Out in the water are some prime floating docks. Taylor points his finger out at one of the docks just in time for us to see a brown-skinned boy pushed into the water by a white boy. I hear Columbus scream.

"I'm not going out there," I tell Taylor.

He laughs, spreading out two beach towels that he keeps in the back of his car for us to sit on. I prop my arms back behind me and watch as Columbus makes the dock rock precipitously, acting as if he's climbing back on but really sending the other eight boys out there holding on for their lives.

"You're pitching tomorrow?" I ask him.

He flicks at his fingernails as if he's not nervous. "Can we not talk about it?"

"Fair enough. How's Amanda?" I say instead.

"Great!" he tells me, his word laced with what sounds like forced enthusiasm. "They think Joe can come home next month. Things are looking really, really good. Which is awesome because Amanda has been such a mess lately. I know you don't like all her over-the-top optimism, but it's honestly a cover-up."

I can't believe he said that. "What are you talking about?" I ask in painfully fake confusion.

He half smiles at me. "Oh, come *on*, Nell, you think I can't read your facial expressions? She acts bubbly like that because she's doing the best she can. Really. She's a wreck most of the time. But things are on the upswing. It's going to be great for her."

"I don't dislike her or anything," I tell him honestly. "It's just, I know she's so sad. I don't know what to do. But I'm happy to hear there's good news. Really happy, Taylor. Honestly, I mean that."

He nods, and I can't make out his eyes behind his sunglasses. "I know you do."

Columbus and one of the other boys are swimming back to shore right then. I watch, a curious arrhythmic thumping coming from my chest area, until I realize the other boy is Jackson. They shove each other as they get out of water, fighting like preschoolers, and walk over to us.

"Making a beer run," Jackson says to Taylor. "You want in?"

"Are you shitting me?" Taylor demands. "We have the state championship game tomorrow. And you two are going to go get beer? Do you know what Coach Montoya would do if he found out?"

"Hold on to your shorts, Reagan," Columbus says, laughing. "Just like one or two."

Taylor stands up, and I can tell he is really getting pissed now. "Do you two care about anything?"

Columbus and Jackson exchange a look and snicker.

"Abso-fucking-lutely not," Taylor says, grabbing up the towel in a huff. "I am not staying out here if you're going to be like that. And I swear to God, if you look so much as one percent off your games tomorrow, I will kill you. We've worked all season for this." His face is going steadily redder. "I'm done." At that, he starts walking up the sand, back in the direction of his car. It takes a moment before he turns back around and says, "Nell, you can stay if you want, but I'm leaving."

I look from him to Jackson and Columbus. "I'm coming," I say, because there's no point in me staying. "But give me a second."

He doesn't bother to nod. Just continues the trek back to his car. The other two boys both still look greatly amused.

"That wasn't funny. You guys know he's pretty high-strung right now," I say.

"It was a little funny," Jackson argues with me.

"Oh, are you speaking to me again?" I ask, and Columbus laughs. "You're not really going to get beer, are you?"

"I guess we're not *now*," Jackson says with a wicked gleam in his eye. At that, Columbus doubles over laughing.

"He's under a lot of pressure," I say. "Why is it so hard to imagine this might actually be important to some people?"

"Oh, boy, here we go. We've officially failed to meet her standards," Jackson says. "Nell here is ready to serve as judge, jury, and executioner of our personal lives." And there's definitely a touch of malice to the way he says it.

It's at that moment a group of girls from school comes pouring out of a car in the parking lot. Lia and Michonne wave when they see me. Columbus's grin grows ten times as he spots them and goes jogging over.

I glance back at Jackson then, and something compels me to say it. "Can we talk for a minute?" I ask.

His eyes narrow as if this is a trick. "Why?"

"You'll find out." I nod my head in the direction of some wooden slats separating a pebbled path to a butterfly garden from the beach. Jackson follows, looking weary. I sit down on one of the slats and he sits down on the opposite side of the path from me.

"We're not friends," I say.

"Yes, thank you, I believe that much is clear," he answers.

"What I mean is—we've coexisted for the past two and a half years without all this shit between us."

"Well, you hated me."

"Don't act like it wasn't mutual," I return sharply.

He sighs. "Nell, I've told you, I never hated you. I don't hate you. I just thought it was funny to mess with you."

"Yeah, I know. I'm so intense, there's no purpose to me." When it seems there's nothing more to add, I do it. "I don't want us to be friends."

He laughs. "Oh my God."

"I mean, I'm sorry," I continue on before I royally ruin the whole apology. "I know you only wanted to vent. I shouldn't have inserted myself into whatever with your parents. You didn't want my opinion and you don't need my opinion and I don't know anything about it."

His mouth is a flat line. "Thanks," he says after a beat.

"I can't imagine what it's like," I say. Though I can imagine some of it. The sound of passive-aggressive taunts, and the feeling that nothing you do will ever be good enough. It's a reality I get a little more of every day.

But I don't tell him that.

"I know why you said it," Jackson tells me. He sighs, doing that thing he does where he stares at his fingers like they might do something interesting. "And you're not completely wrong. Sometimes I go out with girls because they seem to really want me and I want something new, so we both get what we want. But in the back of my head, I know that isn't all they want. It's never going to last and they don't know that. Until they do, and then . . . it doesn't matter. I can't give them what they want so I move on." He laughs darkly. "I know you won't believe this, but I honestly never saw it before. That I did the same thing as him. Over and over again. Do you know how fucked that is?"

He stares off at the river, the people having fun. I know he wishes he were out there with them pretending everything is fine, not here with me, living out painful truths. Part of me wants to tell him how often I wish I didn't have to be in my own head, either.

"But it's more than that. I get a thrill out of it, too. When people do exactly what I want them to do. I enjoy it."

I don't know how to answer that. To tell him I understand wanting that thrill, to feel like you're better than the rest of them. That the world is yours to create.

I can't let myself feel it again. It's too dangerous. Like lighting a match in a room full of fireworks.

I can't be this similar to Jackson Hart.

And I'm about to tell him that, like *good talk, good day, I'm absolved and we are done* when he asks, "Are you coming to the game tomorrow?"

"Of course," I say. I would never miss the state championship with Taylor starting at pitcher.

"Good." One side of his lips goes up, a half smile. "It'll make me feel better to see you there. First home run is all yours."

I know he's joking, but for some reason it bothers me. "Taylor's waiting; I have to go."

"See you tomorrow, Becker."

14

I don't go to the game. I lie to Lia that I'm sick, and I text an apology to Taylor.

I don't know what's wrong with me.

• • •

I spend all weekend studying. Even volleyball is canceled in honor of exam week.

The banner greets me as I walk through the door for my first exam on Monday: *Congrats to the Cedar Woods Baseball Team—Your South Carolina State Champs!* I slap a streamer as I walk in like I'm some sort of monster.

The nice thing is, I don't have time to worry about it too much. Because it's Cedar Woods Prep exam week and everyone knows what that means. A five-day march through Dante's nine circles of hell.

And this is only Day One.

• • •

It's Day Four.

I feel it in every breath I breathe. In the exhaustion sitting behind my eyes, singing from my bones. I haven't slept in days and I don't think I've eaten in twenty-four hours. I don't really remember anymore.

I'm on my back porch leaning against a supporting column with my legs stretched out in front of me, knee-deep in important dates in European history, when my phone buzzes.

Come outside.

I don't recognize the number so I ignore it, going back to my notes. I'm something like three weeks behind on studying for this exam and Dr. Rodgers is a notorious hard-ass. I basically crammed what normally would've been five weeks of studying into two to keep up with volleyball and conditioning and everything else I needed to stay on top of. Only now, I'm so tired and so messed up after multiple nights of three hours of sleep that the dates are turning into each other, the lines dancing into one another as if taunting me. I'm thinking about how irresponsible it was to wait this long and what *assholes* these dates are and my phone is buzzing again.

Nell. Come outside.

I leave everything where it is, shuffling barefoot through the empty house. I open my front door and then heave my whole body into a sigh.

Jackson is walking up and down the sidewalk outside of my house.

I head down the front steps, pushing my hair back from my face. "Can I help you?"

He stops pacing in front of me, biting into his bottom lip. "What are you doing?"

I roll my eyes, propping my hand on my hip. "Studying. I have that huge European history exam tomorrow."

"*Pshaw,*" Jackson says, waving his hand like it's no big deal. "With old Rodgers? That's nothing. Don't waste your time."

I throw up my hands, incredulous.

"I got like a ninety-eight or something last semester," he goes on, like Rodgers isn't infamous for the highest exam failure rate.

I ignore his self-congratulations because he wants the acknowledgment. "And you're here because . . . ?"

He gestures around him at the houses. "I was just in the neighborhood." He looks down at his phone, scrolling through something.

"The neighborhood five miles from your side of the bridge?" I ask.

"Go for a run?" he replies.

My eyes rake over him, in his gym shorts and a cutoff Cedar Woods T-shirt. I haven't been anywhere but school and home all week. Nothing in the world sounds better than a run right now.

I shake my head. "I have to study." I press my palm against my forehead as briefly as I can, only a moment, because I am so tired. So mentally exhausted. So done with this past month.

His eyes flick to mine as if he notices but he chooses not to call me out directly. "It's just the energy boost you need. Nothing like getting the muscles going to wake you up. Your brain will thank you."

He stands there after he says this, looking at me expectantly, a picture of patience.

"Will you tell me what he asked last semester?" I finally say, my words betraying me.

He laughs at that. "Of course. But nothing easy, all right? Henry VIII shit is for chumps."

I swing my arms, already subconsciously trying to loosen my muscles. "You wouldn't sabotage me, would you?"

"C'mon, Becker, if I'm going to trick you, I'd do it in a way where you wouldn't already know what I was saying was bullshit. Besides, where's the fun if we don't settle this fair and square? Well"—he shrugs—"mostly fair."

I half grin. "Fine. Let me go get my shoes. Stay here," I say, because he is definitely not allowed inside of my house. Hell, I still feel as if I'm fraternizing with the enemy.

I'm into my workout gear in less than ten minutes. Even the act of lacing up my shoes makes me feel more alive than I have all week. I meet him down the block where he's wandered off to and we are pounding pavement as soon as we get the chance.

"The Seven Years' War," he says as soon as we start out. "Make sure you don't get it mixed up with the Thirty Years' War, and sometimes he likes to try to confuse you by calling it the French and Indian War instead."

"Right," I agree as we run in the direction of the river. "I need to do some more reading on that. I keep getting dates mixed up."

"How are you on the causes of the French Revolution?" he asks, looking over at me seriously. His dark hair flops over his admittedly very nice eyebrows and alarming blue eyes. I look away quickly.

"Like I can never remember all of them." I feel it building up then, right under my skin. The pressure. The nerves. Sometimes it gets hard to control, to push down the panic to a simmer. Sometimes I'm sure I'm a ticking time bomb. I smooth down the flyaways from my ponytail. "Fine, fine, I'm fine," I say, more to myself than him.

His gaze is on me and I keep exposing these chinks in my armor. "Don't sweat it," he says. "Just make sure you don't get too caught up in how the Revolutionary War was a catalyst for it—Rodgers thinks that's an oversimplification and he'll deduct major points if you rely on it too heavily."

I shake my head. "How do you know that?"

He shrugs good-naturedly. "It's like I keep telling you. Because I pay attention to people."

Far from comforting me, the idea pisses me off. Of course he has no trouble puzzling out that Dr. Rodgers thinks concentrating on how the Revolutionary War led to the French Revolution is an oversimplification and of course he knows Jordan Allen's girlfriend just needed to trust him enough to kiss him, and of course he knows Mrs. Wesley will fall for any absurd reading of *The Scarlet Letter* he throws out of his perfectly shaped mouth, because people just want Jackson to be listening to them.

It makes me more jealous than I'm willing to admit.

"Did you ever read it?" I say. We're making our way up the highest hill in Cedar Woods on the way to the riverbank. There's a trail through the park that leads across the bridge and all the way up to Jackson's side of town, though the winding path becomes more difficult to navigate so as to not run on anyone's very expensive private property.

"You're doing that thing again," he says after a minute. I can tell he's really working and I really don't care. "Where you get all cold to me out of nowhere and I'm not entirely sure why."

"You didn't," I say.

We're almost to the top of the hill. I know the view from there like the back of my hand. The sun fades lazily over the water. The river luxuriates in the end of the day, with the trees bending this way and that in the tepid breeze. It's like déjà vu every time.

"Read what?" he says at last.

"*The Scarlet Letter.*"

He sighs. "What is it with you and that book?"

"Why don't you care?" I answer with a question. "Think of all the things that could be in there. To consider other people's lives. Their perspectives. Think of what it would be like to not be you. I bet you wrote a perfect paper. Got a ninety-fucking-eight percent and your analysis was so well-reasoned, so thoughtful.

"But you don't care what it meant to anyone else—that it's about a woman who's been objectified and humiliated and told she's *different* than everyone else. You don't need to know any of that. Because it's just another thing you can have without working for it."

"You know," he says, "sometimes in brief moments, you make sense to me. But I'm not the one who won't stop judging what everyone else does."

I shake my head, shake him off. He doesn't know anything.

We're at the top of the hill that overlooks the river, the world stretching out in front of us like an invitation, and I make my natural push out to the edge of the grass before it declines steeply into the riverbank, feeling the way the breeze off the water hits my face like it's welcoming me home. I stop, breathe in deeply, closing my eyes, inhaling the scent of the river. It smells like freedom.

I feel him watching me. "That's the first time I've ever seen you look happy," he says. My skin buzzes pleasantly, but I ignore it.

We begin to walk, staring out over the water. He blows out a breath. "I didn't know this was a race." I cut my eyes over to him. "Is that why you didn't show up to the game?" he asks. "Because I don't care what it meant to anyone else? 'Cause I took you at your word. That when you promised to show up, you'd be there, and I'm looking around and you just aren't there. Why is it okay for you to do that to me?"

"Do *what* to you? I didn't make you some deathbed promise."

He stops and stares at me, his dark, dark-blue eyes as cold as I feel. "I don't know."

"Well, let me know when you figure it out."

He laughs at that. "Yeah, okay."

"What's so funny?"

"You. Are. Miserable," he says to me, drawing out the words slowly. We're facing off with each other on the deserted trail at the top of the hill, both of our hands on our hips still working to catch our breaths between words, and I feel an urge to put my fingers around his neck and hold tight so he'll shut the hell up for once in his life.

"Like you're so happy," I snap instead.

"At least I'll let myself try something. Is this your life? School and running and volleyball and impressing your parents? Which part of that do you do because you love it? Which of those things makes you happy?"

I have to work so hard to control myself. "All of it," I bite back. "Why did you come to my house?"

His eyes narrow. After thinking about it for a moment, he says, "To go for a run."

The sun is sinking quickly behind him, the humidity making

droplets of sweat bloom on my skin. "Then let's fucking go," I say, hearing the dangerous knot in my own voice.

He nods then, and we're back at it.

Neither of us feels much like talking after that but our feet fall in unison. Over the dirt path we find ourselves on, up the bank, dodging a branch here and there, keeping a steady pace. After a while, I get lost in the sounds, in breath going in and out of my lungs, and that's what does it—that's what makes me centered. It's as if the world is righted, reality knit back together properly, and I can finally, blissfully, think again.

It's dark by the time we're back in my neighborhood. Jackson stops at the sign welcoming residents to Cedar Common and I follow suit without questioning it.

"This is where I leave you," he says.

I stretch my arms over my head, bending to the left and then the right. "Thanks for the run."

"Do you feel better?" he asks me, and I can't tell whether he's joking, so I ignore the question.

"Bye, Jackson," I say, turning in the direction of my house. His truck must be parked somewhere nearby. I try not to analyze how profoundly weird it is that he went to so much trouble to come over here.

"I wish you would've come, Nell," he says, the words snaking up to grab me from behind. I pause, trying to decide what reply will be bratty enough to send him on his way, but he doesn't stop. "Sometimes it's just nice to have someone around who doesn't expect anything from you."

I leave him there and study for hours, my brain going in and out of focus, hearing him over and over again, tearing the conversation apart. Like trying to draw a map to a place you've never seen.

15

My phone explodes next to my ear, not so much pulling me out of sleep as ejecting me from it. I almost fall out of bed, I'm so disoriented. I scramble to pick up my phone before Lia hangs up.

"Where are you?" she demands in my ear.

I leap out of bed and tear through my hamper, looking for whatever dirty uniform will work. "I overslept."

I can tell she's trying not to laugh. "Are you okay? You're going to make it, right?"

"Yes," I say, buttoning up my Oxford and sliding into boat shoes. "Bye." Then I throw my hair up and go running down the stairs to my car.

I'm at school in fifteen flat, shoving open the front door and sprinting to Dr. Rodgers's class, sliding into my seat right in front of him. I'm completely disheveled, without even a second to gather my thoughts or string together dates in my head. Dr. Rodgers is watching me, unimpressed.

"You're late, Miss Becker."

I give him my most pleading look, which isn't that effective, if I'm being honest. But he lets it go and hands out the test. I feel my brain go completely blank.

Keep going. Nell. Keep working.

• • •

"Time's up, Miss Becker."

I'm alone with Dr. Rodgers, who is sitting at the front of the classroom, watching expectantly. I scribble down one last thing about the damn American Revolution and stand up. I'm nothing but adrenaline and Russian czar ascension dates.

"I'm sure you did great," Dr. Rodgers says as I hand the test over. And it's honestly that more than anything that does me in. I pound out of the classroom, through the empty hallway, trying to get my breathing under control. For good measure, I jog up the stairs and lean against a wall when I make it to the top, working so hard to keep my body under my control, it hurts my chest.

Breathe. Nell. Be like everyone else. Nell.

I stand straight up when I hear someone climbing the stairs behind me, looking down the hall as if something interesting has caught my eye.

"Nell?" Lia's voice rings out from the stairwell. I turn back to the direction she's coming from, willing my face into my idea of normal.

It clearly doesn't work. She frowns. "Are you okay?"

I swallow once, twice, before I can get the words out. "I'll be fine." I take another deeper, near-desperate breath. Lia's looking at my arm like she's thinking about touching it, but she knows better than to do something like that when I'm so on edge.

"What's wrong? I was waiting for you to finish the exam and got kind of worried and then you took off."

I snap my fingers together trying to think think think. "No one else saw, did they?"

"No." She stares up at me, letting me ride it out, and then says, "Nell. What's going on with you?"

I shake my head. "I didn't study enough and I feel like I haven't slept in weeks. I was trying to outline the rise of the Hapsburg dynasty on that essay question and I couldn't keep the names straight, even though they were right there in the corner of my mind and I felt, like, *everything* slipping away from me."

"Everything?" I hear the skepticism in her voice.

I shake my head, running my fingers through my hair. "I know you think I'm crazy, Lia. But, *this*. Being on top of this school and volleyball and I don't know, just seeing my name first on the class rankings when they come out next week—that's everything to me. Because it means we all lined up on the playing field and even though some of us had to start from behind, we found out who was the best. I want that to be me. I always want that to be me."

She sighs, and she sounds sad. "Is it worth destroying yourself over?"

I slump down against the wall, looking at her seriously. "It might be."

"Nell." Her voice is exasperated.

"You don't understand how it will feel for me. For my mom. When I'm up there as valedictorian next year. The All-Star MVP. I've been chasing after boys like Jackson Hart at this school for so long. Girls like me have. And this time, we'll all win."

"You sure it's not just you?"

I swallow. "It'll be me first."

I can tell she doesn't want to let it go, but she does because she knows when she's fighting a useless battle. "You scare me when you have these panic attacks."

I shove off from the wall. "It's fine. It hasn't happened in a long time. Just need to keep everything under my control."

"And you'll tell me," Lia asks, "if it's not?"

I hold up my pinkie for her to grab. "Of course."

She seems to accept that, at last, wrapping her pinkie around mine. "Okay. Well, it's officially summer break, and I want to go get milkshakes and hang out at the river. Do you think you can handle that?" At the look on my face, she says, "And then we can go back to practice tomorrow."

I laugh and follow her out of the building.

16

We wrap up volleyball practice on the first Monday of summer break. It feels good. My energy is back, my body alive and demanding. Final grades are being posted today. I'm feeling slightly better as the days wear on. I was tired and a little flustered when I took Dr. Rodgers's test, but I'm at my best under pressure. Dr. Rodgers would see how much thought I'd put into each of his essay questions.

If Jackson Hart can do it, so can I.

The team huddle is broken with a "Cedar Woods" chant and we head our separate ways. I grab a ball out of the basket and set it up with my fingers, talking to Lia and Michonne. "What are y'all doing today?" I ask.

"Working," Michonne tells us, rolling her eyes. "I'm lifeguarding at the river for the summer. My dad says jobs build character."

"That explains my mother, then," Lia says, and we all laugh uncomfortably. "Do you want to stay and hit some extra balls? I've got time."

"Sure," I say, impressed. Usually I'm the one making that suggestion.

"Can't," Michonne says, glancing at the clock on the wall over the locker room. "My shift starts in two hours and I have to shower and put eye makeup on because God knows if I'm going to sit around life-guarding all summer, I'm going to do it looking good."

We say our good-byes, and after the rest of the team clears out, Lia and I get back to work. She tosses the ball to me, I bump it back to her, and she sets me up. The two of us are like a well-oiled machine. We know exactly where the other will be; we read each other's minds.

Sometimes I think about leaving Lia when I go to college. She'll get a scholarship offer to play at some small school, but I should be able to play Division I and my academics will mean that I can get into any school that wants me. It'll be weird to play without Lia, though. We've been together since seventh grade. When I was younger, I spent a lot of time being jealous of Lia, of everything she had—money and an ease of making her way through the world. Volleyball was the one place I always had a leg up, and though I tried not to let myself revel in it too much, it always felt important to me.

I hate how hard it is to let something like that go.

"Back!" she yells as I send the ball to her in a perfect arc. I run to the spot behind her and wait for the set to come, nailing the placement.

"Hell yeah!" She tosses me a grin over her shoulder, holding her hand up so I can slap it, and hanging on, our hands go down together.

"We're going to kill it in Charleston," I say, feeling almost as confident as I can. The Charleston Invitational is at the end of the week and the top college coaches are supposed to be there. We have to be perfect.

"Obviously," she agrees, walking over to our gym bags we'd brought out of the locker room after practice. She glances down at her phone. "I need to go," she says, picking up her bag faster than is strictly necessary.

"What's the rush? Where are you off to?"

She glances at her phone again, shaking her head. "It's Taylor. We're going to grab lunch." She puts her phone into her bag, her face clearing in the process. It's strange, but I think she's lying. "Him and Amanda aren't doing so hot."

"*What?*" I ask, momentarily distracted.

"Yeah, it's so stupid. Now that her brother is home, she seems so much better and yet he's weird about it. She wants to go out and do stuff. I feel like she's finally kind of . . . normal now, actually?"

"That's amazing, right?" I ask.

"Totally," she agrees. "Only—" Her phone buzzes again. She yanks it out and barks out a laugh at whatever she sees. "Sorry, sorry. I have to go," she says then, not even completely meeting my eye. "Why don't you come over for dinner tonight? I'll make that pizza you like." It's a diversionary tactic. She immediately goes jogging out of the gym like her hair is on fire. My eyes follow her as I spin the ball up against my hands.

What the hell?

I throw the ball violently against the wall and it bounces back to me. I do it a couple more times because it feels good. Like my anger has a life of its own.

"What did that wall do to you?" someone yells across the gym. I look back and catch sight of Jackson, drenched in sweat, making his way toward me.

Great. I turn away from him and throw the ball against the wall again.

He comes to stand next to me, twirling his empty water bottle on a finger and watching the ball with interest.

"Why are you here?" I ask.

"Off-season conditioning. It is truly never-ending, and I feel like I've only got two or three weeks of it before I stop showing up completely."

My eyebrows go up as I catch the ball again. "Of course."

"Working out isn't the same without you, Becker," he tells me.

I take this as a sign from above. I let the ball roll away from me and walk over to my own bag, grabbing my phone to see that no one has tried to contact me in the last twelve hours. Seems about right.

I'm standing there stupidly, looking at the screen like I have received many important correspondences that I need to attend to before further speaking to Jackson. It's while I'm doing that that I get the notification: *One new e-mail.*

I open it up a little bit faster than I mean to. *Updated Class Rankings.*

The Office of the Registrar isn't supposed to send this out until everyone has been notified of final grades, but that doesn't mean much to them, anyway. What is being this rich and successful really about, if it's not about winning? Nothing.

I click into the e-mail and scroll right past all the bullshit at the top. Then I feel my stomach drop.

1. *Jackson Hart—4.87*
2. *Nell Becker—4.86*

It's the first time. It's the first time ever I haven't been number one.

I can't fully process it. Only that I am doing absolutely everything I can to get air into my lungs and I feel like I'm going to vomit and nothing is in my control anymore. I'm a spinning top and there is no gravity to stop me from spinning on and on out of control forever. I rake my fingers through my hair, pulling it back, looking for something to hold on to.

That point, I can't stop thinking. *I'll never be able to make back that point.*

I think I'm being as subtle as possible. Only then: "Nell? Shit, Nell. Are you okay? Hang on," Jackson says, and then he takes off running to the water fountain, filling up his empty bottle and bringing it back to me. "*Fuck.* Breathe. Do you have asthma?"

I try to gulp down water, but the fact that he can see me makes it even harder to breathe and I can't *stop.* I can't force it away and I hate myself so much for it. I'm supposed to be able to beat this.

Stop. Nell. Breathe. Nell. Goddammit what's wrong with you Nell?

"Hey, that's better," Jackson says, his hand just barely touching my arm. I start to get control back, talking myself down.

I'm okay.

I take longer pulls from the water bottle. Embarrassed. Cut to pieces, really, because there are so few things I want less in the world than to cry in front of Jackson Hart because Jackson Hart beat me.

"Nell, look at me," he says, and he puts the side of his index finger under my chin and tilts my face up. "You're okay."

I'm okay.

"Well. Good job," I manage to squeak out at last with tears burning in my eyes. It doesn't sound like me at all—more like some pathetic person who can't hide her emotions. I don't look at his face.

"What are you talking about?" he asks me, and I wish he'd stop looking at me. I pull away from the wall, walking around him.

"Class rankings," I say. "You're beating me."

He scoffs. "That can't be possible."

"Don't play that shit with me," I snap, and the anger actually makes me feel so much better. "Your whole 'I'm Jackson Hart and everything just comes to me, I don't have to work for anything at all and I don't even care' bullshit routine." I round on him. "You know *exactly* how to get whatever you want and you'd rip anything you can get your hands on out of mine. Even if I'd earned it."

"Jesus *Christ*, Becker. I can't even imagine what you think I've done now."

"Oh my God!" I say. "The run. Holy shit. That's what it was all about."

"What?"

"Your bullshit, 'just happened to be in the neighborhood wanted to go on a run' shtick."

"*What?*"

"I was exhausted, at my wit's end, and you show up and run me all over the damn city. You tire me out so much and get in my head and I can't study, I oversleep. I almost missed the exam! You were doing everything you could to get in my way. I am so *stupid*," I gasp.

"Becker, do you really think I care that much?" he asks, like I'm being unreasonable. He takes a step back, feeling the heat of the anger emanating from me.

"*Of fucking course* you do. It's all part of your stupid game and this is just another way that you come out on top, like you always do."

"How was I supposed to know you'd fall asleep? I'm not even convinced you actually need to sleep. I've been under the impression that you run on pure rage most of the time. Listen to yourself."

I do, to the deep breaths I take in and out, to the anger in them. I'm now staring right at him, trying to direct every ounce of hate into my eyes in the hopes that it might affect him in some way.

"It's you, Nell. *You're* the one who works yourself to death. I thought—I guess I just—shit, I don't know," he says like he doesn't want to say something.

"I'm so done with you," I say, not that I ever *started* with him. At least, not on purpose. I march back over to where I'd thrown my phone down, pocket it, and sling my bag over my shoulder. I've got a clear line to the exit until Jackson steps in my escape path and places his hand on my shoulder.

"Wait," he says very calmly, "we can fix this."

I recoil from his touch. "What is that supposed to mean?"

"If they sent out rankings that means all the grades are in the system. How many hundredths of a point am I beating you by? Nudge up your grade on Rodgers's exam by like one or two points, and you're golden. Number one when rankings come out next year. Simple clerical error. That old bat won't notice."

I dig my fingers into my palm, intrigued against my will.

"And why would you do that?" I ask him. I hear some of the anger leaking out of my voice, to my own annoyance. "You wouldn't help me beat you. No one's that stupid."

He shrugs, looking away. "I don't care. It's next to nothing to me, and if you're that upset—I don't know. If it does mean that much to *you*, I don't want to take it away from you."

I scan him, from the tips of his brand-new tennis shoes to his thoughtful face. Is it remorse? I have a hard time worrying about him being a step ahead of me. If the run was a trick, it only got to me because I was so damn tired. Not today—today I'm thinking clearly.

And I can't fall behind now.

"I know how to break into the office," he tells me, reading the interest on my face.

I stand there, staring at him.

"You wanna be the best, Nell?" he asks me after a minute. "Sometimes, you've got to be a little ruthless. Stop waiting—do something. Come on," he says, and takes off out of the gym, heading back through the deserted halls on a mission. I run behind him, the sounds of our footsteps echoing in the emptiness as loud as a roar. I run my fingers over the strap of my bag nervously.

The sensor lights trigger as I follow him deeper into the heart of the building, flickering on us like spotlights until we are walking down the administration hallways. *Alumni Counselor, Guidance Counselor, Donations Manager*. All sorts of ridiculous titles line the hall. And then:

Mary Becker, Head of School.

But instead of going to Mom's door and just picking the lock with a bobby pin or credit card or *whatever* you would assume happens in these circumstances, he backtracks to the other side of the hallway. *Admissions*.

He grabs the handle and pulls, pushing up and away very slowly. And to my amazement, the handle gives until the door I'd assumed was locked is completely open.

"C'mon," he says, letting me through after him.

The admissions office is for prospective students and their parents. There's a waiting room with an open window the assistants sit behind. Farther back down a hallway, there are more offices.

Jackson climbs up onto the admissions counter and through the window. Then he disappears and I hear him rifling through cabinets. Without coming up for air, he puts a bottle of Beefeater Gin on the counter. Right behind that, he plops down a set of keys. And then he emerges looking cheerful.

"Gin?" he asks.

I grab up the keys, unamused. "How in the world did you possibly know how to get in here?"

"Some things are best left unknown." He unscrews the top of the gin and takes a swig, then winces and shudders. "Mrs. Ackley likes the strong stuff."

I roll my eyes, turning away from him and going back out into the hallway and to Mom's door. I feel more than hear Jackson coming up behind me, and even though I know it's him, I shiver. He takes the key out of my hand.

"Watch and learn," he says, testing out a couple of keys before he hits the jackpot.

"This is why the coaches aren't supposed to leave us in the building alone, you know," I say.

"We're Cedar Woods Prep students," he answers, going to sit behind Mom's desktop computer and booting it up. "We're supposed to be on the honor system."

I sigh, hating how much he enjoys my corruption, and go to stand behind him.

"Okay," he says, staring at the screen, "what would your mom use as her password?"

I give him Mom's favorite female politician and then her alma mater, password combinations I know she has used in the past, but we strike out twice. I think carefully as he toggles the mouse back and forth.

"I don't know, Becker," Jackson says after a moment, "you ever think your mom's password might be something to do with you?" He glances back at me.

It hadn't even crossed my mind. But this time, I reach over him and type in *Eleanor* and my birthday.

The screen loads.

Jackson pulls up the grading system. I've seen teachers in it a thousand times. He clicks into Dr. Rodgers's grade book, opens up our class, and scrolls down to where he has keyed in our final scores.

Nell Becker. 94.

My heart constricts for a moment. I wish I'd done better.

Jackson watches me out of the corner of his eye, leaning forward, pressing his chin into his steepled fingers.

"Ninety-four," I say.

He stares at the number like he can't be seeing the same thing as me. "You know that's really good, right?"

My expression doesn't change. My face would give away too much. "It's not as good as yours."

He doesn't answer.

I reach across him and double-click so the override feature pops up. I'll just add two points. That's nothing. It still shows Jackson did better than me, but it puts me right back to where I need to be. Where he *doesn't* need to be.

It's not important to him.

I click on the Update button. A new notification pops up.

Are you sure you want to override this grade?

It had to ask. I glance at Jackson again, feel him watching me as if this whole thing is fascinating.

"You've done this before, haven't you?" I ask. "How else would you know how to get in here?"

"Tristan had too many absent days. I helped her get into Mrs. Regis's office. She keeps her passwords on a sticky note next to her desk." Mrs. Regis, one of the guidance counselors. "I've never changed my grade. Mrs. Regis doesn't have override privileges," he points out, gesturing at the computer, at the mouse my finger is still hovering over.

I drag the box on the screen around with the pointer of my mouse, enjoying watching it moving. Clicking and unclicking like a compulsion.

This isn't how it was supposed to go.

I hit Cancel. The grade reverts. I close the system out and shut the computer down, picking my bag back up violently.

"Let's go," I tell him, my words clipped. I take off from the room like a bat out of hell and slam Mom's door after him, locking it behind me.

"Hey, Nell," he says, doing that stupid thing and putting his hand on my arm to stop me again. I'm shaking all over like earlier and I can feel the day creeping under my skin already. Most times, this makes me want to *go go go* but the only thing I can think of right now is crawling into bed and not getting out of it until this crushing feeling lets me free. "Come do something with me. You'll be all right."

"I didn't do it," I tell him, trying to blink the glassy feeling out of my eyes. "I couldn't."

Jackson looks at me very reasonably. "I know. I'm sorry. It was stupid."

"I have to beat you for real," I say, swallowing hard. "Or else it doesn't count."

This time, his smile is more sad than anything. He takes the keys out of my hand.

"I know" is all he says again.

17

We're walking into the parking lot together, our two cars parked yards apart, the lone survivors of summer workouts. I need somewhere to focus my energy—something to take my mind off my scoreboard loss to Jackson and the undeniable fact that he is starting to find cracks in my armor.

"Are you okay?" he asks me, slowing to stay beside me.

"Why wouldn't I be?" I ask, unable to completely hide the frantic note in my voice. "I need to go."

"And do what?" he asks. "Spend a couple of hours berating yourself? Come on, let's go out. Maybe you could stop—I don't know—hating yourself for a bit."

I grind my teeth against one another. I don't *want* to go with him, but I don't want to go home, either. Lia blew me off and Michonne is working and some terrible part of me is so endlessly interested in him—mostly in arguing with him, but . . .

I'm lying to myself. I do want to go.

Despite the fact that Jackson seems to be involved in every problem I run into, something about him helps me let go, just a little. Which is stupid.

"Why do you even want to hang out with me?" I ask him.

"Look, I'm going to hang out with some friends—just, like, Doug and Columbus and Tristan. You want to come? I think it'll be fun. It usually is."

I stare at him. "I'm not falling for any more of your shit."

He sighs deeply. "What exactly is it you think I'm doing?"

"As of now?" And then I have to think for a few seconds before I come up with an answer. I have to say something or else I'm just full of shit. "Trying to ruin my life is my best guess."

He tilts his head to the side, watching me. "Then this is quite an elaborate plan I've got going on. I'm much smarter than I give myself credit for." He reaches up and ruffles the bottom of his hair. "That's not true, I know how smart I am. Do you want to come or not?"

"Fine. I'm riding with you," I say, marching over to his truck—a mint-condition four-door, deep green with leather seats, shiny and perfect like him. He unlocks the door before pulling it open and getting inside. I glance over at him in time to see him smiling to himself as he gets in.

Asshole.

• • •

"You guys know Nell, right?"

I look from Jackson to his friends, feeling like I'm under scrutiny. Together, they're like some sort of extremely judgmental firing squad. We're on the deck behind Columbus's enormous Southern Gothic house. Doug Rivera is lying on a long chair, everything but his head horizontal so he can sip on a beer. Tristan Kaye has her legs propped up on an outside coffee table, crossed. And Columbus is standing, leaning against the railing of the deck. The boys are wearing what looks like loungewear, gym shorts and T-shirts, and Tristan has on a pair of short shorts with a loose top that exposes her bare stomach when she lifts her arms.

"Do we know Nell?" Tristan says with an eye toward Jackson, her voice almost a singsong. She nods to me. "We meet again. Aren't you two like Cedar Woods Prep golden twins?"

"Right." Jackson walks over to where she's sitting, lifting her beer off the coffee table and sipping it himself. There's something very intimate in the way they interact with each other, like they know exactly what the other is about to do.

"Nell," Columbus says, his mouth breaking out into that bright smile of his. "How you living?"

"Significantly less painfully without baseball conditioning," I say to him with a sympathetic smile in return.

"Welcome to the Proctor household," he says. "Would you like the tour?"

"Later!" Jackson calls. "Get the girl a drink."

"You didn't offer her a drink, Hart?" Doug says, barely moving his face, though his eyes slide almost imperceptibly as he speaks. The sun glints off his olive skin, sweat matting down his wavy black hair. "You're such a dick."

Jackson plops down next to Tristan and I can't help but watch how close they're sitting. He practically fell into her lap. "Nell doesn't like when I do things for her," he says. He puts his feet up next to Tristan's and his big toe rubs against her leg.

"Ew, Jackson, don't be disgusting!" she says, shoving him and pulling her legs away as he laughs.

"I'll get you something," Columbus tells me before disappearing back into the massive house.

I eye Jackson and Tristan flirting effortlessly with each other as I go to stand where Columbus was a moment before. I feel Doug looking over at me.

"They always do that," he says, sitting up a little straighter, his voice soft. I don't know much about him. It seems pretty clear he's a scholarship student, only here by the good grace of Jackson and crew. I had kind of guessed, just on how he acted. Different from the rest of them. More understated. There's a certain way rich people carry themselves. That's how you can tell the rest of us apart.

"Why don't they just screw?" I say, even though *screw* is not a word I ever use.

He takes another sip of beer and licks his lips. "Who says they haven't?"

I ignore the twist in my stomach. It's not like that isn't part of Tristan's reputation.

"Hey, Nell!" Jackson is leaning across Tristan now, his eyes all over me. "You ever seen a Super Bowl ring? You'd be so into it."

Columbus comes back out and puts a can of beer into my hand. I don't recognize the brand but it's definitely nicer than the stuff my dad drinks. "Bottoms up," he says, knocking his can against mine.

The can is cold and the condensation drips all down my fingers. I turn the can up and take a drink.

I sputter.

Tristan absolutely cackles at the sight of me spitting beer out. Columbus giggles to himself and even Doug cracks a smile. But Jackson is still watching me, this thoughtful look on his face.

"That's the good stuff," Columbus says, this time banging the top of my can with the bottom of his. He laughs again. "Don't worry, Becker. Dad only keeps those beers around to make all the white 'I prefer IPA' Prep parents feel at home. That's why he doesn't mind me drinking it. Last year, I saw the NFL Rookie of the Year spit that shit out."

It wasn't personal, but I don't like them laughing at my expense, their little naïve toy to play with. In fact, it kind of pisses me off. I set the beer aside.

Columbus cranks some music up. Tristan asks everyone if it's "that time" and I'm not sure what that means until Doug, Columbus, and Tristan take off into the house and I smell the sweet scent of weed swirling out of the open window on the second floor. Jackson stays behind and I can't decide if it's for my benefit or not.

"You don't have to stay with me, you know," I say, lying down in the lounge chair Doug vacated.

Jackson shrugs like it doesn't matter to him either way.

"Hey, losers!" Tristan is sticking her head out of the window with a smile on her face. "Get off your asses. We're going for a joyride." Then she disappears back inside with a laugh.

Jackson reaches a hand out to help me up. I take it, not sure if I actually want to. "We can walk around the house," he tells me, setting off down the deck stairs. I follow after him.

"What's up with you and Tristan?" I ask, catching up to him.

He gives me a look. A look of some sort of significance. "What does that mean?"

"Do you guys hook up?" I ask, walking with him across the cobblestone path to the front of the Proctors' home.

"Why do you want to know that?"

"I mean, you're always dating someone or other but there's clearly something going on between you two."

"We're friends," he tells me. He pauses. "Who may have hooked up a couple of times."

"Of *course* you did," I say, realizing a moment too late my voice sounds more annoyed than it should.

"When we were younger," he says dismissively. "And not while I'm dating other people, so don't give me that shit."

"Whatever."

He throws up his hands. "What have I done to offend you now?"

And I realize I can't verbalize it. But I can think it, and what I'm thinking right now is that even though I know exactly who he is, I've become so infatuated with the idea of him and he's been leading me around like some sort of wild mare he can break and I'm *following* him. It's not because I trust him—it's because I'm so sick of everything, some part of me doesn't even care if I fall off a cliff.

"Nell?"

At that moment, the other three come tearing out of Columbus's front door. Actually *tearing*, Tristan getting a running start and leaping onto Columbus's back. Doug takes the steps three at a time behind him, and then they start piling into Tristan's Jeep, the doors and top removed for summer. Nothing but the skeleton of the cage between them and the world.

I grab on to Jackson's arm before he gets in. "Are they okay to drive?"

His eyes search from one of their laughing faces to the next. Then his careful gaze rakes over me. Finally, ever so uncertainly, he says, "It's fine. They haven't had that much, and besides, we do it all the time."

I blink at him. "You love the feel of reckless abandon."

Clenching my fist, I find myself climbing into the backseat between Jackson and Doug anyway. Most of the horrible thoughts fly out of my head as soon as the wind is on my face and music is playing again, but I can *feel* Jackson next to me, alive and close and so very tangible.

I hate him. Or at least, I wish I did.

Cedar Woods is a perfectly quaint suburb, but there's plenty of empty roads along the river near the trails, and that's where Tristan drives. We're on one of those little back roads when she pulls over to the shoulder and looks to Columbus in the passenger's side with a dark smile. "You thinking what I'm thinking?" she asks. There's something so vibrant about her, and I think to myself *she's so carefree*, and wish something about that wasn't so appealing to me. That temptation in her smile—I can't help but wonder what guy wouldn't want someone like that.

Columbus seems mostly unaffected. He climbs out of the Jeep and walks around it, clambering up on the bumper and then standing on the back of the car, his arms out wide. "Go, go, go!" he yells then.

And Tristan *goes*. I scream in shock. Columbus shifts as the car takes off and grabs on to the roll cage, holding tight. But he's laughing, the sound like a bell in the night. Everyone else joins me in screaming like I did it out of some sense of excitement, and all I can think is *holy shit, he's going to die.*

But he doesn't. In fact, he looks vital.

And then Tristan is next, her black hair flying behind her in the wind, and she looks so perfect and so happy, I hear myself say it as Columbus rolls the car to a stop.

"I want to do it," I tell them. I feel Tristan's eyes on me.

"No, you don't," Jackson answers. "It's not as fun as they make it look."

"He's a wuss," Tristan says.

"No, I have a healthy sense of self-preservation," Jackson rebuffs.

"I'm not scared," I tell them.

"This isn't a competition, Becker," Jackson says to me.

I turn to him, my eyes narrowing. "You can't tell me what to do."

"Let her go, man," Columbus says, shifting in his seat to look at the two of us.

"He's not going to *let* me do anything. He's just a person I go to school with," I tell them. Columbus's eyes catch mine like he thinks that's bullshit before he turns back around to face forward. I can still see his eyes glinting with amusement in the front mirror.

Tristan climbs over the body of the car and onto the already extremely cramped seat Doug, Jackson, and I are sharing.

"Doug, you go," she says, looking right at me. "I'll give Nell some pointers so she'll be ready next."

"All aboard, Rivera," Columbus says, patting the roll cage.

"Y'all are idiots," Doug says, crawling up from his seat as Tristan scoots in behind him. "Watch and learn, Nell Becker."

He takes his spot at the back of the car, standing up straight. Columbus starts going slow, like the other times.

"The start is the worst," Tristan tells me. Jackson keeps making annoyed sounds beside me. "Once you get going, you're just on for the ride. You gotta take it all in, you know? But Columbus is really good. He's scared to go any faster than a grandma, so you're totally safe in his well-manicured hands."

Columbus does seem to be taking this very seriously. He doesn't acknowledge Tristan in any way. She reaches up across the console, to turn the music up. At that exact moment, we hit a bump or something. Columbus reaches for the stick shift but Tristan is in the way and in his hurry, the shift sticks and jolts violently, sending us all flying forward.

Over the volume of the music, I barely hear Doug scream.

Columbus steers off the road and practically throws himself out of the car in his rush to get to Doug. We're all screaming his name, running as fast as we can, and tears are flowing down Columbus's cheeks before we even can get to him.

"DOUG! Doug! *Doug!*"

His eyes are open when we all reach him, though, and I am able to find my first breath since the jolt. "Doug." Jackson crawls onto the ground next to him. Doug's rolled over from his side onto his back, the part of his face and scalp that took the brunt of the fall skinned all to hell by gravel. "*Fuck.* Can you move? Get away from him, Tristan!" he yells as she goes to move closer. She backs off at the look in his eyes.

Doug bites hard into his bottom lip as if distracting himself from something else. His eyes are glassy and one tear escapes down the side of his cheek. "Hurts. Like a bitch," he coughs out.

Columbus, who is full-on hysterical now, tries to string words together. "D-D-Doug, I'm so sorry Doug I'd rather die than—I'm so sorry." I want to reach out to touch him, the ache of his wail cutting through me like a knife.

Doug grinds his teeth. "Fucking. Asshole," he says. Jackson gives him a smile.

"You're okay, Rivera," Jackson tells him, the voice of reason. "Nell," he says, looking at me as if I'm the only one he can trust with instructions. "Get my phone."

I nod, running back to the car and fishing it out of a cup holder. As I sprint back, I hear Doug saying, "It's my shoulder. My head. And shit. Maybe my leg?"

"Call nine-one-one," Jackson tells me. He's softly holding on to Doug's other shoulder, the one that didn't take the blow of the fall.

"Columbus, you need to leave," Jackson says, his voice particularly cold.

"I'm not leaving him," Columbus manages to get out through his sobs.

"Tristan, get him the hell out of here," Jackson says again.

"Jackson—"

Jackson stands up, talking under his breath, his words weaving into one another like a hiss as he tries to ensure that Doug can't hear him. "Columbus's mom is the district solicitor, and he's a black athlete from a rich family. If the cops find him, he's fucking done for. Get the hell out of here." His eyes find mine. "All of you. Tristan, you need to drive. I don't want them catching anyone else driving your car. Get me?"

I turn away, dialing. My hand is shaking violently. "Nine-one-one, what's your emergency?" the operator asks me.

I take a breath to answer, but Jackson jerks the phone out of my hand. "I need an ambulance," he says into the receiver. "Cawood Road, where it meets the river."

Tristan grabs on to Columbus, pushing him toward the car as he continues to cry. "Let's get the hell out of here," she says, keeping her voice even.

Columbus climbs into the backseat and Tristan into the driver's side. I'm watching the two of them and watching Jackson, who is crouched next to Doug on the phone and Jackson and Doug look so sad and I think I can't leave him, so I turn to Tristan and say, "Go without me."

"Are you out of your mind?" she demands of me.

My eyes flash as I turn back toward Jackson. "You better get out of here."

She waits for half a second more before swearing loudly and taking off. The music is still blasting from the speakers.

Jackson looks up as the taillights get smaller in the distance, sees me, and says, "What are you doing?" Then to the lady on the phone: "No, no. Yes, ma'am, I'm listening," he continues, trying to keep his voice calm.

I ignore him, crouching next to Doug. "Doug? Sorry, Jackson is on the phone," I say, staring down at his beaten face. "Can you hear me? Stay with me, Doug."

"Only need a nap," he mutters. I grab on to his hand and hold it.

"Maybe later," I say instead. I don't know what I'm doing, but my dad watches quite a few emergency-room shows, so I try to do what it seems like they would. "Tell me something. Tell me something you like," I say.

"The twins," he says. "My sisters. When they sing."

I have no idea what that means, but it seems like a good direction to go in. "What do they sing?"

"Christmas songs," he tells me. "No matter if it's one hundred degrees outside." He squeezes my hand back. "Thanks," he says. "Fucking Columbus."

"They'll be here in five minutes," Jackson says over my shoulder, phone still pressed into his ear. It's not long after that we hear the sirens approaching. As soon as they arrive and get to work on putting Doug on a stretcher, they're asking us questions. "What happened to him?" the EMT asks. She's a tired-looking girl in her twenties.

Jackson answers, "He fell off the back of a car."

"What car?" she goes on, watching Doug as she works.

"I don't know," Jackson lies.

She glances up at him with a face that says she's heard it all. But when Jackson climbs into the back of the ambulance with Doug, she doesn't protest. They let me sit in the front seat.

They wheel Doug away from us when we get to the emergency room. Jackson and I sit side by side in the waiting room, and it's a while before he looks at me. I don't look back but I can feel his eyes burning into me.

"You need to go home," he says after a moment passes. "Somebody, I don't know who, but eventually, somebody is going to come ask me what happened and I'm going to have to lie. I assume you don't want to be part of that so . . . You need to go home."

"You're going to take the fall?" I ask, my voice already prepared for an argument.

"Don't say it like it's noble or something. I never should've let them do it. I've always known something like this was going to happen." He leans forward onto his legs, running his hands over the back of his head. I can feel my anxiety spiking. "And *you* were going to do it." His eyes find me again. "Doug's family can't afford this shit."

There's something interesting about him, then, I think. He's not crying exactly and I'm pretty sure he won't, but his casual confidence is gone. He looks lost.

I hate that it gets under my skin.

I hate myself for hating it. This is bad.

I try to keep my voice even. I'm not going to touch him because I don't do that. I'm just going to speak in calm tones and that's going to make it all go away. "I don't understand you," I say.

"I can't do this right now," he says, jiggling his leg up and down violently.

Fine. So I don't touch him exactly—just put my hand on his leg to hold it still.

"Nell," he breathes.

"I didn't think you cared about anyone but yourself."

His leg jerks ever so slightly so I squeeze it.

"Doug and Columbus and Tristan," I keep on. "I guess you do."

He does the thing I don't want him to do. Like he needs an anchor to hold on to, his fingers creep on top of mine, snaking between them. I can feel my heartbeat all over me.

"I never thought you'd be like this." I flip my hand over so he can really have it and he grips it like a lifeline, holding it against his leg, his eyes trained on the floor. "You work so hard to act like you don't give a shit about anything or anyone. Why? Isn't it exhausting?"

"Am I supposed to trust everyone? Everyone I meet wants to use me," he mutters. "Doug and Columbus and Tristan know me. They won't sell me out for a couple of days in the Cedar Woods spotlight. There's no reason for them to try and get close to me because they've proved they aren't trying to get anything from me again and again. I just—" He lets go of my hand suddenly then, his eyes catching on something on the other side of the room. He shoots up out of his chair, standing straight as a man in khakis approaches us. Mr. Hart.

They could be twins, their height exactly the same. Their matching eyes, perfectly straight noses.

"What are you doing here?" Jackson asks, shedding the vulnerability as fast as it came on.

Mr. Hart glances at me, categorizes me as an unimportant accessory, and turns back to Jackson. "Unlike you, some people know well enough to get in touch with me when something happens. The officer who got the call is a friend of the family and gave me a heads-up. And now we're going home."

"I'm not leaving until I hear how Doug is," he tells his dad, his jaw set.

"A suggestion for you, son," Mr. Hart says in a way that makes it clear it's not a suggestion at all, "act like you have some sense."

I feel more than see Jackson's gaze on me then. He balls his hand up into a fist at his side.

"I'm already going to have to pay Rivera's hospital bill to get you out of this. Don't act like you didn't know I would. He practically lives with us."

"You enjoying this, Dad?" Jackson says through clenched teeth. But, when I think he's finally going to lose it, he laughs instead. "You know what? Maybe I did it on purpose."

"Because your mission in life is to give your mother a heart attack?" Mr. Hart asks, his voice steadily rising.

"Oh, fuck you," Jackson says, but I've seen him build the fortress back up. All his walls are in place. His stance is a challenge. Like never before, I see the two halves of one whole that make him who he is. "Where were *you* tonight?"

"We're going," Mr. Hart says. "It's not a negotiation. And if it was, I'd still fucking win. So go get in the car and shut the hell up. You," he continues, pointing at me. "Who are you? Actually it doesn't matter, you have to come, too. And you can both thank your lucky stars that I heard about this before anyone else did."

Jackson holds his dad's gaze. I'm sure he's not going to relent, but then his shoulders fall ever so slightly and I see the surrender below the surface. "C'mon, Nell," he says, his voice sharp, "we're going."

Jackson is walking aggressively fast and I have to use every inch of stride my long legs can give me as I follow him out of the waiting room. He pulls open the back door of a black Escalade and walks around to the other side of the car without a word. I get the hint.

Anger is radiating off Jackson as his dad climbs into the front seat of the car. Mr. Hart cranks the engine. "Where do you live?" he asks, and I realize it's directed at me.

I give him the address in my smallest voice. I don't like authority figures talking to me like I'm insignificant—like I'm nobody. It's everything I'm constantly trying not to be.

It's twenty minutes before we pull up in front of my house. I realize my car's still at the school. Not sure how I'm going to explain that to my mom.

I get out of the car and don't look back.

Well, only once.

18

My phone is buzzing when I get out of the shower after volleyball practice the next day. *I'll take you to get your car.*

I stare at the number. Even though I deleted all the texts he sent me before, it's not a hard mystery to unravel. *How is Doug?*

Fine. He went home last night. Let me take you to your car.

Lia took me to get it this morning. Practice.

In fact, Lia had quite a few words for me after I didn't show up for dinner last night.

Then let's go do something.

Mom is knocking on my door then. I throw on a pair of cutoffs and a volleyball T-shirt. I pull open the door, shaking my hair out of my face.

She strolls into my room like she owns the place. Which I guess she technically does. I throw my towel into the hamper. "What are you doing today?" She gives my casual outfit a look of distaste.

"Going out," I say, because that sounds like something I could be doing.

"With who?"

"Lia." The lie rolls off my tongue without a thought. I don't know what Mom would say if I was doing something with Jackson, but I probably don't want to find out.

"You still thinking about doing some volunteering this summer?" She puts some of my clothes away, and I wish she wouldn't. It feels invasive at the moment. "I know you were going to just focus on volley-ball for a couple of weeks, but I think it would be good for your résumé."

"Sure," I say, trying to escape.

"Where were you last night?" She's looking point-blank at me, through me. I know she knows. I came barreling in late and threw an excuse about where my car was over my shoulder at Dad. I was tired. *I went to Lia's and we went out to dinner and we figured it was stupid to go back and get it tonight since we had volleyball first thing in the morning. Blah blah blah.* Dad didn't ask questions.

I sigh. "I was out with some people from school. And someone got hurt."

"Doug Rivera went to the hospital, you mean," she tells me. She crosses her arms over her chest. "Why were you there?"

"Lia thought I needed to unwind and a couple of people from school were hanging out. Honestly, it just escalated. Everyone was having fun and then it went wrong." I hear how absurd it sounds com-ing out of my mouth. If I were listening to me right now, I'd think I was full of shit. And I see the way she sees me, like someone not smart enough to know better. "I'm sorry," I say, and then almost wish I could take it back.

"I know you are." She closes one of my drawers. "That could've gone really badly."

I push my fingernails into my palms, knuckles tight. "Is this about the rankings?"

She looks down, and I swear I really feel like I know her in that moment. "You have an entire school year, Nell. I'm not worried about it." But I can tell she is. Me losing to Jackson Hart would be the end of her world. That's why she was brought to Prep to begin with—to break down the culture people like Jackson produced. To see girls' names on the rankings list and start shattering all the barriers between *us* and *them*.

My phone buzzes and I glance down at it.

I'm down the block.

I stow my phone in the pocket of my shorts. "I've got to go," I tell Mom, half apologetically.

"Nell," she says, right as I'm about to pass her. I stop so we're side by side, me going one way, she the other. "Be smart," she finishes.

I head down the stairs and out the front door, hustling the two blocks to where Jackson's truck is idling. I jump in. He turns down the music and drives.

"You look wound up," he says after a moment.

Well. That's reassuring. "Mom knows I was with y'all last night," I say.

He nods, pulling to a stop at the exit of our neighborhood. Cold air is blowing from his AC, embracing me like an old friend. "What do you want to do?" I ask him. "We could run."

He sighs. "Nell, I cannot go running today. It's over one hundred degrees, and I'm not built like you. I can't."

I lean back against the seat, tilting my head up toward the roof. I love when he admits I'm better than him at something. "Let's do something fun, then." I don't remember the last time I said that and wasn't referring to something involving volleyball. "What do you think?"

He grins at me from the driver's side. All traces of last night are gone. "I have an idea."

Twenty minutes later, Jackson is walking backward with both hands around mine, tugging me into a bar on the water.

"This is a terrible idea," I say.

"Of course it is," he returns. "That's why you have to do it. Come on, Becker, live a little."

"Why do you think this is fun?" I ask him as he drops my hands, and we walk up the steps of a deck and into the bar.

He holds the door open, mostly, I think, so he can hold my gaze. "It's nice to play pretend sometimes. That I'm older. Free. Just another twentysomething wishing his life away."

"Yes, we're terribly mature," I say, and he laughs. I stop just inside the door and take in the scene. For a restaurant that clearly allows underage drinking, it's not so bad. The wood is old but looks like it once could've held some grandeur. The back area opens onto a huge deck on the water, trees shading it invitingly. There's all sorts of signed memorabilia from local sports stars and older musicians posted up on the wall. *Love Raven's*. And *thanks for the best Manhattan this side of the Mason-Dixon*. I allow myself to be pulled to the bar.

"Look, this is a controlled environment," Jackson responds smartly. "We're not going to do anything stupid. It's just me and you and a whole lot of forgetting we've got to do." He raises his chin toward me. "Don't I at least owe you that?"

I stare back at him. "I guess you do."

"So, Nell Becker," he says, sitting down in a stool and waiting for me to sit beside him. "Let me buy you a drink. A real cocktail, like the rich kids in movies."

He's giving this big, exaggerated performance and I'm unsure whether it's a show. I eye him warily. "I don't trust you."

His eyes light up. "This is brand-new information. Why don't we make a drinking game out of it? Every time you doubt my intentions, we'll drink."

"There's not enough alcohol in the world," I tell him, and he laughs like what I said is really and truly funny.

"Okay, then let's drink and we can both pretend we're someone else."

"Who would I be in this scenario?" I ask, watching him carefully. "Someone more like Tristan, do you think?" I think back to the Jeep—to that moment I found something so appealing in her. She's the cool girl—certainly too cool for the straitlaced girls of Prep—but she doesn't care what any of us think of her.

"Not in a million years. No, look." He leans into the bar. "You're in college studying abroad in some generic European country and you have no responsibilities. I'm, like, I don't know, some uptight recent college grad who goes to work every day who's replaced feeling anything with money and a drug problem."

"Unlike now?" I ask him.

He rolls his eyes.

"Fine." I hit the bar. "Let's do it. I don't want anything gross."

He throws up his hand. "Well, now I have no idea what to order. Lois!" he calls out, cupping his hand over his mouth. A woman who has to be in her sixties with bushy white hair haloing her face and tattoos up and down her arms comes over, laying out two napkins in front of us. "My friend here wants something not gross. Any chance you could oblige?" I bristle at the word *friend*.

Lois inspects me with a neutral face. "You been talking shit about my bartending, Hart?" she asks in a pack-a-day voice.

"Lois, if I didn't talk shit about your bartending, I would be lying, and I know how you feel about that," Jackson returns.

Lois's eyes smile. "Where's the rest of them?"

"Exclusive Tuesday. This is Nell," Jackson tells Lois. "She needs to be eased into all things fun as she is not very familiar with the feeling."

I give him a look.

"I got what you need," Lois says smartly. And then she turns to the bar and starts dumping ice into a glass.

"So, is that who you want to be?" I turn back to Jackson. "The son who grows up and stops acting the fool? Does something that will really impress your dad? Makes good but suffers doing it?"

He almost laughs.

"And that's what you want me to be? Someone who finally follows a whim?" I trace my finger across the bar. "So, if I'm going to be more like you, tell me—how do you even do this?" I look around doubtfully. There's an older couple splitting a bottle of wine in one of the corners but other than that, we're all alone. It's two PM on a Tuesday so that mostly makes sense, but still.

"Well"—Jackson speaks very slowly, as if I am terrible at comprehension—"first you walk into the bar, then you order the alcohol, and then you drink it."

I give him another look to show I am not amused. "You know what I mean."

He sighs. "Things are just different for me, Nell. I get what I want. I bring in a fake ID and Lois pretends it's real because the tip I leave is going to be real. No one asks questions of me. They just do what I say." He tilts his head toward me. "It's not like it's something I'm proud of—it's just true."

The ego is staggering. I don't look at him. "I think you're a little proud of it," I say, watching my finger draw circles on the dark wooden surface of the bar.

His eyes flash up at me, catch me. Pretty blue.

Lois sets two glasses in front of us with bright, colorful liquid splashing against the edges.

"Go on," Lois tells me, and I slowly take a sip, ready to gag like I did on the beer yesterday. But the concoction touches my lips and it's sweet but a little tangy and goes down easier.

I nod with a smile.

"Okay, then," Lois says, sounding as close to satisfied as I can imagine her getting. She points at Jackson. "Don't get me in trouble, Hart." With that, she leaves us alone, heading to the other end of the bar.

"Is it really good?" Jackson asks, looking at my glass doubtfully. "I don't even know what this shit she gave me is."

"You want to talk about last night?" I ask him.

His jaw tenses as he drinks from his glass. "No."

"That's not true," I tell him. "If you didn't, you would've gone and gotten some random girl to come drink with you, but you picked me."

His eyebrows go up as he takes another swig before setting his glass down. "Yes, you've found the flaw in my plan. I should've gone and gotten literally anyone else."

"But you didn't. So if I were you, I'd reflect on that." I don't know why needling him gives me so much satisfaction.

"You're a lot to take," he says, scraping at the bar. "But you wouldn't have come if you didn't want to. You know that as well as I do."

I don't like it that he's right. "Before this all started," I say, outlining a pattern into the condensation on my glass, "I wondered a lot. About what it must be like to be you. This idea that people *like* you, that you get to be successful and smart and mean and everyone still wants a piece of you. That's incredible."

"Nell," he starts.

"But it gets boring, doesn't it? Getting whatever you want all the time?" I sip my drink, watching him with interest. When he doesn't answer for a beat, I go on. "I think that's why you act the way you do. You know, with the girls and all the games you're always playing? You don't want to admit it but you're filling some empty space in your life where you need a challenge. I mean, even school is easier for you than it is for me, and God knows the teachers like you better."

"Oh good. More conspiracy theories." He downs his drink.

"What good do you think it does when you pretend you're something you're not? I mean, that stuff with your dad and Doug. You're a mess, Jackson, and you just act like everything is f—"

"I just don't think about that part of my life that much, Nell, all right?" he says, and it's weird. Before, Jackson always looked so comfortable, so completely in control of every situation, but lately, I can't help but think he's fraying at the edges. Even now, his fingers dance across the bar and his eyes shift back and forth.

"Why wouldn't you think about it?" I ask, and I wonder if he can hear how invested I am, how completely fascinated I am with who he is and *how* he is. How I want free of this fixation. But he's achieved this impossible ideal of perfection I've been chasing all my life, and I don't see how I can let a thing like that go, even if he is faking it.

"Do you think about why you're so obsessive?" he asks me very seriously. He watches me over his water-streaked glass.

"Yes," I say, meeting his eye. "If I didn't think about why I am the way I am, I wouldn't be me."

"You wouldn't," he says darkly.

"I hear that tone in your voice, you know. But I would never treat people as collateral damage."

"Goddammit, Nell," Jackson says, banging down his glass against the table. "Can you just leave it alone? I know! I compartmentalize the fuck out of everything so I can do whatever I want. There, are you happy?"

"You told me I was miserable, remember?"

His eyes don't leave me. "You could get whatever you wanted. You know that, right?"

I half smile. "That only happens to people like you, Jackson. With nice hair." I twirl a piece of my own long auburn hair around my finger, my eyes going to his perfectly tousled dark hair. I think it looks soft, and then I think that I'm appalled at myself for thinking it. I take a sip of my drink and let it sit there a little longer, tasting the liquid swirling around in my mouth. My limbs feel looser already, my mind whirring pleasantly.

"I like that you don't take my shit," Jackson says instead after a minute. "Nothing's ever boring with you. It's, like, when I realized you could see right through me or whatever . . . I hadn't realized up until that moment how transparently obvious everything in my life had become. How much I had stopped seeing the point in anything."

I laugh a little.

"What?" he asks. "Spilling my guts here, Becker."

"It's just funny to think about," I say, smiling at him. "We're both so good at our roles and who are we trying to impress?"

"I assumed it was each other," Jackson says, and we both laugh. Then he asks me, "You think this is a bad idea?"

"What?"

"Us."

"There is no us," I tell him. I know it's not exactly true. We keep pulling together like opposite poles—part of us wanting nothing more than to fight every bit of pull we feel. The rest snaps together like it's nature. Magnetism.

"Of course there's an us," he says.

"It's definitely a bad idea," I admit at last, and he smiles and clinks our glasses together.

It goes down so easy.

•••

"ANOTHER!" Jackson calls, and I destroy the disgusting shot of tequila, slamming the shot glass upside down on the edge of the deck.

"Shit. God, I'm good at drinking!" I yell, turning to face him. He looks very nice, I think then. I rub my thumb over the fabric of his Polo shirt and he watches it. I look up at his eyes, glassy in the fading sun.

He gives me an almost smile as if something has made him sad. "You're good at everything."

"Exactly." I remove my hand from his shirt-sleeve but then immediately swat at him. "How did it take you this long to figure that out?"

He grins. I gaze out over the river, the sun making its descent on the horizon. The bar is built up on a hill in the trees like a hideaway. Birds dip into the water, hungry, and off in the distance, I can see some kids kayaking. "Alcohol makes me happy."

He stares for a moment, and then says, "You won't be saying that tomorrow," as he picks up my empty shot glass. We have amassed a couple of them that he has stacked on the table—they are starting to list dangerously to the side.

"I will," I tell him, my eyes refocusing. "I feel so light. I feel so . . . not like myself. It's nice."

"But I like yourself," he says in a very serious voice that I don't believe.

"No, you don't."

"Because I know you're drunk right now—"

"I'm not drunk," I interrupt him, my words slurring into one another.

His expression doesn't change. "Because I know you're drunk right now, I'm going to tell you something."

I sip at a water. "Tell me."

He tips back his seat—one of those brightly colored barstools that looks like a day at the beach—and tangles his feet up in the slats of the deck railing in front of us. "I really like you, Nell."

I laugh so hard, I spit a little water out, a loud guffaw that makes Lois turn around and glare at me from the outside bar where they've stuck her for the evening shift. I keep giggling and Jackson is watching me with his stupid neutral expression, so I try to pull myself together. "You do not *like me*, you disillusioned rich kid. And I am one hundred percent not going to fall for your shit."

He rubs his jaw, still looking at me all thoughtful, as if this isn't the most ridiculous conversation of lies two people have ever had. "I like that you don't know your own depths."

Something courses through my veins. Something dark and fully alive. "Depths," I repeat.

"You're dark somewhere deep down in there, Becker. Like the hidden parts of the ocean. You're not sure what's lurking beneath the surface and you're not sure if you want to find out."

The metaphor clears my head slightly, the precise way he strings the words together. A shiver goes up my spine. "I don't think that's a compliment."

"It is from me."

"I want," I start, glancing over to be sure he's watching, then turning back out to the water, "to be you, I think. To . . . I don't know, touch you. To beat you. To crawl inside of you and have your power."

"My power," he repeats, his voice slightly strangled. I stare straight ahead because I don't want to see the way he's looking at me. "I hear it, you know, what you won't say. You hate me so much, Becker."

"That's the sad part," I say. "I don't actually hate you at all." I face him then, his dark-blue eyes catching mine, knowing he'll pull me under like a current. But that's not the whole story; there's something else here. Something more real than I let myself imagine.

A sad lady is singing about her broken heart over the speakers, and I watch Jackson's long fingers as he runs them along the railing of the deck. I see the way they're constantly moving, as if they can't stand the stillness, the idea that they may not touch every molecule of oxygen floating here in the sunset.

"Dance with me, Nell," he says in some gruff voice he's been hiding all along, and I don't really have a choice then, do I? He pushes off from the deck, sure that I will follow, and I don't know, I'm pretty sure I will, too, because there's a breeze blowing off the river and even though he's so sure, there is something so profoundly sad about him.

Maybe there's something sad about me.

He takes my hand and I let him, and then I put my other hand on his shoulder so we're not too close. Everything is happening fast and slow all at once, as if the alcohol has given me more clarity than I normally have, but less time to plug it into my brain and understand what it means. It's so easy not to think and only to feel for that one moment.

"I meant what I said before," he says at last, leading us in a circle. The dance is so proper, like he's been trained to do this, and I think he probably has because he pulls our clasped hands over our heads and spins me around and then pulls me back, closer to him than before. "About you."

"I don't remember," I tell him because it is all getting kind of hazy.

"I like you, Nell. I like the stupid way you obsess over everything and how intense you are and that you never fucking let up, no matter how badly I want you to. I thought this was just some stupid *thing* to get under your skin at first and now I keep wondering when I'll see you again and what you're doing and why your mouth is constantly in that line like you're thinking about something important, only not every little thing can possibly be as important as you make it look."

I blink and keep my eyes closed for a minute, feeling all of it. The smell of his cologne and the pulse underneath his wrist and the way my fingers graze the fabric of his shirt. "I'm terribly sorry," I say at last, opening my eyes again.

He barks out a laugh then, his eyes shifting to a spot over my shoulder. "Why?"

"Because you don't know how to turn a feeling like that off."

"You do?"

"Of course," I tell him. I couldn't survive if I didn't.

"It's so messed up. For me to want this. It won't work." He spins me again and I swear he pulls me back even tighter, where neither of us can escape the reality. And it's all a dance—not just the way we're moving with each other but our words and our bodies and everything in between.

"Jackson?" I say.

"What?" he replies.

"You talk too much," I tell him, and then my mouth is on his, all sharp lime and slow boats on a summer breeze.

It registers with him like a shock to the system. His body falls into mine and his fingers tangle up in my hair. I could crawl inside the feel of this kiss, the perfect symmetry of our mouths. And I'm drunk, anyway, so what does it matter if I let myself enjoy it? And I mean, *really* enjoy Jackson Hart without obsessing about all the rest.

He pulls back.

"Don't say anything," I tell him, keeping my voice clear.

He laughs. "Wasn't going to."

The songs ends and we both stop, moving away from each other. The fairy lights come on then, strung over our heads across the deck. People are coming in to eat at the restaurant. I want to call what just happened something like magic but I know it's really the alcohol.

"So what now?" Jackson asks me, his dark hair glowing in the light.

"Now nothing." I shrug. "The day's over, Hart. Sometimes, it's just over."

He nods, glancing toward Lois behind the bar. "Yeah," he says at last. "I guess it is."

19

Coach Prince—our club volleyball coach—blows a whistle and the sound is so shrill, it can only realistically be happening directly inside my head, which is pounding in such an unpleasant way, standing up doesn't even seem like something my body is made to do and vomiting has to be preferable to not vomiting right now.

"Becker!" Coach Prince screams. "Look alive."

I try as I left-right-left to hit the ball. It falls pitifully into the net. Lia's eyes catch mine right before she goes for her next set. It's way too low and Michonne doesn't stand a chance as she tries to hit it.

"That's it!" Coach Prince hits her whistle again like the sound is my punishment. "Everyone get in here," she says, and all the balls roll away as we huddle around her. I can only half listen as I try to keep my breakfast in.

"This is pathetic," Coach Prince tells us. She's so right. "We have our first big tournament in *two days* and you look worse than your first day of practice. Do you think this shit is going to get you into the top five teams? Do you think you can win any matches like this? This group I see won't even make it through an elimination match, much less win a championship. This isn't about you as a player or who you impress or what honor you get. This is about the team. And the team I'm seeing will be wiped off the floor by any other team in Charleston. Is that who you want to be?"

"No," everyone else says with conviction. I can't even force the word out.

"Then get out there and work like it," she tells us, her voice poison. "Becker, Reagan," she calls to the two of us as the huddle disperses. "I expect you to be leaders out there."

Lia nods resolutely and I follow suit, feeling like the absolute lowest person on the planet. People are expecting things from me, and I'm letting them down. I blew off all my responsibilities so I could hang out with Jackson Hart yesterday, of all people. That isn't the kind of person I want to be.

I go back to my hitting line, clenching my teeth.

I pick up the pace considerably then, hangover be damned. We break off into teams and I yell the younger girls into place, making sure their formations and coverage are perfect. I'm not one hundred percent but I can give it all I've got.

I have to.

A ball goes sailing onto our side of the net right at Lia, and even though she's supposed to take the second pass if at all possible, she has no choice but to take a shot at this one. Only, it goes sailing away in the other direction. She calls out "Help!" and I spring into action, taking off in the direction of the ball, running as fast as my body can carry me. I make a desperate dive at the ball, pushing it over my shoulder and hopefully back toward my teammates. As quickly as I can, I roll back over my shoulder, jumping onto my feet and running back to the net so I can block as we make the absolutely phenomenal save. The second-string team does their best but can't return it and the point is ours.

That's when it happens. I hit my knees and throw up on the gym floor. And it's really horrible, as if my guts are coming up from inside, and my head is pounding even harder than before, and once it finally stops, I fall back onto the floor and hold my sweaty palms on my sweaty forehead.

Dear God.

Coach Prince and the team come running over as I push my hair away from my face. There's echoes of "Nell" from all of them, but then Coach Prince is keeping everyone back, giving me my space or protecting them from hazardous materials, I'm not sure which.

"Nell," she says, sinking down next to me, "are you all right?"

"Just dehydrated, I think," I tell her. True enough. Lia is right over Coach Prince's shoulder, watching me with an unreadable expression.

"You need to go home," Coach Prince tells me.

"I don't . . . ," I start to argue.

"Now," she says over me. "Can you walk?"

I nod, allowing her to pull me up. "I'll just clean up and get out of here," I say, the words floating around my brain like a haze.

"Let me walk you," Lia says.

Coach Prince nods. "I'm going to talk to the team and send everyone home so I can get this cleaned up." My face burns. "Thank you for working so hard, Nell. I don't want you to be sick, obviously, but I know the girls felt your energy. You always push everyone around you to be better. Rest up, okay?"

I nod and she walks away from Lia and me, back to where the other girls are standing around, looking concerned. Lia grabs my arm, steering me toward the locker room. She doesn't say anything until after she's opened the door and let it fall closed behind me.

"What's wrong with you?" she asks at last. "You look like hell. What did you do yesterday? My dad's in *The Post and Courier* again and I don't even get a text from you?"

"I'm sorry," I say quickly. I really don't want to talk about it. I push past her and into the bathroom, letting water run onto a paper towel and holding it against my forehead. When I open my eyes, she's standing to my left, her back leaned up against the counter with her arms crossed.

"Jackson Hart posted a picture of a bunch of shots," she says, the accusation in her voice.

I look at her quickly. "I wasn't in it, was I?"

She laughs in a way that is clearly not amused.

"Fine." I push my fingers through my hair. "I'm a jerk. I got drunk and showed up to volleyball hungover. I've completely lost the fragments of my mind that held me together." I shake my head. "I can't explain it to you because I don't know. Why am I doing all of this?"

She relents, a small amount of sympathy creeping onto her face then. Lia is the patient one between the two of us, always has been. Like a true setter, she sits back and waits, bails everyone else out if they mess up. I'm all passion and nerves and she's steady. *I'd be lost without her*, I can't help but think. "You've been killing yourself since April. It could wear on anyone. But why Jackson?"

I dip my head down to the sink again, taking a gulp of water from the faucet.

"It's not a great look," she adds. "If people from school found out you were together. Girls with Jackson don't always get the best reputation." She tilts her head, looking at me. "Or have you forgotten?"

"We're not *together*," I say. "He just gets it, in some weird way. The pressure."

"He's still Jackson."

"Nothing's going on," I say so forcefully, I almost believe it. "He's vile."

"There's something about him you like. I see you. I *know* you, Nell."

"I know him," I return. "I know what I'm doing."

She sighs.

"Okay, not today, obviously." I glance toward the door that leads to the gym, watching it. "They're going to be back soon. I need to get out of here. I can only imagine what they'd think if they saw me like this."

Her eyes narrow. "This isn't over. I'm trying to look after you."

I shake my head, shaking her off like a bug as I walk back out into the main part of the locker room, grabbing my bag from my locker. "I don't need to be looked after, especially when you've got so much going on. And you're being paranoid—I tell you everything." I smile, trying to make it casual. "Usually it's to your detriment."

"Yeah," she agrees. "It's just . . . Don't trust him, okay?"

This I can answer with confidence. I swing my bag up on my shoulder. "Of course not," I reply.

Her eyes meet mine as if looking for a sign. Apparently, it's a good one because she finally says, "All right. Feel better, and drink lots of water."

I nod, giving her a small wave and leaving her behind.

20

I feel something vibrating next to my head. I sit directly up, thinking I'm late. I've been waking up on and off all night, terrified of over-sleeping and not arriving on time for the tournament tomorrow. But the clock on my nightstand says it's one AM and my phone says JACKSON HART is calling me.

I slide my thumb across the screen and put the phone to my ear. "Are you dead or dying?"

"Is this some sort of psychological test?" he returns.

"What do you want? I have an early wake-up call."

"Shit, sorry," he says, throwing his voice like he is. "I'll go."

"Go?" My voice cracks. "Are you here?"

"In my car. Down the block."

"Dammit, Jackson," I hear myself saying, but I'm already out of bed because I can't stand the thought of him driving away. I slide into a pair of flip-flops and put a T-shirt on over my tank top. I think about putting a bra on, but screw it—I don't care what he thinks of me.

I tiptoe down the stairs and out the door, jogging over the side-walk to get away from what feels like my parents' prying eyes.

His headlights are on and he's leaning back in his seat with his eyes closed as if holding up his body is too much work. He jumps in surprise when I open the door.

"Nell Becker, silent assassin." He cranks the engine and we're off again.

"This is starting to feel familiar," I say, more of an out-loud thought than anything else. I see him half grin to himself. "You've got like five minutes to tell me what you're doing here. I have to be up at five thirty."

"Why?" He taps his fingers against the steering wheel. He's leaving my neighborhood again.

"You always do that," I say. "Drive right out of the neighborhood. Like you can't wait to get away from this part of town."

"Don't be dramatic," he says. "I don't like your house because it makes me remember who your mom is."

I roll my eyes. "She's the head of school, not a monster. But seriously, I have a volleyball tournament in Charleston. A lot of scouts will be there, so it's a great opportunity. I should be in bed." But I want to be with him more. Even though I know I need to go to sleep right now, I can't help but feel wired. I realize it's not just the potential of the tournament that has my adrenaline racing—it's him. I feel wired about *him* and I don't know why that's so shocking, but it is.

Why hadn't I noticed it before?

"Your life is just a continuous series of opportunities, isn't it?" he says.

"That's a nice way to look at it," I answer, although I'm not sure that's what he means. He's driving close to the river. It seems like he always is. We're near where Doug had his accident.

Navigating his truck down a boat ramp, Jackson pulls over and opens up the door, getting out without saying anything to me. I take this as a directive to follow.

He leans against the hood of his truck, watching the water lap sadly against the cement as if it can't be bothered to try. I lean next to him and cross my arms. We stand like that, a breath between the hair on our arms when he says, "I was at this party at Marcus's. The usual, you know?" He glances over at me. "Same old people, same old drinks and music and conversations, and I was like, God, I wish Nell were here. She'd know what to do."

"Imagination is a powerful gift," I say, working as much disdain into my voice as I can muster. The worst thing I could do is hint at my epiphany—tell him I *want* to be here, together.

"It's okay," he says. "You don't have to wish me into your life. I'm the one who keeps showing up at your house." I could say it out loud, make it real, but I'm afraid he might realize that I'm just like everyone else.

I'm afraid *I* might realize it.

He walks forward, scoops up a rock or a broken piece of cement or something, and skips it across the water. Three. Four. Five. I put my hands on the hood of the truck and push myself up to sit on it.

"What do you want me to say?" I call to him. The moon is bright tonight, shining like a promise. I can't tell if it's waxing or waning, but I know it's so close to full. Like it's waiting for some other part to fill it up.

He turns back and looks at me. "Everything. Say everything, Nell." He walks toward me, leisurely. I feel my heart pounding against my chest like the night is demanding something from me—something hot and angry and absolutely terrifying. So when he's close enough, I grab on to the front of the button-down shirt he's wearing and pull him to me, between my legs, and I lean forward to kiss him like I did when the feeling of alcohol was destroying my brain cells. He doesn't seem surprised. He doesn't hesitate because he never hesitates. He grabs the back of my head, forcing my mouth down on his, our bodies pressing into each other. I wrap my legs around his waist, and he lets go of my neck to grab my hips with both hands. Our mouths aren't sure if this is the only chance we'll ever have or if we're never going to stop touching.

I slide from the hood of the car, pushing him away as I do and then pulling him back to fill the finite amount of space that was between us. Every inch of skin feels electric. We're supposed to *stop*. We're supposed to want to stop, one of us is supposed to jump back and say this is wrong. Say this is a mistake.

I'll be damned if I'm losing this one.

I link my fingers through his belt loops, pulling us away from the front of the truck. He follows me, pushing me up against the back door, his teeth scraping against the skin of my collarbone. I reach blindly for the door handle, pulling it open, and shove him into the cab until he's sitting on the seat. I keep reaching for him, falling into the cab, into him, my mouth frantic. It's been like waiting to dive into the river on a hot day, realizing the cold water on your skin is all you needed from the start.

I love how in control I feel, how in control he lets me feel, like I get to decide whatever comes next. And I feel it in myself that I don't want to stop, I want to touch him. I don't care if that's what other girls would or wouldn't do. I work at the button of his khakis. I feel like a thousand fires that won't be put out, like a raging bull rushing head-first into red. His whole body tenses as I slide my hand under the elastic of his boxers. His mouth moves considerably more eagerly over any part of me he can reach as I explore. I love this moment, where he's so vulnerable, wants me so badly. My hands on his body.

I've never felt like this before.

So when I finish with him and he falls back, panting, my smile is so small, hidden, as I scrape my teeth against my lower lip. I climb out of the truck and into the fresh, hot air of the Cedar Woods summer night, my heart pounding and the buzz all over my skin inexplicable. I glance back as he fixes his shirt and his pants and does the hair rub before he climbs out to stand next to me. Leans next to me again.

He sighs deeply. Starts to say something. Stops.

I shove away from the truck, walking down the slope toward the water. I leave my flip-flops where I stand and wade into the river, down the slick boat ramp, my athletic shorts soaking straight through. It hasn't been hot for long enough yet so the water offers a little chill that raises goose bumps all over my body. He follows me down once he sees what I'm doing, leans over, and rolls up the cuffs of his khakis.

As he's doing that, I kick the water at him, splattering it all over his outfit.

"*Fuck*, Becker," he says, and I can tell he's not referring to the splash. I laugh and laugh until I have to tilt my head back, I am laughing so hard. He watches me in my manic state like he's waiting for something. It feels like a game. Like a challenge.

Make your move.

I grab the bottom of my T-shirt and pull it over my shoulders. The bottom is soaked through anyway. I walk back and toss it carelessly against the boat ramp before I wade back into the water, my white tank top clinging desperately to my skin. I feel Jackson watching me and I think there's power in this. In being reduced to my barest self in front of him and knowing I'll survive it.

With his eyes still on mine, he unbuttons his shirt, shrugs out of it, and pulls off his white T-shirt underneath. Then he runs at me, knocking me completely into the water and I drag him down with me. Both of our heads bob back up and we keep laughing. I push my fingers through his hair, his face floating in front of me.

"What?" he asks, shaking his head to get his hair out of his face.

I shake my head. "Your pants. You rolled them up and everything. God, you are so stupid." And even that seems especially funny.

"What's wrong with you?" he asks, incredulous.

I go all the way under, water filling my ears and the space between my fingers, and I tug at my tank top, pulling it all the way off. I float back up, pushing my hair out of my face, the water covering me from the shoulders down. I toss my top back toward the shore. We stare at each other across the few feet of space between us.

Now what?

We're in a stare-off, our faces completely devoid of expression, and I know I have to make the first move, always touch him first. I push the water with my hands, swimming slightly closer to him. He treads water. The moon reflects all around us and the night moves in a way that calls

138

to be felt. I put my hand forward, the moonlight shining off my pale fingers, and place it against his warm skin, right above his heart. His heartbeat is steady against my skin. He covers my palm with his own, his fingers creeping around it and pressing my hand into his chest.

We both wait, the water dripping off us, making rivers down our skin. I'm unsure of what to do next, a thrilling, unfamiliar feeling. Without giving it the amount of thought I usually give to things, I take his hand and put it on my face. He trails his fingertips over my cheek, down the skin on my neck and across my collarbone. He plants his palm against the middle of my chest. I swallow.

"Look at you, Nell," he says to me, his voice coming out choked. I hear the way his mouth curls around my name. Most things he says come with an air of derision—like he knows a secret he won't bother sharing with you—but not my name. He says it like he means it.

It's in that moment that I know so clearly that I want him to touch me. To feel fully alive in my skin. I move to kiss him again, and he meets me halfway, his hands desperate for every part of me. I love how much he wants me to touch him. I love how vital I feel—I am a part of the river and I'm apart from everything else about me. And the only sounds in the night are the trees and the waves and our breathing, mixing together.

It's not unexpected, but Jackson's mouth moves exactly how the rest of him does—with confidence. The more I kiss him, the more I want to kiss him, to feel the way his fingertips dig into my skin and his mouth demands mine, the way he strays to my neck and my collarbone but never for too long. I can't help but think that this is where I always want to be and this is how I always want to feel.

Our bodies are pressed too close together and there's a chance this may swallow us whole. I shiver, and promise myself it's only from the chill.

He pulls away. "Nell?" he asks.

"Yeah," I say, my voice an octave higher than normal.

"This water is *cold*."

We both start laughing and I wrap my arms around myself, suddenly way too aware of how naked I am, even under the cover of water. Jackson gets out and pulls some towels from his truck—no one ever travels without them in a river town. He turns so I can get out of the water and wrap one around myself.

We lie next to each other bundled up in our own towels in the bed of his truck, watching the sky. Watching for stars, for unidentified flying objects.

"You kissed me," he says, acknowledging it at last. "Twice."

More than that, I think, but who's counting? "One could argue that Lois's concoction kissed you the first time."

"Why?"

"Seemed like a thing I could do," I tell him.

"Another frontier to conquer." I see him turn toward me out of the corner of my eye. "Can I ask you something?"

"Fine," I say.

"I didn't, like, know"—he swallows—"I didn't know you had been dating people or whatever." He waves his hand afterward as if to wave what he just said away.

"What does that mean?" I ask, baffled.

"Nell, you just." He coughs. "You took charge."

"Is there something wrong with that?" I ask, trying not to sound upset by his words.

He laughs. "Are you kidding? No, no." Then he looks at me and away. "Sorry. Most girls . . . they don't . . ."

"Wow. Jackson Hart rendered speechless. What do *most* girls do?" I ask, my voice growing more dangerous by the second, the moments before losing their shine.

"I didn't mean it like that. You're fearless, that's all," he says quickly.

"Do you categorize them?" I ask. "Shrinking violets? Secretly aggressive? Knows what she's doing?"

"I'm not apologizing to you for having sexual relationships with the people I date. And I would never expect you to do that, either." He bends one arm at the elbow and rests his head on it. "It's none of my business. Sorry I asked."

"Asked what?"

"Who you'd been hooking up with."

I almost don't say it. I really don't want to, only then the words are forming on my lips. "No one," I say at last.

He stares at me. "No one?"

"I mean"—I keep my face toward the moon—"I'm not some never-been-kissed girl or anything. But just now? I felt like doing it, so I did. Because it felt *good*."

"It did," he agrees. I feel his eyes leave me until we're looking in the same direction. "I'm glad it's not Taylor Reagan, to be honest."

I purse my lips. Taylor. How obvious. "I need to go," I say, pushing myself up. His eyes follow the curves of my body as I shake out my wet hair.

He raises an eyebrow. I think he's going to ask me to stay—some small part of me wants him to—but then he grabs on to the edge of the truck bed and sits up next to me. "All right," he says. "Let's get you home."

21

I'm chugging the coffee I sent Mom to get me once we'd gotten to the gym at College of Charleston. "You don't drink coffee," she told me, like there was some universe in which I was unaware of this fact. But I can barely keep my eyes open. I'd drifted in and out of consciousness on the hour ride here and now just the thought of being alive seems a burden too large to bear.

Lia runs up to me and bends over, whispering as I drink. "Are you okay?" I glance behind me at where the other girls have already started bumping balls to one another. *Time to look alive.* I roll my head around on my neck a couple of times.

"I couldn't sleep last night," I tell her. It's mostly true.

She puts her hand on my back, rubbing it sympathetically. It just makes me feel like a bigger, more irresponsible jackass. "Don't get sick, okay?"

"Me? I would never."

I try to pull myself together. To put my nose down, turn off my mind, and let my body do the work. And I almost convince myself it will be that easy. Until the first whistle.

The important parts of my brain all seem to be napping. I'm in the wrong places at the wrong times. I miss simple calls. Hit things out of bounds that I usually nail. In the second game of our first match, Coach Prince benches me.

"What's gotten into you, Becker?" she demands as I walk past her to take my place on the bench. "Get your head on right."

I nod, wiping nonexistent sweat out of my eyes. Briefly, I look behind me at the people in the stands, trying to pick out the scouts in the crowd. They'd be the ones with clipboards, pausing every couple of minutes to write notes down. I twist the orange bracelet signifying me as a rising senior around on my wrist. I imagine the words they might be writing down. *Unfocused. Lazy. Unaware of her surroundings.*

I'm out the rest of the game and we take the second loss of the day. Coach Prince tells me I'm going back in for the must-win set. I make a couple of good plays and feel myself coming back to life. But I can't sustain any kind of momentum and soon, I'm weaving stories in my head about what a complete failure I am. Ball after ball sails out of bounds. Mistake after mistake. I know this oppressive feeling that I'll never be good enough like the back of my hand.

At the end of the day, our record is a paltry two wins, two losses. I look like an outstandingly average middle hitter. Sometimes I run into the net. Sometimes I steal balls from my teammates. I never look polished, never finish all the way. I sit on the bleachers behind our empty bench, running through all the mistakes in my head, reliving them, getting them right.

I get so lost in the act, in picking myself apart. I wonder if any scouts will bother showing up for our games tomorrow.

Lia plops onto the bleachers next to me. "Don't do this. Get out of there, Nell," she says, pulling a hand away from my head. "You're fine. You know you can be better and you will be tomorrow."

"I suck," I say, pulling my hand back and resting it against the side of my head, scraping my fingernails over my face. "All I had to do was take this seriously. But no, I couldn't be bothered to get a proper night's sleep. I just went out there and personally *fucked* myself, Lia. Do you see that?"

She does not return the self-pity I wanted. "What did you really do last night?"

I shake my head. I'm not telling her, not when she'll judge me for it. I don't need that on top of everything else. I want to talk about the game. I want to talk about how bad I was.

"If you don't tell me, I'm going to assume it's something worse."

"That's doubtful," I say, not looking at her. "I don't want to talk about it."

"Did you sleep with him, Nell?" she asks, sounding somewhere between disbelief and mistrust.

"*No*," I tell her. "I couldn't sleep and we were just . . . on the phone. Whatever, it doesn't matter."

"You're right," she says, her voice betraying her relief. "It doesn't. *Stop* thinking about it. And I don't mean him. I mean, if you get down on yourself, you'll never get out of your head. Have fun, but play your game on your own terms. I know how important this is to you."

"Yeah," I agree. "If they see me bounce back tomorrow, that's even better. Phoenix rising from the ashes and all." I don't really believe it, but Lia gives me a half smile, nodding back encouragingly. I squeeze her arm affectionately. "Your setting was really strong today," I tell her.

Lia shrugs. "Honestly, I don't feel right, either. Not like I have at my best. This is usually my favorite tournament. The whole family comes and we get a hotel and go out in Charleston for the night. And now, I keep looking back on the past couple of years, wondering where all that money came from."

"Lia . . . ," I say, not sure what to do.

"It's fine. Not a big deal."

"No, it is." I grab her shoulder. "I can ride back to Cedar Woods with you. We can blast really bad music and scream."

"What about your mom?" she asks.

"She'll be fine," I say, waving my hand dismissively. Mom had driven up by herself today, since Dad had to work. I wait for her as she makes her way down the bleachers. She's keeping a straight face for my benefit—she knows how terrible I was today.

"It wasn't that bad," she says at the look on my face.

I almost laugh. "Wasn't it?"

"You made a couple of great saves." I don't believe her. "You look tired. Like you don't feel like yourself. When you get home, why don't you ice your shoulder and go to bed?"

I stretch out my shoulder, surprised she noticed. "Sure," I say because I always go along with her. "I'm going to ride home with Lia."

"Nell, I'm not going to nag you," she says.

"Lia needs company."

Mom looks over at her, then back at me, her expression clear. "Oh. Okay." She gives me a close-mouthed smile. "Make sure you get something for dinner with lots of protein. I'll see you at home."

"Sure."

She touches my face. "Love you."

I grab up my gym bag and call behind me as I head off, "See you later!"

• • •

The phoenix does not rise from the ashes.

I know from the first ball I touch. I don't have it. I've lost my magic.

I can feel the fury building behind my eyes, growing as the day goes on. I can't blame lack of sleep—not exactly. I decided I would ignore the buzzing of my phone last night, no matter what. Only no buzzing ever came. I checked my phone again and again, but the screen didn't change. And then I couldn't sleep because I wondered *why* my phone wasn't buzzing. And why it mattered.

It was another excuse. Not a very good one.

By the afternoon elimination game, I can barely hold in my frustration. I hit a ball into the net to lose the final point of the set, a perfect pinnacle of my downfall. When the ball rolls sadly back to me, I pick it up and slam it into the gym floor.

"BECKER!" Coach Prince calls after me. "You're out for the next set. Evans, get over here, you're starting."

It's punishment, and I deserve it.

I watch as they lose the final game and the match. Well, watch is probably an unfair way to put it. I can barely make myself pay attention, fuming, wasted on the bench. *I hate me when I'm not perfect.* I don't say anything as Coach Prince debriefs us after the game. She's disappointed. We could do better.

I've been listening to it on a loop in my head for the past two days; that song is tired.

When I get in the car at the end of the day, Dad's eyes are all over me.

"You didn't have your best stuff today, kid. It happens to everyone."

I shake my head, rolling my eyes in the direction of the window so he can't see me.

"You're not owed success, you know," he says, and I hear a touch of annoyance in his voice.

"I know," I answer. Even my voice sounds like an eye roll.

"But that's not what embarrassed me. What embarrassed me was you throwing a tantrum. Slamming the ball like a brat."

I look over at him. "I'm acting out like a regular teenager. Isn't that what you want?"

"Don't speak to me that way. You have to be a team player. You have to accept defeat."

I cross my arms over my chest. "I can only imagine if Mom heard you say that."

"Well, she's not here, is she?" he asks, starting the car. Classic rock plays in the background. "The kind of treatment you act as if the world owes you now . . ."

I stare up at the car roof. "Don't give me this."

Dad holds on to the steering wheel tightly. "You're stuck in between two worlds," he tells me, his voice annoyingly calm. "You get to decide, Nell. You get to decide who to be."

I turn to stare at him, my jaw clenched. "You sound like a fortune cookie," I say.

He puts the car into drive. He doesn't speak to me as we ride to the sandwich shop where we're meeting some of the girls before we head back to Cedar Woods. I can feel his disapproval radiating from across the car and I already feel terrible about what I said.

It's the attitude I take as I get my sandwich and sit across from Lia. She seems just as mad as I am, which at least fuels me on. I'm angrily spreading mustard onto my sandwich when she says, "Can you stop pouting? You're making my food taste bad."

"I'm not pouting," I say, which is completely irrational because I'm definitely pouting. But I'm in the mood where being accused of doing what I'm doing only makes me more indignant.

"So you played like shit. It's not like you're the only one."

"Right? Because I didn't blow up my expectations at all."

"So what, Nell?" she asks, chucking down her sandwich so that it falls apart. She keeps her voice low but frustration sharpens her tone. "Do you know how much better I would've looked if you were out there killing it? What about me, Nell? What about my scholarships? I want scouts to see me, too. Don't you get that? Don't you get that *my* life is a disaster? It's always—*always*"—she grabs up her tray, and I see so clearly that she's leaving and I want to tell her not to, but I don't find the words—"about you." She finishes brutally and is gone from the table in an instant.

I slump back in my seat, defeated.

Taylor falls into her empty spot. "That looked fun," he says, biting into his sandwich.

I sit in silence, contemplating my own terribleness. Taylor throws a chip at me and it hits me in the middle of the chest. "Cheer up."

I grimace at him.

"She'll get over it," he says. "You'll be fine."

"She's right. I'm being an asshole."

Taylor shrugs like he's not so sure. "Lia's not mad at you. She's mad at Mom and Dad. Her anger manifests outwardly while I fall apart on the inside." He bites into his sandwich. "But life goes on."

"I shouldn't be so self-involved."

"It's who you are. You're always focused on you because you're the best." He shrugs again, turning back to his sandwich. "Just do something for her to show you care. That's all she needs. She can't sulk forever."

"I'm not sure that makes me feel better."

"Join the club," he says.

"What's up with you?" I ask.

He shrugs like it doesn't matter. "Amanda. She's different lately."

I attempt to eat as well. "Different, how?"

"It's, like, she loves to go out to parties and socialize and she's—I don't know. Shallow or something? Not how she used to be."

"She went through a lot," I tell him, trying to be reasonable.

"I know, I know," he says, as if he's convincing himself. "I want to be patient. That's why I came down for the games today. So I could zone out and get some perspective or something. I'm sure it'll all be fine."

I'm not so sure. Taylor has a pattern with the girls he dates. Once he's decided things have gone south, it's hard to turn it around.

Taylor's looking at me and keeps biting his lip as if to stop himself from talking. "Can I ask you something?" he says at last.

"Shoot," I say.

"Is there something to the rumors floating around? I heard you were with Jackson Hart when Doug got hurt."

I sip my water, not looking at him. I can feel the heat creeping up my neck. "Who told you that?"

"You know how he is, Nell."

"Oh, not you, too," I say, setting my cup down. "It's nothing. I'm just blowing off some steam. That's what I told Lia and that's what I'm telling you. It's. Nothing."

Taylor doesn't say anything for a minute. And then, "I'm not here to tell you what do."

That seems fair, so I say, "Good."

We mindlessly chatter through the rest of the meal, about college visits and summer plans. I go to clean off my tray at the trash can when I see Lia headed toward me.

"I'm sorry," I say quickly, before she can speak. "I know the tournament is important to you, too, and I wasn't respecting that at all. You're right."

"S'okay," Lia says. "I'm sorry, too. We'll do better next weekend, right? You're fine. We'll be fine."

I nod.

She holds up her hand as if for a high five, but I lace my fingers through it and pull our hands together and we both laugh.

22

I enter the next week with new purpose, able to focus all my energy on volleyball now that school's out. I'd let myself get distracted, by grades and class standing and Jackson. But this is the last summer to play with my team, my girls, my best friend—next year will be all college camps and new teammates.

I *want* to be able to enjoy this. And I couldn't, not for the past month—in fact, I'd almost become convinced it was a burden, weighing me down. I needed this reset.

The good news is, distractions are eradicating themselves from my life faster than I can catch up to them. I find myself checking my phone constantly, holding it close to me, as if it will vibrate and tell me something. And every time it buzzes and I look down and see the name on the screen, I feel my stomach drop.

It's never him.

Sometimes, without thinking about it, I watch the hall of the gym during volleyball practice, waiting to see if he will walk by from weight training. I probably wouldn't see him if he did. Pathetically, I even find myself parking my car close to his in hopes that it will act as a reminder or something. He'll see it and be like—*oh yeah, her.*

But the days drag on and nothing happens. Nothing changes. I want to not want him so badly.

If I'm honest, I don't even know *what* I want. Some acknowledgment. Some proof that I'm different, like I've always thought I am. It happened, didn't it? I was there.

That can't be the end of the story.

After volleyball on Wednesday, I'm changing out of my sweat-soaked top in the locker room. "Where are you off to?" I ask Lia as she stuffs things into her bag in a rush like she's running late.

"Oh, come on, Nell," Michonne calls from the row of lockers opposite us. "Haven't you figured it out?" She looks over at Lia. "Who's your secret man, Lia?"

Lia stops abruptly, knocking one of her sneakers off the bench in surprise. She looks over at Michonne, her face turning red. "My what?"

"The guy you keep running off to see."

"I'm not—" Lia glances over at me and shuts her mouth. "It's not like that," she says instead.

"Seriously?" My voice cuts across the distance, an accusation.

"I can't talk about this right now." Lia shoots Michonne a dirty look. "I'm already late. I'll see you both later. And you can talk to me about keeping secrets *then*," she finishes. She picks up her shoe, shoves it into her bag, and takes off as if that settles the conversation. I'm standing there in nothing but my sports bra and spandex, looking stupidly after her.

"Knew it," Michonne singsongs, turning back to her locker.

"Do you know who?" I ask her, pulling a T-shirt over my head.

"Nah, I've just seen her headed out of here." Michonne throws a piece of gum in her mouth, blowing a bubble loudly before continuing. "Yesterday, it was eyeliner and perfume. And I saw a dress fall out of her bag earlier this week."

"Someone from Prep?" I ask, waiting for Michonne to close her locker. When she does, I pick up my own bag and walk out beside her.

"Probably." She rolls her eyes. "These families and their scandals.

You gotta stay away from them," she goes on, like she's not one of them. "That's why I only date public schoolers and tourists."

I laugh, cracking open the locker room door into the blazing heat. "Like there's so many tourists in Cedar Woods."

"Gets the job done," she says. "And it's always the prettiest boys and girls who stay for the whole summer. So many potential love interests, so little time." She gives me a wicked grin.

I almost stop dead in my tracks when I see them. Some of the baseball team milling around Jackson's truck, talking post-conditioning. And he's right there in the middle with that dark hair and dark-blue gaze in the light of day. Michonne laughs mischievously, popping her gum.

The guys wave at the two of us and I feel Jackson's eyes meet mine. The moment it happens, the temperature drops precipitously. He averts his gaze like he doesn't recognize me at all.

My heart pounds out an angry staccato rhythm against my chest. "You want to go over there?" Michonne asks. I barely hear her.

I know this part—can put the pieces together like a puzzle. When boys like Jackson are done with a girl, they don't deal with it. They hope she fades off into the distance, humiliated. Too ashamed or proud to confront them. He thinks he can make me disappear.

Fuck that.

"No," I tell Michonne. "I'm going." I get in the car, try to stop myself from shaking. I'm not going to make a fool of myself in front of all those boys.

When it's time to burn it all down, you can't let them see it coming.

I slam the door of my car.

• • •

The house is both exactly as I imagined it and not like anything I imagined at all. It's gorgeous, all the signs of money and time poured carefully into the foundation but with something that so distinctly feels like home. A hand-carved stone fire pit is surrounded by welcoming wooden chairs with a stone walkway leading up to the stone porch. Wood mingles with the stone and floor-to-ceiling windows give the whole thing an open look.

This would be a hard house to burn down.

I walk up the steps like I have some sort of authority and ring the doorbell. The sound chimes all over the house. Someone on the inside pounds down steps, a cacophony echoing in their wake. The door opens and there he is.

He looks like he could be going for a run, aside from his bare feet. His entire face changes when he sees me, and not in a good way.

"What are you doing here?" he asks, exasperated.

I give him a humorless laugh. "Are you kidding me?"

He presses his lips together as he looks at me, and then he stops, staring off into the distance over my shoulder. "I can't talk to you," he tells me.

I've taught myself in my years being dismissed at Prep that if you get angry enough, you won't leave room for hurt. You can mow it down in its tracks, fill it with something so much better. Get rid of those places where hurt feelings are supposed to go and douse them in kerosene instead so they'll burn better. "You can't talk to me. That is perfect."

"Dammit, Nell," he says, pushing the door all the way open like he's trying to frame himself in a better light. "Don't do this—don't get into shit you don't understand."

"Oh my God, fuck you," I spit out. "Find someone else to condescend to."

"I will," he tells me, starting to close the door. "Go home, Nell."

Who gave him permission to dismiss me? I think. I brace my hand against the door—I'm for sure getting called crazy by everyone in his social group after this anyway, so damn it all to hell at this point—and push the door open after him. The house opens into a huge great room, two stories high with a balcony overlooking the main floor. Everything is wooden and beautiful and glossy and perfect and I am just me. Tall and abrasive and too much. Too much ambition, too much competitiveness, too much girl, too much everything. "You are not going to throw me aside like a piece of trash, Jackson Hart," I say, my voice holding steady. "Because I'm not."

There's something else in his expression. It's not contempt. I'm not even sure it's regret. It looks like *hunger*.

"It's not like that," he says. "This has gone way too far."

"*Too far?* You had no problem showing up at *my* house unannounced, and at all hours of the night. So, fine. Is it me? Or is it your reputation? What do you even think *this* is?" I'm to the point where I know I should stop. Close my mouth and go. Step back and sort through my thoughts.

Easier said than done.

He rubs his hands over the silky material of his shorts. "It's none of that. It's *not* about any of that."

"Jesus Christ." I put my forehead into my palms, the realization hitting me like a brick. "Fine. You're right. You proved your point. You can pull me in just like every other sad girl on this planet. It's clearly my problem. I'm the one who thought I was somehow better than everyone else."

"There's nothing wrong with them and there's nothing wrong with you, okay? I don't know what more I can say. That's all of it."

"I was pissed," I say, putting myself back together. It's sinking into my shoulders, weighing the rest of me down. Hating myself for my own false sense of superiority. "You know what? Never mind." I turn back toward the door and then stop myself. One last thing before I go. "It does hurt, you know. When you do this. Just for future reference, you should at least say something nice at the end."

He puts his hand flat against the door right as I go to open it, stopping me. "This is not what you think it is."

I twist around so that his arm is next to my face, sun-lightened hair on tan skin, my back against the door. "What is it, then?"

He closes his eyes as if he's in physical pain, luxuriating in the drama of the moment, making me feel so unsure. Then he opens his eyes and I think he's going to say something.

He doesn't. He kisses me.

There must be some word for it. For when you have always felt like the most logical, rational person on the planet, and the feel of someone else's body against yours turns you into something famished for connection. I wrap my arms around his neck, linking them below the collar of his T-shirt. His mouth is everywhere and our bodies are everywhere and there's nothing but me and him, him and me, and I can't remember what I was supposed to feel before.

I guess that's the thing about kerosene veins. Lots of different things can light you on fire.

"Don't stop," I mutter into his hair when his mouth is on my neck.

He doesn't show any signs of it. Our hands want to touch every part of each other, and I love that I don't have to think about anything when it's happening. Nothing's ever felt this simple in my life.

"Where's your room?" I ask then, and apparently, that's what stops him. He gives me a look like he's just remembered who I am. "What?" I demand.

He motions his head in the direction of the stairs, up to the balcony, and ushers me through the first door on the right when we reach the top. The room is green. It has all the signs of being carefully decorated by a professional with tiny moments of rebellion thrown in throughout: A group picture on the shelf with Jackson and all his friends flipping off the camera. A fake stuffed head of some mythological creature, part

155

lion but with antlers and a jaunty hat. A collection of trophies displayed upside down for some reason or other.

It's weird, but for the first time, I think he's not just Jackson Hart. He's a person. That's what all these disparate pieces equal. For the first time, I really *see* him.

He's watching me and when my eyes catch his again, there's a different intimacy than was there before. I don't like the space between us. It's like room to think, and that's the last thing I want. I take one step closer. His fingers tangle into my hair, his palm resting against my cheek.

"You know," he whispers, and his voice sounds a little strangled. "For someone so innocent, your eyes look like you want to take me apart."

I don't know if that's what does me in or if it's everything else. I kiss him quick, once, like a question. And he kisses me back again like an invitation.

I know it's supposed to be a big moment. Some epic flash where you consider all your options and come to the right conclusion. That you're ready.

But I've never been the type of person to wait for something I want.

I throw my shirt over my head because it doesn't matter. And neither do these shorts. They're all just an impediment, one more thing between him and me, keeping us from each other. He follows my lead, his eyes never leaving me as if this is a mysterious, unbelievable thing he must track through every moment. Until we're both on the bed and my whole body is screaming *stop making me wait so long*, and finally he reaches over to his nightstand and grabs a condom and he stops right after he does it and looks down at me, at all of me.

It aches everywhere.

I wait for him to say something like they do in movies—*Are you sure?* pops to mind. Or maybe *I've wanted this for so long*, but instead he's like, "Is this a huge mistake?"

"If you make me wait one more second, I will kill you," I say, and my voice aches, too. I push him over so I'm on top and wait for him to get the condom on, and then I figure the rest out on my own. He lets me take the lead, like I know he knows I like, and the feel—my God, the way my whole body feels. It's uncomfortable, the way everyone always talks about in the whispers of locker rooms and bedroom conversations, but it's something else, too.

It's two people from the inside out. It's nothing and it's everything. And I never want it to end.

But that's the thing, isn't it? Everything ends.

Then you're left trying to reach that high. Over and over again.

23

"This is supposed to be the weird part, right?" I ask. Jackson reaches to the top of his bed and grabs a pillow; I raise myself up slightly so he can put it under my head. He puts the other pillow under his own and we lie there next to each other, across the bed instead of using it properly because we can never do anything properly. It takes me a couple of seconds to become self-conscious over how very, very naked we are before I grab a velour blanket from the end of the bed and drape it over myself. And then him.

Jackson talks a lot with his body, I've decided. His thumb presses into the spot between my collarbone and throat and his fingers wrap around the back of my neck. "Is it weird?" he asks, his thumb in constant motion.

"It felt right." I turn my head so I'm looking at the side of his face. "That wasn't how it was supposed to go."

"Says who?" He leans to look at me, moving our faces close together. "You don't worry very much about how things are supposed to be. You always do everything like you're sure."

"I am always sure." I frown and shift away, watching the ceiling fan spin in circles above us. "I feel like I've been missing something."

"That makes two of us." He releases me. "I'm sorry. About before. Downstairs. And in the parking lot." He almost has to force himself to say it. "For not telling you last week."

"Telling me what?"

He doesn't answer immediately. Like he has to work himself up to it, he says, "That there are few things worse in this world than watching you walk away from me."

I swallow. That sounds like a big declaration. Or maybe just a line.

"I don't control myself as well as you do, but I guess I somehow thought I could prevent the inevitable." Inevitable. As if we're two freight trains set to collide at full speed and nothing we do can change that.

"I completely freaked the hell out," he goes on, "and that's why I was avoiding you. This isn't a good time for *this*."

"What?" I ask, twirling an artfully frayed piece of the blanket around in my fingers.

He eyes me.

"Don't freak out, Hart," I say, lacing my voice with bravado. I push the blanket off then as if I haven't a care in the whole world, and re-dress. He stays where he is, staring up—not necessarily giving me privacy, but like he can't stop thinking about something.

"You know it was real, right?" he says. I don't know what that means. I pull my shirt back over my head, watching him. "Offering to change your grade on the test wasn't a trick or anything. I would've let you have number one."

I pull my hair from under my shirt, looking at myself from afar in the wardrobe mirror on the other side of his bed. "I won't let you give me anything because I'm not going to owe you anything."

"I just mean I wasn't playing a game. All of it, like, wasn't just to get you here. Do you believe me?" he asks, like my answer is of the utmost importance. And he's looking at me—really looking at me—like it matters.

I sit down at the edge of the bed, at his feet. Play with another piece of the blanket. "Okay," I say, feeling like I'm agreeing to something else. Something I'm not sure I understand. I watch him as I answer. "I believe you."

He sits up, the blanket pooling at his stomach. I watch the taut muscles of his abdomen as he moves. He pulls his legs up close to him, reaching out and pushing my hair away from my face. It feels too intimate.

"I have to go," I say. Then I meet his eyes meaningfully. "I'll be back."

He looks disappointed. Or relieved. How am I supposed to be able to tell?

"Okay," he says, keeping his voice void of either of those emotions. "Let me get dressed. I'll walk you out."

"Don't worry about it," I say, standing up. "I'm already probably going to be late," I continue, glancing at the clock on my phone screen like the number means something to me. "I can show myself out."

Right as I say that, I hear something moving downstairs. A person. Right, he has parents. I assumed they weren't home.

He sees the look on my face. "It's only my dad," he says. "He doesn't care." But then, "Just let me put my clothes on."

"I'm fine," I say, rushing out of the room before he can change my mind and taking off down the stairs with my head held low. It doesn't matter because my footsteps echo through the house like it's a cavern.

I slam the front door behind me, only chancing a look back when I'm a couple of yards from the porch.

I see his dad's face in the window. Watching me.

I don't know what else to do, so I wave.

24

"You did *what*?" Lia demands of me, her face drained of all color. She goes to sit up from her bed, then thinks better of it and falls back down. "But why, Nell?"

I shrug, leaning against the wall of her yellow bedroom. "Because I wanted to."

She unleashes a loud laugh. "Of course. Because you wanted to." She shakes her head in disbelief. "Because you go take whatever you want when the thought occurs to you."

I'm a little confused about why that is a bad thing. "And that's never been a problem because usually I'm taking the thing that I'm supposed to want, as per you and Mom and Dad, only now I want something that just *I* want so it's wrong."

"You want Jackson?" she asks, her voice skeptical. Now that I don't have quite as snappy of an answer to. Because I do want *something* about Jackson. But I haven't quite figured out what that means yet.

I'm not ready to admit that.

"Couldn't you have at least waited to have sex with him?"

"Waited for what?" I ask, daring her to judge me.

"I don't know," she admits, throwing up her hands. "You said you don't trust him."

"Who says that's changed?" I throw back.

"Oh, okay, fine. Why would it matter if you trust him? You trust him with your whole body."

"He doesn't have that," I tell her sharply.

"Fine, you're right. I'm sorry," she says at last, rubbing a spot on her temple with her finger. "I just—didn't expect this," she tells me, her voice more even.

"I don't love him," I say. "It's not like that. I'm not confusing the two."

"Good," she says then. "That's good." I can tell she's weighing her words carefully. "It's only that I'm worried about you, Nell."

"He's just a boy. I have complete control of the situation," I assure her. That part feels true. I have complete control. I've been in control for seventeen years of my life and very few things deter me now.

"You'll tell me what's happening, right? You'll always tell me." She's looking at me hard, her eyes sharp. "No matter what it is."

"Of course," I agree. "I just did, didn't I?" I push off the wall, walking closer to her. "Now you tell me."

She sighs, as if this was expected. "You're not going to like it," she says, curling her legs up, making herself smaller. "It's Columbus Proctor." She momentarily buries her face so I only just hear her mumble, "It's a train wreck."

"Are you serious? What? *How?*"

She shakes her head. "I know. But everything has been awful with the trial, and I needed someone to talk to. You've been working so hard and I don't know—Columbus *wanted* to talk to me. I don't know why, but he's such a good person. My parents would kill me. Taylor would kill me. You can't tell anyone."

I twist my hair in my fingers. "Wow."

"Guess I shouldn't be so critical, huh?" she says with a laugh.

After a minute, I join in. "Oh my God, you are sitting here judging me about Jackson Hart and you are dating his best friend."

"I'm not sleeping with him, though," she tells me in a quiet voice. "We're just—I don't know—together sometimes."

I go right past it. "And you're using him to spy on me."

"He knows we're best friends. He wasn't spying. He was talking about you because he thought I already knew." She looks away.

"I'm sorry," I say. "I'm still trying to navigate all this. I don't know what it is."

She leans her head against the wall. "Trust me, I understand. But"—she holds her pinkie finger out to me—"no more secrets, okay?"

I reach out to grab her pinkie with my own. "You know the depths of my soul," I tell her with a smile.

"Gross," she returns, dropping my hand. And for the first time in a long time, something feels like normalcy between us.

"You wanna go to the park? Practice serving?" I ask, and her eyes practically roll out of her head.

A few minutes later, we're in our workout gear and headed out the door. As we pass by the kitchen, Taylor's voice floats in. "I'm not *mad* you're happy," he says to someone. When it's a moment before I hear anything else, I realize he's on the phone. "For the love of everything, Amanda, I did not like you better when your life was in shambles."

Lia gives me a look, an eyebrow raised. I shake my head at her and pass through the side door into the bright sun, the sounds of Taylor's pleas echoing behind us.

25

Do you want to go run after you get done with volleyball?

"What are you grinning at?" Mom asks. It's the next Monday. Five days later. We won our tournament yesterday—it was a smaller tournament in Newberry, a town right outside of Columbia—but still, it felt so good. I'd been the consensus tournament MVP. It was a start.

I look at Mom on the other side of the kitchen. She's turned back toward the sink washing dishes just like she was a minute ago. I guess she had to take a peek, see what I was doing. But I hadn't realized I was smiling so I immediately stop. "Lia," I tell her, my new perpetual lie.

Sounds good, I type back.

I haven't seen you all weekend. Please give me something more than that.

I set my phone down.

"What are you two up to?" Mom asks me about two decibels from her reasonable Mrs. Becker voice. "You're acting strange."

I hate that she's noticed.

"Volleyball." I shake out my hands. There's so much nervous energy running through my veins. So often, my nerves act like an impetus, driving me, forcing me to test my boundaries, but I can't let them in too much or they swallow me whole.

And God knows I can't let Mom know that.

"I have book club tonight," she tells me, letting it go. She dries the wineglass she was washing. I hadn't seen her drinking when I came home last night. I chance a glance toward the recycling bag but there's no telltale sign there, either.

"Again?" I ask. "Didn't you just have it?"

"It's a bunch of teachers," she tells me. "More frequent in the summer."

"Oh." I nod. "Well, have fun," I tell her.

"You'll be able to find something to eat?" she asks.

I almost let myself smile again. Dad left a note earlier that he had a late showing. It's just another hour I can be out of the house without anyone noticing. "I'm sure I'll think of something," I say.

• • •

One of the best parts about this new thing between Jackson and me is that it's okay to watch his body now when we run side by side, to see the way his calf muscles flex and release, carrying us both over the dirt paths of Cedar Woods.

"You're doing it again," he says, pulling my eyes back to his face.

I stare ahead then, caught. "What?"

"Watching me like you wish I didn't have clothes on."

One side of my mouth quirks. I pick up the pace because I know he can't hold it as long as I can. It only takes him a couple minutes more to feel it.

"Okay, okay, okay," he tells me, falling back and putting his arms over his head. I slow to a walk next to him, keeping my breathing as steady as possible. In through the nose, out through the mouth.

As we walk, our breath catching up with us, he falls behind me, tugging on my sweaty white tank top. He licks my shoulder because he's disgusting. I push him away. "What is wrong with you?"

"It could not be more fortunate that you're so tall," he says.

I rub my sweaty arm, trying not to look self-conscious. *Tall.* I've always been the tall girl. "And why is that?"

"More skin to touch," he says, and I feel myself shiver all over.

"Are your parents home?" I ask. We've had sex three more times since the first time. I don't see myself growing tired of it very soon.

He doesn't answer right away, and we walk in silence for a minute. "I like you when you're near the water," he says. "You look happy." We're on a nice flat bank overlooking the river. It's after six, and still probably too hot to be running around the way we are.

I avoid his eyes. "Don't do that. Try and analyze me. I hate that."

"Unless you're doing it?"

"Yes," I say.

"So is this, like, a secret?" he asks me.

"Me and you?" I ask, pointing a finger between the two of us. "Which part?"

"I don't know," he says. "Like if Doug says, 'Why the hell aren't you coming over to bring me snacks from my refrigerator since I can't walk on my shattered leg?' can I tell him it's your fault?"

"I guess," I return. "As long as you tell him we're not . . ." I trail off, unsure how to finish.

"We're not what?"

"I don't know," I say then. "I don't know what we're not."

"Okay," he says. "That's fine. If that's what you want."

"What do you want?" I ask, and it sounds like a challenge. Something I don't know the right answer to.

"Nell Becker," he says, "if I knew what I wanted, there'd be nothing but fire and blood in the streets. But right now? I kind of just want to be with you."

I don't grab his hand or anything dramatic like that. I just wing my hands so our fingers brush against each other's. He reciprocates with a twitch of his own finger.

"I'll race you back to your house," I tell him, a glint in my eye.

He looks like he's not sure what to do for a second, but then he smiles. "You're on."

26

Two weeks go by like that. Two weeks of summer we'll never get back, and I don't even care. Because those two weeks fly. There's still so much summer left to live and I could probably live this way forever.

Volleyball. Jackson. Tournament. Jackson. Best friend. Jackson.

Everyone's told me—even my guidance counselor suggested it during a pretty tense meeting last semester—I have a tendency to obsess. And right now, I think I may be obsessed.

"What does pot taste like?" I ask as Tristan sucks on a joint by the fire pit at the Harts' house. She has a boy with her. He has sort of dull eyes and a crooked nose. I can only imagine what the other girls at school would say if they could see him or any of the other guys I've seen with Tristan in the past few weeks.

Then again, they'd probably just say the same things they already say about her.

Doug has two chairs to himself, his huge cast propped up on one. Columbus is notably absent. Jackson gave me this ridiculous wink when he informed me. He's leaned back in the wooden chair with his ankles resting on the edge of the empty fire pit. I'm sitting in another chair, next to him, our feet almost touching. He keeps nudging my big toe with his big toe and Tristan has seen us do it several times, sighing and rolling her eyes dramatically.

"You want some?" she asks me. She's wrapped up as if pulling her limbs into herself. One leg tucked under her and the other knee bent, her arm wrapped around it.

"No," I say. "Can't chance getting drug tested."

She laughs like that's the most hilarious thing she's ever heard. "That's what Hart's always saying."

"Hart's welcome to do whatever he wants," I return. She might be good at her game, but it's always dangerous to come at a winner.

"Give it a rest, Tristan," Doug says, shifting his leg as if uncomfortable. "You're being a damn pill."

She cuts him a look, inhaling again. The dull-eyed boy doesn't defend her.

I turn to Jackson. "My parents are going to be out of town this weekend since we don't have a tournament."

He looks intrigued by this information. "Where are they going?"

"Greenville, to visit my aunt, but I still have practice, so . . ." I shrug innocently.

"You're a deceptively bad person," he says.

I raise an eyebrow. "What's deceptive about it?" He nudges my toe again.

"What the *fuck* is wrong with you two?" Tristan calls again. She's picking a fight. I feel it pulsing through me without actually knowing what it's about.

"Stop drinking dark liquor, Tris," Jackson finally tells her, his voice several octaves lower than normal.

"No, I mean it," she says. "Suddenly the two of you are in love or something? You couldn't fucking stand her guts two months ago."

"We are most definitely not in love," I say as Jackson says, "*Stop, Tristan.*"

"She won't let me intimidate her like your other playthings, will she, Hart?"

"I'm right here," I tell her loud and clear, locking on her eyes shining in the starlight. "If you have something to say, you can address it to me."

"You're so stupid and you don't even know it," she says then.

"Will you leave her the hell alone?" Doug implores like he's exhausted. He's picking up the slack so Jackson doesn't have to.

"He'll get bored with you, just like everyone else. It might take longer and it might go down uglier, but it'll happen. And we'll always be here, like we are, to laugh and pick up the pieces."

I push myself up from my chair as Jackson reaches out to grab me. I pull my arm away, step forward, and crush a soda can, tossing it into the empty fire pit. "It's like you think I'm so easily entertained, I'll just be hanging around hoping y'all love me. Hell, I'm already bored with this conversation," I tell her, and then set off away from them, up the walkway and into Jackson's house, shaking the anger out of my fingers as I go. Approximately ten seconds later, I hear Tristan's Jeep crank and watch as her headlights zoom out of the driveway.

I lean against a couch in the great room, watching the two dark figures work together in the distance. Jackson is helping Doug toward the house, where I've finally figured out he usually sleeps in one of the spare bedrooms. I should go to help.

I don't.

It takes them a bit to maneuver through the door. "I'll be just a minute," Jackson tells me when they hobble in together. "Gotta get Dougy in bed. He needs his rest and relaxation, isn't that right, Rivera?"

"You can ignore her, Nell," Doug says to me instead. "She's always a bitch when she starts drinking whiskey."

I give him a weak smile.

I fall down on the couch. Neither of Jackson's parents are around, but that's normal. His older sister is at school on the West Coast and skipped the whole "coming home for the summer" thing—or presumably, ever again—per Jackson.

I avoid his dad as much as possible. When his mom is home, she never leaves her room. She has things going on a lot of nights— philanthropy events or girls' nights or whatever. Sometimes, he'll tell me that she's home when we're coming in after a run, but she's always in her bedroom. He'll poke his head in her room before we go upstairs. And I'm nosy enough to listen in.

"Mom, I'm home," he'll say.

I'll hear her light reply. "Hey, sweetie."

"I'm with a friend," he always tells her like that is a code and she knows what it means.

"Do you two need anything?" she asks every time.

"No," he says. Always no.

I get the distinct feeling he doesn't want her to meet me.

Now, he comes out of Doug's room, wearing one of his sincere expressions, his mouth a straight line, his dark brows close together.

"Can we talk for a second?" he asks.

I shake my head. "I don't want to talk about it."

It's clear he does so I keep my own expression as resolute as possible, snaking my finger into his belt loop and taking a step closer. I hold his gaze until he has no choice but to look away, taking the loss in stride. He fishes my fingers from the loop and links them through his and we go upstairs. It's our place. Hallowed ground.

After, we're under a sheet, the comforter thrown off at the bottom of the bed days ago, though I suspect someone keeps putting it back for him to take it off again—it changes positions every time I come. I haven't moved from the spot next to him where I'm lying on my side, so my whole body is turned to face him with one leg wrapped around his. He lies on his back. I'm not ready to leave yet. I want more.

That's the thing about the wanting, it always leaves you with the *more*.

He swallows. Something is working behind his eyes, I can see it.

"You okay?" I ask.

He looks at me, then back up. It's too warm under the sheet even. We need to crawl out of it, but he says, "C'mere," and wraps his arms around me, pulling me on top of him, me pushing away so I have to brace my knees on either side, leaning into him. I think he's going to do something, that he's thinking what I'm thinking, that we can't be in motion again soon enough.

He grabs my hand, holding it against his chest with both of his own. "Do you feel that?"

"What?" I demand, tugging my hand out of his.

He laughs, a loud quick sound. "It's my heart. Hammering." He carefully takes my hand back and presses it to his warm skin again.

I do. Feel it. The steady beat against my fingers, the way it propels him forward, keeps him going, so easily vibrant and beautiful.

"Why?" I say.

He rolls over onto his side, dislodging me. "I don't know."

I go with it, sliding off him to sprawl on my back; he reaches for me, then stops with his hand in midair when I shift away from him. "You always look at me like you're scared I might get too close to you," he says.

I roll my eyes. "I think you've gotten plenty close to me." I sigh, pulling the sheet back over my body. I watch him out of the side of my eye for a moment. Sometimes, I find myself thinking about him so much, the way his collarbone dips into his shoulder and the perfect symmetry of his face and how he always looks so calm, like nothing is hard or complex. I ask him, "Has anyone ever told you that you might do well if you kept your head down?"

"What?"

"That's what they told me when I started Prep. Sit down and shut up, little girl, and if you're lucky we'll make some good things happen for you." Without thinking about it, I roll over, too, so we're looking at each other.

He pushes a strand of hair out of my face. "You've got a chip on your shoulder."

I shake my head. "It's not *about that*. I want to be loud, to be *seen*. I get so tired of being told to sit down and play nice and say '*please*' and '*thank you*.' So apparently that's a chip on my shoulder? I'm sure no one would say that about you."

"Oh, Becker, I've got a hell of a chip on my shoulder, too," he says, a wicked gleam in his eyes.

"So I can't play this game with you. I can't feel your heart and tell you how beautiful you are and beg you to tell me what you like most about me. I don't do that, Hart."

He's looking at my fingers where I have them bunched up in the sheet. "So don't," he says, his eyes going to mine. "Tell me a lie."

I scoot closer to him, push my fingertips into his cheek, and lean my face against his. "I love you," I breathe against him.

He laughs, hard, threads his fingers through my hair. "You're a good liar." And then he kisses me, his mouth hungry against mine, his teeth scraping against my lip, not violent but wanting and having.

Every time I kiss him, it feels like a battle of wills, like a competition one of us is trying to win. I stop and pull away, grabbing my phone off his nightstand to check the time.

"Stay," he begs. I love the sound of him begging.

But I turn to him and he's watching me and he looks so startlingly earnest, I swear I can feel his heartbeat again even though I'm not touching him. I want to stay, so much, but *this*. This look on his face stops me. There's something too true in it. I feel splintered, afraid if I stay, a part of me will never leave, and I have to escape before I accidentally get pulled in. "I have to go," I say.

He stares up at the ceiling. "You don't." He glances back once, gives himself away.

I sigh.

"I'm sorry, Becker. I'm sorry to inconvenience you by being an actual person. My mom hasn't gotten out of bed in three days, and I don't know where my dad is, yet he's somehow found time today to text me what a shithead I am *because* Mom hasn't gotten out of bed in three days. But don't let me bother you."

So his mom is here. I stare straight ahead, digging my fingers into the tops of my thighs.

"Say something," he tells me.

"That's not," I begin, "what this is. *That's* what I'm trying to tell you."

"I don't know what to say to you, Nell," he tells me then. "Fine, you don't want love. But you have to give me a little more than whatever this"—he gestures between the two of us—"is. I need *something* from you here."

"You don't get that," I say. "It's nonnegotiable. I'm mine."

"That's what I'm telling you. It's not *like* that," he says, his voice practically desperate.

"I'm not here to validate you."

"I want you more than I've ever wanted anyone. See? I did it first—that's what you want to hear, right? Is that enough *validation* for you?"

"Let it go," I snap.

He breathes exactly like he's trained to do, like he's just run a mile. In through the nose, out through the mouth. "I never knew you were like this," he says. "I mean, I knew you were competitive but . . ."

"Like what?" I demand.

"You win things," he returns. I can feel all the energy he isn't exerting. His constant need to be on the move. He's speaking to me like a child now. "You can't win a relationship, you know."

"What relationship?"

He laughs. "Oh my God, you're doing this on purpose."

I've had enough. "Jackson, I just don't want to hear about your daddy issues or whatever the hell your problem is. It's *always* something with you."

"Really, okay, wow. What the fuck is wrong with you?"

I don't dignify that with a response, just stand up and start looking around for my clothes.

"Fine," he says after a moment. "Leave, then. I'm really not in the mood for this, anyway."

"So now you want me to go?" I ask him like it doesn't matter to me one way or the other.

"Do whatever you want," he tells me.

"Okay." I put my clothes on with my back turned to him. I should say something before I leave, can feel him waiting for it.

Instead, I grab my bag and take off out the front door. The frame shakes behind me.

Only I don't make it very far. There's headlights in the driveway. The sports car pulls in behind my sensible one, blocking it in. And Jackson's dad gets out. We stare at each other across the expanse for a moment. I hear Jackson clattering down the outside stairs, shoeless, and then he's beside me. "Shit," he mutters. I glance at him out of the corner of my eye. "You need to go."

His dad comes over to the two of us, his eyes barely stopping on me. He's in regular clothes—khaki shorts and a button-down. He looks disturbingly like Jackson that way, out of his normal clothes, like looking into the future. "Two thousand dollars this week," he says, his voice low.

I glance at Jackson, whose jaw clenches imperceptibly.

"What do you want me to do, son?" Jackson's dad steps closer to him. "Hit you?"

Jackson shrugs. "Sure."

"Jesus Christ," I say, grabbing the back of Jackson's shirt and pulling him away from his dad.

Mr. Hart is looking at me again and I'm guessing he hasn't forgotten a six-foot-tall girl. "So this is the girl you have at the house every night. Guessing she doesn't know your extracurriculars."

"Nell, I like to go to wherever my dad is skulking around and make charges to his credit card. There," he says, "now she knows."

"Don't do this right now," I say.

"Leave her out of it," Jackson says to his dad.

"You think you're so smart," his dad says.

"I know I am," Jackson replies.

I bite into the inside of my cheek.

"I'm not going to hit you," his dad tells him. "You think you're so much better than me, but nothing's real for you, son. That's my house and my truck and my clothes you wear around every day. That's even my brain that you're always using to try and outsmart me. My town, my family. Hell . . ." He trails off as he looks at me. I grab on to Jackson's forearm instinctively. His fist is clenched so tight, his arm shakes.

"You're drunk," Jackson says spitefully.

For a second I think his dad is going to say something else, but he just gives the two of us a long look; then he turns away and walks into the house, closing the door behind him. My heart is racing, my body unsure the danger has passed. I drop Jackson's arm. Immediately, he pulls both of them up over his head, reaching for his back, taking in a deep breath. And then he lets go, releasing a loud, *"Goddammit."*

He looks over at me, his face pure misery. "Please don't go."

I stare at the ground, something like guilt eating at me. "I have to."

"Then let me take you. I don't care where we go," he says. I don't like this noncharming, dark Jackson.

Only I do. I think it might be my favorite Jackson.

"I'm picking the music," I tell him, and walk past him toward his truck.

When I don't hear him moving, I stop and glance back over my shoulder. His eyes are on me. "Don't do anything you don't want to," he says.

"I never have."

He snorts and catches up with me.

27

My hand is out the window, riding the waves of cool evening air as Jackson's truck rumbles along the road. Night buzzes around us, loud and quiet all at once.

"Where do you want to go?" Jackson asks, pushing the pedal hard. I know all he wants to do is escape. "You want to eat?"

I shrug. "Whatever you want to do."

He laughs. "Dangerous."

I watch him across the console, a smile playing on his lips like it's all a game, his shoulders tense. And I see right through him, right to his core.

The ease of it is both shocking and satisfying.

We drive around like that for a while, putting nothing but miles on the truck and time between then and now. After about a half hour of aimless driving, he pulls off the road abruptly and into the parking lot of a small café nestled into a corner on the outskirts of Cedar Woods, near where the town ends and the highway begins—this side of town is supposed to belong to me. A little hanging sign out front says EDGE OF THE RIVER, paint peeling off the Es and Rs. The parking lot is small, almost empty, but there's a side lot with a couple of eighteen-wheelers pulled in.

"Food," he says, killing the car. He rolls his hands over the leather of the steering wheel a couple of times, hanging on to it tight. Then he lets go, shaking his hands out. I watch him with interest, feeling like I should *do* something but not sure exactly what that should be. He fishes a pair of worn sneakers from his back seat and then, with a deep exhale, pockets his keys and opens the door.

I follow him into the place, a dive, to be sure. A few men are sitting by themselves, sipping coffee, and there's two boys—maybe college age—at a corner table, one laughing loudly while the other tries in vain to shush him. Jackson slides into a booth a few tables down from one of the older men.

We sit across from each other, and I think how, if we were a normal couple, we'd want to touch in some way, our fingers finding each other's across the expanse of the table. But Jackson's hands are just doing what they're always doing—tapping and fidgeting and alive in a way that seems out of his control.

"Good evening, Jackson," an old waitress says, coming over to our table to hand us menus. "Haven't seen you here in a while."

Jackson attempts his best charming smile, but it doesn't quite touch his eyes. "I've missed you most, Madeline." He tips his head to me across the table. "This is Nell."

He always does that. Introduces me to people. Everyone except his family. And I never know how to look like someone he would be with, but she smiles at me all the same.

"You want the usual?" she asks him. Her voice is all warm honey, comforting in some way.

"Please."

She turns to me. "And you, hon?"

The menu is five pages, and I haven't even glanced at one. I panic. "Fries?" I ask desperately.

"Add cheese," Jackson whispers like he's telling me a secret.

"With cheese," I say quickly. She smiles and takes our menus as fast as she brought them. I stare at the tabletop.

"You know every hole-in-the-wall in the county?" I ask him after a moment.

"As I'm sure you can imagine, I find a lot of reasons to not be at

178

home." He scrapes at a stain on the tabletop with his fingernail. "Late-night Edge of the River is a gift, Nell." He's still doing that thing, trying to be the biggest and boldest—sucking all the energy out of the room. He's imitating the person he usually is.

"You don't have to do that, you know," I say instinctively. "Pretend or whatever, for me. I'm not your audience—I'm just me. And it sucks." I shrug. "Like, what I said at your house, before. That was shit. I'm sorry. You don't have to pretend it doesn't suck."

He glances up and looks back down. Sighs. "My dad's a dick. No point in dwelling on it."

"Feeling isn't dwelling."

He laughs, eyes catching mine. "C'mon, you know the trick. Always gotta have on the game face."

I pull my feet up into the booth, tucking them under me. He knows. "Fair."

"I wouldn't want to mope too much anyway. It might ruin the illusion of who I am for you."

"Look, I really didn't mean—"

"I know what you meant, Becker."

"You *think* you know what I meant."

"You want to have sex with me, not talk to me. I get it. It's not like it's a new or complicated concept. It's like my dad said."

I bristle. "Don't you dare put his words into my mouth. Look, this is all happening really fast, and I just . . . I need some space. I need to feel in control. Don't you get it?" I hold a hand out as if showing him. "I know everyone always loves you immediately. It's not real, but it's what you expect. That's why this is so difficult for you—it's not because of some special thing you feel about me."

He sighs, shaking his head. "People don't love me, they just want something from me. They always have. You might want a different some-thing from me than most people, but it's all the same."

"That's not what I said," I try again.

He shrugs. "You didn't have to say it for it to be the truth."

Madeline the server stops by then, leaving waters on our table. "You know, on second thought," Jackson says to her right before she leaves, "I think we're going to want to get two milkshakes, too. The birthday ones," and Madeline gives him a knowing smile.

The two boys get up from their table, one of them still carrying on. As they pass by us, the loud boy stops, his arm pulled tightly around his companion. "This guy," he tells Jackson and me, pulling the other boy closer, "is this not the best-looking guy you've ever seen?"

I laugh as the other boy blushes. "Truly," I say.

"You're a lucky man," Jackson agrees.

The talking boy grins. "It's a beautiful night to be in love, y'all." His boyfriend excuses him and they leave together. Jackson and I meet each other's eyes across the table and then look away.

Madeline returns soon with our food and milkshakes, placing them in front of us without fanfare. I grab a cheese fry, and it practically melts in my mouth.

"Oh my God, Jackson. These are incredible."

The smile he gives me this time is real. "That's the happiest I've ever heard you sound when you say my name."

I throw a fry at him and cheese splatters on his T-shirt. He looks down. "You didn't."

I bite into my lip, resisting the urge to laugh, and nod.

"Nell, I swear to God," he says, and then he grabs across the table at my fries, and I put them into my lap so he can't reach. He stands up to try and reach over my edge of the table and I attempt to use my body as a shield for the fries.

"Watch out for my milkshake!" I yell at him as he comes dangerously close to toppling it. The other five people in the café are all watching us but no one really seems to mind. I swear I see one of the truckers chuckling. Jackson finally stops, and then he reaches out and slides his fingers into my hair on either side of my head, holding my face. We look at each other. After a beat, he falls back into his seat in defeat, attempting to wipe the cheese sauce off with a napkin.

"That was dirty," he tells me solemnly. "That could get you killed in some places."

I suck on my milkshake straw, watching him, feeling where his hands rested against my skin like a burn. "This is nice," I say after a minute. "Not, like, being around your house or your friends or at school or whatever. I don't feel so . . . watched."

"People are always watching you, Nell," he says. "In case you don't remember, I spent the past three years unable to ignore you."

I look down. "Not like they watch you. Everyone's just watching me waiting for me to fall on my face. You included."

"Why do you keep acting like I'm your two-dimensional enemy?"

I stare down at the stain he was picking at earlier. "Because it's easier," I say at last. When I look up at him, he's staring at a spot outside the window, his face unguarded. And I can't believe he's real. He's like an ideal of a teenage boy, and even in the unflattering diner lighting there's something almost impossibly beautiful and effortless about him. Like he's in his own movie everywhere he goes. Everyone loves him, everyone knows him, and he's rich and smart and comfortable in his own skin.

And he's so deeply unhappy.

We sit quietly after that, the minutes ticking by until Madeline finally approaches us again. "Can we get the check?" Jackson asks her.

"It's covered," she tells us, nodding at one of the truckers. He tips his cap at us.

"You kids have fun," he says, a strong bayou accent coating his words. Jackson tosses down more than the price of the meal on the table for Madeline anyway and we thank the man profusely as we leave, taking the milkshakes to go.

Out in the parking lot, I glance at my phone to see it's after midnight. I'd originally been planning to go to Lia's after I left Jackson's but I'd texted her I would be late after the blowup with Jackson's dad. "Let's go to the river," I tell Jackson instead.

We leave Edge of the River and Jackson drives back closer to town, along a road hugging the water. He pulls into some area designated as part of the state park and positions his truck so the bed faces the river. It's a wooded area, pretty far off from the road. We climb out and sit on the tailgate, our legs dangling over the side, music from the cab playing in the background. Jackson slurps on his milkshake loudly.

The moon is bright enough to see the water in the distance—the exact spot where the sky hits the river continuing the darkest navy forever up into it. The feeling is all over me then, the singular joy the sight gives me every time. The current sings to me in the way nothing else does, begs for me, and I breathe in every scent of a rain that wants to fall and earth that thirsts for it.

Here on the water is where I really feel it: the possibility of the world. In Cedar Woods, the river is always a barrier—a separation between them and us. But from here, I can't see the gabled roofs or the shiny cars. I see only the water for miles until the end of the world.

"What's going on in that head of yours, Becker?" Jackson asks me.

I crash back to reality, startled. "Thinking about the river."

He doesn't say anything.

"It's not that I don't like talking to you," I hear myself say. "I do. It's just—"

"A lot," he answers for me. "It's fine. You don't have to explain yourself to me. Sorry I pushed it so much."

I nod. Then, after a moment, I lean back, watching the current lap the shore. "Tell me a lie," I say.

"No," he returns, and I feel like I've lost this one based on how sharply he says it. But after a moment, he faces me. "That game is tired. Let's play a new one."

"Your pick," I say, pretending I don't care.

"Tell me a secret."

I glance at him. "You first."

He looks toward the sky and then back to me. "Should've seen that coming." He releases a deep sigh. "Every time I'm talking to you, I feel like you're digging, and I'm worried one day soon, you'll want to stop," he says, his voice touching each of the words as if he's giving them thought. "You'll have me all figured out, if you don't already, and it'll be just like you told Tristan earlier. You'll get bored first."

I half laugh, dry and hollow. "None of that counts as a secret." I try to grab the words back immediately, shaking my heard. "Sorry, I ruined it again." I push off from the truck, walking out to the edge of where the land overlooks the water. There's a simple wooden fence there, easy to climb, and then you hang on the brink, a twenty-foot drop into the water below.

"No, it's okay." He startles me, standing a few feet behind me with his hands in his pockets; I hadn't heard him coming. "I've got another."

I stare straight ahead, waiting.

"I finally hit him last year. I think that's when he really wiped his hands of me."

I glance back at him and he shrugs it off.

"I mean," he continues, "it was exam week so I was maybe getting a couple of hours of sleep a night. But anyway, he came in late, and honestly, I don't know if he'd even been out screwing around or whatever, but I didn't speak to him. Just kept reading. And he . . ." I feel Jackson moving, unable to stay still, his hands in his hair and then rubbing against each other, and then sliding over the fabric of his shirt. "He was like, 'You'll do all right, you know. These games you play, how you act like being successful is another way to get back at me, but I see right through them. I see you.' And then he, like, touched my shoulder and I could smell that stale scent of booze that had settled on him, and Jesus, I think I fucking saw me for a minute, too, so I hit him."

He's looking at me again. I feel his eyes. "Of all the people I could be and all the secrets I could tell, I choose this. So, I don't know, you're probably smart to not talk to me."

I can't stand him like that, like he's been defeated, and it's not fair that he can make me feel this way, but I turn around and stand in front of him. His hands slide into my hair until it's tangled up in his fingers, and then he tilts my face ever so slightly to kiss me. Soft and chaste, not like how we usually kiss. There's nothing hungry in it. When he pulls back, we're still looking right at each other and I'm so sure in that moment that we're here on the precipice of something like that twenty-foot plunge into the river and the last thing I want to do is fall.

I'm not sure I can risk the drop.

28

I'm lying upside down in a lounge chair in the Reagans' immaculately designed backyard reading a book, my head and hair hanging off the bottom of the chair. I feel someone sit down in the chair next to me.

"You look like you're having a good time."

I shade my eyes with the book to look up at Taylor, wearing brightly colored swim trunks with Ray-Bans covering his eyes. It's a Friday, the sun is bright, and I have decided I have very few cares. "You don't," I say, pushing myself up on the chair and sitting cross-legged to face him. "Haven't seen you around all week."

"Yeah." He leans back on his chair, putting his hands behind his head. "Me and Amanda broke up."

"So Lia said." I reach down, grabbing the cup of water below my chair, and sip it with a straw. "How are you doing?"

"I'm all right. It was a long time coming. She changed."

That's something Taylor has been saying about girls since I knew him. *She changed.*

"Do you guys have practice?" I ask. I already know the answer.

"Just running some drills at, like, four." He looks at me. "But you probably already knew that." *Dammit.*

"Who told you that?" I ask him sharply.

"I ran into Doug Rivera at the river last week and he mentioned he'd been seeing a lot of you. I don't think he would've said anything if it wasn't me."

I breathe out a sigh of relief. "It's not a big thing," I say quickly.

"Well, it's not like I'm not going to go tell everybody. But I don't get it."

"You don't have to get it," I return.

"You *know* how he is. Hell, you're basically the one who explained it to me."

I wave a hand dismissively. "I'm not worried about it. I've got him figured out. We're just having some fun with each other. Jackson's addicted to the chase—no one is falling madly in love here. I know that's not the game."

"Doug made it sound like Jackson was really into you," Taylor says, watching me with interest.

"That's because Doug has Jackson's back."

"You know the thing about rich people, right?" Taylor asks me.

"They're really good at getting off for murder?" I deadpan.

Taylor looks at me sadly. "Nell, rich people aren't used to people who don't do whatever they want. People who aren't just like them. Who don't want to bask in their glow. I remember when Doug started at Prep, I used to see Jackson tailing him, desperate to be friends with him. And he was constantly going on about how Doug wasn't his charity case. Jackson wants to believe in his own redemption."

"I'm not his fake redemption, if that's what you're implying," I say.

"Look at my dad," Taylor goes on. "He was going to save the city, do it for the good of everyone. And we both know where he is now.

"You don't need any of us. You never have. And if I were you, I'd escape it all while I could. Getting involved with Jackson is . . . the opposite of that."

"This is my life, Taylor," I say, daring him to challenge me. "I can't escape it."

He shakes his head, getting up to move away from me. "I have no idea why you'd want to be a part of this world. There's so much more out there."

I watch him fade into the distance, dropping down to lie across the lawn chair again, letting the sun warm my skin.

• • •

It's five PM in my empty house when my phone starts ringing. I check the name on the front before sliding my thumb across the screen to answer. I'd been expecting a text from Jackson to tell me when he's coming over after baseball. I'd planned for him to be over most of the weekend with my parents out of town. "What?" I ask into the phone.

"Hey, Nell." His voice sounds a little shaky. "I can't come over tonight. I wanted to tell you myself, and I can't—uh—exactly see the words on my phone screen right now."

I stand up straighter. "*What?* What's wrong? Are you okay? Where are you?"

He laughs. "Ow. If my head didn't hurt so much right now I would be touched. I, uh, kinda got hit in the head with a ball and seem to have suffered. Um. Some sort of concussion."

"*Shit*, Jackson."

"I know, right?" he asks, making light of the situation. "Anyway, now I'm feeling *super* fucked up and I gotta get home somehow. Doug is trying to figure out some way to drive over so he can pick me up. I'm probably going to be out of commission all weekend."

"Don't," I say, already grabbing up my keys. "He doesn't need to do that with his leg. I'll come get you."

"You will?" he asks, skeptical.

"Of course," I say, and I'm pounding down the porch stairs. "Don't move. I'll be there in fifteen."

"Okay," he says, dragging out the word a little longer than is necessary.

I try not to feel any panic as I drive over the bridge to get him. He's fine, of course he is. I pull into the athletic complex parking lot and see the guys are still running through some drills out on the baseball field. Jackson sits with one of the assistant coaches on the sideline. I get out and walk over to him, trying to draw as little attention to myself as possible in the process. Even still, I feel eyes on me. When I look up, I see it's Taylor.

"I'm his ride," I tell the coach, who is watching me like I'm up to something. I point at Jackson for emphasis and the coach still looks suspicious.

"Okay, fine," he says at last. "No physical activity for at least a week. He can sleep some but he needs to be woken up at least once to check his symptoms."

"So I don't die," Jackson interjects wisely.

"Watch for the usual stuff: irritability, short-term memory loss, headaches, dizziness. He should be fine in a few days."

"Define 'fine,'" I say, and the coach doesn't laugh but Jackson does.

"Any heavy vomiting or difficulty waking up, call an ambulance. Otherwise, we'll just get him checked out by the team physician again next week to make sure he's all right to come back. You okay, Hart?"

"Yeah. I thought I was dizzy for a minute, but then I remembered Nell Becker just does that to my head." The coach looks more closely at me when Jackson says my name, and I have to get us out of here, like, now.

Jackson leans into me as we head back to my car, his gym bag hanging off my shoulder. I open the door and I'm about to shove him in when he leans forward and presses the top of his head against my forehead. I push him into the car. "That's quite enough."

I've been driving in the wrong direction for a little bit before I realize where I'm going. "I'm taking you back to my house. Mom and Dad won't be home until Sunday so you can stay with me tonight."

"I have parents, Nell," he says.

I don't say *I don't trust them* or *I'll take better care of you*. But my hands are on the steering wheel and he pretty much has no choice but to do what I say.

It's not easy, but I manage to get him into the house.

"Are you tired?" I ask, touching his face. It's hot. "You probably need to lie down."

But his eyes are all over the place, taking in every square inch of our house. "This is how the Beckers live?"

"Yes," I say, fighting to keep the annoyance out of my voice. "Not quite up to your standards, I'm sure."

"It's nice," he tells me, making his way over to a family picture on an end table in the den. He studies it carefully, and I don't like the way he examines everything like he can see something I can't.

"What about food? Have you taken anything for the pain?"

He turns back to me. "Yeah. And I'm nauseous as hell, so pass."

"Sleep?" I ask.

"Yeah, okay," he agrees. "And can you turn all the lights off? They're kind of making me want to die."

I oblige quickly.

"Come on," I tell him, nudging him up the stairs with my hands on his back. He goes. "You'll have to sleep in my room because I can't deal with the complex of you in my parents' room."

He chuckles darkly. "Who would have thought it? This is all it took for you to care." I continue to push him, not amused. I wish he'd stop trying to read me, stop trying to figure me out. I wish I didn't care.

My room is practically dark thanks to my thick blinds, so I toss his gym bag down and pull back the covers of my bed. I grab on to the bottom of the T-shirt he's wearing and pull it over his head. He takes one step toward me and I take one back. "Okay," I say. "I'll come check on you in, like, an hour. Start slow, right?"

I wait for him to climb under the covers, feeling an absurd desire to tuck him in. To make sure he's all right.

It's like I don't know myself at all anymore.

I'm about to leave when he says, "Nell."

"Yeah."

"Will you lie down with me? Just for a minute."

I almost laugh, he's so good. I go over to the other side of the bed and climb under the covers in my clothes. He ropes an arm over me, moving in closer, always closer. I find that I don't mind it so much.

"What happened?" I ask him.

"Speak quietly, if you don't mind." His face is resting so close to mine, I'm able to turn my head and watch his eyes flutter open and closed in the dim light sneaking through small cracks in the blinds. "Proctor hit a damn foul ball directly at my head. I wasn't looking and Reagan didn't even do me the courtesy of a heads-up. I think he's in love with you," he mutters, trailing off.

"Shut up, Jackson," I whisper. I run my thumb over a piece of his hair on his forehead.

"I would've done it to him if the situation was reversed."

"You're so full of shit," I tell him, a grin in my voice.

"I'm so in love with you," he says.

My hand stills at the words. I pull away, but his hand reaches out and catches me before I can evade him. "Please don't stop," he says. I remember saying those words to him when we kissed. Afraid I might lose him.

It's only been about a month since we danced together at Raven's, when he talked until I kissed him so he'd stop. I've known Jackson for years, known everything about him: his GPA down to the thousandth point, the number of varsity letters he has, the girls he dated, even sometimes how he spent each one of his wonderful, perfect weekends, filtered through gossip. But I've never *really* known anything about Jackson at all.

"Jackson," I say, so quietly, I wonder if he'll be able to hear me. "I can't give you everything. You get that, right? But I can give you something."

His hand comes to my face, his thumb rubbing over my cheek, his long fingers curling around the back of my neck.

"You have to promise not to suffer short-term memory loss because I'm only going to say it once and if you forget, you forfeit it, all right?"

"I won't forget," he promises me.

I breathe softly in his face. "I've been fighting every day for as long as I can remember—me against a world that I was sure would never want me. And now when I'm with you, for the first time in forever, I want someone to *see* me. Not the version I've created, but reality. I don't know, I have to exist to do more than succeed, right? I have to be *somebody*. And you make me feel like maybe I am or always was or something.

"Before, how could I tell you? I was so afraid I'd lose a part of myself in the process."

He's quiet for a moment, his fingers still playing with the fine hair at the back of my neck. Then he says, "I promise I'll never lose any parts of yourself, Nell Becker." He sounds exhausted. I take his hand away from my face and do something I swore I'd never do. I stay with him. I throw my arm over his torso, cross my leg over his, and hold on to him tight.

It's like that we both drift to sleep.

29

I wake up at five the next morning, having gone to bed far earlier than any reasonable person would. Jackson is still sleeping so I get some food and Tylenol and make my way back up the stairs. When I get there, he's awake. I throw his T-shirt over the lamp next to my bed to soften the light and turn it on so I can see. He sits up and already, some color has returned to his face. He looks more alive.

"Can you eat?" I ask him. "I brought you toast."

"I can try," he says, first taking the Tylenol with a swig of water. He breaks off a small piece of toast and nibbles at it. It's almost painful to watch. "Look," he says, after a minute. He grabs up another piece. "About last night."

I brace myself, my heart rate jumping. It had seemed all right to say those things when the lights were out, when he was so vulnerable, but now I have nothing. Nowhere to hide. "What about it?" I ask, keeping my voice even.

"I wasn't trying to freak you out. I just—I don't know why I said it."

Oh. I feel relief flooding through me because what he did was worse than what I did. "It's fine," I tell him. I want to touch him but I don't. "I know you didn't mean it."

He gives me a look and just as quickly, hops up from the bed and pushes past me, heading in the direction of my bathroom. He runs some water, taking a while before he comes back out.

"I still feel pretty nauseous. I'm sorry for ruining your weekend," he says, standing in the doorway of the bathroom. There's something utterly defeated about him, about the soft sleepiness of his eyes and the curves of his shoulders.

"Don't be. I'm sorry you got hurt," I say, getting up from where I'm sitting and going over to him, having no choice but to wrap my arms around his neck and press my forehead into his. He accepts it, his arms snaking around me.

"S'okay," he says at last. "I know you didn't mean it." I'm not sure which part he's talking about.

He's finally able to get a couple more bites of toast down and then, as if fighting it, falls back to sleep. I have to leave for volleyball practice, so I write him a note to eat whatever he'd like when he wakes up.

When I get back, he and the note are gone.

30

I come in from volleyball practice a few days later, sweaty and hot. I haven't heard from Jackson since his concussion. I shot him a couple of texts but he messaged me back that his screen was giving him a headache, so I let it go. Well, as much as I can let things go.

My after-practice T-shirt is soaked through from the blazing heat—outside is only tolerable near the river. When I walk over the threshold into my house, I get that uncomfortable feeling that something is wrong. Running both hands through my hair uneasily, I head up the stairs to my room. Mom is sitting on my bed, looking like the Grim Reaper come to call.

Then I see what's set out on the nightstand next to her.

A box of condoms.

Great. I slowly lower my bag onto the floor as she takes me in. "Hey," I say.

I can tell she's going to keep her cool about this if it kills her. "I found these on the floor near your bed when I came in to get your laundry hamper."

I glance down at the floor. *What the hell?* "I'm not sure how they got there."

"Are they yours?" she asks.

"No," I say quickly, immediately regretting the answer. If they're not mine, they must belong to someone else. Ten seconds ago, I probably could've lied and said I had gotten them for curiosity or proactive safety or something.

Mom sighs deeply. "You're too old to lie to me about something like this. Can you please just tell me what's going on?"

I feel my whole body turning red. I stare down at my bare feet, in bad shape from a summer, a lifetime, of volleyball and running. "I'm, uh, seeing someone," I go with.

"Who?" she asks, her face still a mask of calm. "If he's been in my house, I deserve to know who he is."

I don't want to tell her. This would be different for anyone else. For a girl whose mom didn't know the ins and outs of Cedar Woods Prep's student body. For a mom who wouldn't know exactly what the next words that leave my mouth mean. "Jackson Hart."

I keep my eyes trained away from her, closing them as I wait for the blow to come. But it doesn't. I glance up after it's been quiet for too long. All color has left Mom's face, to the point where I'm almost concerned. "Are you okay?" I ask.

She stands up immediately, like she can take control of the situation. "You can't *do* this, Nell," she tells me, her voice sharp.

"Do what?"

"Jackson Hart. Have you lost every bit of good sense you came into this world with? This isn't just you sleeping with some random boy." I blanch at the horrible way she makes it sound. "This is a way to ruin your entire life. Jackson Hart is one the most manipulative people I've ever met. He's dangerous."

The words instantly make me feel like the world's biggest idiot, someone unworthy of her.

"It's not like that," I say, playing the part of every petulant teenager ever.

"You're supposed to be better than this," she says, and I don't know that I've ever heard her voice sound so purely mean, like I am a complete waste of space in her perfect house.

I feel them, then: the tears forming behind my eyes. She doesn't wait for me to say anything.

"Do you want to be like the rest of them? Like those girls? You've never wanted that before. You've wanted to be the best, and you know what happens to girls like that."

A tear leaks down my cheek. I don't remember the last time she made me cry. "I am *still* the best," I tell her, my voice strangled. I won't let her take that away from me.

She shakes her head. "You're better than this. Than whatever he's made you believe."

I look away. Another tear squeezes out. "This is not about you," I tell her.

"You're damn right." Then she grabs my chin, bringing my face back to look at her. "Don't do this, Nell."

"It's not about him, either! It's about *me*. Something is *mine* for the first time in my entire life. Something *I* decided."

"I got married young. Was a mother young—because I thought that was what I wanted. Thought other people could make me happy. Please trust me on this. You have to be your own person before you can be anyone else's."

I bend my head down, feeling like I might fall apart at any moment. But it's the way she says it, the way she *knows* it.

"But what kind of person am I?" How can I be a person—a good person who does charity and works hard and is smart—and still want all the things I want? I don't feel like I can fit it all in this body.

"You're a person who rises to the top. You're a person who's better than all the rest of them.

"You're my daughter."

I wear it like a burden.

"I can't tell you what to do, Nell," she says then, seeming to work back up to it. To pull herself together. "I won't. I trust you too much."

Every day every day every day. She's who I fight for, keep fighting for. That eventually I'll feel like enough. The daughter she deserves. The one who everyone wants so desperately to be.

"It's up to you," she says at last, stepping away from me, giving me space to think. "I need you to be smart." She goes over, picks up the offending laundry hamper. I've never been so ashamed. "I love you" is the last thing she says as she leaves me in the room alone.

31

I get in my car twenty minutes later, after I've had time to compose myself, and drive over to Jackson's house. He's clearly surprised to find me at his door, but instead of inviting me in, he closes the door behind him and steps outside with me. "This isn't a great time," he says. "What is that?"

I throw the box in my hand at him and it bounces off his chest and falls to the ground. He leans down to pick it up, rubbing at the spot on his chest. He gives it a once-over, then looks back at me, a question in his eyes. "Why don't you tell me what it is? Why don't you tell me why the *fuck* it was in my room?" I demand.

He's still confused by my level of complete rage. "Do you really want to have this conversation out here?" he asks me.

"No, I don't," I tell him. "You're the one who shoved me out of your house."

He sighs. "It's not like that. Come on, let's go up to my room," he says, turning and reopening the door, giving me room to enter before he closes it behind him again.

"Jackson!" someone calls from the direction of the kitchen. I recognize his mom's voice. "Who was that?"

"It's a friend, Mom!" Jackson yells back.

"Well, act like you have some manners! Come introduce me."

Something tightens in his face. He throws the box on the stairs and walks in the direction of the kitchen; I take that as a sign to follow him.

His mom is at the breakfast nook, drinking what I suspect is not just orange juice out of a champagne flute and wearing nothing but a bathrobe. My eyes flit to the clock above the stove to confirm it is nearly noon.

"Well, hello," she says, standing up from the stool she's sitting on to extend her hand. "I don't think we've met before. What's your name?"

"I'm Nell Becker," I say, trying to erase some of my anger, to be polite. Only her face changes at the sound of my name, like I said the wrong thing. She pulls her hand back quickly and retakes her seat, busying herself with her drink.

I don't know what I did.

"Mom," Jackson says, standing right behind me. "Nell's the girl I've been dating all summer. You know that, right?"

"Yes, yes," Mrs. Hart says dismissively through sips of her drink. I feel like she's purposely not looking at me, to the point when I have to wonder what exactly I've done. Was it one of those days I came in with Jackson and kept him to myself all night? Or maybe she knows I didn't bring him home after he got his concussion.

I comb my hand nervously through my hair.

"Jackson," she says, as if she can see right through me to him, "get me some more before you run off, would you?"

He nods and walks over to the fridge. I keep chancing glances at Mrs. Hart. Before, I'd only ever seen her from afar at school events and fund-raisers and ceremonies. But she doesn't have any makeup on right now, more wrinkles visible on her face, her roots showing on top of her lank hair. Jackson reaches over the counter, pouring the flute nearly full of champagne and then topping it off with some orange juice, as I suspected.

He puts everything back and says, "Come on, Nell," so I follow him back out through the great room and up the stairs.

"Is she okay?" I ask under my breath.

"She'll be fine," he tells me nonchalantly.

"Did I do something?"

He closes the door behind me as we go into his room. He tosses the box of condoms on his bed. I'd almost forgotten that was why I was here. "She doesn't want me to date anyone right now," he says, and that sounds like a lie. "It's not you."

"She sure seemed chipper before it was me."

He rubs his hair with his palm, back and forth. "The condoms—I just. They were in my bag that I was bringing over after baseball practice because at the time, I assumed we'd need them."

"That doesn't explain how they got left in my room. You can't stop yourself, can you? From always ruining everything."

"Nell!" he exclaims, throwing his hands up in exasperation. "I wasn't thinking straight, in case you don't remember. They probably fell out of my bag when I was getting dressed or something and I didn't notice in my concussed state. I don't understand what you're so pissed about. I was trying to be responsible."

"I didn't find them," I tell him. "My mom did."

He leans back against the bookshelf right behind him, releasing a breath. "Oh."

"So now she knows. About us."

He crosses his arms, not saying anything for a minute. Finally, he says, "Good."

My heartbeat picks up considerably. "Excuse me?"

"You heard me loud and clear. Good. I'm Jackson fucking Hart. I'm first in our class, I'm going to whatever college I want, and I'll grow up to live in a huge house *just like this one*," he says, opening up his hands as if to show me around. "I'm not the kind of person you need to keep a secret."

I shake my head. "You're unbelievable, that's what you are. Things don't belong to you just because you were born this way!" A beat. Too long for me to sharpen my response. "I hate you like this."

He pulls back, struck. The look on his face changes. "But I'm so *damn* tired," he replies, softer. "What do I have to do for you to take me seriously? How can I prove to you I don't want to own you?"

I sit back, watching him.

"Look at me, Nell. I'm desperate." He takes a long, slow breath. "What do you *want* from me? For a change, can you tell me what *you* want?" He trails off then, giving it all to me. The decision. The control.

He's always known what I like.

I hear Mom in my head telling me I'm smarter than this, than *him*. Sometimes, I can see the elegant way he weaves stories, pulls people into him. He's so good that he's won most games before the cards have ever been dealt.

But then I see the cracks. Like walking past a series of fun-house mirrors until you are finally standing in front of your true self and suddenly don't recognize it at all. *That* is what it's like, looking at Jackson.

I do everything right. School and sports and *life*. I love the adrenaline rush of competition, always chasing the high of a victory.

But when's the last time I gave myself all the way into something? I'm always calculating.

And I'm so damn tired of it.

"*Say it,*" he says like he can see everything written on my face.

I breathe in and out like I've just gone on a long run. "I'm in love with you," I say.

Everything about his body language changes, comes to life. I can feel it like a palpable energy, the way the dark blue in his eyes softens; he straightens and comes over to me, putting one hand on my lower back to bring me closer to him.

"Say it again," he tells me, every spot our bodies touch like a live wire.

"I love you," I say. I close my eyes, scared, and almost laugh. "Goddammit."

He tilts his head, ever so slightly, barely pressing his lips against mine. "I love you, too, Nell Becker," he whispers right next to my mouth.

And then we kiss for a long time after that.

Game. Set. Match.

32

Not much changes after that. Well, strictly speaking, that's not entirely true. We were already spending most of our time together, but now it feels like we're rarely apart. I stop lying about meeting Lia and start telling my parents where I am and who I'm with. Dad doesn't seem to mind much, aside from insisting he meet Jackson, and Mom keeps her word. She won't try to stop me. Soon I hope to work up the courage to ask her to take me to the doctor, but I'm not ready to see that disappointed look on her face yet. Lia never says much when Jackson's name comes up, but I can't help but feel like she's avoiding me—her schedule has suddenly gotten much fuller.

Jackson drives an hour the next weekend to our volleyball tournament. He doesn't say anything to me, just sits up in the stands the whole time with his hands in his pockets, watching. Columbus is with him, but there's too many people around for me to ask Lia how their relationship is progressing. I feel like we're living worlds apart.

We don't post anything on social media, either. Not because it's some big secret but because right now, it still feels like it's just ours, something no one else can have. Only our best friends really know about us and part of me wishes no one knew at all.

I did lie last night, though. I told Mom that Lia and I were going to a slumber party at Michonne's but I spent the night at Jackson's. Mom didn't believe me anyway, so I'm not sure why I bothered.

I wake up to the dull sun shining in through the shades covering the massive window at the front of his room. I reach an arm out for him and come back with nothing.

He's missing from his side of the bed, but his phone sits on the nightstand as if signaling he'll be right back. I get up and dress, heading for his bedroom door. I open it, but stop at the sound of voices, echoing up from the kitchen.

Someone is crying.

"Mom, Mom, it's fine. I'll clean it up," Jackson is saying, and I hear something that sounds like broken glass being shifted around. *Shit.* His parents weren't supposed to come back last night.

"I told you, Jackson, I don't want that *girl* sleeping in my house."

I lean my forehead against the doorframe, listening.

"We are not doing this right now," he tells his mom, and I hear the sound of glass falling violently into a trash bag.

"You want to be like him?" she demands. "After everything."

His voices goes lower. "This isn't about that."

"You're supposed to be my baby, Jackson," she says, and she starts absolutely wailing then, so I can't hear anything Jackson is saying to her. I close the door as quietly as I can, going back over to sit down on the bed.

It's at least fifteen minutes before Jackson comes in, looking tired.

"Oh," he says, seeing me immediately. "You're up."

"Yep," I say.

"Look." He rubs the back of his neck. "That was . . ."

"Why does she hate me?" I cut back over him.

"She doesn't even know you," Jackson says quickly. "She's just going through a lot. Can you imagine what dealing with my dad is like?"

"I can't imagine sitting in my bathrobe crying about it all day," I answer icily. "You *told* me this would be okay. You've begged me all summer to stay with you, and then your mom acts like I'm some kind of *trash* you dragged in off the street." I can feel myself trembling, trying to hold it together.

"Don't do that," he says, a warning in his voice.

I grab my purse and stand up. "I'm leaving," I tell him. "I'm obviously not wanted here."

"Wait, wait, wait," he says, backing up and stretching his arm across the doorframe to stop me. "Don't worry about that, okay? I'll figure out some way to put it right, it's just going to take time. Let's go do something fun—me and you. No Doug or Columbus or Tristan."

I relent slightly. "What do you want to do?"

He gives me a smile. It looks a little wicked.

• • •

The boat club is on his side of town, not that it would be anywhere else. I wait while Jackson and one of the boat hands gets the Harts' boat ready for the water, untying ropes and checking fuel levels.

I stopped at home to get a bathing suit. Mom saw us walking into the house together and didn't say a word, despite Jackson's "Hello, Mrs. Becker." I emerged from my room fifteen minutes later dressed for a day on the water and she'd taken a look at me.

"Don't you have volleyball practice this afternoon?"

"I'll be there," I say.

She glanced over at Jackson, and then turned back to the morning show she was watching. He said, "Good-bye, Mrs. Becker," and we left.

"That's as good as it's going to get," Jackson says, passing the boat hand a tip. It's a speedboat, with two long bench seats running up on either side to meet at the bow in the front, and a canopy covering the captain's and passenger seats in the back. I set my bag down in the shade and go lie out on one of the seats at the front of the boat.

It's a perfect day on the water, a crisp breeze in the air. It's a Wednesday, so the water is almost completely clear of boats, save for some rentals from the marina and a couple of retirees fishing. After we drive around for a bit, taking in the sights, Jackson finds a spot to anchor at a sandbar on the edge of one of the many islands on the river. We're utterly alone, my favorite place to be.

He walks up to where I'm lying down, my body stretched out on the seat. "Hi," he says, leaning down and nudging my hip so he can crowd onto the edge next to me, even though there's really no room.

"Hi," I whisper back.

"I missed you," he tells me, because we are so that couple now. I grab his sunglasses off his face so I can see him. In return, he grabs the string tied around the back of my neck and tugs at it until the bow comes loose. One of his fingers trails down my collarbone after the tumbling string of my bikini.

I try to reach out for him, but he stops me. "Don't," he says. "You trust me, don't you?"

"Why should I?" I ask, my voice tripping over itself in my effort to be cool.

He laughs. "Because I want you to." His finger trails down the center of my chest, over the middle of my now-loose bikini top, down my stomach. I close my eyes for a moment.

"I could give it a try," I say, gazing back up at him.

His eyes light up, the dark blue after a storm. "Well, try not to make a move. Let me." He tugs at the strings of my bikini bottom, and I grip my fist into a tight ball at my side, digging my fingernails into my palm to resist the urge to take back control.

He trails his hand lazily over the bottom of my stomach, and I hold on to what's left of my good sense with everything I have. *Don't let go.* "Make sure no one's around," I say to him, trying to catch my breath.

"No one's around," he answers, and then dips his hand to touch me. He takes his time, watching how I react to him. And I'm afraid he might notice at last. That my walls are down. That it scares me.

In one movement, he shifts over me, his knee between the seat's backrest and me so he's straddling me, still with one foot on the floor of the boat. The situation is out of control in a way that both thrills and terrifies me. He leans over me, pressing his mouth into mine, hungry.

"Let me touch you," I tell him.

"You can't," he says. His voice sounds like he might laugh. "That's the game."

"You picked something I can't win," I say, shifting my body up to more fully meet his. "It's not fair."

I can tell he doesn't enjoy the next words as much. "I didn't bring a condom," he admits, and I hear the regret in his voice, the frustration he's trying to hide.

"Pull out, then," I tell him without thinking about it.

"Nell . . ."

"I trust you," I say again, more forcefully this time, more truthfully. "*Please*, Jackson. That's what you want to hear, right? I trust you."

The words do him in. I feel the way they make his body change, like *this*, right now, is all that he has. I know I'm going to get what I want. He draws his hand back and I want like no one has ever wanted before, like I can't believe I thought something was important before this, and then finally, thankfully, the wanting is over and the having is happening. He plants a hand next to my face, his other pressing into the hot skin of my cheek, my neck, and I can feel the way his fingers dig into the seat, the way our bodies find each other, desperately, searching for a place in between.

There's something I've never felt before, an intensity that is so alive between us, and it has nothing to do with the physical act of it. *Trust*, I think, but not too hard. It feels different. Some barrier is down that was between us before, something that wasn't truly and really right until this moment when I finally surrendered the thing I held closest—control. I can tell he feels it.

I feel it.

"Nell," he's saying, and I'm lost in it. The air and the water and every breath in between. "Nell, I can't—"

I don't let him go. A moment too long.

He pulls away from me, grabbing a towel from the floorboard. "Shit," he says. "*Shit.*"

I press my fists into my forehead, still reeling. "Oh my God," I say. "I'm so sorry. I didn't—I just . . ."

He sits back down on the edge of the bench. "No, no, it's not your fault."

"Yes, it is," I tell him. "I'm the one who . . ." But I can't finish it. I'm too embarrassed. I completely let the situation get away from me. I let down my guard and now . . .

"It takes two," he says, but I still think he might be mad. I don't blame him. But he just leans his elbows on the top of his legs and puts his head down. "Shit."

"It's fine," I say, thinking as fast as I can. "I can go get Plan B in the morning. It'll be fine."

"Are you sure?" he asks, looking at me, hope in every line of his face. "You can do that?"

"Yeah," I say, even though the idea makes me a little nauseated. Not the actual Plan B—just the being *that girl*. "I Googled it. It's easy." That girl who doesn't use a condom. That girl who doesn't protect herself. I *had* Googled it, but just in case a condom broke, not in the case of me turning into a hormonal idiot.

"I'm sorry," he tells me. "It was dumb." He reaches down to retie my bathing suit for me, now that we've solved the problem I created. I watch him do both sides of the bottom.

"I'm sorry," I whisper.

He sits up, reaching his fingers expertly behind my neck to fix my top, and then presses his mouth to my sweaty forehead once he's done.

"Everything's fine," he tells me then. He presses two fingers against the pulse point of my neck. "Are you okay?"

I breathe in and out slowly. He must've seen the attack coming on. *Nell. Breathe. Nell. Think. Nell. Rationalize.* "Yeah," I say at last. He sees me. I know he sees me without me having to say the words.

He stands up, looking down at me. "Have you ever told anyone about your anxiety?"

My eyes flit away from him, out to the water. "Lia knows." He's still watching me, I feel it. "Look, I've researched it. I use techniques, I'm fine."

"You don't always have to be fine. Sometimes, you can ask for help." I want to bite back at him, tell him he sounds like a television therapist, but I can't find it in me to lash out.

I'm tired.

Finally, he lets it go and moves to lie on the other bench seat opposite me so that our heads are next to each other, and if we were to hold hands across the deck our bodies would form the shape of a letter A. We stay like that together for a while, faces to the sun, not saying anything. I keep replaying the incident over and over again, from when it started to when I stopped thinking to his last words. I don't want *help.* I don't want to need help.

After a while, Jackson reaches out to play with my fingers. "What are we going to do when we go back to school?" I ask him.

"What do you mean?" he says. I look down at our hands; his skin is significantly darker, tanned by hours in the sun at baseball and on the riverbank, mine pale in comparison from too much sunscreen and time in the volleyball gym.

"Things are going to be different. I mean, I have all the volleyball stuff now but double that once we have school and varsity. We're going to win the state championship, so I'll be busy. Not to mention college applications."

He laughs. "Nell, come on. I know you've already got all your college applications filled out."

"Whatever," I dismiss him. "There's also the small matter of settling valedictorian. And, I mean, there's all the people."

"Yeah, I'm super unconcerned about them, to say the least."

"What about me?" I say. "I can't be *this* once school starts again. All boats and screwing around. I have a plan. Will you even want me then?"

He hides his face in his arm. "It's so nice here. Do we have to talk about this right now?"

"I'm just saying, it's going to be different." I turn my head to the side to look at him. "Have you read it yet?"

"Read what?" he asks, shading his eyes to look back at me.

"Surely you know what I'm talking about."

"No idea."

"*The Scarlet Letter.*"

He laughs. "No."

"Of course not," I say, irritation coating my voice.

"You weren't serious about that." He doesn't say it like it's a question, but more like I couldn't possibly have been.

"I just don't see why it's so difficult for you," I tell him, my voice doing that lilting thing it does when I'm annoyed. "It's only one thing. It wouldn't even take you that long—it's not like anything's hard for you."

He still sounds amused. "Why do you care so much about *The Scarlet Letter*? Was it, like, transcendent for you?"

"I don't even *like The Scarlet Letter*," I tell him. "I don't know, it's the principle of the matter. That I work so hard and yet, somehow you're still beating me. That fucking Hester Prynne was humiliated for doing exactly what the men did and everyone turned on her." I flex my leg and then straighten it. "*This* is what school's going to be like."

"Hester Prynne figured it out and we will, too," he answers, not a

care in the world. "That's what people like us do. We rise to the top."
I've heard those words before, only it was Mom saying them.

"What time is it?" I ask Jackson a second later, still annoyed.

"Almost four," he returns, lazily.

"*What?*" I sit straight up. "I had practice at three. I thought we
had plenty of time."

Jackson doesn't sit all the way up, instead angling himself against
the bow. "Well, you're not going to make it now. It's at least a half-
hour ride back to the marina."

"Shit," I say, running my hands through my hair. "I don't know
the last time I missed a practice. And I didn't even tell anyone. Lia doesn't
have any idea where I am. I'm going to have to pretend I was sick and,
like, fell asleep or something."

Jackson is watching me with that infuriatingly calm look. "Is it
that bad?"

"What do you mean?"

"I mean that you missed one practice. All summer. Don't the
other girls go on vacation and stuff? Aren't they out sick sometimes?"

"It doesn't matter what other girls do," I say. "People are expecting me."

"It's one practice, Nell," he replies. He sits all the way up and turns
so he's facing me, his bare feet against the floor of the boat. "Remember
when you got those scores for the class rankings? And that caused a
panic attack?"

I frown at him. "Vividly."

"*This* is why. You treat everything like it's the end of the world."

"Don't condescend to me," I snap.

He sighs, falling back against the edge of the boat dramatically.

"Seriously, don't be like that," I say to him. "Like I'm your annoying girlfriend."

"You're not my annoying girlfriend. You're my annoying obsession. It's, like, a hundred times more tragic."

I grab a bottled water from its cup holder and sip it furiously. "Fine," I finally say, screwing the top back on. "It's *fine*."

"Seems like it."

"What does that mean?" I ask. "About me being an obsession."

He gives me a look, all eyes and straight lips.

"What?" I say.

"You're the one who used to ask me about all the girls I dated. Why it didn't last. I always thought it would eventually. It would stick.

"This isn't that," he says. "This is goddamn consuming."

"How?" I ask, curious.

"Like I'll never get enough. Like if I go a day without seeing you, then what was even the point of the day? Like if I'm not breathing the same air as you in any given moment, then something's wrong. I feel like I've been drunk for two months straight. I don't even know what it would mean to sober up anymore."

I sit back so I'm facing him the same way he's facing me. "That doesn't sound like love. That sounds dangerous." The word is thick against my tongue.

He puts his hand against my cheek in the way he is wont to do. "It *feels* dangerous."

We watch each other. A beat and then two. A steady wave rocks the boat and we both just hold on.

33

It's another hour before we make our way back to the marina. Jackson is steering into his dock when I notice the man standing there waiting for us.

It's his dad.

Mr. Hart waits until Jackson docks the boat with help from another boat hand. Once everything is secure, Jackson walks over to him. I stand behind at a safe distance.

"Where have you been?" Mr. Hart asks, his voice deadly calm.

"Out for a nice leisure ride," Jackson says. He's doing his fake-confident voice now. The one he uses as armor against the outside world.

"You took the boat without my permission," Mr. Hart says. Everything about him looks cold to me. He's in a pair of business slacks but his button-down is untucked and the sleeves are rolled up. His hands are in his pockets as if this is some casual conversation.

"Yes, that is correct," Jackson says.

"I was going to take an important business partner out on the boat," Mr. Hart continues. "And you knew that."

Jackson snaps. "Knew I was forgetting something." I feel heat building in my face. This day hadn't been about us or making up for the way Mrs. Hart treated me—it was about pissing off his dad. Every time I think we've finally finished with all the bullshit . . . I can't believe he's put me in the middle of this.

"Don't test me right now," Mr. Hart says. "I should've called the police and reported it stolen."

"Well, that certainly would've added an additional twist to the soap opera we are all currently living," Jackson tells him, his voice about one octave from complete joy. "Exactly how long have you been waiting out here to make this as dramatic as possible? Or should I say," he continues, looking over his dad's rumpled clothes, "how long have you been waiting at the bar?"

"You are an ungrateful brat," his dad says. I think he wants to slap him and is reining himself in.

"At least we agree on something."

"I can't believe you'd ruin a business opportunity for our whole family for your flavor of the week."

"I beg your pardon," I say. That he thinks he can treat me like that tells me everything I need to know. If your average net worth doesn't have the proper number of zeroes behind it, you might as well be another decoration on the wall to them. If you're a female, you're an accessory.

I'm not something to be had.

"That flavor of the week is my girlfriend, and I need you to apologize to her."

Mr. Hart sneers. "So you've found another slut. Like there's any teenage boy in America as rich as you that can't get some desperate girl to screw him."

I move forward but Jackson puts his arm up to hold me back. "I think you have a bit more respect for the Beckers than that, don't you, Dad?" he asks.

His dad's eyes go to me then, looking closely. I feel my heart pounding. I don't know what I was going to do. Probably not go off and hit him, but I'd at least like to have had my chance.

"If you'd like to apologize, I have a name," I say. "I don't usually go by 'slut.'"

"I'm sorry, Nell." This comes from Jackson. He should be so sorry. I'm not done with him, either.

But Mr. Hart has somehow shot straight up into apoplectic. "Get out of my sight," he tells us, jabbing a finger into Jackson's chest. "The next time you pull a stunt like this, I'm enrolling you in military school."

Jackson clasps his fingers around mine and leads me away. I'm shaking so hard, I can barely put one foot in front of the other to get away from him. When we're safely in Jackson's truck, I don't even know why, but I lose it. I put my face into my hands and start crying.

"Nell," he says, his hand rubbing slow circles on my back. "I'm so sorry."

"How can he just . . . degrade me like that?" I hear myself saying. "I am so many fucking *things*, but all he sees is a slut. All he sees is something for a man to stick his dick into."

"Nell," he tries.

"And you." I turn to him, pointing. "You used me in one of your schemes against him. You knew what would happen if you took that boat and you did it anyway. You *used* me and to what end? So you could have your little moment of victory. You . . . You treated me the same way he did."

"I never meant to do any of that. I'm sorry," he pleads. "Look, yes, I wanted to piss him off, but I didn't think he would turn on you like that. I wanted to be with you before anything else."

"You are such a liar," I tell him. My hands are still shaking. "You always have been. 'I thought you respected the Beckers.' You knew *exactly* what would happen."

"Nell. Come on, we are so far past that."

I shake my head. "I'm not a pawn in your game, Jackson. I *am* the goddamn game."

"I know," he says. "I'm sorry. I fucked up."

I don't look at him, staring straight ahead out the front window, trying to become steel again. They're nothing but *words*. Nothing but empty words from men who have to assure themselves exactly how much power they have.

"Take me home," I tell him. "Just take me home."

34

I'm coming over.

Lia had sent me that text right after volleyball practice.

When I walk into my house, she's sitting on the couch, watching TV with Dad.

"Hello," he says to me when I walk in. I feel both of their eyes on my skin, slowly turning red from too much sun. "Did you have a nice day?" he asks.

I shrink under his withering glare. "The boat ran out of gas," I lie.

"People are counting on you, Nell. If something comes up, you need to let them know."

"I called your mom," Lia says, throwing her hands up in defeat. "I didn't know where you were. I was worried."

I swallow. "Thanks for being worried. You don't have to apologize," I tell her.

"Your mom is not happy with you," Dad says. "You need to talk to her when she gets home. She's working late and then going to book club."

I put my fingers against my temples as if holding my head in place, a ghost of a tremor still living under my skin. "Can everyone just give me a break right now? I'm sorry but . . . I can't." I'm barely keeping it together, after the scene with Mr. Hart.

"I need to talk to you," Lia tells me, standing up from the couch. "Thanks for entertaining me, Mr. Becker."

"You're always welcome," he tells her.

"Let's go out back. There's finally a breeze," I say. We walk through the kitchen, through the screened porch, and out into the backyard where a wooden swing still hangs from the big willow tree.

Lia's barely been over at all this summer, I realize. Even though we've always spent more time at her place than mine, it's the first summer I can remember when we haven't gotten giggly in my room and run outside, pushing each other on the swing, standing on the wooden slat like we are brave.

The swing looks awfully lonely now.

I sit down in the grass, lying back and staring up at the fading sunlight, the stars fighting to take control of the sky. She lies in the opposite direction, our heads perfectly in line. We've done this more times than I can remember.

"I covered for you," she says. She glances over at me. "What happened to you? You look like shit."

I rub my hand against my sunburnt arm. "Jackson's dad called me a slut," I tell her. "Well, first, his mom insinuated I wasn't welcome in their home and then his dad called me a slut." I feel my eyes welling up and almost tell her what happened on the boat, but I'm too embarrassed to admit it.

Lia sits up, staring back at me. "Are you kidding?"

I shake my head, unable to fully meet her eye. "Jackson dragged me right into the lion's den. He was taunting his dad and . . ." I trail off. Part of me wants to take it back because I know she'll judge me for it. I'll lose her respect.

"Nell," she says, "you are not a slut. And you are far better than what Jackson Hart deserves."

"Please don't do that."

"Hey," she answers, and I stare up at her, upside down and blurry through my unshed tears, "no one gets to talk to you like that. No matter who they are."

She lies back down next to me, brushing a piece of grass from my face. "Sometimes I wonder if you even realize what you've gotten yourself into."

A plane is moving through the sky, pretending to be a comet. "What does that mean?" I ask. "You think I can't handle him myself?"

"I just think there's things about him you don't know."

"Of course there are," I tell her. "I think there's things about *you* I don't know. Is there something specific?"

"No, I just—" I feel her shift, fold one arm behind her head. "Columbus is always so uncomfortable when he talks about things Jackson does and says—and that's his *best friend*, Nell. I feel like there's more to all this weird shit with his parents than he's letting on."

"You always do this," I say. "When I admit I got hurt or messed up, you infantilize me. As if I'm somehow incapable."

"Seriously? You have, like, the most bizarre set of rules for yourself. You think too much about everything, but you always *defend* him. How can you not see what I do?"

"You're such a hypocrite." I sit up. "You and Columbus and that star-crossed bullshit? You think that's all on the up and up?"

"That is *completely* different," Lia tells me, volume rising. "It's not even his choice. My family has already lost everything, and now you want me to throw this on top of it, too?"

"Your family hasn't lost anything. That's the thing with you people," I say, taking something out on her that isn't her fault. "You still do whatever you want and you're still rich and the way it hurts anyone else doesn't matter at all." I can still feel the way Jackson was watching me in the truck earlier. Like a flip-book, it runs through my mind—all the clothes I could never afford and all the trips I could never take and opportunity after opportunity I won't have.

I have everything I need, but as long as I know that life exists, I'll never be enough.

Lia sits straight up, twisting around to face me. "How. *Fucking.*

Dare you? I have been bending over backward to accommodate you despite the fact that *my* life is falling apart. But all I ever hear about is Nell's volleyball and Nell's class ranking and Nell's rich boyfriend."

"Lia," I say. "*Don't.*"

She gets to her feet and stands there looking down at me. "Do you know how shit I feel all the time?"

"No, because you don't tell me. You won't talk to me, and half the time, I wonder if you even like me. Besides," I continue because I can't stand to miss my kill shot. To get the win. "Imagine how Columbus feels. His parents are the good guys."

Her face closes off, her hair bouncing behind her. "I think I need to . . ." She pauses to compose herself and I realize it's because she's about to start crying. ". . . not talk to you for a couple of days. Which should be just fine with you, right?"

I want to take it all back, and I don't. "Wait, Lia. I only—" I start to say, but the look on her face stops me. Because it wasn't an accident and she knows me well enough to know it.

"I'll see you at practice tomorrow," she says. Then she walks around the side of the house, purposely not going back in, not having to face my family, which she is basically a member of. I curl my legs up into my body, burying my face in my knees. Take deep breaths. I start, ridiculously, running over important dates in European history in my head. I wonder if I can drown my brain in important dates in European history until I forget everything else about this terrible fucking day.

Minutes or hours pass. By the time I hear the porch door opening, it's completely dark. "Hey, kid." *Kid*—I'm always a kid to him.

"Please don't lecture me," I beg him. "I can't take anymore. I can't take anymore *anything* at this point."

"Honey, the only thing I'll ever ask you to do is not purposely hurt somebody else and to apologize if you unintentionally do. Not too much, right?"

"Simple," I say, pressing my mouth into my knee. I look up at him. "How do you ever know when you're wrong?"

He laughs. "You don't. You just hope you're not and pray like hell. That's what my dad always said."

I nod.

"Do you know why I hate this place?" Dad asks me.

"No," I return, though I've always wondered.

"This town never gives anyone room to grow. You are who you'll always be. I could sell a thousand million-dollar homes, but I'll always be an upstate hick to them. We're always going to be on the wrong side of the river. Your mom thinks she can fight it, thinks you'll beat it. It's a worthy cause, but it's like hoping the Earth will reverse course on its axis.

"Some boys are always going to be revered in Cedar Woods. And that is why your mother hates that boyfriend of yours."

I blink a couple of times. "I could be revered, too."

Dad looks at me, tall and straight-backed. "I want you to do everything you want. But don't forget that one day, you're going to look back and realize what a small part of your life this was."

I stand up. I can't stay here. I feel suffocated. Expected to pick a path without getting to look down them both, find any balance. "I know today wasn't my finest hour, but I need to go for a drive or something to clear my head, if that's okay? I'm not going to Jackson's, I swear. I need to be alone for a little bit." I probably could've gone without asking, but for some reason in that moment, it feels important to ask. To ask for that trust.

"That's fine," he tells me. And then just to add some extra parental authority: "Can you please be back by eleven?"

"Sure," I say. I turn to go, but then: "Do you think I should break up with him?" I ask, stuck somewhere in the middle of leaving.

"That's the thing," he tells me, hands in his pockets. "I think for a change, you should do whatever you want."

35

I don't know where I'm going. The roads between my house and Jackson's feel too familiar. I find as I'm driving that I'm so sick of the roads of this town. Of the endless gossip. Of the rich kids who prey on the kids who want to be accepted into their graces. Who want, more than anything, to *be* them.

There's nothing so extraordinary about them.

I think about driving to Lois's bar. I wonder if she'd remember me. But then I think, just like everything else in this town, she belongs to Jackson. Everything belongs to him.

not me not me not me

So I follow the river. Southwest, the way it flows. Fishing boats make their ways across it, herons dipping in sometimes to scoop something up. It's not long before I hit the next town, Morgan. Right on the outskirts, there's this little riverside restaurant my family used to go to. It's beautiful but not pretentious like most of the nice places in Cedar Woods. Morgan doesn't have the average household income Cedar Woods boasts, so there's no one around to impress.

I pull into the parking lot, staring at the side of the building. It hasn't changed at all and I haven't been here since middle school, at least. Back then, it was Mom and Dad's favorite place, and sometimes, they'd bring me along. There's a sidewalk trailing the river out back. It opens to a dock with a small schooner that hosts fishing trips through the summer season.

I crunch through the gravel parking lot to the river, walking along the dock to its end, out in the water. The wind is blowing hard off the river, fish bobbing up to grab pieces of bread left floating around from the dinner crowd earlier. But it's after ten now.

I push my body against the railing at the end of the dock, mostly wanting to fling myself over, in. Just to feel it. The fall. The splash. Swim back to shore dripping wet and with nowhere to go.

When you have everything so perfectly under control, so tightly held all the time, sometimes you only want to follow your impulses.

That's what Jackson is—an impulse.

I pull my phone out of my pocket, sliding open the messages.

I'm sorry. It was stupid.

Would you call me cliché if I said the l-word?

Don't answer that. Of course you would.

Can you answer me? Like the second you're ready to talk to me again, will you talk to me?

I'm sorry, Nell. Not for earlier but for all the texts. I promise, I'll give you space. Take all you need and then I'll just be here. Waiting and all that.

Love you.

I press my palms against my eyes. Then I turn around so the water is at my back and lean against the railing, tipping my head up to look at the sky. It's different here, still a few miles from the heart of the town, only the river and me. The stars demand one's attention. They don't ask.

I'll answer him, I decide finally, heading down the dock. I'll answer him when I get home. I'll decide if I want to forgive him. I can't keep living in the in-between. At some point, I have to acknowledge that I can't go back to before.

I will figure out how to make things right with Lia. To make things right with my parents. To make things right with *me*.

I stop short when I get back to the riverwalk leading to the parking lot. Because there is my mother's car, parked as innocuously as could be. Dad didn't say anything about her going out. Why would she be all the way out in Morgan?

I backtrack, walking the other way down the riverwalk. The restaurant deck is closed but with all the lights out, I'm able to see through the huge windows—they're rolled up to give the back bar open air. I move closer, creeping up the stairs that lead from the restaurant's deck to the riverwalk.

I spot her then—her reflection in the mirror over the bar as she sits on a stool. She's alone.

Why?

She has her usual glass of white wine, holding it as if it's a precious commodity. It's strange to watch her like this, unguarded. Not trying to look proper for anybody else. Not perfect. Just being.

She looks like she could be someone like me.

She's talking to a man sitting a couple of seats over from her. Not in a flirtatious way at all. Very casual. She points to something behind the bar and she and the man both laugh. I can't see his reflection from my angle.

I move forward until I'm on the deck, not more than a few yards from them, hidden in the dark. Not that they're looking. I should let this go. Leave well enough alone.

But I think anyone in my shoes would do the same thing.

I'm at the right angle to see his face, and I do. I grab on to the back railing of the deck, my mind not completely understanding.

It's Mr. Hart.

They're talking like they've never met in their lives, like they're brand-new people. There's no way they just ran into each other here. Mr. Hart would never waste time on Morgan. Not without a reason.

Mom stops laughing. She turns back to the bar, saying something to the bartender as he goes by. He nods at her. She's completely ignoring Mr. Hart now, sending my brain into spirals.

It's once they're not looking at each other that it happens. He passes something to her under the bar and she takes it. A gesture so smooth that I notice it only because I'm watching them so closely.

This exact spot. Where everything changed.

I take the steps three at a time, almost twisting my ankle as I hit the bottom and run to my car. I have to get out of here. I have to get out of here before they see me.

I'm trying to unlock my car so fast, I drop my keys. Twice. I finally get in and take off, driving forty miles over the legal speed limit out of town. I'm panting so hard, I can't catch my breath, my heart racing faster than an Olympic medalist crossing the finish line. I'm not even sure how I'm driving, only that I have to get away faster faster *faster*.

I take a violent left to get off the main road as if they might follow me there and when I see a long driveway up ahead, I pull off the road. I wrap my hands around the steering wheel, holding on for dear life, the panic attack fully having its way with me. I feel like I'm going to be sick, except I'm not a tangible enough person to be sick right now. I can't breathe so I'm sure I've died. I pull my feet up to my seat, wrapping my arms around them so I'm in the fetal position, waiting for it to pass. *Please let me go please let me go please.*

I start running through dates. But dates keep fading into memories and memories into realizations.

Mom.

Jackson's mom and how she reacted to my name.

His dad's face when he heard it, too.

I think you have a bit more respect for the Beckers than that, don't you, Dad?

He knew.

I'm sorry. About before. Downstairs. And in the parking lot. That look after the first time we slept together. *For not telling you last week.*

He always knew.

It all clicks into place then, one piece falling after another. The boat. The condoms. *Hello, Mrs. Becker. Good-bye, Mrs. Becker.*

I am so. Goddamn. Stupid.

I don't know why, but something about that calms me. Makes me find my center. Tells me to *pull it the fuck together.*

I run my fingers through my hair, thinking. Wishing I could hold on to my thoughts as fast as I can think them because it's all coming together into one solid story. I wipe the skin under my eyes clean with my palm. Left then right. Pick up my phone and type out a text.

Meet me down by the river. Where we hooked up that first time.

I text Dad that I'm sorry, but I won't be home until midnight. *I'm sorry*, I type again just to see the words, knowing I won't send it.

I'm sorry I missed it.

I'm sorry you're married to a conniving bitch.

I'm sorry I'm not as smart as I thought I was.

Jackson's reply comes fast.

That sounds a little ominous.

I answer: *I'll see you in twenty.*

He's already there when I drive down the boat ramp, parking behind him because there's not enough room next to his truck. He's leaned onto his hood like last time. But he stands up straight when I get out of the car and walk toward him. I keep as much distance as I can between.us, walking to the edge of the water and watching him from there, with my hands buried in my pockets.

"I know why you didn't want to come over to my house," he says, and I almost feel the desire to laugh. "But Mom apologized. And he's not even there."

"I know," I say.

His expression shifts ever so slightly.

I shake my head, looking away from him. "I'm not here to make nice. All I want to know is when you knew."

226

"When I knew what?" he asks, nerves progressively edging into his voice.

"That our parents were fucking," I say, not letting the slightest bit of hurt or pain or anything touch my voice or face.

His expression changes completely. "Jesus Christ," he says, burying his face in his hands.

"Don't act like you didn't know," I say, holding on to that feeling. It's the only way I'll keep all the pieces of myself together.

He throws his hands up. "Of course I knew. And when exactly do you think would've been a good time for me to mention it?"

"Oh, go fuck yourself right up the river," I tell him. I have an overwhelming desire to shove him, to *hurt* him. It's a feral urge deep under my skin. "How long have you *known*? Was it that day you told me that sob story about hitting your dad? Or maybe when we were carting your best friend to the emergency room. Or even better"—I clap my hands together—"the day you took my virginity."

"Do *not* put that shit on me," he says. "That wasn't exactly the seduction of the century I was running there."

"Oh my God," I say, actually letting out a laugh. "You did know then, didn't you? That was what all your 'you don't understand' bullshit was about. You actually had a conscience for half a second."

"You wanted it as much as I did, Nell."

"So why didn't you STOP me!" I yell at him. "Say 'by the way, Nell, our parents are having an affair and that's why I need you to leave the damn premises.'" I curl my hands into fists. "How did you even know? Did he *tell* you? 'Just so you know, I'm banging that Becker girl's mom so you might want to stop screwing around with her.'"

Jackson takes a deep breath, working hard to build up to it, to keep his always-perfectly-maintained composure. "I realized Mom knew who he was having an affair with and since she knew, I made it my business to know. So I followed him around for a couple of days before I saw them together. Well, I saw him go into a hotel, and then I waited and saw your mom come out. But I wanted to be sure so I kept following him, and by the third time I saw your mom . . . I knew."

"*When?*" I demand.

He rubs his eyes. "The weekend of Alston's party. I started following Dad around after the bonfire. After you cornered me about my parents."

I run my fingers through my hair. "So all of it? The whole thing was a lie?"

He shakes his head. "I just wanted to know more about you. So I'd know about your mom. And then—I swear, I wasn't ever planning any of the rest of this. Once I really knew you, I always wanted to be with you, Nell, and then that night we were here at the river, I realized it was getting so out of control. I tried to end it. I did."

"All you had to do was tell me." My voice is so raw. "You got me to sleep with you, proved you could get any girl you wanted. That could've been the end of it."

"I didn't want *this*. I thought I could give you up, eventually. But by the time you came to my house—Jesus, Nell," he says, his voice edging on desperate. "We'd already gotten in so deep."

"Do you have *no* self-control? You couldn't stop sleeping with me, stop trying to make me love you?" I take a step toward him, remaining calm as I do. "It didn't take me that long to figure out. Everything. You'd let every other girl go in a minute, but you weren't going to let me go, not when you could see that look in my mom's eyes, feel that victory. The condoms? Genius. The boat thing today. You were just getting started. This was going to be Jackson Hart's best ever con.

"Tell me," I say as if I'm a teacher moving him along in class. "Tell me the truth."

He swallows, stopping and starting. Finally, he manages to get it out: "Look, fine, I knew—I knew if I could get close to you, like, really close, it would be punishment for both of them. And yes, I saw opportunities or whatever, I guess, to mess with them, but there's so much more to it than that." His voice cracks. "I need to sort everything out because it's not like that. If you only understood what my family was really like."

He's crying, I can see that now. Everything in me goes numb and I can't think anything but: *He's ugly when he cries.*

"*Your* family? *You*, Jackson. It's YOU. Goddammit, what is wrong with you?"

"I don't know."

"And you're just going to stand here and cry like that somehow absolves you?" I take a step toward him. "You still wanna fuck me?"

"I'm not going to fight with you," he tells me.

"Not even if I tell you that's the only way I'd feel even the smallest bit better?"

He sighs, taking a shaky breath.

"You know, there's one small comfort I take in all of this," I say. "When I told you I trusted you earlier, it was a lie."

He doesn't say anything as I walk past him, doesn't try to call me back. He stands there, still, like this is where he'll always be now.

My amazing calm lasts long enough for me to drive away. I go the opposite of the way I know he might leave and pull over again, this time in a random patch of grass because I can't go any farther. I call Lia, hysterical to the point that she thinks someone's dead.

"I don't know what you're saying," she finally says, "but I'm in my car already. I'll meet you at your house."

That's where she is when I get home, parked on the street and waiting on me. I'd gotten it together enough to get home, but I lose it all over again when I see her. She goes into the house before me to make sure she hears the sound of Dad snoring before she pulls me inside, flipping off the porch light he left on behind us, and taking me up the stairs.

I try not to let myself wonder when Mom will be home.

Upstairs, I crawl directly under the covers, willing my breathing back to normal. She sits cross-legged in front of me, running her fingers over my hair. "You're okay," she keeps saying, and I want to tell her *I doubt that very seriously.*

It's a while before I dry out. She's had time to change into a pair of athletic shorts and T-shirt to sleep in since it's clear she'll be spending the night. "Do you want to tell me what happened?" she asks.

Sometimes it's the worst thing in the world to have to say *You were right.*

I have to tell her in pieces. The drive. The restaurant. Mom. *His* dad. She doesn't say anything at that part, which is good because otherwise I might not be able to finish. Her face grows steadily darker as I tell her everything else, ending on murderous.

"You were right," I finally finish, turning the loathing inward. "I was his masterpiece, perfectly played, never seeing any of it. I told him I loved him." I close my eyes, a tear leaking out. "I'm a pawn in some sick game between our parents. And he got every single piece of me that he wanted. Like, a complete skeleton, sinew and all."

Lia winces. "Nell, I am so sorry. I—I"—she trips over her words— "I don't even know what to say. Only I wasn't right at all. I never imagined this. He's a damn sociopath."

I cling to the comforter on my bed.

"*Shit,*" she says. "We have to spend an entire school year with him. With his smug face every day. I'll kill him."

"Lia." I reach out and grab her arm, hanging on tight. "You can't tell *anyone* about this. I am humiliated."

"Of course," she says, squeezing my hand gently where it's touching her, despite my deadly grip.

"I want to pretend this never happened. To make it go away. I want him to be nothing."

"He's less than nothing," she tells me, pulling my hand down carefully. "Nothing has substance. You can't ignore *nothing*. He's something you stuffed in a drawer when you got it three years ago and threw in the trash while spring cleaning without even considering it. Nell, he's a black hole and you're the best damn person I know."

Her voice is steady, vibrating into my skin. "Thanks for being my best friend," I tell her, lying with my head facing her, cuddled up close.

"You can't get rid of me that easily," she whispers, leaning down and pressing her lips against my forehead like I'm a child.

36

I become a permanent fixture at the Reagans' house.

I stay there as often as I can, sharing a bed with Lia more nights than not. Otherwise, I sneak home, trying to avoid both of my parents. The Reagans don't seem to mind. Mr. Reagan's in and out of the house; I have no idea where he goes most of the time and I don't think anyone else does, either, frankly. He isn't supposed to leave the state as he's considered a minor flight risk due to his business interests and money. Lia gets this look on her face when I ask and says he's probably with "Meemaw," rolling her eyes. Mrs. Reagan is back to her charity routines and the liquor cabinets are locked, the key stowed away in Taylor's sock drawer.

Here's the first thing I discover when I'm left at the Reagans' alone: Taylor's bedroom window is missing the screen and has a low slope on the porch roof that makes the perfect perch. It's where I am now with a huge water bottle I've filled with red wine. I can't stand the taste of Mom's beloved white wine, so red it is.

It reminds me of what Jackson said to me that day at Raven's. About being someone else. About pretending.

But then I guess he was always pretending.

So I'm on the roof watching the day go by in a lovely haze. Taylor pokes his head out, his eyes widening when they meet mine. "Nell!" he calls, climbing out onto the roof with me. "I didn't think there was a chance I'd find you here. It's hotter out than the floor of hell."

I shrug, sipping from my bottle. "I didn't notice."

He comes over and sits next to me. "Give me that," he says, trying to pull the water bottle out of my hand and taking a sip. "Ugh. That is terrible."

I pull it back. "I don't mind it so much."

"This is, like, the third day in a row you've only left the house for practice. How much longer are you going to do this?" He means sulk, I guess. Or be useless.

What Taylor knows is this: Jackson and I broke up. I am not handling it well. It's sort of embarrassing to think that I'd sink to these depths over a simple breakup, but Taylor is practically family, so I've let him witness my self-destruction. He's earned that trust.

I consider Taylor's question. I feel nothing but happy right now, calm, *not a problem*. Last night, I'd gotten a text from Dad and had a minor breakdown. Lia had gone off somewhere with Columbus so Taylor was left to clean me up.

I saw the accusation in his eyes when I cried.

"I think I'll be done soon," I tell Taylor. "Or never." I twist my head around to look at him. "Who knows?" I drink again.

He sighs, but doesn't try to take the bottle from me this time. "He really did a number on you, huh?"

"Very astute observation," I agree.

"I don't know exactly what happened," Taylor says, "but just remember, he's done this a hundred times before. Don't let him have the satisfaction of seeing you like this. I know you might need time to process, but you have to go into school focused, like you always do.

"And I know you, Nell. You'll come out on top."

I nod at him, as if what he's just said is remotely wise. "I was wrong about him," I say. "Remember what I told you in the parking lot during baseball season?"

He nods, his eyebrows drawing together in confusion.

"I was wrong," I continue. "I said that if he thought he deserved something, it would come to him. That's not true." I shake my head, taking another gulp of warm red wine. "If he wants something, he'll do whatever it takes to get it. He's the hardest-working person I know."

Taylor looks at me curiously, maybe scared—I'm currently too drunk to determine—and then glances over the edge of the roof. "You're not going to, like, jump, are you?"

"I would probably break my leg," I tell him. "And he'd get way too much pleasure out of that."

"Nell," he says, very seriously. I sit still to show him that I am listening. "I'm sorry," he says.

I take another sip. "Thank you. Me, too."

• • •

You know what's funny about the end of something? You don't realize how much that something took from you, and how much you gain back when it's gone.

The end of Jackson and me leaves me with something I hadn't considered all summer: time.

Time, time, time. To put together all Mom's lies, to track her movements, check her mileage meter when she gets home to see if she could've possibly gone where she said she did. Time to think about Jackson, time to reconstruct everything he said or did. Time to wonder why I let myself believe in anything to begin with.

The biggest irony of all is that I was built specifically for this kind of obsession.

The clock says one AM and I am wide awake.

It's impossible to describe my state of mind, because for the past two weeks, I've rarely been able to *think* at all. My life feels like a series of events that's happening to me. I had no choice but to hit Pause. I don't want to run or think about school or volleyball or anything except my parents and Jackson's parents and Jackson and how I solve this problem. Lia saw me doodling some ideas earlier—*publicly out affair* (crossed out), *have Jackson arrested for credit card fraud???*, *graduate early*—and took the notebook away from me.

Betrayal is a curious thing. Because it's so much more than one moment of stabbing pain—it's like losing your truth, your guiding principle, your *self.* "You'll have to work harder than them to get what they'll get," Mom told me the first time she'd seen me bent over my shiny new Cedar Woods Prep books, her fingers tugging at the end of my braid.

I hadn't known exactly who she'd been talking about. The other students. The rich ones. The boys, the ones who'd gotten off free after Bryce McCabe had died. All I'd said was "I will."

But Mr. Hart is the worst of them. So Mom has been a liar all along.

Mom, Jackson.

I keep chasing fragments of light. They bend before I can get my hand around them.

My brain pounds against my skull. I'm considering getting some wine, but Mr. Reagan asked who had been in the wine cabinet at dinner tonight, and Taylor took the fall so I'm *thisclose* to being busted.

I get out of bed, sneaking down the hallway. And then, I nudge open the door to Taylor's room, navigating the maze of clothes on his floor. I pull up the covers and get into bed with him.

His eyes open ever so slightly at the movement. He doesn't jump, too sleepy to fully care.

"Nell?" he mutters.

I throw my arm over his torso, cross my leg over his, and hold on to him tight.

He presses his cheek against the top of my head.

"You were right about what you said on the roof," I tell him after a moment. "They can't have me. I have to keep going."

"Of course they can't," he tells me, sounding more awake. He doesn't push me away.

I wake up the next morning and go for a run.

• • •

I sneak into Taylor's room every night for the rest of the week.

37

I'm scrolling through people's pictures on my phone, pretending not to listen to the conversation Lia and Columbus are having. Lia is sitting against a propped-up pillow on her bed with Columbus's feet next to her. He's sprawled upside down on the comforter, looking like he owns the place. Lia's parents are out of town for the next two days, and the look in Lia's eyes had dared Taylor to say something when Columbus came in the door. Taylor just smiled his pretty Reagan smile and shook Columbus's hand.

"I heard Erin Clark has been running around with some CW High boy all summer," Lia is telling him, staring at a picture on his phone, which he's holding to her face, and smiling at the screen. "That's no good at all."

Columbus throws his head back, laughing. "How do you even know that?"

She smirks. "I know things."

He uses his bare foot to nudge her ribs and she giggles, pushing him away.

"What about you, Nell?" Columbus calls across the room to me. "You ready to be back at school?"

I set my phone down, avoiding answering. It's the perfect time to leave, as I feel like I'm in their way anyway. "Doesn't really matter if I'm ready, does it?" I ask, pretending to smile. Lia shoots me a sympathetic look.

I flex my tennis-shoed foot out in front of me. "You think Taylor would go running with me?" I ask, watching my lime-green shoe.

"No, Nell, you're not using my brother as a replacement," Lia says. I cut my gaze to her, and she returns it, her face dead serious.

"Lia," Columbus chides her. He sits up straighter. "Nell, you probably don't want to hear this," he continues, looking over at me, "but he's currently a disaster in human form."

"Jackson?" I ask, though I still hate saying his name out loud, the way it sits on the edge of my tongue like a taunt.

"Look, whatever went down between you," he goes on, taking a second to look back at Lia as if for encouragement, "I don't know what it was exactly, but I know it was messed up. He's always done some stupid stuff, had a self-destructive streak or whatever, but now he just seems like he doesn't care about anything."

I keep my head down. "He never did."

"I don't think that's true," Columbus responds, a little defensive. "He meant well sometimes. I'd never tell you he was a perfect person, but there was good in there." He blinks, licking his lip. "I hope there still is."

"You don't owe me any explanations," I tell him.

"Someone sure as hell does," Lia chimes in. She puts her hand against his leg, holding on tight. It's nice. I only wish it didn't make me so sick to my stomach.

"All I know is I've never seen him like this," Columbus says, shaking his head. "Every. Night. He's out of control. Always wasted or with some girl—" He stops himself, glancing over at me.

I get up abruptly. I can't hear this. "I have to go," I say.

Lia looks up, surprised. "I'm sorry. I didn't mean what I said, about Taylor."

"I know," I answer, pushing my hair behind my ear.

"I'm sorry, too, Nell," Columbus says quickly. "I shouldn't have said any of that. I just meant, it's not worth it, you know?"

I push open the door with my toe, taking some pleasure in the scuff mark it leaves on the white paint. "Trust me, I've learned that lesson enough for a thousand lifetimes."

38

It's amazing how something you feel like you've been preparing for your whole life can just happen. You wake up one day and you're seventeen with the end of this godforsaken high school journey in sight. You're left wondering how something so arbitrary used to feel so important, wishing it was easier to care less.

That's how it feels walking into Cedar Woods Prep on the first day of senior year. Like I don't know the girl who walked out at the end of last year. I put on that crisp Oxford, slide on the plaid skirt, stare at that same girl in the mirror. I slept at home last night and woke up to my uniform laid out, ironed. Mom's work.

Some days I see her now, and I feel my whole body shudder, as if rejecting an essential organ.

As I walk through the doors of Cedar Woods Preparatory Academy, I find myself clenching and unclenching my hands, dreading the moment when the whole thing goes up in smoke.

We received class schedules last week, but every first day at Prep begins the same way, with a school assembly. And, as everything at Prep is an overblown production, there's no way out of it. Like being forced to attend your own funeral.

I catch up with Lia, Michonne, and the other volleyball seniors and we walk to the auditorium together. The ones of us who didn't play ball together during the summer are all *oh my gosh, tell me everything you did this summer*, and I do my best to stay on the fringes of the conversation, nodding along with Lia like we were absolutely on the same page the past three months.

When I finally sit down in the auditorium, my hands are shaking. I'm not ready for this.

Lia reaches over, putting her hand on mine. "Are you okay?"

I nod my head, even though I'm not sure. She clings to my fingers tightly, and I think *I love her so much.*

Mr. Rochester—dean of students—takes the stage to welcome us back to another wonderfully exciting and challenging year at Cedar Woods Prep. Usually, I hang on to every word of these ceremonies, but today, all I can think is that everyone will know. Everyone will see my vulnerabilities, written into my skin like a scar.

"And without further ado, please welcome Cedar Woods Preparatory Academy's head of school, Mrs. Mary Becker."

Mom comes out then in one of her perfectly tailored pantsuits. I can't help but watch; she looks the same as ever—beautiful, smart, ready for battle as needed. I still seek her out like a homing beacon, waiting to be called home. To myself.

I have to turn it off. That's not who she is. She's a fraud.

I'm a fraud.

"Welcome to another year," Mom says. "I want to especially welcome our incoming freshmen and rising seniors. You're going to see some highly accomplished individuals on this stage today, and it's important to remember they were all in your place at one time. Our seniors will go through a lot this year—a hard-fought battle for the top of the class, acceptances into college, the last moments of high school. Saying good-bye. We can only hope that we here at Cedar Woods have prepared them as they take the next step in their lives. I'm very excited to welcome some of our top senior classmen to the stage to take part in the traditional pinning ceremony. Mr. Rochester, if you wouldn't mind."

Of course he wouldn't mind. He's already standing by the table of pins, looking so damn pleasant. Mom starts with number ten in the class, listing off accomplishments as she goes.

Lia leaves when they call for Number Nine, and I watch as Doug makes his way up for Number Six, down to only a boot on his leg. And so the countdown goes.

"Eleanor Mary Becker," Mom reads off a piece of paper, looking up with a smile. "With a 4.876 GPA, captain of last year's lower-state runner-up Cedar Woods Lady Knights volleyball team, South Carolina All-State Volleyball player and Region Seven MVP, an active member of the Cedar Woods Guild and Beta Club, cochair of Cedar Woods Students for the Betterment of Mankind, Cedar Woods yearbook coeditor, National Merit Semifinalist, Honor Society, and National English Honor Society." I'm already up to the stairs by the time Mom gets done reading off my list of accomplishments. So many of them sound hollow in my own ears, meaningless padding. But that's Summer Nell talking. Each and every victory means something. It has to.

Dr. Rochester pushes the pin into the collar of my Oxford and I fake a smile as people applaud politely. I go to shake Mom's hand, too, which I do without ever meeting her eye, and then move to stand next to Number Three, Ellen Ng.

"And the current valedictorian for the rising senior class." Mom says like it doesn't pain her at all. "Nathaniel Jackson Hart the Second, with a GPA of 4.877, National Merit Semifinalist, and a member of the state champion Cedar Woods Knights baseball team." His list is short, pathetic in comparison to mine. But the applause doubles because who doesn't want a seemingly slacking guy to beat a girl who works her ass off for everything she gets?

I see him loping slowly up the aisle and I look down at the floor as if it's the most fascinating thing on the planet. It betrays weakness, but I don't feel ready to look him in the eye, not until I've secured my place on top again. Not until I have my edge back.

Besides, he doesn't deserve to meet my eyes.

He gets his pin and goes behind the rest of us to shake Mom's hand. She won't break because she's a damn pro. She can look him straight in the eye and not blink.

I want that.

I glance up and our eyes meet for the briefest of seconds before he comes to stand beside me. My hands are shaking again, but this time it is rage and not fear driving them. We're too close together, molecules displaced in the universe.

I stay there, frozen in hell as Mom finishes up and forces everyone to applaud us. When she lets us go, I take off from the stage so fast, I almost knock him over, and I don't stop. I keep going straight out the door and into the hallway. I turn one corner and then two to make sure no one can see me and then I command myself to breathe. To stay above water. To stay.

My mind is racing. It has been for the past two days, and I can't deny it any longer.

Nell. Breathe. Nell. Stay. Nell. Hang in there.

"Don't give anyone anything," I tell myself out loud, pressing my hands into my abdomen.

"Sounds about right," says a voice from the other end of the hallway. And he's right *there*. How is that a thing he can be? "We need to talk."

I can't believe the way he looks in his untucked Oxford and rumpled khakis, his tie knotted crooked. Carefree. Making a mockery of an honor.

For Jackson Hart, nothing is ever real.

"No one can see us."

He steps around me, giving a violent shake to the handle of a door on the other side of the hall, and it gives. He pushes it open with the toe of his scuffed shoe and waits for me to go in. I do it, head held high, and he follows me and closes the door behind us.

It's a janitor's closet. I hit the light switch and a dim bare bulb blinks to life overhead, lighting the contours of his face only enough for the familiarity of it to feel like a punch in the gut. The closet is small, way too small for us to be in together. There's hardly room for the few inches between our chests and I hate it. I hate that still after everything, I can feel the effect of his gaze all over.

"What do you want?" I ask, trying to remain as still as possible so that not one part of my skin chances to touch his.

"We can't be like this," he tells me. I catch something then, in the space between us. The smell of alcohol on his breath.

"Are you *drunk*?" I demand.

"No matter how much we both hate it, we have to live with each other for the rest of the year. All year," he says as if it pains him as much as it does me.

"Aren't I so damn blessed?" I bite back.

"I don't want this any more than you do," he tells me.

"Pretend I don't exist and I'll do the same." I reach for the door handle and he grabs my arm, but releases it as quickly when I set my eyes on him.

"You know how it is here, Nell," he says, and I *dare* him to let my name cross his lips again. "It's not going to work like that."

"Figure out a way to make it work like that," I hiss. "Isn't that what you told me—that ignoring things, pretending they never happened, was the way to survive this place? Pretend I never happened."

"Jesus Christ," he says. "You're so damn cold." His voice comes out different from before—more like I'm used to hearing.

I feel my heart pound. Once, then twice.

"Does anyone mean anything to you?" he asks. "Or are you always figuring out who will be most advantageous on your climb to the top?"

I suck in a breath. "We're still in the same place we've always been. And it still bothers you that I won't roll over and love you the way I'm supposed to."

He laughs. "Of course you don't. I'm only the guy you spent all summer fucking. Which, if we're honest, was just another means to an end for you."

I try and laugh back, match the cruelty. Double it. "You'd know all about that, wouldn't you? You've used so many girls for sex or approval or something. Don't shame me for getting what I want and please, just this once, spare me your sob story, Hart. The game is over."

I can't stop, not now that I've started. "You pretend you have everything, but you just keep hoping someone will finally really love you at last. Your friends are sick of your shit, your dad can't stand you, and your mom? Don't even get me started on how pathetic she is. No wonder you can't deal with a girl who has a backbone."

I think that's it. He's done. I hear him swallow, and my hand is turning the door handle when he speaks softly through the darkness. "You think you're so special."

"Make your point."

"I will say one thing for you, Becker. You act like you're some paragon of being top bitch in charge but I've never met another girl in my life who would do the things you did. I could walk out of this door right now and tell every guy in this school what we spent the summer doing, and you'd be the biggest slut at Prep by the end of the day. Is that, like, something you're proud of? Because it wasn't even to please me, was it? It's because it's what you wanted. I could get you a couple of thousand dates if you want. You could fuck your way through the school because I can guarantee they aren't getting that from any other girl here. An actual guarantee because I've done some sampling."

I'm holding the door handle so tight, my fingers have gone numb. "You wouldn't dare," I say, not turning in his direction.

"There you go again. Seriously underestimating what I would dare do."

"How much do you love that, huh? Holding it over me that you can run around doing whatever you want because you're a boy and my reputation is a ticking time bomb."

"More than you can imagine," he tells me. "Are you going to let me out?"

He puts his hand on top of mine, forcing me to open the door, and then pushes past me, fading away into the distance. I feel it under my skin, the rising panic. Of what he could do. Of what he has done.

Trying to be as subtle as I can, I escape to the closest restroom—a blessedly empty restroom—stuff the janitor's wedge under the opposite side of the door to keep everyone out, and let it all go, every ragged breath and panicked thought. I lock myself in the farthest stall, bent over with my hands on my knees. And then I throw up, which just makes me panic more. I sit on the ground catty-corner to the toilet and wrap my arms around my legs, panting.

I'm so angry he can make me feel this way. That he would call *me* a slut after everything he's done—after everything he told me he's done. There's no consequences for him, never anything that touches him. He'll always be everything Cedar Woods loves, no matter who he sleeps with, what he breaks. But I'll always just be a girl. And a girl who wants sex will never be anything but a slut. Despite everything else she is.

He's right. He can turn around and ruin my reputation without losing a step. Without suffering at all.

I'm *so angry*.

Someone taps on the outside of the stall and my eyes go to the door. The wedge is still jammed under the door to the bathroom. "Becker," a voice says.

I know that voice. I get up and open the door of the stall, using the back of the same hand to wipe my mouth.

It's Tristan Kaye, her black hair hanging limp around her pretty, perfect face.

"How did you get in here?" I ask, heading toward the sink and running the water. I look like something that was hit by a truck.

"I followed you. You suck at wedging the door and then you were vomiting so you didn't notice," she says cheerfully, "and then I put your sad little wedge back in place the right way so no one else will have to witness this."

"What do you want?" I ask, wetting a paper towel and rubbing it under my eyes, dark rings reflecting in the mirror, telltale signs of my sleepless nights. I look back at Tristan, tilting my head to the side. "Just to see the show?"

"Hardly."

"Right. Because no one wanted this to happen more than you did. So I'm sure you take *zero* pleasure in this."

"Fine," she says. "You want me to say I didn't like you. I didn't. But considering where we are now, I'd say that's neither here nor there. What the hell was that?" she asks, glancing back at the bathroom stall.

I brace myself, holding on to the counter in front of me. "I believe it's called a panic attack."

"Look, you need to steer clear of him," she says then, and I turn on her, my rage running over.

"So you can have him all to yourself? He's yours."

"Please," she says, waving a dismissive hand. "As if I would ever do that again. That shit," she says, pointing at the stall, "is why. You're somebody with something in this world. He's—I don't know. The way he is with girls right now . . . He used to at least, like, pretend to date them—it was fake but he played his part." She's staring straight at me. "There's nothing for you there, Nell. There never was. Whatever went down between you has made it that much worse. And trust me, you don't want to end up being hated by every girl in this school like me. I'm giving you a damn warning before you do something you really regret."

I stare at her, feeling smaller by the second. "Too late for that."

If Tristan could feel pity, I imagine that's what's behind her eyes. But I don't want that, either. I shoulder past her and into the hallway to face the day.

It shouldn't be a problem. I've seen worse.

39

The next morning, I crank up the speed on the treadmill because there's too much space to think in my head right now. I feel like the days are running together, only they can't be because I've been tallying them on my calendar, each and every one. Tracking myself. My workouts. My moods. *Me*. Constantly trying to grab back some control I've lost.

My feet pound the treadmill when I command them. They give in to me.

I try to clear my mind, keep moving, but it's tangled up in what Jackson said in that closet. What he implied.

Boys get to have it all. Girls are either sluts or saints.

The thoughts keep pushing in. I run faster.

"Nell," Mom said to me when I was fifteen, "did you hear what happened to Shauna Meyers this weekend?"

I looked up from my bowl of cereal. I was light-years apart from the Shauna Meyerses of the world. The parties and boats and blank, easy smiles.

"No."

"Apparently she blacked out at Jordan Allen's house. There's pictures and videos of her all over social media."

My heart clenched. "Is she okay?" I asked.

"She only made a fool of herself, thank God. Rebecca Hart took her home so no one would take advantage of her. That girl is too smart—if she hadn't been so concerned with smoking her way through high school, she'd be on her way to Stanford and not UC Riverside."

I continued eating my cereal, thinking about what those boys could have done to Shauna. What boys like them do every day. "She didn't deserve that," I said. "Shauna's a nice girl."

"I'll tell you right now, my dear, being nice gets you nowhere in this world. I've known too many Shaunas." She leaned down in my face, hesitating. "It's not Shauna's fault, but . . . when you're a girl alone in this world, you have to be smart. Keep your guard up. If you let it down, they'll always be right there, ready. They'll always take advantage."

My treadmill alarm goes off and I nearly jump out of my skin, my heart pounding furiously against my chest, my mom's words singing to me across time. I wipe my hand across my cheek, clearing away the sweat. I need to take a shower and get ready for class, but I can't stand the thought of the quiet, not when there's a scream ripping through my chest.

Keep moving. Nell. Keep going.

I grab my towel, running it over my face as I head toward the locker room. The soccer girls have an away game tonight so it's a ghost town, and I don't run into anyone on my way to throw up. *Again*, the silence reminds me, but I ignore it as I exit the toilet stall to rinse my mouth. I stop as I see myself in the mirror above the sink, my nerves frayed to breaking point. Wide eyes, slender nose, hair flying all around me, sweaty and dark. How long had it taken me to build that confidence behind my eyes, develop that shield? It looks faded now, almost gone completely. I feel abandoned. I feel different.

My body doesn't *look* any different from how it normally does, of course. Too tall with shoulders too broad. A figure that will never be petite or quite feminine enough. Before, I never particularly hated or loved my body, I just knew what it was. It was for something very particular—made to be pushed, made so I could be a winner. I loved what it did for me. Who it allowed me to be.

Ever since the thing with Jackson started—from the first time he touched my shoulder in the gym—I'd been sure. I always trusted my body completely.

Add it to growing list of things that have betrayed me.

I feel tears well up in my eyes and jump when I hear the locker room door open. "Nell," Lia's voice calls from the front room. "Nell, are you in here?"

I take a deep breath to calm myself, stepping out to meet her, my sweaty hair sticking to my neck. I don't look good. "What are you doing here?"

"I brought you a biscuit from Grady's," she says, handing over the greasy package from my favorite diner. But she stops when she gets a better look at me. "Christ, Nell," she says in that worried voice she's always using, as if I am someone who must be taken care of. "Are you okay?"

I look away from her so she won't see my eyes.

"What is it?" she asks.

I run my hand over my face.

"Is it Jackson? What did he do?" she asks, even more urgently.

"I did this," I tell her.

"*What*, Nell?" she demands. The panic in her voice hurts more than anything.

A tear creeps out from under my eyelid as I say it. "I'm late," I tell her.

She goes completely silent and another tear forms. I grab a paper towel, trying to avoid her gaze at all costs.

I can feel her working up to it. Then finally, "But you always used condoms, right?"

I look up at her, the tears flowing more freely now. "Yes, except for—" And then I completely lose it and she doesn't make me finish but pulls me into her shoulder, letting my tears soak into her pristine light blue shirt. I don't want to hurt like this. I want to shut it down, and it's only a feeling—turning it off can't be that hard.

"It's fine. It's going to be fine," she says, running a hand over my back. Then she pulls away, looking up at me. "Come on. We need to go take a test right now. You should clean up."

I stop, pause. Feel the words coming before I give them thought. "I can't." I go over to my locker and open it, slipping into a pair of shower flip-flops, wiping at my tear-streaked face. "I have to go to class. It's too important."

She stands in front of me, bewildered. "You can't *go to class*. Look at you. You're barely functional."

"There's nothing we can do right now," I tell her reasonably, my back to her as I crumple up my shirt, throwing it violently into the locker on top of my running shoes. "If I'm pregnant, I'll still be pregnant tomorrow." I wish I hadn't said it out loud. It seems to mar me, break down the myth I'd built for myself. Prove that I let myself lose control of my story.

My body is mine my body is mine my body is mine.

I can't face the alternative.

"So when do you plan to deal with this?" she asks. I hear her getting angry, losing patience with me.

I grab my shower bag and turn to face her. "When we don't have class," I say. "Can I please just take a shower?"

I try to shut it out, but I can hear my mom's voice pounding in my head. *Smart girls don't get pregnant. Smart girls don't get tricked by a rich boy with a nice smile.*

"I'm not stopping you," Lia says. She shoots me a look that promises she's not done as I turn away from her and head to the shower. But she tries one last plea. "Please don't do this to yourself," she calls behind me. I close my eyes, turning the spigot and letting the hot water burn everything away.

• • •

Lia catches me at my locker as I'm getting ready to leave the next afternoon. I've been avoiding her all day and am heading out early, our afternoon volleyball practice canceled. My avoidance has nothing to do with her and everything to do with the fact that she reminds me what I'm running from. I've become so adept at compartmentalizing since the end of summer, but her blue eyes burn right into me, not letting me forget or pretend any longer.

I'm getting so good at it.

As soon as I see Lia, it becomes clear she's not willing to play this waiting game any longer. "We need to talk," she says.

I lean into the locker next to my open one, plastering on a playful look. "Are you breaking up with me?" I ask.

Lia's not amused. She holds a plastic bag out to me. "Take this."

I grab it out of her hand and glance inside, closing it again just as quickly and thrusting it back to her. It's a pregnancy test. "Are you serious?" I ask, my voice as soft as I can make it.

"Nell, take the damn test. I cannot *believe* you're trying to ignore this. I haven't seen you eat a meal since we've been back at school."

I step closer to her, trying to hide the bag between the two of us. "Why are you doing this to me? What if someone saw me with this?"

"I don't know. They'd realize you're not fucking perfect? You think this has never happened to anyone else at this school?"

I turn away from her. "I'm not everyone else."

She sighs, impatient. "It doesn't suddenly become not true if you don't think about it."

I feel myself disappearing and try to grab hold, protect myself. "Stop it."

"I'm just trying to help," she says. "I don't understand why you think you're so much better than the rest of us. You made a mistake. *Everyone* makes mistakes, and they deal with them."

I close my eyes, breathe in deeply. "If you really want to help," I say at last, "leave me the hell alone." I slam my locker shut and turn to her.

We both go quiet, staring at each other in a face-off. I ball my fist

252

into the edge of my skirt, holding on desperately. Holding on to everything left.

It can't be real.

"I need to go," I say at last.

Her eyes flash. "Goddammit, Nell."

"Make sure no one sees you with that," I mutter as I take off.

I'm out in the parking lot so fast, I'm not sure if I ran or not.

My instinct, as ever, is to keep moving. I'm on my way to my car to go God knows where when I spot Taylor sitting in his SUV. Through the windows, I hear the music and see him playing an imaginary drum set against his steering wheel. He doesn't notice me as I approach and jumps when I knock on the passenger's-side window. I pull open the door when he signals for me to get in, sitting next to him as he turns down the loud classic rock he'd been listening to.

"You're good," I tell him, eyes scanning his dash.

He shrugs. "I try." He's looking over at me. "You okay, Nell?"

"I've been better," I admit, returning his gaze. "I've been doing what you said. Faking it. Putting on a show."

"I never would've guessed," he tells me, and I think it's supposed to be a compliment. I push my hair back. "You always look perfect and that's all he sees."

I take a shaky breath. "What about you? What are you doing out here?"

"Killing time until practice," he says. Taylor's on the cross-country team in the fall—not because he's a particularly good runner but because he needs to fill out his college résumé and it's not a good idea for pitchers to play contact sports like football.

That's the thing about us Prep kids—it's not about what we like. It's about what we have to do.

"You want to go to the river?" I ask after a minute.

Taylor turns the key in the ignition. "Let's go," he says.

And that's how we end up down by the bank. We're standing

beside the water together in our uniforms. It's still warm but there's a breeze in the air, unusual for this late in August. I slide off my flats, poking my toes into the cold water. I shiver and pull back.

"Do you want to talk about it?" Taylor asks after a moment.

I don't. Some part of me wants to go back to before Jackson, to before Mom, to live in that world I don't believe in anymore. But I think about that time and wonder if it's all the same misery with different perspectives. It's only looking into the water that I see something like truth. I've lost everything; I can't lose me.

I want to come out on the other side. Clean.

"Let's go out to the docks," I say, pointing to the floating dock out in the water.

Taylor glances at me with one eyebrow raised. The wind blows his curly hair into his face. "I don't have a bathing suit."

"Me neither," I say, unbuttoning my Oxford and tossing it off; it falls onto the riverbank where the water runs over it. I watch Taylor's eyebrows continue their upward journey as I dash out into the water in my tank top and skirt. It takes a little extra work to swim in the skirt, but I'm an athlete. I pull up to the dock pretty quickly and climb out of the cold water, wringing the water from my thick skirt. I lie back against the deck and a few moments later, Taylor surfaces, the sun reflecting off his pale chest as he pulls himself over the side and tilts the deck precipitously with his weight. He sighs.

"I'm taking my pants off," he says, and I laugh out loud by accident, a sound I've become unfamiliar with cutting through the silence. He stands up on the deck and starts undoing his soaking khaki pants, sliding them down his legs until he's left in a pair of boxers covered in jalapeños.

"Shut up," he warns.

Once I've started laughing, I can't stop.

Finally, he spreads the pants out to dry and lies down on the deck right next to me, putting his arms behind his head. My hair hangs over the edge. We stay like that, in silence.

"Do you see me differently now?" I ask Taylor after a while. My eyes are closed and the world is still. I feel him shift beside me.

"What do you mean, 'now'?" he asks.

I think about that for a minute before I say, "Since Jackson. I can't help but feel like everyone who knows—even your sister—sees me as, like, someone something *happened* to. Not interesting enough for my own story, just a page in someone else's. I don't know."

"Do you see yourself differently?" he asks.

"In some ways, I guess," I tell him. "Like I got fooled. Another girl who fell for a boy's lies. Like during weight training last year, I felt like I fit in automatically. I was sure, confident. I never would've let something like Jackson get in my way. I was *different* and now . . ." I trail off, trying to send all the thoughts to the back of my brain.

"There's no you and them, Nell." I feel his eyes on me. "That's never how I saw you at all. You've always been Nell to me. . . . Stop trying to be someone you think you're supposed to be. You're you."

"No one deserves this," I say after a moment. I close my eyes against the sun, thinking of them. Mr. Hart. Jackson. Our mouths. Mom's hand touching Mr. Hart's. Us laughing. The boat. After the boat. I feel Taylor's hand on mine.

"They'll always take advantage," I tell him, repeating my mother's words back to myself. "He called me a slut." I open my eyes. Taylor stares at me, disgusted.

"I'll kill him," he says, sitting up straight.

"It'd just be what he wanted," I say, and Taylor stares at me, eyes hard against mine. "Jackson knows—he always knows exactly the best way to dig into you."

I look up at the sky, thinking. In competition, you find your opponent's weakness and try to exploit it. Jackson knew that better than anybody, studied people like a book, pulling them apart at their edges.

He knows what I care about. Control.

But him. His weakness is want. It's always been want. Wanting to win, wanting to be seen, wanting to be good. In odd moments, I still find myself trying to live in his head, be him. But I think too much.

At the end of the day, I'll always just be a girl.

And he'll still be the boy who has everything.

40

We spend the rest of the afternoon lying side by side on the dock, and only return to the shore as the sun begins its retreat from the sky. Taylor doesn't even say anything about missing cross-country practice.

"What are you doing tonight?" he asks as he buttons his white shirt back up. He saved my shirt, too—from the watery grave I had hoped would claim it—but I don't put it back on.

"Studying," I say automatically. It's Friday night. The football game is away so I don't have yearbook duty, and Coach Madison gave us the day off.

Taylor gives me a look. "You're not studying," he says, as if that's the most ridiculous thing he's ever heard.

"I've got a couple of quizzes coming up next week. I need to keep up with my reading," I say, rolling my shoulders as the anxiety the water had washed away creeps back in.

"You can take one night off."

"And do what?" I ask.

"Well . . . ," he begins, his face immediately turning apologetic. "There's a party at Alston Marcus's house."

"Taylor."

"I don't know. He doesn't own this town, right? He doesn't own you. Why should you hold back just because he'll be there?"

I shut my eyes tight. Something about going to Alston's feels dangerous, but running is getting pretty tiring. From him. From what's happened. From a truth I don't want to face.

Maybe at Alston's, I could be somebody else again.

And then maybe after, I could face who I'd become.

• • •

It's early when we pull up at Alston's—Taylor, a begrudging Lia, and me. Early enough that we get a parking spot right in front of the house. And I'm staring at this stupid house, thinking it's a perfect microcosm of everything about this town. Every weekend there's a party at Alston Marcus's house because nothing ever changes here. You keep showing up at the same place every weekend, drinking the same beer, and trying to kiss the same people, lost in the same patterns.

Because even if there were no Alston Marcus, there would always be an Alston Marcus.

I've never actually seen Alston before, but he's there on the front porch when we walk in, mixing up jungle juice in an oversized cooler. My nose wrinkles in disgust at the sight of it. He's a big, burly guy, almost too big for the crumbling porch, but he looks like a teddy bear when he smiles. He's also wearing a hemp necklace and drinking kombucha. "It's important to properly hydrate," he tells us solemnly.

"What do you want?" Taylor asks me, reaching to pull a beer out of an ice-filled kiddie pool near Alston's feet.

I shake my head. "I'm fine."

Taylor gives me a look but doesn't say anything as he pops the top on his beer.

I hang back with Lia as Taylor steps through the threshold into the house. I hold out a pinkie to her. "I'm sorry about earlier," I say. "Truce?"

She looks from my hand to my eyes. "Promise," she says. "Tonight. Promise you'll take the test."

I resist the instinct to recoil. "I promise."

"Nothing changes between us either way," she tells me, and then she wraps her pinkie finger around mine and we walk in side by side.

The kitchen looks bigger without all the people inside. Doug and Michonne are standing around the island with Taylor, all taking a shot together.

"Hey, Nell," Doug says, subdued, as if he's not sure how to talk to me. Taylor gives him a look and then shudders like the liquor is hitting him all over again.

Michonne gives me a scrutinizing once-over. I'd bailed on lunch every day this week, so I want to make it up to her.

"Let's go downstairs," I say, grabbing on to her hand and pulling her behind me. "We can pick the music. C'mon, Reagan."

He follows obediently, playing the part of protector he loves so much. But once I open the door, music is already blasting. It almost knocks us down as we take the stairs into the basement.

I should've known—somehow known—what I'd be walking into.

I know that soft dark hair and that hand splayed against the wall next to a girl I've never seen before. I know the way his head moves when he kisses someone, and worse, when he looks up and sees us, I know that glassy look in his eyes that means he's not really there at all.

The girl giggles, covering her mouth with her fingers. I feel Taylor's hand wrap around my arm.

Jackson's eyes don't leave mine as he drops his hand from next to her and marches over to where the three of us are standing, frozen.

"What are you doing here?" he asks me, pushing his hair back out of his face. His hands don't stop once they've started.

I keep my voice even. "It's a party."

"What's your problem?" Michonne asks, looking him up and down.

"It's a party," I repeat, my words clipped. "And I get to be here."

Jackson looks from Taylor to Michonne and then to me. "May I speak with you privately?" he asks.

"No," I answer. Then I can't help it. I shake my head. "I can't believe you."

"Just let me—" He puts his hand up like he's going to touch me and Taylor shoves him away.

"I think that's enough," he says, his voice lightly menacing.

Jackson steps back, his eyes glazed over, looking at Taylor. He sighs deeply. "I think you're right," he says at last.

And then he walks around the three of us and up the stairs, not looking at the girl again.

"Hey!" she calls after him.

My practiced calm deserts me, my heart hammering in my chest. I shake off Taylor and Michonne and escape, upstairs and back outside where there's oxygen by the ratty old swing set in Alston's front yard. I have to find Lia.

"Old habits die hard." It's his voice in the dark, a tenor that makes me shiver involuntarily, my body responding like one of Pavlov's dogs. Jackson Hart. "Always trying to run away."

He pulls against the rusty bar holding the swing set together. I take a step back, my arms crossed protectively. I should've guessed he'd find me out here; he always finds me.

"Don't act like you know me," I say, because at this moment I really have no idea what I might do if I have to spend another moment with him, and that scares me a little.

"I like to run, too," he continues. He puts his hands in his pockets. "Just give me a minute. Look, I get that you must hate me, but I just need you to know that I didn't—"

"No," I cut him off, my mind suddenly clearing. "No, you don't," I say, and I feel like I've just stepped onto the court. I push forward again, nearer to him. "You have no idea how much I hate you. How watching you suffer would give me the most intense kind of pleasure imaginable. You threaten my reputation and you threaten every-fucking-thing I've worked for in this world and you think you have a single idea of how much I hate you?"

He swallows. "I know."

"No, you don't!" I scream. I want to scare him. I want him to feel what I feel, this ache cutting through me every day. The way I'm being torn apart.

"I think I'm pregnant."

Those are the words that change everything. The bored way he's standing and the faraway look in his eyes vanishes and he suddenly jerks forward and feels *much* closer to me. "You *think*?"

I swallow, command myself to maintain my composure. "Yes."

"Jesus Christ," he says. "Jesus Christ." He runs his fingers through his hair. Again. And again. "I thought we always— Shit, the boat? Weren't you going to . . ." But even he can't make himself finish saying it because there's a limit to that kind of gall.

"I got a little distracted," I tell him, keeping my voice neutral. And I see it then, his weakness. "In case you don't remember, my judgment was clouded around that time."

He takes a deep breath in and out. He struggles, caught the way I have been.

"Okay," he says at last. "Okay. You can't be *sure*." He stands stock-still, like he can't even make himself move.

And the truth is, I can't make myself say it. That I'm not sure. Not when I have the power.

"I have to go," I say, and he lifts his hand toward me.

"Nell—wait—"

I hold my spine straight and I take so much pleasure in my height then, in how close we are to matching up face-to-face.

"There's nothing you can say, Jackson. *It doesn't matter.* If the world ended tomorrow, I'd pray more than anything that you survived because that would be too easy of an out for you." The rage creeps back into my voice. "If I'm still here, all I want is you along with me so I can watch you suffer."

He swallows, his Adam's apple going up and down.

"So, no, don't presume to know how I feel. Don't follow me. Don't even *look* at me. Stop, Jackson! Just stop!"

And I can feel I'm about to cry angry tears, and he's standing there like he has no idea what to say, how he's going to try and trick me this time, and I want to *run run run*—

I head in the direction of the road, walking away as if with purpose, and he doesn't call after me the way someone who always has a game plan would.

Then I do hear someone calling my name. Running toward me.

It's Lia. She catches up to me and is quiet because she knows— she can tell. She slides her hand into mine and squeezes.

"Let's go home," she says.

41

"It's negative," Lia tells me.

I fall back against the wall of Lia's bathroom in relief. I'm sitting on the floor, the lowest place I can reach. Lia sits next to me and wraps both arms around me, holding on tight. I sit still, letting her do what she needs to, my mind continuing to spin. Finally she says, "You should do another one. Just to be safe. I'm sure it's right but . . ."

I nod, not really listening to her.

"You know, nothing means anything to him," I say instead.

"I know," she answers darkly.

"I'm going to destroy him." I stare ahead, the words coursing through me, filling up the empty space left behind.

She hesitates. "Nell . . ."

"Just this once, he needs to lose something real." I glance at her. "He needs to have consequences. It's not just about me. Think of all the girls he treats like they don't matter." I close my eyes. "Jesus, I used to think his room was our holy ground, Lia. No telling how many girls he's ruined there. But that's not me, and I can't *let* him."

"Nell," she tries again, her voice perfectly calm. "You've got to put him behind you. You can do that now. There's no good that's going to come from having anything else to do with him and you know that. You can't save the world from people like Jackson."

I stare up at the pregnancy test on the counter. I remember the way he walked up to the stage. In my spot. On my stage. Sloppy. Drunk. The things he said to me in the closet. The way he kissed that girl at the party tonight. Because it didn't matter at all to him.

"He called me a slut," I say. "He wanted me to hate myself. He wants us all to hate ourselves. It makes his life easier."

Lia takes a deep breath, as if restraining herself. "He knows what he is. You don't have to sink down to his level." She spins around in front of me, kneeling down and pushing my hair back from my face. "This is all going to be a distant memory soon."

She's looking so hopeful, I have no choice but to give her what she wants. "I know," I say at last. "It's all still so raw. I don't want other people to have to feel this way."

"Me neither," she agrees, grabbing on to either side of my head and pressing her forehead against mine. "Love you, Nell."

"Love you, Lia," I answer, more robotically than I mean to, and when she pulls away, we pinkie swear on it again.

42

It's Saturday. It's Saturday and I should tell Jackson that I was wrong. It's a relief, I know, but I hate thinking of his voice on the other side of the phone, the way he might draw his words out lazily. The way he might tell Tristan and Doug and pop beer tops to celebrate the victory.

I can't stop feeling sick to my stomach.

There's a knock on the front door and I sit up, going to answer it. No one comes without warning around here.

But it's him, as if summoned here by my thoughts. It's Jackson standing in front of me with a grocery bag and a determined look on his face. "Come on," he says, walking past me into the foyer.

"Get the *hell* out of my house," I tell him. My mind, outside of my control, flashes to the day of the concussion. How can he be that person and this person, all rolled into one? I wanted to protect him or shelter him. And every time I had let that instinct take over me, he had played me again.

"I'm sorry," he says. "I've been driving by for the past hour and a half, waiting for your parents to leave. Dad said he has a lunch meeting, so I kind of figured," he says, his voice completely breezing over the implication that our parents are still screwing. "We need to make sure you weren't getting a false positive or something. That can happen, I've been reading about it. And we're not doing this at school."

"Oh yeah, wouldn't want any of those girls who have been drooling all over you to find out there might be some extra baggage to deal with."

"Don't go there," Jackson says to me. "I can only imagine how you would feel if someone at school got wind of this. I was trying to respect your privacy." He thrusts the bag out to me. "I bought the test."

I laugh. "Wait. *You* don't believe *me*? Are you joking?"

"It's not like that," he tells me. "Look, they can be wrong. This is for both of us to know for sure."

"You don't think I took three tests?" I ask him.

"I know you did," he says, sitting down on a decorative chair in our foyer and resting his forearms on his thighs. "Can you please just do it?"

"Fine," I say, going into our guest bathroom and slamming the door behind me.

Shit.

I stare at myself in the mirror, waiting for my own reflection to tell me to do what I know I should. But she looks just as clueless and desperate as I am.

I could take the test. Let him have his way, tell him he was right and say I got a false positive. But that feels hollow. If I refuse to do it, he'll just label me as crazy. I should tell him—tell him now that it's not happening. That I took the tests and they were negative.

It's like everything else in his life, coming together the way he wills it. I can't be pregnant because everything that Jackson Hart does is part of a plan he's been constructing. And it doesn't matter if he's lying or cheating or hurting anyone else, it will turn out in Jackson's favor.

But I'm a person. Not a pawn to be maneuvered and not a mess to clean up.

And the truth of the matter is, Jackson knows me. He knows what I care most about in life, and he knows the one thing I would never let him see.

So I dig my fingernails into my palms until my eyes water, and I let myself live through it. Every ugly thought and broken promise and lie someone's told me in the past four months. That moment, waiting for the pregnancy test yesterday, when I thought I had finally fucked up bad enough that I'd ruined everything.

All of it all of it all of it.

And then I'm crying. Crying until my throat's raw, until my head hurts. I'm tearing myself apart, outside in for a change.

It's a second later before I hear Jackson outside the bathroom, tapping on the door. "Nell, are you okay?" he asks, though he has to hear me wailing. I try to stop, wiping the back of my hand over my mouth. He pushes open the door. "Jesus, shit," he says, as I reach up to flush the toilet for show and fall back against the cold tile of the bathroom floor, pushing my head against the wall and crossing my arms over my stomach.

"I thought I was going to be sick," I lie, my voice thick. "I have been all day and I just . . . another test? I lost it. Sorry."

He takes another step into the bathroom and I see him glance at the counter and then at me. "What are we going to do?" he asks at last, defeat in every line of his body. I can feel my heart pounding. I may actually be sick but that may be worth it.

My breaths become shallower as I try to rein myself in, but now that I've started crying it's hard to stop. My cheeks feel hot, splotchy, my hair sticking to my neck. I can only imagine how I must look to him.

Broken. Like he wanted.

"You mean, what am *I* going to do, because this doesn't seem like any of your business."

"Look," he begins. "I know you don't want me here and I don't begrudge you that. I am the biggest jackass of all jackasses, which I know only touches on how you feel about me. But I'll support whatever you want to do, okay? I'm not going to leave you hanging."

I laugh bitterly.

"*Nell*," he says, and God, it's wrong but I love hearing the desperation in his voice.

"I haven't decided what I'm going to do yet." I put my hand over my mouth, pulling myself back together. "I still think I'm going to be sick. Can you go?"

"I'm worried about what this means. For the future. For both of us." He tries coming closer, like he might think he's allowed to be near me again, so I put my hand up.

"Great. Well, the good news is that you're a guy," I say. The more I talk, the more the lines of truth and lie, fiction and reality start to blur. "You can do whatever you want. They'll say boys will be boys and sweep it under the rug. You can leave, go off to the wonderful future you know you're destined for with half the work I've done. Hell, I'm sure there will be girls who are really attracted to the 'hot single dad' thing." I look toward him, a tear creeping down my face. "I think your future is fine, Jackson."

He has the decency to look ashamed.

I stare back down at my lap.

"I don't care about me," he insists. "But you have *everything* to lose. Everything you've worked your entire life for. And I can't be the reason behind that. Not when you're everything you are. To hell with me. What about *you?*"

"Don't play that card with me," I tell him. "You gave sooooo many fucks about me when you were putting your hands on whatever you could get below the Mason-Dixon for the past month. Don't even try to pressure me."

"I didn't— Shit, Nell," he says. "Please don't cut me out, that's all I'm saying. Have you even talked to your parents?"

"Of course not," I snap at him.

"I just want to make sure—"

"I don't need you," I tell him.

"I *know*, you never needed me, but I—" and apparently he doesn't know because that's where he stops.

"I need space to think. Go," I say.

"Can I at least make sure you get in bed before—"

"You're not a good person," I tell him, and he winces, hard, like that hurt. I press my sweaty face into my knee. "And nothing you say is going to change my mind. Leave."

I hear him shuffle to the door and then stop. I hope he's not looking at me. I'm glad *I* can't see me.

"I'm sorry," he says, and I wait to hear him leave, the echo of the front door closing.

I'm going to be sick.

43

That night, I'm lying on the chaise longue on Columbus's back deck staring up at the stars painted against the sky. Columbus's parents aren't home and he and Lia disappeared twenty minutes ago. Someone's deep, mournful voice is warbling out from the speakers.

I stare up at my fingers, tracing the stars one to the next on a clear path.

The silence is like a buzz all around me. I hear accusations in each call of the crickets.

Liar.

Pathetic.

Loser.

Sad sad sad.

They all sing. If I lie here too much longer, I will finally lose my mind.

I push myself out of the chair and bang down the steps of the deck, walking around the house, springing on my toes to fake movement, tugging at the ends of my hair. *Don't think Nell don't think Nell don't think.*

I hear the back door open and blow out a breath. "Nell! You ready?" Lia yells for me. "We're going."

"Over here!" I call out.

"Lia," Columbus says behind her, as if he's the voice of reason. Lia comes stomping down the stairs and Columbus—a foot taller than her—follows behind. "I didn't mean anything."

"I'm calling Taylor to come get us," Lia says, stopping in front of me. "Wouldn't want to have my bad blood in Columbus's car."

"You know that's not what I meant," he says. "Lia."

"I don't need your holier-than-thou shit!" she spits back, holding her phone in front of her face. "I know what my family is, and I know what yours is. Jesus *Christ*, pick up your phone, Taylor." She's on the verge of tears, and I see the first one escape, shining down her face. I rush over.

"Lia," Columbus says calmly. "Lia."

"Hey, Columbus doesn't think your family has bad blood," I tell her, touching the ends of her hair. She grabs at me and pulls herself into my side, crying quietly against my T-shirt. Columbus watches the two of us as I press my face against her hair.

"I don't, Lia," he says carefully. "I think you're the best person in all of Cedar Woods."

She snorts. "Don't lie to me, Columbus Proctor."

A shadow of a grin plays on his face. "Lia." He tugs on her shoulder, pulls her away from me. She looks down down down and then looks up at him. "There she is," he says, smiling. I want to look away. Things like this, they don't happen. Not to girls like me.

Just another reminder that I should've known better.

She's so tiny next to him, like I'd never be. He pushes her hair back, his fingers splayed out across her petite, pale face and then he has to lean down to kiss her, and I don't know, she's my best friend. She looks out for me.

Part of me doesn't want anyone else to have her.

"All right." Lia pulls away. "C'mon, we need to get home."

"You got it," Columbus says.

I climb into the backseat of Columbus's extremely nice SUV. He heads out, turning the music up on his stereo, reaching over to grab Lia's hand across the console. Even though they're on the same side of the bridge, Columbus's house is farther from town than Lia's, almost on the edge of the county. As we drive toward the Reagans' house, Columbus fishes his phone from his pocket. "Hang on. I'm getting a call." He turns down the radio, pops in a Bluetooth headset, and answers with a less-than-enthusiastic "What?"

He listens and then answers, his jaw tightening. "He did *what*? Right now? Rivera, I've got—" He glances over at me and cuts himself off. "Let me take Lia home first— Seriously? And I'm supposed to drop everything and come now? Y'all should just leave him there. Let his ass get arrested." A beat. "*Fine*. Shit." And then he pulls the headset down from his ear, looking tired.

"What is it?" I ask, watching him in the front seat.

"I've gotta go get him, Nell. I'm sorry." And I know exactly who he's talking about.

"You aren't," Lia breathes.

Columbus takes a deep breath. "You don't know what his dad will do to him."

I close my eyes and take a deep breath. Lia pulls her hand away from Columbus, clenching it in a tight fist.

Columbus isn't driving for long before I figure out we're headed in the direction of Alston Marcus's house—of course. It's a weekend night in Cedar Woods, an event playing on a loop.

I've never even believed Jackson liked parties at Alston Marcus's house. It was just another place to be, another part to play.

Fifteen minutes later, Columbus pulls up to the street outside of the house, the yard packed with cars as always. Off to the side, I see shadows holding someone between them. It doesn't take much to figure out the smaller, lithe frame is Tristan and the bulkier one is Doug. Columbus unbuckles his seat belt, shaking his head as he gets out and goes over to meet them. I watch as Columbus fusses at the other two, then looks down at Jackson like the sad excuse for a human being he is.

He puts Jackson's arm around his neck and walks him toward the car, opening up the door and pushing him into the backseat next to me, where he kind of falls sadly forward. Lia looks over her shoulder at him like some sort of offensive stain on the leather.

"He hit Marcus," Columbus tells us apologetically. "Someone called the cops. Doug and Tristan can't drive. He was supposed to be their ride. He's belligerent again. I couldn't leave him." His last words are somber as he looks behind him at the miserable form of a boy who is his best friend because you can't shut that off.

Jackson turns his head against his seat, his eyes falling on me, glazing over like he's not sure if I'm real. "Nell," he whispers, seemingly finding talking particularly challenging.

Columbus turns the music up in the front seat, trying to drown out Jackson's words, but I can practically read his lips, can feel the way my body comes to life when his eyes are on me.

"Every time I see you, I start counting the minutes between," he whispers then, so close I find myself leaning in to hear him. I dig my nails into my fist until I feel my pulse in my fingertips. "When I know you're going to disappear all over again."

"Shut the hell up back there," Columbus says, his voice a warning. "I will drop you off on the side of the road." He cranks the music up even louder, rattling the windows.

"You're supposedly so obsessed with me," I tell him, and he watches me, as if mesmerized. "But every time I see you, you're all over another girl."

Jackson lies back against his seat, pressing the heels of his hands into his eyes. Then he turns his head toward me, watching me quietly, not looking away.

"Stay," he says. His hand falls open between us. "Please stay."

I stare back at him, my eyes welling, the music banging in my ears. "You're so drunk." A tear starts to fall and I wipe it away with the pad of my finger before it escapes. "I could be anyone."

He curls his fingers up into his palm. "Of course you're not."

Columbus glances behind him when he hears Jackson speaking again, seeing the state we're in. "Hart, stop!" he yells at him, jerking him away from me. "You've got no damn shame, man."

Jackson pulls away from me and closer to the door, grabbing up his shirt to rub against his face. He shoves forward onto the middle console, taking Columbus by surprise, and punches the radio knob. Silence devours the pounding music. "Tell her about the girls," Jackson says to Columbus.

"I'm not telling her shit," Columbus replies, the cold cutting through his baritone voice.

"I didn't want to have to think anymore, Nell. The last person I want to be alone with is myself."

"Columbus, make him stop," Lia orders.

"I'm a walking catastrophe," he goes on. "I'd destroy myself, and my dad, too, Nell, if I could change this. I'd fix it for you and anything else. I want you to do everything you want to do. You deserve that. You don't deserve what's happening."

"You *are* destroying yourself," Columbus says. Then to me: "Nell, I'm so sorry; we're almost at his house."

"I don't know what to do," Jackson continues as if no one else is here. "I feel like I'm drowning."

"*Stop*," I say, because he can't tell Columbus and Lia about my lie. They don't know the girl in that version of my life, and she's too crazy for me to show them.

"I wish I hated you," he says.

I blink. "It's not so hard."

"We're here," Columbus says, slamming on the brakes at the end of Jackson's driveway, refusing to drive up it. He unlocks the doors. "Walk."

Jackson opens his door and practically falls out of it, struggling to regain his balance as he moves toward his driveway. I'm doubtful he's going to make it.

"Do you think we should help him?" Lia asks, sounding a little concerned.

I turn away. "No."

No one answers that.

I can feel them, judging me and trying not to judge me, and I hear myself without really thinking about what I'm saying. "I know you both think I should feel bad for him, but his self-destructive streak is just another way he can get what he wants." I breathe fog onto the back window and draw a heart. "Everyone feels sorry for him because he acts so hurt and he's a boy, but I keep up my armor to survive, and then I'm the bad guy. It's never enough for anyone, is it?"

"No one thinks that," Lia says, but I hear the lie in her voice.

Columbus turns his car around in silence and drives us back to Lia's, giving her a peck on the lips before we get out. Lia walks into the house with me, quiet. Her parents are either not awake or not home when we get there. All I see is the light on in Taylor's room.

Lia and I are together in her bathroom brushing our teeth. She spits out her toothpaste and looks at me sideways. "What did you do to Jackson?"

I pause brushing my teeth, watching her sideways. "What did *I* do to him?"

Lia puts her toothbrush back on its stand. "The way he was talking about fixing everything for you and how you didn't deserve what was happening. What was he talking about?"

I spit into the sink, too, washing off my toothbrush under the faucet. "He was shithoused!" At the look she's giving me, I look away, shrugging. "Maybe he grew a conscience."

"It felt different than that. He sounded scared. I almost felt bad for him."

"*Why?*" I demand.

Lia crosses her arms, staring at me in the mirror.

"So what did you do?" she asks. She's watching me too carefully and she knows me too well.

"I did what he does." I look down. "I looked at the pieces on the table, assessed what I had, and made a move."

She puts her hands up, looking like she's holding something back. "So help me God, do not bullshit me right now, Nell. Did you tell him you were pregnant?" Her voice is so quiet, it feels deadly.

I don't meet her eye in the mirror. "I just said I thought I was. I *did* think I was. That's it."

"And then? You told him you took the test?"

I shrug.

She takes a deep breath, reaching her hand up as if to steady herself. Finally she says, "You have completely lost it."

"Don't do that," I say, though my defense sounds weak to my own ears.

She turns on me. "How can you look yourself in the mirror? This isn't a *game*. I don't even know what to say to you."

I keep my face as neutral as possible, but it hurts. Some deep, buried part of me knows she's right. But the other half needs this—needs to see him brought to his knees once and for all.

After what I've been through, who would ask me to give that up?

"Why should I tell him the truth?" I ask her. "He never cared enough to tell me the truth about our parents and our whole relationship, but now I have to be a bigger person? It's not fair that I have to throw in the towel."

"I know you don't think it's that simple. Just this once, Nell, can you talk to me? Can you please talk to me instead of"—she throws her hands up in front of her—"whatever you're doing."

"He has all the power. He *always* had all the power because he knew," I tell her. "He controlled everything about our relationship. He chose me and knew how to play me. It was all *fake*. It was all fake and I fell for it and he gets off free? He doesn't lose anything? That's not the way the world is supposed to work!"

"Of course that's the way the world works!" she yells back at me. "Look at this goddamn *world* we live in! We get twice as much for half the work because we were born into this family. Look at the inflated sense of importance of our family and Jackson's family in this town. My dad is going to get off on probation and everyone will be surprised but *that's the way the world works* when you're wealthy and you're white and you're a man. So of course, Nell. There will always be someone like Jackson to ruin your fucking life and never be punished for it, and if you're lucky there will always be someone like me to pick up the pieces."

"So I just accept it? Because I wasn't born with money? Or because I'm a girl?"

She shakes her head and looks away again. "This is going to end with you being humiliated, and then you're only going to feel worse. Do you know how it would look if all this got out? What everyone would *think* of you?"

I do, actually. I finally step outside my pain and look at it. Probably exactly what I've been thinking of every other girl who's gone out with Jackson since I stepped through the door at Cedar Woods.

What a judgmental bitch I've been.

I nod at Lia, sinking my front teeth into my bottom lip. "Because it doesn't matter how far I've climbed. It'll never be quite enough. I'll always be just a little bit less to them. The girl who can't accept her fate. Who won't stop fighting."

Her eyes flash in the mirror then, glancing up at me. "You're my *best friend*. And that's all you've ever been to me. It'd be nice if you acknowledged that for a change."

I deflate, running out of room to hold my anger. "You are my best friend," I say simply.

She closes her eyes, a beat and then two. "I'm sorry."

"You're right," I say. "Of course you are. Stringing him along isn't going to change anything. I can't stop the Jacksons of the world. It's never going to end in my favor. Instead, I'll end up like Mom. Chasing Jacksons my whole life only to finally have one catch up to me." I almost laugh. "I guess I already did."

Lia is frowning but she nods anyway. Whatever it takes to stop me.

"But not this weekend. I can't see him again, not when I don't have to. Please don't ask me to do that."

She surveys me momentarily before her eyes change into something like acceptance. "Just get this fixed," she says, walking behind me and pushing open the cracked bathroom door to leave me alone. I turn back to my reflection, tracing the outline of my face with one finger. Finding all the flaws, the imperfections I can't hammer out. Sometimes I want to start over. To be someone else. Someone simple because that's what people want.

Not *me*.

I leave the bathroom, following her to her bedroom, where she's already turned the lights out. I climb in beside her, just like always.

• • •

I wake up at two AM.

There's no running into side tables or hitting my knee on doorframes. I know the way. I slink through the darkness, across the hallways, and so quietly open Taylor's door, closing it behind me just as softly and climbing under the covers next to him.

It only takes moments before he moves, his arms sliding around me and pulling me to lie against his chest. He's never pulled me to him so quickly before.

Right then, I don't know what makes me do it. Desperation or some feeling of belonging or just missing the way someone else's skin feels, but I press my mouth against his. I feel his fingers tangle up in my hair in a way that feels so safe, our legs wrapping around each other.

It's so comfortable, I don't even think about how strange it is to be kissing Taylor. The way his tongue feels against mine. The way our bodies fit so nicely together.

"Nell," his voice creaks as he pulls back from me. I wait for him to tell me to go. He's so warm. "Are you . . . pregnant?"

My throat closes. How can he be holding me this close and not notice I have stopped breathing? He heard Lia in the bathroom, misunderstood. And now he thinks—*dammit.*

"Taylor, I—" I don't know how to finish the sentence. I freeze. Press my eyes closed, crushing them together like perhaps it will help me escape this mess.

What if he tells Jackson before I do?

He takes the whole thing—my stiff body, my cringe—the wrong way. He takes it to mean something it doesn't and, if anything, holds on tighter. I wonder if I cannot say anything at all, become nothing but silence, and this will pass completely.

His thumb caresses the back of my neck, pushing against it tenderly, tangling my hair. I hold myself against him, listening to the sound of his steady-beating heart.

44

I wash my hands in the restroom sink at school on Monday morning, then shake them out and grab a paper towel from the dispenser. I'm supposed to talk to Jackson, but every time I think about it, I find it almost impossible to breathe. As I work to comb my fingers through my hair, watching myself in the mirror, the stall behind me opens and Tristan comes out reflected over my shoulder, her eye makeup darker than the night sky.

"Oh," she says, walking over to the sink. "It's you."

I toss the paper towels into the trash. "It's me."

She cuts off the water. "Heard a nasty little rumor about you."

I stop, facing her. She takes her time, pulling her own paper towels out. "Don't you wanna hear it?" she asks at last.

I go to leave instead of sticking around for her to gloat and she calls back to stop me. "Jackson thinks you're pregnant." I turn back around, all the way, so we're looking right at each other. She balls up her paper towels and tosses them in the trash can. "I told him it was bullshit."

"Because I'm the liar," I say.

"Because you're the one with something to prove," she returns.

My blood boils. "Must be nice to know it all." I tug at my bag. "Did he tell everyone when he was drunk?" I can imagine it running through the basement of Alston's house like an electric current, finally giving everyone something to talk about. Someone new to tear apart.

"He told me yesterday when he wasn't drunk." She gives me a dark look. "Because he knows I know what it's like."

I pause. "Tristan . . . ," I start to say, but she's already walking around me.

"Just have your fun with him and cut him loose," she calls behind her. "I can't take the angst. But, Nell"—she turns back around so I have no choice but to face her—"this is a dangerous play, so you better know what you're doing."

I meet her eyes. "I don't know what you're talking about."

She nods, once, and closes the door behind her.

• • •

I can't believe he sicced Tristan on me. That he *told* her.

He had to do one thing—keep *one* secret for me, after everything he'd kept from me. He couldn't even let me have this to myself.

So I take it all out in volleyball. Like I always do.

I can feel the chill from Lia, without her saying anything. Things aren't going to be the same until I come clean. And I can't help but feel like she knows about Taylor.

What she knows about Taylor—I'm still not sure.

I'm too anxious to leave after practice. Need to tamp it down, get it under control. Get myself under control. *Breathe. Nell.*

I walk around the back of the school, edging toward the athletic complex. The sound of a pitching machine throwing balls out echoes from the baseball field. I feel the eyes on me before I see him, watching me instead of the ball flying by him in the batting cage. My heart goes into the pit of my stomach.

"Wait," he says, barely dodging a ball the machine pitches out, tossing his bat and helmet aside at the edge of the fence. He runs over to me before I can get away.

"What could you possibly want from me now?" I ask.

"I don't know how stuff like this works," he says, stopping ahead of me. "Is it safe for you to be diving around on the floor like you do? Don't guess I could convince you to slow down."

I look at his face. Clear, like nothing on Saturday night happened. And here he is, so proprietary over my body. As if he's in charge of that, too.

"You're unbelievable," I return, looking out over the baseball field. "Like you care about my well-being or anyone else's."

"You act like I'd prefer you dead."

I unleash my fury. "Of course not, because you can't screw up the lives of dead people. How *dare* you tell Tristan? And how dare you have her threaten me?"

"She wasn't supposed to do that," he returns. "I'm worried, all right? Is that what you want to hear? That I'm worried about you?"

"Is that what you have to tell yourself to sleep at night?"

"*What do you want from me?*" he demands. *Nothing*, I think. And then, *Everything you have.*

I shake my head, running my hand through my sweaty hair as I do. "Just a little bit of honesty," I tell him. "One single moment where you admit that you don't care. That you got to see my face that day by the lake and that was all you wanted anyway. You controlled me, Jackson. You controlled me, you controlled our parents, everything that happened. And even after everything, you still want to control my body?"

"Please," he says then, "it's not like that."

I chuckle darkly. "It's always like that with guys like you. You always win."

But I'm not playing by his rules anymore.

He closes his eyes for a moment. I wonder, despite myself, what's back there. What gets through to him. How much of his emotions he can fake. I wonder if he's ever felt anything real.

He got me to put my guard down. But did I ever, *truly*, see him without his?

"I'm sorry," he says at last, "but I can't let this go. I have college applications staring me in the face and I don't know what to do."

"You should've thought of that before," I tell him. It's a specific kind of satisfaction, one I might go my whole life and never understand again. To finally own that feeling of power that I always knew he had. To watch his sad eyes and his sad posture and to know that he feels as hopeless as I did staring at myself that day in the locker room.

He gets money and power and safety.

But I'm the one thing he can't make disappear.

"Beg me," I return, watching his downturned face. "Say it."

"What?"

"What you want me to do. Ask me to fix your problem."

"Nell . . ." His voice is a warning, a question.

"It's what any guy would want in this situation. So beg me." I step closer to him. "Fucking *beg me*, Jackson."

He's staring at me. "You can't be serious."

I have never been more serious in my life.

"I'm not doing this with you," he says at last. "Because it's not a fucking competition. It never *was*, Nell."

I take one last step. "Wasn't it?" I ask at last. "You still haven't apologized. Not for lying. Not for Saturday night or the girls or even"—my voice catches a moment—"or even for that day in the closet. I don't think you've ever truly apologized for anything in your life."

He swallows slowly, starts to speak. But I don't wait to hear his reply. I don't *want* to hear it, not when his hand has been forced. A stick cracks somewhere in the distance, beckoning me, and I take off. Running my troubles away and holding on to the look on his face.

I can't hear anything but the whirring pitching machine behind me, trying to keep throwing out baseballs that aren't there.

45

I'm sitting in first period the next day when Lia comes bursting into the room. She tries not to look it, but I can tell from the set of her jaw. She's angry.

"Ms. Macintyre," she says with a big, fake smile, "can I borrow Nell for just a quick second before class starts? Official student council business." She doesn't wait for an answer before she motions me to follow her into the hallway. I do.

Once the door closes behind her, she continues walking down the empty hall before turning back to me, taking one step forward, and stopping. "Nell, I know you're avoiding me. And I am so done. You let my *brother* believe you were pregnant?"

"Lia . . . ," I try.

"Nope." She puts up her hand. "No more talking for you. Time for you to listen."

I watch her, already trying to figure a way out of it. Calculating the odds. Constructing my narrative.

She holds up one finger. "You're going to tell Jackson." Another finger. "You're going to tell my *brother*. You're done jerking Taylor around." And one last one. "You're going to tell anyone else you've pulled into this. And we're going to pretend it never happened because *I get it*, Nell, I do. And it's not okay. But neither is this. Don't you see what you've become? And what about me? What about your best friend? I can't deal with any more. I've been dealing with this shit for four months and it has to stop. I'm watching you come goddamn unraveled. We're supposed to have each other's backs."

I take a deep breath.

"When you promised me on Saturday night, was that another lie?"

I think back, turning it around in my head. "I . . . I don't know. When I said it, I meant it, but it's not as easy as it seems. Once I do this . . ." I trail off. Once I do this, it's over. He's free.

I close my eyes, taking it in. Because I'm not sure I'll ever really be free again. Always watching. Waiting for the other shoe to drop. Fearing I'll be played again. At least this had been a distraction. From Mom. From the thrumming ache in my heart.

"Nell," Lia says, her voice softer.

"Okay," I say, putting my thoughts on pause. I nod. "Okay, you're right. I'll tell them."

She exhales. She already wants to apologize, I see it in her features. Put things back right again. Lia's my constant, my person. I spin in circles. She's fixed.

"I'll tell Jackson at lunch. And then . . ." I swallow. "I'll talk to Taylor."

"Tell him everything."

I nod. "I'll be completely honest."

She closes her eyes for a second, letting it all roll off her. Finally, she opens them. "Okay."

46

When I walk into fourth period, I slip a note written in blue ink onto Jackson's desk.

Tennis court. Lunch.

Nothing changes in his posture when he reads it. He leans back like he always does and watches everything move around him like he always does.

When the lunch bell rings, I take off without glancing back. I stuff my bag in my locker and then hide in a bathroom stall, my head pressed into the door, listing dates, counting backward, breathing breathing breathing. It's like that for a couple of minutes before I go outside, walk the length of the athletic complex and through the woods toward the forgotten tennis court.

He's sitting on the clay, scrolling through his phone. Even looking at him now, I can't help but think it—how easy everything looks for him. How simple it must be.

Jealousy still burns through me whenever I see him.

When he feels me watching him, he stands up, stuffing his phone in his pocket.

"Thanks for waiting," I say, and a crease forms in his forehead. Confusion.

"Thanks for"—he searches for a word—"talking to me."

I nod, walking down the length of the crumbling fence, running my hand over the rusted chain link. I'm trying to speak, to form the right words, when he takes the pressure off.

"I have to tell you something," he says.

I turn back around to face him, grateful for the distraction. "Oh."

"Look." He glances up at the sky, as if praying for help, before looking back down. "I don't even know if I should tell you this. I know this whole mess is my fault. And I treated you like some sort of collateral damage, but I mean, you know that. I treat everyone like collateral damage."

My heart beats against my chest in a way that makes me unable to decipher between anger and nerves. I don't want to hear whatever's next but I *need* to hear it.

"Nell, you're right, I never did apologize. And I'm so desperately sorry for lying to you about our parents and putting you in the middle of it. For throwing other girls in your face when I'm the one who was so fucked up. And for Saturday night. For dragging you through my depression like you should feel sorry for me.

"And most importantly, for what I said in the janitor's closet. I didn't mean a word I said that day. Can't you tell? I'm stupid fucking in love with you." He does that thing with his hands where they won't stop moving. The fence and then his chin and then his hair. "It was just—that night by the water. I couldn't tell you then. I couldn't look you in the eye and then admit something like that, like, that I'd always been in love with you, even before I really realized it. I knew it wasn't fair to put that on you when you had earned the right to hate me but now with the mess we've created, I can't *not* tell you the truth. You don't deserve to have to listen to my shit, but I can't let you keep thinking I meant a word of it."

"You called me a slut," I say, holding on to it so tight.

"I resorted to the worst parts of myself. I knew exactly what I was doing and I know I'm the world's biggest hypocrite. I never once thought you were a slut. I've never thought anyone was a slut because I thought I'd evolved past that," he tells me. "But you turn off so damn easy and I wanted you to feel something. I know what I did. I thought of the first thing my father would say and I said it to you."

"Guess what I feel now?" I demand of him.

"I never meant for any of it to happen the way you think I did. It wasn't all some elegant scheme, I swear. After everything started happening with us, I thought . . . I thought it would disappear, the thing with our parents. I don't know. When I was around you, I was never thinking straight, I was only wanting you right there. And then the whole thing blew up and I panicked. Look at me. I'm pathetic."

"It's like, once again, you've made my pain about you," I say. "All you had to do was *stop*. Would you ever have told me about the affair to remember?" I ask, working to keep my voice calm. "Once we got to college, maybe?"

"I don't know. But now here we are. I know what I did, I'm not going to deny it and you don't have to forgive me. I've spent the last five weeks in misery and you're right. I fucked that up, too, just like I do everything else. I don't know what you want from me because I know you don't owe me shit, but I'm not going to stand here and watch this whole thing happen and keep lying to your face. I am fucking in love with you."

"You're so full of shit," I say, my mouth in a straight line.

"Fine, you know what?" he says, taking one step closer to me. "Do you know why it was so hard to talk to you, to be honest with you? It was always dangerous because I never knew what would shut you down. I never knew how to get through.

"Do you know what it's like, loving you? Even before, when I was giving you every humiliating truth about my useless life? Like loving a natural disaster. You'd ruin something that made you happy if it meant you were the winner. And it feels like, no matter what someone does or who they are or how long they chase you, they'll never get your attention. They'll never get all the way in. That's what you want. How could I ever—*ever*—have an honest conversation with you about our parents and still keep you?

"I had already lost before it started. How does someone make up for that?"

I breathe as slowly as I can, taking it all in, running it methodically through my system. Blink. "Say it again," I tell him, my voice barely more than a whisper. "Say what you said before."

His face changes, softens. There's that feeling behind his eyes— something like hope. So easy to crush. Because he knows. He remembers, and he thinks maybe for a second that this is where he can finally get it right. "I love you," he tells me quietly, his eyes dead on mine, the words close enough to touch.

This. This is what I've been waiting for. The key.

I turn away without another word and take off back toward school.

47

I get the text from Taylor right after school. *Party at the cove tonight. See you there?*

I study it, running over it in my mind all through volleyball practice. Jackson showing his cards at last. Taylor and the cove and everyone else.

I think I know how this ends now.

As we're leaving I admit to Lia that my conversation with Jackson had gone completely sideways, but it's over. It ends tonight.

She says, voice cold, to talk to her when that's happened.

I go home to change, eschewing my usual jean shorts and T-shirt for an underutilized tight top and skirt. So many of the clothes I wear are an attempt to hide, make myself smaller.

Not tonight.

The hidden cove is right on the river, through some of the trails I run, owned by some rich family or the other. The beach is packed with Prep kids—too many Prep kids—drinking out of Solo cups and groping one another while pretending to dance and feeling generally superior, the way Prep kids do. Something about a weeknight party makes the whole thing feel that much more rebellious.

I spot Taylor before he spots me. Tall and blond, a breeze off the river ruffling his hair. I look at the people around him, pretty, perfect people with their pretty, perfect, fucked-up lives.

I sneak up behind him, place my hand on the middle of his back, and he turns around to face me. I keep moving my hand upward, snaking it into his hair, and I bring his face toward me and kiss him. He realizes what is happening fairly quickly and he slides his arms around my waist, kissing me more thoroughly. He pulls back after a second, all eyes at the bonfire on us.

Someone whoops, and then someone else yells, "Reagan!" and people are laughing around us and Taylor's staring straight at me, his eyes full of questions.

I smile. "You looked so good standing over here."

His eyes rake down me, my outfit, taking me in as if he's not quite sure who he's seeing. "It's good to see you, too. You're . . . looking confident."

He's so kind, it almost hurts.

The thing is, I *do* like Taylor, always have. The way he makes me feel. His almost-constant kindness, and even those little moments where he breaks just like the rest of us.

He makes me feel safe.

I want it to be real.

"I'm gonna go get a beer," I tell him, and then, at the look on his face, "for you."

He nods and I head over to the keg on the other side of the beach. Michonne is standing there, and she claps her hands together when she sees me. "You did *not* just do that." I glance around and when I see other people watching me, a grin slides onto my face.

"Nell Becker," she says, impressed.

I shrug.

After that, Taylor is a steady presence and he won't leave my side, the perfect protector. He keeps his hand placed on the small of my back, like he's worried what might happen to me.

Taylor's been chasing broken women his whole life, hoping to catch them.

Later that night, we're standing together talking by the water, the waves washing up to the beach, soaking our toes, and I see Jackson over Taylor's shoulder. Drinking. Watching us. And when he sees me seeing him, he throws his cup down and walks toward us.

"Well, this is a new one," he says once he's close.

Taylor turns at the sound of his voice. Exasperated, Taylor says, "What do you want, Hart?"

"Why don't you tell him, Nell? What my problem is?"

Electricity crackles to life in my chest. "He knows," I answer.

"About today?" Jackson asks.

I drop my gaze. "Not that."

"Did you immediately go make out with him?" Jackson asks, disgusted. "Was that the play?"

"Go away," I tell him dismissively. "You don't get to tell me who to kiss."

Jackson bends over, pushing both of his hands through his hair like he's going to scream before he stands back up straight. "How can you not see how wrong this is? Dragging this out? Leaving me hanging?" He points. "Bringing Reagan into it."

"Back the fuck off, Hart," Taylor says then in a gruff voice that doesn't suit him. I can feel how close Jackson is to crying, and I hate it when he does that.

"Don't pick me if you don't want to pick me," Jackson says, "but stop this. Please end it now and put every last one of us out of our fucking misery, Nell."

"You think everything is yours to take," Taylor says, pushing in front of Jackson. "Why?"

"Tell him," Jackson says, looking at me over Taylor's shoulder. "Tell him why you kissed him. What you're using him for."

"I kissed him before," I tell Jackson, my eyes boring into his.

"What is wrong with you?" Taylor asks him.

To my mounting horror, people around us are watching. The sides are closing in, and I need to stop before too much of me is on display.

I need to turn into one of those herons on the wind and fly away. Evolve.

"I told her I loved her," Jackson says to Taylor. "I told her I'm ridiculously, outlandishly in love with her so she went and found you."

"Can't imagine why she didn't throw herself at your feet like she was supposed to," Taylor bites back.

"Taylor," I say softly.

Jackson is looking at me again. "If he can't track the movements of your game right now, he doesn't really know you at all. Did she even tell you, Reagan? Did she tell you she's pregnant?"

And that's what finally does it. Taylor hauls off and punches Jackson directly in the jaw.

If I weren't so deep in despair, it might be satisfying to finally see him laid low, unwilling to fight back. And he goes down hard, landing on the solid dirt of the beach. He has the dignity not to say any more. Taylor turns back to me. "C'mon, Nell. Let's go."

I swallow, glancing down. Jackson's eyes meet mine; he pulls himself up, wipes the dirt off, and walks away. I look back to Taylor. "I can't."

His face remains totally passive. "Why?"

Because Jackson is right, I don't say. I finally got what I wanted—I broke his heart. Or as much of one as he ever had. And that—that'll be for every girl he's ever hurt or used or laughed about once she's gone.

It'll be for me, most of all.

I'd thought, for some reason, that maybe I'd get out of this the good guy, righteous and victorious. That anyone else caught in it would understand eventually. But Taylor is watching me right now, and he's loved me for far longer than I've deserved it.

I used him.

I blink. "He's right. About why I kissed you."

Taylor sighs deeply. "Are you kidding?"

"He told me he loved me and I wanted to make him bleed. I thought

293

if he saw you and me together . . . I wanted to break him, so he'd know what it was like. Can you understand the impulse?"

He turns away and spits into the dirt. "No," he says, not looking back at me. "I can't."

And that's where he leaves me at last.

Momentarily in a daze, I stand there, alone, the wind whipping my hair. I only have one clear thought: *I need a drink.*

I push my way through the people gathered around us, ignoring the murmurs that follow me as I walk in the opposite direction from the way Jackson left. I take the first cup someone hands me and down it so quickly, I don't taste what's inside.

This is not the proper way to deal with my emotions. Even I know that.

But I never knew what it was like before. To not know how to stop a thing you started. I've ruined my relationships with the two people who are my surrogate family. I can barely stand to be in my own house. The only boy I've ever loved believes a lie I told and is possibly the most terrible person alive and some part of me doesn't care.

And worst of all, I hate myself.

I guess I always did.

I'm in a group of people, riding the wave of the crowd. Everyone, having seen Taylor punch Jackson in the face, is now staring at me. Someone hands me another drink and I take it.

Everything is loud, but I can't *hear* any of it.

Someone grabs my shoulder.

"Nell," she says. Lia is alone and in the shape of something angry. *I'm sorry*, I should say. *You were right you're always right.* "Where the hell is my brother?"

I shrug sloppily. And some deep, dark part of me knows I should care, but I can't. I don't want to. I'm so goddamn sick of caring about everything so much.

"He's supposed to be my ride home."

"Guess you'll have to find another ride," I say. "He left."

She grabs on to my arm. "What did you *do?*" she asks, her voice edging into desperation.

She's always thought I am too much, even if she'd never say it. Someone to be looked after. Someone who would never fit in.

I think she's my best friend because she was afraid what would happen if she left me on my own.

I feel someone else come up beside me then, Michonne's skin shining in the light from the fire. "Are you okay, Nell?" she asks, looking at my cup of some kind of alcohol. Her face is serious, but she had been laughing with me a couple of hours ago. "You shouldn't be drinking that. I mean, everyone is saying . . . that you're . . ." She drops her voice. ". . . pregnant."

My heart stops.

Someone else hears her. Some boy laughs. "So Hart *did* get Nell Becker pregnant. God, I can't wait for school tomorrow."

No.

Someone else is like, "You're LYING," and there are voices, voices everywhere.

Sad Nell Becker. Pathetic, try-hard Nell Becker. Look at her now.

Nonononono.

"No one is pregnant. I'm *not* pregnant." Then I take a huge swig of my drink as if proving the point. When I move the cup away from my lips, I see him like a blurry mirage through the fire. Jackson. Watching me and seeing me and I see the way his face changes when he watches me, the way the anger falls away to . . . nothing. He's glowing in the firelight, tan and easy and blank, his eyes locked on mine. Then he's gone.

There are so many people staring at me, picking me apart with their eyes. Seeing who I was and who I am now and thinking they're so glad not to be me. And there's Lia right there, waiting for me to say it. Admit that I'm a liar. That I'm *that* girl, the pathetic one who would use my body as a weapon—even if it was the only one I had left.

Everything I've done in my life and *this* is what I'll be remembered for.

I grab a drink out of the closest person's hand and down it, too. "See?" I toss the cup on the sand, swaying ever so slightly.

It's an odd silence around us. Quiet enough in our immediate circle but conversation buzzing from outside and even more from outside of that. I make myself look at Lia, who is looking back at me. I've never seen her face so closed off. So done.

"The nerve of you to call Jackson the liar." I can feel how much she doesn't want to look at me. "You used Taylor, after how much we've always cared about you. After this summer. You are the worst kind of narcissist. No wonder you and Jackson think you're made for each other."

"Lia, wait—"

She stands in front of me, fists clenched, daring me to speak. The fire is burning in the distance behind her, haloing the tendrils of her wild hair. I realize I don't know what to say.

"That's what I thought," she says. "God," and she gets choked up. She blinks one time, a tear escaping her eye, and says to me, "I am so finished with you," and then walks away in the other direction. I want to call after her but I've got no more explanations. I know what I did. I planned it, calculated. Jackson's words from earlier run through my mind. *I treat everyone like collateral damage.*

I have to get out of here.

Jackson is walking toward me and Michonne is watching me like she is both sad and disgusted. I get that. I open my mouth to tell her just how fucked up I am, but instead I say, "Will you please take me home, Mich?" and her face softens a little and she nods and walks me over to her car. We pile in and she nicely doesn't talk until we are in front of my house.

"It doesn't have to be like this," she says.

"Like what?"

"I don't know," she tells me. "Like, you don't always have to win every argument."

"You don't understand," I tell her.

"Don't I? You think you're the only one at this school who has to protect herself? Me—I'm not straight. I'm not white. Money doesn't fix everything."

My stomach turns over. I'd never even considered that. "I feel like shit," I tell her.

"Don't," Michonne replies, her voice easy as ever. "Just stop acting like the rest of us are removed from all of this. You're not a damn island, Nell."

I swallow and open the door of her car to walk on unsteady legs to my house.

I should probably do something. Hide. Try to sneak in. Anything so my parents won't see me the way I am. But shit, I'm tired. And I don't care.

So I go through the front door.

It looks dark but when I go into the den, I see Mom sitting next to a lamp, reading a book and sipping a glass of wine and looking perfect. We both stare silently at each other for a minute. I push a piece of hair back behind my ear.

Mom stands up. "It's a Tuesday night. Where have you been?"

I blink. "With every other fucked-up teenager in Cedar Woods," I tell her. I'm so tired. I only want to go to bed.

"Are you drunk?" she demands. "What is going on, Nell?"

I do some mental math in the "what is going on" department. The reputation I've worked for my entire life is shattered, and I've lost my best friends.

It's all her fault.

I laugh.

The sound catches her by surprise, I think. I watch her face change, fall, looking at me like an unsolvable problem. "What's wrong, Mom?" I ask. "Don't you think this is *hilarious*?"

"I don't know what's wrong with you," she says, sounding like a person who can be hurt. "Your father and I barely see you. You don't talk to us. You can . . . You can tell me anything." She braces herself.

I can't, I realize. Tell her anything.

If she knew who I was, it would probably break her.

Instead, I say, "*You?* You don't know what's wrong with *me*? How can you ask me what's going on?" My voice rises, hatred the last thing I have to hold on to. "Every terrible thing that's happened to me this year is because of you. I don't ask about your terrible choices."

She blanches.

"Look at me, Mom," I finish, my voice breaking. "Being a selfish bitch runs in the family."

She doesn't answer me. I head up the stairs and collapse into a heap on my bed.

• • •

I wake up to my phone ringing. My head spins, my brain pounding angrily against my skull. For a minute, I'm not sure where I am. I answer my phone.

"Nell?" someone says on the other end. Taylor.

I'm so shocked to hear his voice, I wonder if the past twelve hours were a dream.

"Yeah?" I answer. It's still dark outside.

"Have you seen Lia?" Taylor asks me. His voice trembles precariously. "She never came home from the cove."

I miss a breath. I throw back the covers. "She's not answering her phone? Did you try Columbus?"

"No one knows where she is. I've been driving around for an hour."

"I'm going to go back to the cove," I tell him, sliding on a pair of shorts. "Call me."

"Okay," he says. "You, too."

I'm back at the cove in record time. It's after three in the morning—Lia would never stay out this late without telling anyone. I feel my hands shaking.

Embers remain where the fire burned earlier, driftwood collapsed, cups thrown into the sand. The moon is bright on the beach and the water, the night eerily still. Someone is lying on the beach next to the burned-out fire, staring up at the sky with their arms behind their head. Like a person that time forgot, waiting for the night to give them answers. I hurry forward, calling out "Lia!"

The person gets up, looking at me as if I'm a mirage. It's Jackson. Because of course it is. Of course he'd be here posing like the happy ending. But it doesn't seem like the time to rehash the past—none of that is particularly important right now.

"Lia?" he asks.

I feel near tears. I had been so hopeful for that moment between heartbeats when I'd seen him. "Taylor says she never came home from the party. She was mad at me. I don't know, she walked off and now no one knows where she is."

"Okay," he says, his voice the embodiment of calm, "it's okay. We'll find her." And he says it so confidently, I actually believe him. *We'll find her.* He's always been good under pressure. "Do you know which direction she went in?" he asks.

I'm not sure, which almost sends me into another panic.

"Okay," he tries again, "where were you standing?"

I point in the general direction, mentally position myself and Lia, but it's all blurry. "That way, I think," I tell him at last, pointing to where the beach curves out of the cove and continues on. The other way turns into vegetation in the back of someone or another's property.

"Come on," Jackson tells me, and I follow him.

"Lia!" I call out down the beach, my voice echoing in the night. This area of the beach is abandoned, hilly with enough rocks to make it dangerous running terrain.

"She's going to be fine," Jackson tells me again.

I hear something then. Barely audible, a shift so small it could be a mouse. But it's enough. "LIA!" I yell again, and then someone definitely yells back, a struggle, and I take off running despite the landscape.

"Nell!" Jackson calls, on my heels.

But nothing will stop me. I see her. She's lying partway down a drop-off, sitting up straight with her legs out in front of her. I run to her side and crouch down next to her, grabbing on to her arm. I glance back at Jackson. "Call for help and then call Taylor."

"What happened?" I ask, my attention back on Lia.

She grinds her teeth. "Lost my footing. Phone's down there." She points to the bottom of the drop-off. "Been trying to crawl to it but I think my ankle's broken." A tear creeps down her face. I hug into her side, burying my forehead in her shoulder.

"It's fine, Lia," I say, holding her. "You're going to be okay."

She lets me hang on, but deep down, I know.

It's only because I'm the one there.

48

Jackson and I are sitting together in the hospital waiting room in uneasy silence. A door on the other side opens and Taylor comes through, holding two cups of coffee. He walks to us and we stand at the same time as he shoves coffee into both of our hands. I think he'd sooner be done with the pair of us.

"She's fine," he says. "Coming out of surgery on her ankle and then setting it. There's nothing more y'all can do, so you can go home now." It's not a question. He's sending us away. Lia doesn't want to see me.

"Tell her . . . ," I start, and Taylor cuts his eyes at me. I stop. Lia doesn't owe me anything, especially having to hear from me right now. I nod.

"Thanks," Taylor says then, effectively ending the conversation, "for finding her. We're all really grateful." It's strange to be spoken to so formally by him.

I'd tell him I'm sorry but it's not the right time. So I let him go.

Jackson and I had ridden together in my car, which means we have to leave together. Unsure of what else to do, we walk into the parking lot side by side.

"I called Tristan to come get me," Jackson says as the doors slide closed behind us. He takes a sip of coffee. The sun is starting to peek out, turn the lights on the night.

I continue walking down the sidewalk. "Of course you did," I say.

"Nell," he says. "About yesterday. Tell me."

I stop on the sidewalk down from the entrance and turn around. It's completely silent out here right now, no ambulance or people. We are utterly alone. The coffee cup burns the inside of my hand pleasantly.

I start counting backward. I say, "Tell you what?"

He takes a step closer to me. "Are you pregnant or not? Were you *ever*?"

Breathe. Keep breathing. "No," I answer him as quickly as I can. "I thought I might be and I panicked. The test was negative. All the tests were negative. Everything spun out of control and I kept trying to tell you, but I . . . I couldn't stand you and the way you kept kissing those girls right in front of me and the way you called me a slut and the way you did everything. I thought I was pregnant and you thought nothing. You felt nothing.

"I wanted to hurt you the way you hurt me. I had to do something to . . ." I seek out the word, but it's right there. It always has been: "Win."

His face goes completely blank, whitens, as he stares at me. I watch his fingers as they curl and uncurl into a fist.

"Say something."

"I'm thinking," he finally answers, "about how to react to the fact that you're just as horrible a person as I am."

"I know," I say. "But—"

"See," he says, "your 'but' doesn't matter. Just like mine didn't to you. It was malicious, designed to hurt. So." He looks away. There's a car idling in the roundabout that feeds into the hospital entrance. It's Tristan's. His eyes find mine again. "I can apologize again, if you want. But I don't think you do." He salutes me with his cup. "Congratulations. You won." He walks away, gets into the car, and they drive off.

I won.

I only wish it hadn't taken so much of me in the process.

49

I'm about to reach my car parked way in the back of the hospital lot when someone pulls up beside me. It's my mother. She has on a pair of sunglasses she doesn't actually need and is staring at me through her passenger's-side window. I'm about to get the lecture of a lifetime.

But she just rolls down the window and says, "Come on, we're going to breakfast." I climb into the passenger's side and buckle up.

She drives for almost twenty minutes, leaving Cedar Woods behind, NPR telling stories in the background. The farther away we get, the more relief I feel. She pulls into the parking lot of a Waffle House off an interstate exit and we go in together.

Mom orders me another coffee and enough food to feed a large family, much less the two of us. A couple of people are in booths, up too early or too late, but we are alone on our side of the restaurant.

"How's Lia?" Mom asks me. I had texted her once we found Lia to let her know where I was.

I shrug. "I didn't see her. Taylor told me she was going home later today."

Mom nods.

I sip my coffee and stare down at the paper placemat. "It's my fault she got hurt. I've been lying to everyone, and I got caught. I was horrible. She couldn't wait to get away from me." I grab a napkin, pressing it to hide my tears. "That's why she was alone."

"Nell." Mom grabs on to my hand and I pull it away from her. I see the shock cross her face and another tear escapes.

I can't keep staring at her and pretending I don't know. I take a breath. "Anyway, you should know that I know you're sleeping with Jackson's dad, so." I blow my nose. "So I'm having a little bit of a hard time with you right now."

Mom's face loses all color and that is, of course, the exact moment our waiter comes over, handing us plate after plate from behind the counter. I try to do everything I can to look normal but there's no hiding it, which is likely why he leaves us as quickly as possible.

"You should have told me," I fire at her. "As soon as you knew about Jackson, it had gone too far. It wasn't just your life anymore—it never was. It was mine." I fight to keep my voice as steady as possible but I've lost so much of my essential truth, a compass that's lost its north.

"I'm sorry," she replies in her shaky voice. "Nell, I—I can't imagine what you must think of me."

"That you were supposed to be smarter than that?" I reply. I violently break a piece of bacon in half. "That you always said you expected *me* to be smarter than that? To be better than all the other girls?"

"You must think me such a hypocrite," she says.

"A hypocrite?" I laugh. "I think you didn't care if I was happy as long as I was who you thought I was supposed to be. As long as I didn't make any mistakes. But my life has been nothing but mistakes. You're so much worse than a hypocrite to me. You made me believe in an impossible standard and all I could ever do was fall short. And then hate myself for it. I can't let anyone in because I just see them as competitors or dangerous. I've been judging everyone for so long."

She grabs at a napkin. "I never meant for you to feel any of that."

I hiccup. "But I did. I still *do* and I've been doing whatever I can to come out on top. Most days I look at myself, I feel like I don't even know who I am."

"But I was never saying you weren't enough. You did it naturally. You were the best and I just—I wanted to make sure you knew it. That you used it. Because I couldn't."

"Don't." I hold up my hand. "Don't do that. You showed me every day that you were perfect. You made no mistakes. You told me I wasn't like other girls so when I wanted to be, when I wanted to have feelings, I *hated* myself for it."

"Nell." She almost tries to grab my hand again, I can tell, but she thinks better of it. She swallows. "I've been doing this my whole life, you see? I remember what my mom used to say. *Sit up straight, smile more, wear makeup, find the right husband. That's all you need to be happy, Mary.*

"But that wasn't what I wanted. And when I met your father . . . it was a whirlwind. I didn't want her idea of being a woman. I wanted to be free and in love and live on a currency of happiness or whatever you think when you're young and rebelling against everything you've been told to be.

"But then there was the real world. With a baby and bills and getting my first teaching job at a prep school. And I had to learn what it was like to deal with people like your classmates. That first year teaching, I was going to fail one of the big donor's sons. He deserved it.

"But the dean of students came to me, and he told me I couldn't. He said that boy—that teenage boy who thought the world would hand him everything—should get whatever he wanted. And that was how it started. Me realizing that I'd always be serving people like him.

"I never wanted that for you. The compromise. I never wanted you to have to go find the right husband or think love would be a cure-all. I wanted you to be a woman who didn't answer to anyone but yourself. Who succeeded at everything you did. You would never serve them, and you would never need them. But I guess I pushed you too far. I pushed you away and I pushed your father away. We used to be happy. Now most days, I feel like I don't remember what that ever felt like."

"When did you meet Mr. Hart?" I ask, still not entirely sure I want to know.

She glances over my shoulder momentarily, ashamed. "Last spring. His wife was supposedly sick and he came in for a conference after something Jackson had done for attention. I saw the connection right away. Suddenly, that boy made so much more sense to me."

I take a deep breath. "Why?"

She sighs. "Why? Isn't that the question?" She takes a long gulp of orange juice, I think to give herself something to do. "Part of me was wondering what my life could've been, I think, if I . . ." She looks away as if resisting saying it but goes on, "I hadn't gotten tied down so young. Or if I'd married a man like Atticus Hart like Mom wanted, if I could've lived that life and wasn't always trying so hard to impress people who would never be impressed with me.

"But I think the other part of me just wanted to feel *something* again. Your father doesn't see anything worthy in me anymore, and you'd stopped talking to me a long time ago. There was some connection."

"Do you love him?" I ask her, my eyes filling with tears.

"Oh, Nell," she says, her hands reaching across the table to cup my face. "He is a man who's never satisfied with what he has. And I was, too. That's all it takes."

A tear falls from my eye and onto her hand.

"I never would've let you get involved in this. None of this is fair to you and it wasn't fair to Jackson, either—I should've called this off when I realized you felt something for him. When you called me selfish"—she drops her gaze to the table—"you weren't wrong."

"He's such a mess," I whisper. "And I guess I am, too." I blink another tear out of my eye.

I can't stop staring at her. Cardigan, still in perfect shape, still with total authority. *She's perfect*, I think, a line that's always played on repeat in my head. I want to be perfect, too.

She's not supposed to be like this, with all these harsh edges. Such a mess.

I've been trying to live up to a standard that didn't exist.

She's just a person.

I shake my head, and she drops her hand. "I've been wanting to hurt you so bad—not just you. Jackson, who I thought deserved it. And everyone else, too, who didn't deserve it. Because I felt so betrayed by everyone. Everything I thought I knew. I don't want to be so trapped in my own skin anymore."

Mom watches me over the table, waffles going cold, butter melting into grits, and I think she's going to say something really profound or offer redemption but instead she says, "It's okay, Nell."

"I did it, though. I turned it around on him, I treated him and everyone else like pieces in a game," I tell her, wondering if she might take some small pride in it. But I see in her face that she doesn't. "And it didn't feel any better," I admit.

"I know," she says, reaching out and pushing a strand of my hair back. "But you're not the mistakes you make. You're my girl. And you've got so much time."

It's different but I feel it then, for just a moment. The bone-deep connection between two generations of women. Never quite enough. Always trying to live up to the person her mom wanted her to be.

And that deep connection—mine to that girl she was—I hold on to it like a balloon in the wind, afraid it might fly away, leave me alone and untethered.

And for a change, she holds on right back.

50

Lia isn't at school the next day, or the rest of the week. The halls are abuzz with what happened at the cove. Everyone seems to have finally put together that something went on between Jackson and me over the summer but if that's the worst they can figure, then why should I try to stop them?

I want to call Lia or go see her or even just lie face-to-face in opposite directions one more time, but I've lost my privilege to do that. I find Columbus in the hall between classes. He shakes his head when he sees me. "You're acting like him, Nell. And look what he's done to himself."

"I know." I look down at the ground. "I've got to fix myself."

"You both do. Look, I'm not going to absolve you," he tells me then. "That's for Lia to decide. And she's pretty banged up. Not just physically, know what I mean?"

I nod.

"Give it some time is all I'm saying." He looks at me very seriously with his dark brown eyes. "Let her have her time."

I thank him for the advice.

Friday dawns stormy, thunder jolting me from sleep earlier than usual, not even bothering to offer any reprieve from the heat. I can't sleep through the noise so I head to school.

There's plenty of time before homeroom so I hop on the treadmill in the weight room and plug my headphones into my phone, blowing my ears out with music in the process. I get lost in the feel of it, in my sneakers hitting the belt. So lost that I almost trip when someone slams the Stop button.

I yank my headphones out of my ears, turning to see who's interrupted me. It's Jackson, sporting wet hair and a damp Cedar Woods tee. I lean back against the edge of the handles of the treadmill, panting as the belt slows.

Here's the thing: I knew he'd come to me eventually. I knew we weren't done after the hospital—we were in shock, running on nothing but caffeine and adrenaline, and something like that can only last for so long.

Something like us always demands a reckoning.

"Get off the treadmill," he says to me, his voice neutral. "We should be outside."

I follow him, intrigued.

Outside is all mud and electricity, and it'll always be where I feel most alive. I don't need my headphones because the rumbling thunder keeps the beat. We match strides, the way our bodies are trained to do, racing like we've got somewhere to be. Once we get out under the trees, almost completely shielded from the rain, I stop, panting again, my shirt sticking to my body. I feel every inch of my skin right then, all six feet of my body that is always, always completely under my control.

Except I don't think it has been in a long time.

I shove my hand against his white shirt, and he grabs on to my forearm like he was anticipating it. "*What?*" I demand of him, pulling back. "Put me out of my misery."

"You already know so don't ask me to say it," he answers, and I watch a raindrop slide off his face.

I nod, lacing my fingers on top of my head. "Like what I did was so much worse than what you did."

"You wanna do this again, Nell!" Jackson yells at me then. "You wanna take out the scoreboard and see which one of us is worse? Are you going to do this forever?"

I push my palms under my eyes because I'm afraid he might see me cry. "You tossed it in my face. All of this. This summer and everything—the river and the diner and even the godforsaken boat— and those things might not have meant anything to you, but they meant something to me. You said you'd tell everyone."

He breathes and blinks and the rain keeps falling. "Of course they meant something to me. All I wanted the whole summer was to get through that armor you wouldn't drop. Everything I said that day was—"

"Meant to hurt me, I know," I cut over him. "Call a girl with everything a slut and that's all she'll ever be. Call a boy with everything a slut and he's the perfect package. But it wasn't just that. It was all of the rest of it. You made a game out of my life. And then you made me feel like *I* was wrong. After—after you'd torn me apart, you kept hurting me a little more with the girls and your self-destructive guilt that was all about you and I never, ever knew if what we had was real. So I wanted to take whatever was left. I wanted your freedom and your happiness and that carefree thing you have that makes you all you, Jackson. I wanted *you.* And I didn't care how crazy I looked when I got it."

"What about what happens to you, Nell?"

"You said it yourself," I answer, trying to keep my voice steady. "It doesn't matter what happens to me. As long as you lose."

He pushes his wet hair out of his face. "Jesus, shit, don't you see? I thought you had me all figured out. I lose every day to this bullshit. To some urge to feel control over something because I can't feel control over anything that matters. You're *always* in control. You tell yourself to feel nothing and you don't. Of course I used the last desperate gasp of air I had to try and burn you down."

"I'm a goddamn mess!" I yell at him. The rain picks up then, too much for even the trees to hold back. "I've got nothing but empty accolades and that hatred everyone here feels for a girl who wants it all like I do. You think I don't know what they think of me? That I think

I'm too good for anyone else. That I can't feel fun, feel *anything*—can't breathe. You knew it. I'm still not *enough*. The only time I've ever felt the littlest bit of space to an imperfect person since I came to this hellhole four years ago was when we were together! So damn you, Jackson Hart. Damn you for being a liar and damn you for convincing me you weren't and damn you for making me realize I was never more than another game to you."

His face changes as I say it, yell it, let myself live out every bottled-up emotion of the past month. His eyes are serious, and he says, "Of course you weren't a game. You were mine."

"I'm nobody's," I tell him.

He laughs sadly. "No, I guess not. That was my desperation talking." He inclines his head toward me. He slides both of his hands into my hair on either side of my head, tilting my face up to look at him. Inches away from my face, he tells me, "I know what you think, but it was never about the chase. It was never about having you or winning you or anything else. It was always about you. I never felt like I played you—I never wanted to.

"I only ever wanted to be right there, wherever you are. There wasn't a game between us—there was just *us* and everything else in between."

And so fast, he kisses me soft, too quick, and it feels like a last time. That's the funny thing about kisses and looks and moments stolen under covers—that you never really know while it's happening that it's the last time and you'll always be trying to catch hold of it like a lightning bug on a summer evening, that one last memory, wishing to feel it again.

But summer always comes to an end.

He lets go and steps back from me, turning to run away from the school, mud splashing up his calves. I don't watch him, though; instead I tilt my face toward the sky, letting the rain soak my hair and wash away what was left of yesterday's makeup that I hadn't bothered to rinse off, his words echoing behind him.

51

Everyone crowds around Lia as she limps into school on crutches the next Monday morning. I know she won't want the attention but she'll let everyone fawn over her anyway so they feel better. Columbus walks beside her, carrying her bag. Apparently, that secret is out, too. And I watch from afar like the spectator I've been relegated to.

I texted her over the weekend but didn't push when she didn't answer. I realize exactly how deep the hole I've dug myself is, so I keep my distance. From her. From Taylor. From Jackson.

It's like if everyone you've ever known forgot you were alive.

We have a volleyball game Tuesday so I head to the gym after school to warm up. Lia sits on the bench with her leg propped up, watching us with longing in her eyes. Right before we go out to start the game, I run to the locker room and change jerseys. Into her number. Her jersey is too tight on me, but I don't care. I run back out and the other girls are excited about it, to see her represented.

I sit down on the bench next to her without saying anything. She hands me a water.

"You don't have to do that," she says like she doesn't want me to. "I'm not dead."

"You should be out there," I tell her.

"I know," she answers, icy.

"You should be out there because you really love it. Because volleyball means more to you than it does to me, and I've been taking that from you for longer than I can remember."

She doesn't answer, staring straight ahead.

"I want to win, Lia. You know that. It's everything to me. That doesn't make anything I've done okay. But this is for you, okay? I'm going to play for you and the team and the game. Not for me, for a change."

She sighs. "It's about you, Nell."

"What?"

She glances at me, taking in the jersey. "Wearing that isn't for me. You're doing it for you. Because it's always about you."

I swallow.

"It's your world and the rest of us will always just be living in it. I've always thought I had to live with that. To live with Nell's scholarship and Nell's panic attacks and Nell's valedictorian spot."

"I never meant for you to feel like that."

She laughs. "And then Nell's boyfriend, only that wasn't good enough, either. Nell's dramatic breakup. Nell's *fake pregnancy*. And you never, ever own up to any of it. You couldn't even stand the fact that *I* had something going on in my life. That wouldn't work for you and now look where the hell we both are." She stares back at the court. "So, fine, go play in my jersey and let everyone soak up your Nellness. If only we could all be so fortunate."

"Lia—" I start.

"Get out of my sight," she says, crossing her arms, and I feel my heart break like a glass. Or maybe like a bone.

I know it's time for me to stop arguing so I nod and push off from the bench, heading to the court.

I try not to think too much about what Lia said while we play, and we win. I do what I promised—try to make everyone else look good. Not worry so much about my own stat sheet, about who everyone will think is the best player.

And I feel okay.

The fans are getting rowdy by the end and run out onto the court to celebrate when the last point lands. I run into a group hug and as I pull away, I spot Taylor standing right there next to me.

"Hey," I say to him, my voice cracking.

"Hi," he returns. My teammates dance around us.

"I'm sorry," I say.

"It doesn't matter," he tells me. "I just wanted to say—thanks. You came through when it mattered. You found Lia. You're like family to us, Nell."

I feel my eyes watering. "It was my fault it happened to begin with."

He inclines his head. "Maybe."

"And what I did to you—that wasn't okay."

"Nope," he agrees. "But you know, when you can't find your sister, it kind of puts things into perspective."

"Yeah," I say. "I guess it does."

He almost laughs in a self-deprecating way and glances up at the ceiling. "I can't believe you let me believe you were pregnant. You were supposed to be the one out of us who had it together."

I shrug. "I don't." But I keep standing in front of him and he looks at me, waiting for me to say whatever it is I'm thinking. "What did it mean to you?" I ask him, curiosity bubbling up inside of me. "I know that I needed someone who would hold on to me and not ask questions and I'm grateful for that—you honestly helped so much—but did you feel anything for me?"

"What do you mean?" he asks.

"You love to save people, Taylor. You aren't as good when they don't need the saving."

He thinks about that for a moment, eyes trained on me. "I guess I do."

"We've known each other for so long," I say. "But it was always simple before."

314

"I don't know, Nell," he answers. I can feel the chill return. "You never needed anyone to take care of you before and when you did . . . I couldn't leave you hurting." He shrugs. "What you did sucks, but also, I kind of feel better just knowing you're okay. I guess when I thought you wanted me, I had just broken up with Amanda, too, and yeah, sometimes it's nice for someone to be there." But he only shrugs again.

"Yeah," I say. "It was nice." I pause. "I never thought about it before everything happened with Jackson. What a part of my life you are. You'd always just been Lia's brother and you'd never needed anything and I never had either but we both did. You didn't leave me alone. Thank you."

He looks down. "You matter to me. I'm sorry you didn't see it before."

"I'm so sorry." I grab on to my hair right above my ponytail, thinking of how much Taylor did for me, how many times he'd been there when I needed someone. I'd been so lost in myself for so long, in *proving* something to people who never asked me to begin with. "I ruined everything."

"Things have been bad enough. We can't splinter our family any more. We'll be okay," he tells me. "One day."

One day feels like a very long time away right now. But there's one thing I know about Taylor. Well, two.

That he's too nice. And that he means it.

52

It doesn't take long for school to kick into high gear. My GPA crawls up a hundredth of a point to tie Jackson and me in class rankings, but I see him. Lying in the grass behind the school, scribbling notes into his books. He's trying.

I spend most of my time when I'm not playing volleyball studying. There's something satisfying about getting lost in a monotonous routine.

Oftentimes, I find myself adrift but somehow still afloat. Without Lia, I'm anchorless, but at the same time, I know I'm coping better; the panic attacks have stopped and I guess if they start again, I'll finally have to tell my parents.

That's the nice thing about falling from grace in such a truly disastrous manner; there's something freeing in it. Everything still matters, but it doesn't feel quite as attached to my personhood.

Cedar Woods' homecoming dance falls the day after the homecoming football game at the marina in town. As I'm getting ready, Mom walks into my room and puts a hand on my back, fussing with the hook on my dress. "Is Lia coming with the other girls?" she asks me.

I shake my head.

"I remember when I broke up with my best friend," she says, her fingernails scraping my back softly. "In college. She used to always look at me before I went out and say 'Are you wearing that?' or 'It doesn't look like you're ready.' I finally told her to go to hell."

I glance back at her. "Lia would never do that."

She looks at me in my reflection, her eyes dark and serious like mine. "I know. But you cut out the bad people in your life. And then you fight with all you've got to keep the rest." She cups my chin. "And no one's better at fighting than you, my dear."

She kisses my cheek, having to reach up to do it, and goes.

Sometimes it's hard to adjust to this version of her. The one who goes to therapy, who doesn't know whether she wants to stay married, who doesn't know if she wants any of the things she always has.

It's like putting together the pieces of a puzzle I've never seen completed.

Michonne and a couple of other girls show up and we take pictures at my house before the dance. Right before I go, Dad grabs on to my arm and pulls me back.

We're standing outside in the sun of our perfectly suburban lawn and his eyes scan my bright orange dress, picked to make me stand out. I'd never shied away from my height or from being intimidating, but it was time to finally stop shying away from not being *perfect*— or someone else's idea of perfect.

In this dress, I'm a force to be reckoned with.

"Your mom and I have been talking," he says to me, and my heart pounds. "She says you're still feeling some guilt. About what you knew and when."

I swallow.

He slides his fingers up so they rest on my shoulder. "I would never, ever blame you for anything. What's been going on between your mom and me has been going on for some time and it was unfair of us— irresponsible of us—to let what's been happening the last few months continue without talking to you about it."

I shake my head, unable to look at him. "I never meant to get in the middle of anything."

"You aren't. But I should've talked to you. I shouldn't have left it all on your mom. I've put too much on her shoulders. Whatever else was going on, I haven't been an easy person to live with, but you know it, don't you? All I've ever wanted is for you to be happy."

A deep, shuddering breath comes out of me, louder than I expected. "I do know," I say.

"You're good at everything you do. And I'm so proud of you," he says, "but never forget to be who you are. And never stop doing things that make you happy."

My eyes water. "I love you, Dad. Whatever happens."

He squeezes my arm. "Same, kid."

Someone is laying on the horn in their car. I laugh. "Guess I better go."

"Have fun," he says, and I take off running, badly, in my heels.

• • •

Twenty minutes later, we roll up to the dance like a girl gang, Michonne in a green halter dress with a low back, leaning into my arm, laughing, as we go through the lobby and into the ballroom area. My eyes find Jackson as I pass him, sitting at a table with Tristan, who is in a strapless black dress. Someone as effortlessly badass as Tristan doesn't need colors to stand out.

I spot Lia on the other side of the room sitting with Columbus and Taylor, a long white dress hiding her ankle from view. They wave at our group as we come in, but turn away just as fast. I feel a small pang, but it's quickly forgotten as my friends and I take to the dance floor. One of my volleyball teammates grabs my hand, tries to spin me around, and I have to dip to make it under her arm. I throw my head, my hair flying out all around me.

It was never like this before, when I felt so self-conscious, so protective of myself, so hidden away, and God, it's so much fun.

I'm not so afraid of *who* I am.

We break off after a little while, some of the girls dancing with

Prep guys or, in Michonne's case, flirting with the pretty new girl. I grab a cup of punch, sip on it, and watch the dance.

"You didn't hear it from me, but you look nice," a voice says next to me. I look up and laugh at Tristan in spite of myself.

"You, too," I tell her, and she clinks her plastic cup against mine.

"Are you having fun?" I ask her.

She nods. "Not as much as you, I guess."

"But I'll never look as cool as you," I reply. We lean into a wall together, comfortable.

"That's true," she says. "But I'll never get invited to hang out with a group of girls because I'm an evil slut, so I guess we're even."

I lock eyes with her and then look away. "You can come hang out with us if you want, Tristan. No one's going to stop you. I just didn't think you wanted to."

She shrugs.

"It could be fun," I suggest. "I know having to listen to Jackson and Doug talk about whatever they talk about all the time is enthralling but . . ."

She laughs. "We're here together, but not like together or anything. Me and Jackson. Just so you know."

"I know," I say, watching everyone dance and taking another sip. "C'mon," I continue, inclining my head toward our table. "Let's go." And I take her over with me. Everyone eyes her as if she might be up to something, but it fades fast. I even see her laugh.

The DJ comes in over the sound system. "Let's slow it down. This song is for couples only," he says as something romantic starts playing. People are looking desperately around, trying to pair off, to not be left alone. "So find that person—the one who means more to you than anyone else in the world—and tell them right now. This could be your only chance."

Tristan glances at me as he says that and goes, "That's, like, super fucking profound," in that wise voice she has, and we laugh. But it's digging into that hole in my heart. I hold myself back as long as I can but there's a magnetism, a *need* to not stay. To move.

This time it feels right.

I get up and go across the room. And then I crouch down next to my best friend—injured and solid and beautiful. I hold out a hand to Lia. "Can you dance?" I ask.

Her eyes go to mine, shocked. Then she glances down at her leg and then behind her at Columbus. Then back to me. "I can put a little weight on it now."

She takes my hand. Columbus immediately catches on to what's happening and is out of his chair, helping to pull her to her feet. I take one step back from the table and he gives her over to me. I can almost see the laugh in her eyes.

"Let me know if y'all need anything," Columbus says, sounding ridiculously happy.

Lia puts her hands on my shoulders to help support herself and I grab her around the waist. We sway back and forth, barely moving. I can feel people watching us.

She laughs, her face scrunching up. "This is so embarrassing," she says, glancing at her boot.

My giggle join hers. "I don't care. You're my person. They'll never get that."

"Damn," she says after a moment, running her fingers under her eye, pushing away a tear trying to escape. "I miss you."

"I miss you," I tell her, my voice somewhere between pleading and hysterical. "I screwed up bad. I know this . . . rift between us is my fault. I know I treat control like some kind of addiction, and you *told* me everything was spiraling. I was a tornado of destruction. I was toxic. And I'm sorry."

"Yep," she agrees with terrifying simplicity. But then she smiles. "But God, Nell. You look so good. Happy for a change. This dress." She rubs her fingers over the fabric.

"Is it too much?" I ask.

"You look like you—fearless and comfortable and *you*."

"It's nice," I admit. "To feel something like an entire person and not a series of accomplishments."

"You always were to me," she says.

"I know." I look away for a moment. "So, how are you?"

"The injured daughter of a disgraced politician who's going to be impeached by my boyfriend's mother? I'll be okay. It could always be worse."

We sway a bit longer in silence. "I'll be rehabbing soon," she tells me. "I'm not telling anyone yet because it's a long shot, but I might be back for the championship, if we make it."

"We'll make it," I promise her.

"Anyway, there's still a lot going on, but, I don't know. With Dad and the press, it all starts to run together. I'm just trying to stay focused on right now, this year, getting better. And I see you doing okay and it makes me glad, like I have one less thing to worry about." She looks away. "Not that I don't worry."

"We were best friends for years for a reason." I hate using the word *were* and I see it cross Lia's face, too, but we don't address it. I go on, "Things seem good with Columbus. Now that it's not a secret."

She turns red, nods. "I guess they kind of are. It's not perfect—our parents are just ignoring it, but it's nice not to have it hanging over my head all the time. It's weird that you don't know all this stuff."

I shrug. "It's my own fault."

"I guess so," she says, and I hear the song starting to end. It sends me into a near panic. When the song ends, it might mean this truce is over. It might mean we never go back to how we were. Lia seems to sense that and tells me then, "Taylor says you're family."

"But family doesn't mean close," I reply.

"No," she says. "God knows mine never has been." Her blond hair curls around her face, no makeup smudged. She's perfect in her own way, my best friend. "I never saw you as lesser, but I maybe didn't want you to be so much all the time. You didn't deserve that. I'm sorry, too. Some of this is my fault. There's no one culprit, you know?"

I don't answer, enjoying our moment together. The song ends and we stop swaying. Drop our hands. People never think about it with friendships, but you can spend so much time touching one another. Standing side by side, putting an arm around one another, holding on after a bad day. It's the most specific kind of intimacy.

And now it's gone.

Lia looks tired from the effort of being on her leg for too long. "I'm sorry," I say. "I shouldn't have made you do that. It was too much."

"Nell," she says, reaching up and brushing hair out of my face. "I'm glad you look so happy. And I'm sorry for the silent treatment. It's not—I don't want it to be like this. But it's never going to be the same, you know? We're going to have to figure out how it is now."

I nod. "That's what happens when you get older, right?"

"I guess so. But," she continues, "I still love you. Nothing can ever change that."

I bend down and hug her as tight as I can. She responds in kind. I whisper into her ear, a shared secret, "I love you, too." And it's not everything, but it's something.

I feel like, one day, we might be able to put us back together again. And that seems good enough for now.

53

I leave Lia after that. Slide my shoes off at the back door of the marina's ballroom, the one with the path down to the river. Tristan passes by and hands me a note scribbled on a ripped-up piece of paper. I look at her, my face a question, but she just winks and walks away. I uncrumple it and read, a smile finding its way onto my own face despite myself.

No man, for any considerable period, can wear one face to himself, and another to the multitude, without finally getting bewildered as to which may be the true.

I laugh then. Finally. Loudly. Because of course it was that one. Of course.

I walk outside onto the trail behind the marina. It goes down for a while to a dock leading to the river.

The river. Where everything in this town seemingly ends.

The only place where it's ever felt like I begin.

The wood is cold against my feet. The night is overcast, the water even darker than the sky. I breathe in deeply, feeling a steady calm for a change. Sure in the silence.

I turn around at the sound of footsteps behind me.

Jackson is in an ever-faithful pair of khakis and an Oxford I know is red-white-and-blue checked like the All-American boy he is because I saw it in the light earlier. The top three buttons are unbuttoned, his tie hanging untied and loose.

"You read it," I say, waving the paper.

"It's a metaphor."

"Everything's a metaphor," I return.

"It was a little stuffy," he admits. "But I get it. The historical dystopia was a *really* bad analysis."

I laugh, studying the contours of his face.

"People like us," I finally say, "we're too much for most people, you know?"

"I know."

"I used to feel like, when we were together, like I didn't know how I could feel so much at one time. Like, I'd always heard about people completing each other, but you and me, we were more like a match and a stick of dynamite."

He presses his lips together. "More likely to light one another on fire," he finishes like he knows exactly what I mean.

I half smile. "Dangerous," I say, and he nods.

After a moment he says, "I wanted to take it all back, Nell, from the first time we were ever together, I wanted to unknow what I knew. I wanted to start over, to not have had this happen the way it did. To *prove* something to you."

I stare at my fingers, knowing I'm going to admit it for the first time. "I wasn't happy," I say. "And you were the only person who forced me to see that. I wanted to be a person who was never real to begin with. I was *existing*, but there was no point in it at all.

"So, I don't think I'd take it back. I would change some things the second time maybe, clean up a couple of errors, but I wouldn't take it back."

His eyes narrow. "I'd do it all over again. I'd hurt all the same if I could do it all again."

"But we can't undo what we did to each other. To everyone around us."

"Or our parents," he says like an agreement.

"The whole world," I say. "The two of us together? We might destroy it."

He laughs. "Actually, that part doesn't sound so bad." He walks up to stand next to me, looking out over the water with his hands in his pockets. "I was going to ask for a dance."

I return his laugh, the sound loud and vivid against the night.

"I can leave if you want," he says.

"Don't," I say, glancing over at him. I let the crumpled piece of paper fall into the river, absorbing water, blooming. Our eyes meet.

It's so clear about certain things in life: They're never over.

They're always only just starting.

"It's beautiful tonight," he says, staring back out over the water. He scuffs his foot against the dock. "I remember the way you always looked at the water. That's the first time I ever saw your eyes light up. Like it was in your veins. Like it knew you."

"The only other thing I ever looked at like that was you."

He's quiet, thoughtful for a moment, eyes glued to me. "No one ever saw me that way."

And somewhere in that space between heartbeats, I know what needs to happen. He meets my eyes, and I know he knows, too. I offer him my hand and he takes it.

"One," I say.

"Two," he replies, glancing at me with that old grin I miss so much.

"Three!" we say at the same time, both of our feet leaving the dock. My scream is the prelude before we hit. The water is like a shot of electricity, brilliant and intense. The river deep, cold, unknown. I've wanted to jump so many times and held myself back, waited. But the water rushes over me now, cold and clean and demanding. Everything is bright and new.

It's like coming alive.

AUTHOR'S NOTE

Dear Reader,

You have in your hand a book that's about a lot of things—river towns and summer and sports and that first obsessive love and how parents shape their children. But mostly, it's about girls.

In today's political climate, I find myself thinking a lot about how differently women are judged versus men, whether in fiction or the public stage. We, as a society, expect boys to want it all and encourage them to have it: competition, glory, sex, victory. And if those same boys make some mistakes along the way to get what they want, we don't mind forgiving them. In fact, we often write their apologies for them: *He meant well. Boys will be boys.*

Girls aren't offered the same leniency. *She should've been smarter than that. Was too ambitious, too unkind, too overtly sexual, too much too much too much.*

I wrote *Winner Take All* because I wanted to challenge this. To present a deeply flawed heroine—a girl who is not just intelligent and thoughtful, but also messy, mean, competitive, anxious. And I drew her carefully against her love interest, a boy who she sees as the ultimate entitled antagonist—rich, smart, and easy to love. Sometimes, I joke that this book is really about two terrible people who fall in love. But more than that, I wanted to challenge readers' notions of why we so often find girls' actions unforgivable but are willing and eager to accept apologies from their male counterparts. I didn't want my main character to always be likable, but I wanted her to always feel real.

It's easy to forget that every day, teenage girls face a massive amount of pressure to be perfect, and every day, they suffer in silence from undiagnosed anxiety, depression, and other mental illnesses. Don't get caught in the trap of thinking mental illness is something you need to handle alone. Here are a few resources to consider (in addition to a trusted parent, teacher, or other adult):

- Anxiety and Depression Association of America (adaa.org)
- Center for Young Women's Health (youngwomenshealth.org)
- National Alliance on Mental Illness (nami.org)
- National Institute of Mental Health (nimh.nih.gov)
- OK2Talk (ok2talk.org)
- Teen Mental Health (teenmentalhealth.org)

At the end of the day, this book is about the girls I love the most. The ones who want the world. And won't apologize for it.

Happy reading always,
Laurie

ACKNOWLEDGMENTS

I can't believe this book exists. Seriously. There's something about the reality of getting to *keep* telling stories after your first book that makes it even more surreal the second time around. Countless people, hours, and daydreaming made *Winner Take All* possible and I can't thank everyone, mentioned and unmentioned, enough. But I will try my best.

First of all, none of this would be possible without my agent, Diana Fox, as ever, for always helping to turn my wild ideas into reality. I am endlessly appreciative of your tireless work to help me shape this book—and I mean "tireless" literally because we both basically stopped sleeping at various points throughout its creation.

My eternal thanks to my excellent editor, Erin Stein, for her guidance and encouragement as Nell and Jackson's story came to life. Also to Nicole Otto for always keeping me on schedule and generally being the best. Ellen Duda did an absolutely incredible job giving this book its aesthetic—I can't imagine Nell without the badass cover you designed. My thanks as well to Alexei Esikoff and Raymond Colon for their work on production, Caitlin Crocker and Amanda Mustafic for marketing and publicity, and Melissa Croce, Lucy Del Priore, Katie Halata, and Amanda German for getting this book out into the world.

Can't say enough about my favorite hag ladies. Kristin Halbrook and Kody Keplinger came to my rescue with notes just when I most desperately needed them. Courtney Summers and Maurene Goo both raved about this book when I was sure no one would ever get it. Veronica Roth is the best listener a girl can ask for—appreciate each and every writing date. And to the rest of the fantastic authors who always have my back—y'all are the light of my YA life.

Thanks to my parents for listening, even when they have no idea what I'm talking about. I promise nothing is based on you. Drew, thanks for being rad. Answer my text. And to my entire extended family—thanks for being so supportive of my book-writing dreams.

To all my friends I blew off because I had a deadline: I'm sorry, I love you, please still hang out with me. Much love to Jamie, Sarah T., Campbell, Sarah W., Felicia, Meisha, Mitchel, Erin, Sarah C., Randi, and the many more generally awesome people I know. My coworkers have always made having a day job not so bad. Rachel, Maura, Mary, Abbie, Audrey, Emma, Claire, and Amanda—you have always been my people.

There's never enough space to mention all the people who help a book to come together so my thanks extends beyond this list—I love you all dearly. And last but not least, I can't say enough for my readers. My gratitude at being able to write weird little stories is so immense and I can't believe y'all are out there, giving my books a chance. So, to everyone who picked up this book, none of this would be possible without you. Thanks a million. XOXO